The
WITCHES'
KITCHEN

BOOKS BY CECELIA HOLLAND

A TOM DOHERTY ASSOCIATES BOOK

New York

The
WITCHES'
KITCHEN

CECELIA HOLLAND

THE WITCHES' KITCHEN

Copyright © 2004 by Cecelia Holland

A Forge Book
Published by Tom Doherty Associates, LLC
175 Fifth Avenue
New York, NY 10010

www.tor.com

Forge® is a registered trademark of Tom Doherty Associates, LLC.

Library of Congress Cataloging-in-Publication Data

Holland, Cecelia, 1943-
    The witches' kitchen / Cecelia Holland.—1st ed.
        p. cm.
    "A Tom Doherty Associates book."
    ISBN 0-312-84886-2 (acid-free paper)
    EAN 978-0312-84886-6
    1. America—Discovery and exploration—Fiction. 2. Haithabu (Extinct city)—Fiction. 3. York (England)—Fiction. 4. Vikings—Fiction. I. Title.

PS3558.O348W58 2004
813'.54—dc22

                                                          2003062627

First Edition: April 2004

Printed in the United States of America

0   9   8   7   6   5   4   3   2   1

For MY MOTHER, FOR BOB BATJER,
JOHN JACKSON, DAVID ANDERSON,
HELEN BEALL, MIKE ALLEN, AND FOR
ALL THE OTHER WANDERING STARS
THAT LATELY WENT TO THEIR REST

The Lost Island

By midmorning they had hauled so many cod out of the sea that the boat could carry no more. The boys coiled up their lines, and Corban stowed the gaff alongside the mast. He went back to the rudder, glad for the chance to sit down. The boys scrambled around the boat, packing the fish away, getting their oars, and their voices rose in a sudden chatter.

"Wait until Mam sees all these fish!" Conn crammed the last of the gutted cod into a basket and wedged the basket under the swell of the gunwale. He had been slicing up the catch, and his forearms were slick with blood; the boat's hull, the wooden frame, the thwarts, even the mast glittered with scales and blood. Conn pulled his oar out from under the bench.

Raef said, "I'm already sick of fish, and we haven't even eaten any." His hair was the color of duck down in the sun. He wore no shirt, and his shoulders were red as a blister.

Conn snorted at him. "You always find something to gripe at! Get your oar."

"Don't tell me what to do."

Sitting in the stern, by the tiller, Corban turned his head to look out over the sea. Their bickering put his teeth on edge. The boat felt too small to hold the three of them; he felt himself leaning back, twisting away. Reaching down behind him into the cleft of the stern, he brought out his shirt, shook it, and pulled it on over his head. His sunburnt shoulders flinched from the light touch of the deerskin. He stretched his gaze toward the eastern horizon and the open ocean.

The day was blooming, warm and calm, the sky fair and blue, the water glossy, lifting in long gentle swells like a giant breathing. A swarm of seagulls dove and flapped around the water just behind them, fighting for the fish guts they had cast out. Corban waited for a swell to take them up higher, so that he could get his bearings; from the peak of the wave he could just see the dark line of land along the northern horizon.

"We'll have to row the whole way back," Raef said, hunched down on the midboat thwart. "There isn't a stir of the wind. I don't think it's such a good thing—" He jerked his face around, staring out to sea, frowning.

"Let's get a start on it, then," Corban said.

Conn sat down on the forward thwart and lowered his oar into the rowlock. A black wing of his hair fell into his eyes, and he tossed it back with a jerk of his head. "You just pull hard, that's all, Raef." His voice rang with threat.

Corban at the tiller headed them toward the low dark seam of the land. Once they got to work, they would stop arguing. They had done well at the fishing; he was proud of them, his son, his nephew, strong and willing when he needed them, and then they had worked together, almost silent, tireless and sure. Burdened with fish, the boat felt reluctant under his hand; he wiggled the tiller bar a little, trying to feel how the water was going.

"We could come out tomorrow. How did you know they'd be running like this, Pap?" Conn said.

"When I was down off the southern point yesterday I saw the whales following them," Corban said. "Get your backs to it, the wind should blow soon." In this season there were often thunderstorms in the afternoon; he wanted to be well inshore by then. He squinted up at the sky, where more seagulls were gathering, their raw cries grating in his ears. A brown wintering gull floated down past them, almost to Corban's eye level. More than one creature preys on the cod, he thought. A long rising sea lifted the boat and slid on away toward the distant shore; under his feet the wooden boat frame flexed as the wave went by.

"She's heavy," Conn said, straining at his oar. "It must be all the fish."

Raef said abruptly, "Let's get out of here."

A tingle of alarm went down Corban's spine. He felt the boat wallow down another long slow sea; it began to climb the next wave, and suddenly his feet were wet.

His gut clenched. "No. She's full of water." He hooked the keeper over the tiller bar and grabbed the bailing bucket. "She's coming apart again." He looked around the boat to see where the water was coming in. The boat's skin, sewn together of many hides, was always coming to pieces, and he had fixed it so many times he knew where every hole was. "It's that patch in the bow again."

Raef sat where he was, his hands hanging and his eyes wild. "I knew it. We're sinking."

Conn said, "Can we fix it?"

Corban thrust the bailing bucket into his hands. "Bail like hell, boy." He scrambled back into the prow of the boat, pulled away a great basket of fish, water sloshing around his ankles, and reached past more baskets toward the box where he kept his spare sail.

"Raef! Help me!"

His nephew came up the boat to him, his face fretful. Between them they spread the sail out, then, each taking one end, they pleated it into a length, and flopped the folded middle over the blunt prow of the boat. Leaning down around the prow, Corban worked the lower edge of the sail around and under the boat, spreading it over the leaky hide hull; he pulled the bottom corner up snug over the gunwale halfway down the boat and lashed it, and went up to the bow again to help Raef on the other side.

Back by the stern Conn bobbed up and down, bailing, the bucket in his hands swinging in an arc that ended in a long brown jet of water flying out over the sea.

Corban fastened down the bottom edge of the sail; he leaned down over the side of the boat, gathering the top edge of the sail tight around the breast of the prow, and Raef said, half strangled, "Uncle, watch out."

Corban lifted his head. Out there across the sleek water a narrow black fin was slicing down through the slope of the wave toward him. He jerked himself up and back, onto his feet and well into the boat. All his skin tingled. The fin veered off suddenly and circled around the prow.

Corban went quickly up into the bow and yanked the edge of the patch as tight as he could. Fastening the edge down, he went to the mast and took the gaff out of its socket. Conn scooped up bilgewater and flung it over the side, and Corban said, "Stop for now. Get the oars out and row."

The boys jumped to the thwarts and swung their oars out. Corban stood by the mast, the gaff in his hand; the boat seemed drier, the sail maybe holding everything together, for now at least. The boys pulled two long hard strokes on the oars; the shark fin slid away through the water, leaving.

Raef's breath hissed between his teeth. "They can smell the fish."

Conn said, "Shut up. Just row."

Corban sat down on the stern thwart, the gaff across his knees. Raef was right. The water they had bailed out of the boat had been thick with cod blood; they had baited the sharks to them. The long dark strip of the land ahead looked no closer. He scanned the glassy water around him, looking for signs of wind, and saw another fin gliding slowly toward them. A moment later something bumped the outside of the boat.

"Pap!"

"I see—" Corban stood up, the gaff in his hands, watched the long gray body slipping along just under the water, and struck down hard. The gaff glanced off the shark, which whirled and fled.

The boat rocked, bumped again. Two more fins prowled along through the water, circling the boat, and the bigger of them abruptly turned in toward them.

Conn said, "Papa, I'll help." He stood up, his oar in his hand.

"Keep rowing, for God's sake. We can't stop," Corban said. He cocked the arm holding the gaff, watching the big shark swim slowly up beside the boat.

Then suddenly the shark lunged; its pointed nose broke the surface of the water and its jaws gaped, and its teeth like saws ripped at the side of the boat. Corban swung the gaff around and smashed the iron head against the shark's nose. The sea churned. The shark flipped around and disappeared into the darkness, green water rolling over its white flank.

"Row, damn it," Corban shouted. "Row!" He gaped at the big hole in the flank of the boat. The stiff resin-soaked hide of the hull was notched with toothmarks; a foot of the top rail of the frame was gone, only the false gunwale holding the boat together.

"Pap—"

"I'll fight the sharks—you row!"

The boys bent to their oars again. The boat waddled along. They were taking on water again. Corban grabbed the bucket and bailed, holding the gaff with his left hand, his eyes on the flat calm sea around them, where now he could count five sharks prowling, thin and black, not the big gray that had attacked them.

"Uncle!" Raef shouted.

Something struck the boat hard from below and rocked it toward the broken gunwale. Water poured in through the hole. Corban lost his balance, teetered on the verge of falling, the gaff clutched in his hand. He dropped the bailing bucket and threw his weight against the high side of the tipping boat; he heard Conn shouting, behind him. The boat rocked back upright again, lifting the hole up out of the sea. Corban could see the frame bowing; he thought it would break entirely and throw them all into the water with the sharks.

The frame held. The boys flailed their oars back and forth, catching air, catching water, pushing them on. Corban scrambled bent-legged toward the hole in the boat, looking for some way to mend it, and then up through the jagged hole a huge maw rose, a pointed nose, a slick pink throat behind a great circle of teeth, coming at him.

He shrank down; he could not get away. The maw reached for him. A carrion stench swept over him. He thought of his wife. He thought of the boys, cast into the sea. He swung up the gaff in his hand, and as the shark's jaws gaped to take him he jammed the gaff inside its enormous mouth, the iron point straight up.

The shark bit down. The wooden handle shuddered in Corban's hand, and he saw the closing jaws stop for an instant, propped apart on the gaff, his arm enveloped in a wet heat, burning his skin. He yanked his hand free, saw his arm slide out between the rows of teeth, his whole arm slick as the shark's gullet.

Something yanked him backward—Conn, hauling him by the neck of his shirt into the middle of the boat. The shark still hung in the gap in the side of the boat, thrashing, its jaws stuck half closed. The boat frame bent under its weight. Green water shipped in past it. Just in front of the great notched fin, the shark's back bulged up suddenly. Abruptly the iron head of the gaff burst out through its back. Blood splattered down its jaw and out the long slits of its gills. In a spasm it lurched back into the water and vanished, and the boat heaved upright again.

"Row." Corban lunged for Raef's oar.

"Are we sinking?"

"Get us out of here."

"Are you hurt?"

Corban looked at his left arm; the sodden deerskin sleeve of his shirt was shredded from the shoulder to the wrist. Silently he bent to the work of the oar. All his muscles were jumping. He saw again and again the wide pink maw, slick, devouring. He imagined himself disappearing whole down that clenching throat. Raef got the bucket and bailed. In their wake, suddenly, the circling fins were clustering together, and the water began to churn; at the center of it the big shark suddenly appeared again, or a piece of it, blood-striped. Corban dragged the oar through the water, his arm throbbing.

He could feel how loose the boat was. With every stroke of the oar he saw how the broken frame opened and stretched and the hide buckled and water trickled in. He could fix that. Tie the frame together and put his shirt over the hole. But he could not do that now, with his heart hammering, his blood racing; all he wanted to do now was get away from the sharks, and he bent his back to the work.

⚓

"It was as big as the boat, wasn't it, Pap."

"I didn't notice," Corban said. They had hauled the boat out on the beach at the southern tip of his island, at the mouth of the great bay, and he was painting resin on the new patches. His whole body ached, exhausted, but he was nearly done: He had mended the frame with rope and green pine; he had caulked the holes in the prow with moss. His hands and arms were sticky with black pitch up to his elbows.

"It was the biggest fish I've ever seen, except a whale," Conn said.

Raef said, "I didn't think it was that big."

"Oh, yes, you were so brave, Raef!" Conn shoved him.

"You get those fires built," Corban said, "and stop arguing." He didn't like thinking about the shark.

He was wondering if it had been, really, just a shark. He had a lot of old enemies, who he hoped had forgotten about him.

He made himself think about easy things. While he had been fixing the boat, the boys had been slicing and hanging the cod, tail up, on long lines of rope in the sun. Now they were making fires to help the fish dry out faster. In a few days they would have enough dried fish to last them well after the cold set in. Nobody liked it, but everybody ate it when there was nothing else. There was still a lot of work, but Corban intended to do little of it himself. He would take the mended boat up around the island to his home on the north cove and fetch his wife and other children back here to help.

He finished with the boat and sat scrubbing his hands and arms ineffectually with sand. He thought longingly of his wife, off at the other end of the island. Raef stamped up with a load of twigs and branches and dumped it onto the fireline. He glanced around, looking for Conn, and faced Corban, holding himself very straight. "I wasn't scared, there, today."

Corban laughed at him. He felt a sudden rush of love for his sister's awkward, gloomy son. "I was. Are you a fool, boy?"

Raef flushed, bright red against his white hair. "Then I was, too, sort of. But I, I, I—"

Corban slapped his arm. "You did well enough. We're alive, we have the fish. Go get more wood. It's getting dark. Benna will be wondering where we are." Conn was struggling down the beach toward them under a great load, Conn, who had to do everything best.

Raef lingered. "You're not sailing up there tonight."

"No." He wasn't mad enough to try to sail the narrow water in the dark in a leaky boat. The tide was wrong anyway. "Let's make a cookfire. We can eat some of this fish."

They roasted a piece of the cod. Corban sat with his back against a log, his belly full, feeling much better. The early summer twilight was deepening to night blue. The stars were coming out, and as if mirroring them the dark rippled waters of the bay shone here and there with ghostly sunken lights. The world was full of things he did not understand. Yet the shark seemed just a shark now. The boat was fixed; tomorrow he would see Benna, and the girls. It annoyed him to have lost the gaff; he had few iron tools.

Conn said, "When the new boat is done, we'll catch twice as many fish as we did today, every time we go out."

Corban grunted, amused. Raef said, "I hate fish. Uncle— when the new boat is done, is that all we're going to do with her? Fish?"

Corban slapped at a stinging fly lighting on his arm. "Hard to hunt squirrels with a boat, Raef."

Conn exploded with laughter. Raef turned redder than the firelight. But he persisted; this was a favorite point of his. "We can't sail anywhere else?" He leaned forward, his eyes glinting. "Couldn't we sail over the sea?"

Corban was tired of the whole issue. "The boat is nowhere near done."

"We're on the last course," Conn said. This was something on which for once he and Raef agreed; they leaned toward him, one dark, one fair, their eyes hot with dreams. "She's beautiful already, she'll be true and fast and strong—why couldn't we take her over the sea?"

"We have to fit on the gunwale, and deck her, and set in the thwarts. She's nowhere near finished."

Raef said, "Why don't you want to go back where we came from?"

"Here there are sharks," Corban said. "There there are kings and priests. I'd sooner the sharks."

The two boys looked at each other. Corban said, "We have to carve oars and the steerboard, step the mast, and make a sail. That's going to be hard."

Conn said slowly, "Ulf said he would bring us a sail, didn't he?"

"Ulf has not come for two years now." Corban got up, stretching his arms. "Help me with these fires." They had piled sticks up in a heap at the end of the fireline, and he gathered an armful and went along the string of fires, ducking down beneath the strings of split cod to stuff wood into the flames.

He had been thinking much lately of Ulf, the Danish captain who had brought them here, when they left their old country behind. In the beginning Ulf had returned every spring around this time, bringing them food and stores and news, reminding Corban always of the old places, Jorvik and Hedeby, and of the people there, and what Corban had done there.

Then their lives here had seemed temporary, a wandering, not a settling. But Ulf had not come the last year, or the one before, and now this third year was late in the spring, almost summer, almost past the time when his ship usually appeared in the great bay around Corban's island.

It was a hard, dangerous trip, and maybe Ulf had lost interest. Or he was dead, and with him was gone also the knowledge for getting here, and the last link between this place and that old world was cut.

If so, Corban was glad. He could turn now wholly to his life here, and not have his mind drawn constantly back toward Jorvik and Hedeby. He went back to his camp and lay down, cradled his head on his arm, and thought sweetly a moment about his wife, lying in their bed, the house they had made. But when he slept, he dreamt over and over of the great shark rising out of the sea to devour him.

⚯

In the morning Benna with the little girls went up into the woods, to the pond, and drew water. Coming back out of the trees, onto the high peak of land above her house, she stretched her gaze out over the bay around her, but there was still no sign of Corban.

She stood a moment looking down past the cove, toward the long strait between the island and the bay's eastern shore, straining her eyes, searching for him. They had gone fishing; he had said they might not come back for a few days. For an instant she let into her mind the thought of being without them, of being alone here, forever, and quickly shut that off. They would be back, if not today, tomorrow. She stared down the strait a moment longer, as if she could bring them to her with her eyes.

Aelfu came after her, carrying the baby. Benna hauled the two buckets of water down to the house, walking in between the house and her little patch of garden, past the new boat on its stout wooden crutches. The long lapped boards of the hull were nearly all attached, and the boat lay like a great fish in its cradle, smelling of wood. Under the swelling keelson was a basket of treenails, like owl pellets; that was how they stuck the boards on. The boat drew her. She had dreamed that it sang to her. Aelfu called out, breathless, and Benna stopped and took the baby from her. Leaving one bucket of water behind, she continued on down to the house. Aelfu ran on down ahead of her, skipping.

The day was warm and calm. She had already picked berries enough to keep the girls happy, and she had grubbed out all the bad plants in her garden; she had nothing to do but sit in the sun and draw, and let Aelfu and Miru make mud cakes and dig in the sandy dirt.

She drew on anything that would take a picture, on shaved hide when she could get it, on split wood and shells and bark. Settling down now beside her house, she picked up a flat rock she had found, and took her brush.

She thought of Corban, sailing over the sea, and drew a sturgeon, leaping up out of the water as she had seen one sometimes do, the long body bent like the arc of the rainbow. With short strokes of the brush she put on its stripes of horny armor, making it a warrior fish, and its long mustaches. On one side of the sturgeon, near its spread tail, she put the shore of the island, three rows of lines, meaning the water, the surf, the land. On the other side, below the long gaping jaw of the fish, its manic eye, she laid down more lines, for the far shore.

She stared at it a moment, enjoying the strong arch of its body. Without thinking she took the brush and with a few quick marks gave the sturgeon Corban's face, above the mustaches.

This startled her, somehow, and she was gazing at it, wondering, when the girls began to fight. Aelfu had made a little figure of packed mud and set it down on the sand; Miru promptly grabbed it up and in her baby fingers broke it. Benna got quickly between the girl and the baby, turned Aelfu's eyes to the drawing of the sturgeon, and said, "Where should I put this? You decide."

"She broke my woman," Aelfu said.

Benna hauled Miru up into her arms; the baby was heavy and squirmed, wanting down. Benna said, "You can make another. Don't let her get near it." She remembered when she had made pictures, as a child, and her sisters had ruined them: She had beaten them, screaming, pulled out their hair in handfuls. Leaning down, she got Aelfu by the chin and tipped her frowning face up.

"It will be better the next time."

"You always say that," Aelfu cried. "It never is." She stamped her foot. Evilly she glared at Benna's fish. "We should throw yours into the water. That's where fish belong." Her eyes glinted. She watched her mother narrowly, to see how Benna took this.

"Very well," Benna said mildly. "I think you're right. Let's go—you carry the stone, and I will carry Miru."

Aelfu's eyes widened. After a moment, she bent down and studied the stone, and then, lifting it, tramped away toward the shore.

Benna followed her, jouncing the baby on her hip. From her dooryard the land sloped down through grassy hummocks to the shore of the cove, a jumble of tide-washed rocks, covered with seaweed and barnacles, wisps and rags of blown sand in among them. The tide was out. As they came down onto the sand, swarms of tiny crabs darted away toward their holes. Holding the rock with both hands, Aelfu marched straight across the beach to the edge of the water; she turned once and looked back to see if Benna would stop her, and then, standing to her ankles in the little waves, she hurled the rock outward. It splashed into the bay only a few feet away.

Aelfu said loftily, "You can get it out if you want." She brushed her hands together.

Benna said, "Let it stay there." The picture was already gone. The soft black stuff she drew with came right off in water. Aelfu was frowning; Benna thought she had given her something to think over, and anyhow she was no longer angry with Miru. The baby got carefully up onto her feet and padded off across the sand, and Aelfu followed, reaching for her arm, saying, "Hold my hand, now, Miru, or you'll step on a crab."

Benna straightened. From here she could look straight across the narrowest part of the strait, to where the river came down into the bay. The last winter's flood had brought down a lot of old wood, two big trees now stranded in the shallows along the far beach there, their roots reaching out everywhere like a mass of wooden arms. Here, at its northern tip, the island came almost within a stone's throw of the mainland, and on the thin yellow beach above the river's mouth, above the beached driftwood, she could see people, two men, it seemed, standing there, staring back at her.

She knew who they were; they came from a village nearby, where she had even been, once or twice, with Corban. Then those people, men and women, had stared at her, murmured, laughed, until her skin went hot and she could not lift her gaze from the ground. They lived here, she thought, over and over. They lived here, and she and Corban were strangers and did not belong.

They never really bothered her and Corban—any of their family—and Corban got on with them well enough, but she was glad to have the water between them and her home.

Then suddenly Aelfu cried out, "Look, Mama!"

Benna straightened, turning around to aim her eyes where the girl pointed; the breeze fluttered her hair into her face, and she drew it back with one hand. Her heart skipped, and she shouted out joyously, "Corban!"

Down the brisk blue water, the little boat was bobbing into sight, the sail cupped over the fist of the wind. Even from here she could see him, by the tiller, black-haired, his shirt flapping. Her heart swelled. She took in a deep breath, as if she had not breathed until now.

"Papa," Aelfu cried, leaping up and down. "Papa!"

"Corban," Benna said again. She bent and gathered Miru up. She cast another look over her shoulder at the two people watching her from the shore, but now with Corban coming she had more important things to do, and she took Aelfu by the hand and went to meet her husband.

CHAPTER TWO

"There they are," Tisconum said. "That is their house, anyway." With the young outlander beside him, he saw the house as if for the first time, and again realized how strange it was, that bump there in the meadow, squat and angular, its tilted slabs of roof all grown up now in green grass.

He had brought Miska as close as he dared come, up to the very edge of the shore, with only the narrow arm of the water between them and the island. Across the ruffled surface of the water, up above the round indent of the cove, he could see the whole green clearing, not just the heavy-roofed house with its half-buried walls of woven branches, but the other strange things around it.

"There's one of the women," he said, and pointed with his chin, polite even at this distance; he knew them for long-sighted.

Miska grunted; he took a step closer, thrusting his head out, squinting, bold and rude.

"The talk was that they were white as birches. I knew that wasn't so."

Tisconum grunted at him. Miska clearly did not see as well as Tisconum did, and Tisconum from here could only see her shape. She was standing on the shore on the point, just above the mouth of of the cove, holding the baby in her arms. For a moment Tisconum had the uncomfortable sensation she was staring back at him. He pulled his gaze from her; carefully, knowing what to look for, he searched along the shore and found the other child, running across the sand.

Miska made another harsh grunt. He said, "She sees us. But she isn't afraid."

Tisconum looked back at her; she had bent to put the child in her arms down on the sand. The lanky outlander beside him turned to look up and down this shore; they were on a thin stretch of beach like a lip above the mouth of the river. Miska squatted and put his fingers into the water, and then tasted them; his eyebrows jumped.

He straightened. He said, "Can we get closer?"

"No," Tisconum said.

"I saw a dugout on the riverbank there."

"No," Tisconum said sharply. "I don't go into their water. You won't either, if you're wise." He snorted, doubting Miska was ever particularly wise.

Miska frowned across the strait; his hand rose to the pouch hanging around his neck. He was slab-chested, gaunt, long-legged, almost as tall as Tisconum, who was tall. He said, "Look—what is that? Hah!"

Tisconum lifted his head. Out there on the shore the woman had turned, suddenly, cast her arm up, looking away down the strait between the island and the shore of the bay.

"Yes—there he comes."

Up the strait the little boat rushed into sight, skimming the water, its wing spread on the air. The wind was blowing hard out of the southwest and the tide was flooding in, the dark blue water spangled white where the wind ripped off the tops of the waves. The boat bobbed and jerked along, spinning a thin white trail across the water behind it, borne like a feather in the stream of the wind.

Miska muttered something under his breath and clutched at an amulet bag hanging from a thong around his neck. Pleased, Tisconum folded his arms over his chest. He said, "They have many magical things. There is a box that makes fire, too. Stone that is not stone."

Miska stared out at the boat. His arm had fallen to his side. "We have much power, too, my people." His voice sounded half smothered.

Tisconum made a derisive sound in his throat. He hated all Miska's clan, who called themselves the People of the Wolf. They had no such power as Corban. They lived a long walk away to the west, off in the deep woods. Even there they were newcomers, although they acted as if they were first in everything, barging into old hunting grounds and wanting to fight all the time.

They had come from the west, only a few summers before this, although their name had gone ahead of them, and Tisconum had heard of them long ago. Ever since they arrived in this country their headman, Burnt Feet, had been pushing steadily into councils and gatherings. Now he had sent this shoot of a boy to see about the white people, who were Tisconum's business, not anybody else's, Tisconum's to decide about.

"Why is Burnt Feet interested in them, anyway?" He asked. "They do no harm, they're just odd. And very few." He stepped back from the little lapping wave before him. The tide was running high, drowning the beach. He felt, for an instant, the whole great dark cold salty bay reaching out for him, and backed hastily up onto the dry ground behind him.

The boat skipped toward him, up past the mouth of the river, into the narrow water, where it fell off the wind. A single man sat behind the wing; as the boat glided up on the current, its wing flapping, he stood and went to the stick in the middle and took the wing down. It was Corban, Tisconum saw, and hoped he would not notice them standing here.

If he did notice, the man in the boat made no sign. Sitting in the middle of the boat, he ran out paddles to either side and let the tide help him float in toward the shore, using the paddles to steady and steer.

Miska let out his breath in a sigh. Tisconum gave him a sharp look. The young man's face shone, intent. He said, "I want to do that."

"It's all different from our way," Tisconum said, exasper-
ated. "It's all magical, and who knows what it means. Come on.
I don't want to stay here, the tide's coming in, the marsh floods,
we'll be cut off."

Miska did not move, still staring hard across the water. The
woman had waded out to meet the boat. The man leapt over the
side; for a moment he and she stood together, to their waists in
the water, their faces touching. On the shore behind them the two
children screamed and jumped. The wind took their voices off
like the cries of gulls.

Miska said, "Is this all of them?"

"No," Tisconum said. "There are two boys, old enough for
the fire ceremony, although, of course, these people—" He waved
that off, remembering belatedly that Miska's people had no fire
ceremony either. "They were born here. All the children were
born here. And there is another woman."

Over there, now, the man and the woman were walking up out
of the water. The woman had hold of the man's sleeve, tugging at
it, talking to him, and near the edge of the water he turned to her
and stripped the shirt off.

Miska let out a cry. "He is white."

Tisconum laughed, pleased. "You had to see for yourself,
didn't you. They are all like that. One of the boys has hair white
as owl down. And there is a pale ring in their eyes. You can see
into their eyes as if into water." He smiled, glad to see Miska
clutch again at the bag of charms around his neck. He glanced
over at Corban, squatting down on the sandy beach to greet his
little children, while his woman went up to the house with his
shirt.

"They're demons," Miska said. He gripped the bag tight.
"They're evil. It's disgusting."

Tisconum snorted at him. "Come along. You've seen them
now, haven't you? What else do you want?"

At last Miska followed him away. They wound back over the

black soggy ground, clumped with tall rushes, alive with crabs. Tisconum was wondering again how many more nights he would have to keep Miska in his house; he wished Burnt Feet had stayed where he belonged.

"How did Burnt Feet hear about them?" he asked.

Miska had been walking along with his head down, frowning at the ground in some effort of thought. Now he darted a glance at Tisconum. "Everybody knows about them. As far west as the Great River country, people speak of them."

Tisconum frowned, unsurprised. "Well, then, why does he suddenly care about them now? They've been here for years." Longer, he almost said, than the Wolves themselves. They came to higher, drier ground, where jumbled rocks broke out of the drifted leaves; the trail pinched down, and Miska walked behind him.

"How did they come? In the boat?"

Tisconum grunted. He wanted no more questions. Especially not obvious ones: Corban and his people had in fact reached the island in a boat, not this one, but a much bigger one, moving up from the world-water, from out past the islands, where the land ended.

So far, though, nothing much had happened with them. Corban and his family were quiet and peaceful, making no trouble, although all around the great bay, in the villages here and there, people muttered darkly of ruined fishing and how no one could go out to the big island anymore. Tisconum had moved slowly, cautiously, to take control of the situation and determine what good could be had of it, and so far his way had worked. Through care and patience he had won Corban's trust—had even taught him to give presents, among them the big clamshells from the heart of the bay, which made the best beads. Of course there were always people who saw evil in everything, but Tisconum had them quiet now. And he needed Burnt Feet out of it.

He stretched his legs, walking faster; they had come in under the trees of the forest. Above all he did not want Burnt Feet or

Miska to come face to face with Corban, perhaps with better presents than Tisconum's. Quickly he led the young outlander back toward his town, on the higher ground behind the marsh.

⸺⸰⸻

Miska let Tisconum lead him away, but in the next dawn he came back, alone.

The forest here was not like his homeland. There were more pines, especially nearer the water, and the great bay, spreading inland with its scatter of islands, made everything seem much more open and wide. The smells were different. The pines and the inland forest sweetened the air, but over it all lay the keen salty tang of the bay and the stinks of rotting stuff cast up along the shoreline. He had tasted the water and it was brine, impossible to drink.

He was close to the world-water, of which he had heard only legends. Something in that made his skin tingle, just to think.

The ground was squelchy and black. Flowers he had never seen grew under the trees. He recognized some of the birds screaming and singing in the trees around him but not all, not that sudden screech, not the weird, high, beautiful warble.

He walked away from Tisconum's village meaning never to go back again. Everything he had carried here from home he had brought with him. He stowed this pack between the humped roots of a tall pine tree, and went down the streambank toward the place where the day before he had seen a dugout.

The log boat was still there, and even had a paddle stowed inside. He dragged it down the stream to the bay.

The sun was just coming up. The dark water spread out flat and calm before him, giving off drifting wisps like smoke rising into the air. The haze obscured the island a little so that it seemed not to emerge from the water but to float above it. The light of the rising sun began to slide along the surface of the water, and the haze thinned before it. The tops of the trees on the island blazed. The wind rose in his face, suddenly warmer.

He hauled the dugout into the water and climbed in, and began to paddle out into the deep water. All his life he had used river boats, and he had no trouble with this dugout, although it was clumsy and slow compared to the slim bark canoes of his people. The sky brightened to a fierce blue above him, while the mists rising from the water still veiled all the island save the points of the trees on the hill. Away behind him in the marsh some cranes began to call back and forth. A fish plopped nearby him. Among the ragged upper branches of the trees he saw the great twig-piles of fishhawks' nests. Through the mist he began to make out the unnatural shape of the house, high on the gentle slope above the shore.

At once he began to think the people were gone. The boat was nowhere in sight, and the meadow was empty. He could smell no smoke; he saw no one moving up there. He touched the amulet bag around his neck, wishing for a sign what to do. He wanted to land on the island and get as close to the house as he could. If the people weren't there it would be easier.

He remembered the man he had seen the day before, how strange he was. Not really a man: some kind of animal. A bear, perhaps. His thick black hair covered his head and his face, too, like a bear. Miska envied the quick sure way he had handled the boat; the dugout seemed almost useless compared to it. Above all he remembered the man's clay-white skin.

He had thought about this all the night, as he planned this trip to the island. He thought it was a curse, perhaps. These people were cursed, cast out, that explained much. Or they were really ghosts, counterfeits, who did not know how people looked beneath their clothes. He felt a little prick of anger at Tisconum, who tolerated them.

They weren't really people, even if they weren't ghosts, just cursed outcasts. Maybe they had sprouted here, like mushrooms, which were also white. Or crawled up out of the sea, water-bleached like fish.

Whatever it was, he hated that man. If he came on him, out on the island, Miska thought, he might try to kill him.

The dugout plowed steadily through the flat water. The mist was clearing; now he saw the house much nearer, the square edges of its doorway, the tangles of yellow wildflowers sprouting on its roof. Beyond it on the trampled meadow were other made things: a small square house with a door set down into the earth, and, off a little by itself, a great long hollow shape, set on stilty legs, its body pointed at both ends, like a kind of wooden fish. He dug the paddle in, driving the dugout toward the shore.

In front of him suddenly the water curled up into a wave, like the wave that formed when a quick-running river plunged over a rock in its bed. The dugout began to jerk and twitch, bobbing back and forth. He drove the paddle down, looking for steady water. The paddle wrenched in his grip like a live thing.

The nose of the dugout pitched up, and the boat twisted. The water whirled around, and the center of it sank down into a well, falling away toward the bottom of the bay, and the dugout tipped forward and swooped down along the inside of the well.

Miska's belly came up into his throat; he dropped the paddle and grabbed the wooden sides of the boat, leaning back to stay upright, looking straight down into a whirling sink of water. The cold and clammy wind rushing up into his face blew the yell back down his throat.

Then from the center of the hole the water whooshed straight up at him. A great foaming fountain exploded up from the center of the eddy, caught the dugout, and flung it into the air.

Miska lost his grip on the boat. He sailed upside down through the air and hit the water on his back so hard it knocked him silly. Dimly he heard the dugout crash down beside him.

The whirling water tugged and hauled at his feet like icy hands, drawing him under. The water closed over his head. He saw the sunlight, wan and green and wrinkled, fading above him. Brine trickled into his lungs. His foot struck something submerged, and he pushed himself up toward the surface as the need to breathe swelled up in him irresistibly.

His head burst through the water; he gulped in the clean pure air. His head spun. He gathered in deep lungfuls of the wonderful air. Steadier, he turned around, paddling with his hands, looking for the eddy.

It was gone. The bay was calm before him, flat and smooth. A little way from him, the dugout floated upside down. He swam to it and leaned on it, still breathless, his skin rough as bark with cold and fear.

He touched the amulet bag around his neck. He whispered a thanks to his grandmother, whose powerful magic had saved him. He laid his head down on the dugout a moment, tired, trying not to think he might have died.

He had not died. He was ashamed of being afraid.

He watched a huge snagged tree glide slowly by him, a root like a long neck stretching up into the air. He lifted his head, looking around. The slow current was carrying him on down past the mouth of the river, clogged with driftwood. He turned to look the other way, toward the island, and saw through the flooded reeds an opening into a cove, sheltered behind the ridge of land where the odd-shaped house stood. He pulled himself higher onto the dugout, more into the sun, feeling better. Above him on the slope he saw the house, and behind it, half hidden, the strange wooden shape, which reminded him a little of the boat. There was no sign of the people at all.

At least no one had seen him, he thought, relieved. He had looked like a fool, but nobody had witnessed it.

His chest hurt. The water was cold and he was not a good swimmer, and the current was carrying the dugout and him far from the little beach where he had started. Now also he considered what might live beneath him in the cold and dark. Grimly he pulled himself all the way onto the overturned dugout, sprawled himself along its bottom, and, paddling with his feet and hands, headed it back where it belonged.

He could try again to reach the island. But he remembered Tisconum's indignant fear when Miska talked of going into the water, and now he understood it. Working his way back to the shore, he went over and over in his mind what had happened, so that he would be able to tell Burns-His-Feet and the others when he got back. He wondered if they would believe him.

Probably not. Stretched on the dugout, straining to turn the clumsy floating log in toward the shore, he felt a sudden despair, and then a rush of rage at the white-skinned man, who had made him look silly.

When finally he reached the shore, his arms were so sore he could hardly lift them. As he hauled the dugout up onto the beach, it slipped out of his numb fingers and fell onto the sand, and he left it there. He was glad he didn't have to go back to Tisconum's village, where someone might have seen his failure, where they might even now be spreading the story around, laughing at him. He wanted to kill the white-skinned man and trample his body.

He left the dugout and went across the marsh, picked up his pack, and started off to the west. He was soaking wet, but he would dry off, walking. He reached the edge of the forest and went in under the trees, following a narrow old deer path beaten through the dense underbrush, and in the deep shadow of the trees he came abruptly face to face with a woman as white as an elder blossom.

He stuck fast where he was, shocked still, his breath frozen in his throat. Tisconum had said there was another woman, and he knew at once this was she. She stood before him, not afraid, staring at him, making signs neither of welcome nor of fear. Her wild black hair hung around her, tangled with leaves. Her face was gaunt and her eyes huge, as if she lived only to see. Around the centers of her eyes were rings of clear gray, like storm clouds. He could hear her breathing. He saw her nostrils flare as she faced him.

He looked into her gray eyes and saw worlds. She swallowed him into her eyes. He swayed, off balance, giddy on some promise in her eyes.

She turned, her gaze leaving him, and was gone, as if when she stopped seeing him she vanished.

He cried out. He leapt forward, his hands out to catch her, and clutched the air. He spun around, sweeping his gaze around him. Gone. Abruptly he stooped down, lowered his face to the earth where she had stood, and inhaled up a long draft of her, a scent of woman and moss and time.

He straightened, his heart hammering. She was gone. Yet she had deliberately shown herself to him. A warning. He gripped the bag of charms around his neck, which had failed.

They had not failed. They had saved him in the eddy, and saved him also when this ghost-woman revealed herself to him. Her scent lingered in his nostrils, his eyes burned to have looked upon her. She had not been afraid; she had meant him to see her.

He stooped and ran his fingertips along the ground where she had stood; something small and sharp turned under his touch, and he picked up a little white pebble. He opened his amulet bag and put the pebble into it.

He would see her again. He had to see her again. A sudden pulse of lust passed through him. She had taken him, somehow, in that look. He would kill the man, but not her. He gripped the amulet bag, promising this. He would take her, as she had taken him.

The wind rose, shaking the trees around him. He was cold. He went off quickly along the little path, heading toward the west, to bear word of all this to Burns-His-Feet and the rest of the Wolf People.

CHAPTER THREE

The tide was out. The boat lay like a stranded jellyfish on the black muck of the beach. Raef followed Conn back up toward the sand dunes humping up just above the wrack line, topped with sawgrass like spikes of hair.

They had dried all the fish and packed it into the storehouse, and as a reward Corban had let them take the boat by themselves until nightfall. Conn had immediately set out for the mouth of the bay, where the long low seaward beach edged a broad stretch of meadows and forest. During the fall and the winter he and Raef hunted there often, but during the summer the local people moved in, built their fishing villages, and did their own hunting, and Corban had warned the boys to stay out of their way.

Nonetheless Conn wanted to lay out some snares, and Raef could not change his mind.

Raef followed his cousin up the gentle slope of the beach. The land here rose away in sweeps of marsh and meadow; the forest took over the higher slopes inland, maple and pine. Raef's feet sank into the dry loose sand above the wrack line, crisscrossed with the forked tracks of seabirds. Saw grass stuck up here and there like big green hairs. At the edge of the marsh was a big gray boulder, and Conn scrambled up it and stood shading his eyes to look inland.

Raef sat down at the foot of the boulder, looking back toward the sea, running in long serene waves in from the south. Out there were other islands. He found his eyes straining to see into the misty distance toward the east. Earlier he had dived for clams, and now the heat of the sun was baking his bare arms and chest, but he shivered. His skin crawled; he felt itchy all over.

He fought the feeling off. He hated being like this; nobody

else felt like this, except his mother, who sang and screamed and lived in the woods and nobody ever saw her and everybody said she was mad. He had felt like this just before the shark attacked the boat. He remembered that—it had come at him in bits and jerks, and he had not understood it then, but now, looking back, he knew.

It hadn't helped. Corban had saved them, as always. He shivered the feeling off and locked his mind to it.

Conn slid down from the boulder. "I don't see anything. There's a village away up near the top of the ridge, is all." He rubbed his broad hands on his chest, looking around.

"Are you sure we should do this?"

"Don't be a girl, Raef."

Conn was afraid of nothing. Conn never shivered. Standing beside the big rock, he pointed this way and that way over the inland marsh.

"There's no sign of anybody, see? We could go over toward the creek, there, and cut up along the bank toward the woods. With the sun up so high there won't be much game on the wet ground, but it'll be easy to see if those other people are around here at all. Or we could just go straight up to the maple grove, there. Maybe we can start a deer."

Stubbornly Raef said, "Uncle says—"

Conn wheeled on him. "Are you going to let my father tell you what to do all your life?"

Raef said nothing. The brown husk of a sword crab lay half buried in the crusty sand by his foot, and he dug it up with his toes.

"Well, I'm not," Conn said. He turned to stare over the meadow toward the trees, where now a brawling flock of birds scattered up into the air like a spray of blown leaves, their screeches faint in the distance. "I want to take some meat home."

Raef picked up the old piece of shell; most of it had crumbled away, only the round rim left, and the sword. They had no way to kill a deer if they did start one. He pulled off the sword of the crab shell and stabbed it into the sand.

Conn said, "Pap goes around everywhere, all summer long. I don't see why we can't."

Raef was thinking about Corban; he said suddenly, "Why do you think he won't even talk about the old place?"

Conn said, "You heard him. Kings and priests. Come on." He started down the side of the dune, his feet throwing sheets of sand ahead of him.

There were kings and priests in Benna's stories, too, not all of them as evil as Corban said. Benna told stories of wonderful lands, Hedeby and Jorvik, Denmark and England, where giant beasts carried people around on their backs, men fought with magic weapons, and people lived in great villages and danced and feasted every day. Sometimes she drew pictures to show them, but Raef thought she made most of it up. He followed Conn into the soggy meadow, tufted with clumps of knife-edged grass.

He was still thinking of Corban, and where he had come from, and why he would not go home again, and without thinking he said, "He must have done something terrible, back there."

He dodged. The blow struck him anyway, hard. Conn said, "Don't you ever say anything bad about my father."

Raef turned the back of his head to Conn. He had no father, which seemed to him the greatest wrong in the world.

They crossed the meadow toward the first scruffy pine trees. The black muck under the spiky marsh grass was studded with pieces of driftwood, broken shells, pieces of dead crabs, dirty gull feathers. Where the ground was drier they crossed a little game trail, hardly a trace along the hard needle-strewn ground.

While Conn fussed with a snare, Raef went in under the pine trees, looking for mushrooms. The air was close and dusty. Under the dense green of their outer coats of needles, the pines were tangles of dead black twigs around the trunks. A bird chattered, somewhere over his head. He circled back and found Conn again, moving steadily up the slight slope, following the trace toward the maple trees. There was no sign of the other people. Raef broke a hairy owl pellet in his fingers, full of tiny cropped bones.

Conn set three more snares, little circles of string tied intricately to the surrounding brush. They pushed their way on steadily into the maples. These trees were higher than the pines, and under their wide heavy crowns scrawny saplings and masses of poison-leaf grew. They went single file along a deer path, ducking under low branches and spiderwebs. When Conn stopped to tie up another snare, Raef walked on ahead of him, toward the sunlit meadow just past the maple trees.

Somebody—the other people—had been gathering wood, all through the maple grove, and the brush was beaten down and all the fallen wood broken up, so that the grove was very open: Raef could walk straight through it under the spreading roofs of leaves. The openness startled him; he looked quickly all around, wary. Then, halfway to the edge of the sunlight, his ears picked up distant cries.

His back tingled. Cautiously he went forward, working his way up behind a tree at the very edge of the wood, and stood looking out into the meadow.

Out on the grass there a shouting gang of boys was running back and forth. They streamed down the meadow like a flock of birds that turned and flew in unison. Raef leaned against the tree, watching. He had seen them do this before, and at first had thought they were fighting, until he saw that they kicked some object back and forth among them. Even now he wasn't sure what they were trying to do. His cheek against the rough bark of the tree, he watched two of them break out of the pack, hurtling down the meadow, the thing they kicked flying away ahead of them, bouncing over the rough ground. The other boys streamed after them, their voices keen as whips.

Conn said, "What are they doing?"

"Playing that game," Raef said.

Conn came past him, almost into the sunlight. "We could do that," he said.

"You want to? Go tell them."

Conn barked a little laugh. "We could beat them. Wait. Why did they stop?"

"Oh, no," Raef said.

Across the grass, the wild stream of boys had suddenly halted. They were turning; they were looking up the meadow, straight toward Raef and Conn, and abruptly, down there, somebody shrieked and pointed.

"Come on," Conn said, and whirled, but Raef was already running. He bolted back into the maple grove, across the broad leaf-cushioned floor, racing for the path downward. Behind him he heard the yips and whoops of pursuit. Conn bounded at his heels. He tore through the brushy edge of the grove and down the slope into the pines. As if he could see them, he knew that some of the other boys were racing out to skirt the maples and reach the marshy meadows ahead of him. He thought of the boat, lying empty on the beach. If the other boys got to the boat before he did—if they lost the boat—

He plowed down through the piny woods, his arms out ahead of him fending off the swinging, toothy boughs. His feet struck rocks and roots and he skidded and slipped. Conn ran into him and they pushed and caught at each other, getting their balance, and then ran on.

Faster than Conn, Raef raced ahead of him, broke out onto the open ground of the salt meadow, and saw, off to his left, the first of the other boys charging in along the creek bank, his arms pumping.

Across the empty stretch between them Raef looked into his face and knew him, that long jutting jaw and high brow, someone he had seen often, playing, hunting, in the bay fishing. He was far ahead of the other boys. Raef had only to beat this one boy to beat them all. He stretched his legs, cutting straight across the lowland meadow toward the great boulder that marked where the boat was. He bounded over puddles and patches of slick mud. Casting a

quick look over his shoulder, he saw Conn lagging behind him and
the other boy racing up, even with Conn, but twenty strides to the
left. After that boy was a gap of a dozen yards and then a long
stream of boys reaching back across the meadow to the creek. One
slipped and fell hard, but the rest came pounding on.

Silent. Not screaming now. Using all their strength to chase
him. Raef used all his strength to flee, stretching his legs long as
deer legs, his arms pumping like wings, his eyes picking out his
course on the stubbly slick ground before him. He dodged
around a slick salt-rimed pool of water and bounded over a
chunk of driftwood bristling with roots.

The boulder loomed up before him like a great gray skull.
His feet sank into loose sand and he struggled to keep running,
heaving himself up against the drag of the slipping sand. Just
past the boulder he wheeled around, gasping for breath.

Conn was a few strides behind him, dashing across the
meadow. The other boy, far ahead of his friends, had almost
caught him. In the shadow of the boulder, Conn whirled around,
and the boy chasing them leapt on him.

Raef yelled. He thought of the boat again and half turned,
wanting to go to the boat, and then swung back to see Conn and
the other boy gripped in each other's arms, straining together, their
faces inches apart. The other boy's gang was streaking in across
the meadow, and now they began to shout again, triumphant.

Conn planted his feet. Raef could see the muscles of his
back bunch together; he felt all through his own arms his
cousin's arms flex and heave, and then Conn lifted the other boy
up off the ground.

The jubilant wails of the gang cut off. The running boys
slowed and stopped, a respectful distance back. Conn lifted the
long-jawed boy up in the air and flung him down, and every one
of the other boys bounded back a step.

Conn spun around and charged past the boulder, out onto the
beach; he caught up with Raef and slid to a stop and twisted

around to look back at the other boys. "He's not dead," he said, disappointed. "He's not even hurt."

Raef had swept his first glance down at the beach, to the boat, rocking gently on the waves at the end of its painter; the tide had come in. The tight panic went out of his belly. He glanced back at the meadow, where the other boys were running off, as if getting away as fast as possible would make everything better. In their midst the long-jawed boy ran as nimbly as ever, unhurt.

"You beat him, though," Raef said. He thumped Conn on the shoulder. "I've never seen you do that before."

"He isn't as heavy as you are," Conn said. "But it didn't even hurt him."

Raef made a sound in his throat. He was glad nobody was hurt. "Do you think Corban will find out?"

Conn laughed. "They won't tell anybody, I think." He spat, smiling, and stretched his arms. "I'm not telling." Sitting down, he took one of his feet in his hands to worry a thorn out.

No, Raef thought. None of us will tell anybody.

He stood there on the dune, looking out the sea, with the salt wind rising in his face. He remembered the boys playing at their game, kicking the thing around on the ground. He remembered the longing to run out there and join them.

They would have driven him away, or worse, fallen on him and beaten him, in spite of Conn. He felt suddenly, unbearably separate, alone, outside, as if everything happened in front of him, and he could only watch. As if he and Corban's whole family lived not in the world at all, but in some magic space, which Benna's pictures made, and that was why they could not join the other boys' game.

Then out on the glinting sea, out past the barely visible edge of the southern island, he saw something red.

He yelled. Beside him, Conn jumped, startled. Raef laughed, pointing. "Look! See there—"

Conn squinted, thrusting his head out, and shaded his eyes with his hand.

"I don't see anything."

"I do—" Raef clapped his hands, laughing. "That's a sail—it's the ship!" He plunged away down the dune. "It's Ulf's ship!"

Conn let out a whoop. "Let's go meet them."

"No—the wind's dead foul—let's go tell Uncle." Raef reached out, trying to catch Conn's arm and hold him. Conn was already halfway down the dune. Raef groaned. They would have to row the whole way. He turned and looked back into the meadow, where the last of the other boys had disappeared.

Conn yelled for him. He went obediently down and waded out after his cousin, to the hide boat.

———※———

The water of the bay was a sleek and glinting surface, the sky a soft blue depth. She drew the line of the trees and the earth between them, the trees feathery, close, manifold, upright against the line of the marshes, flat and low, spiky with reeds. Beyond the trees she drew the tall smoke of the village there.

She lowered her hand with the brush and looked at what she had made. The column of smoke reminded her of a church steeple, and in a rush the memory swept over her, of looking across the river toward Jorvik, and the steeple of the church on the hill there.

The strokes of the bell that called people to prayer. She shut her eyes, drowning in memory.

"Mama, look."

She opened her eyes and turned her head; Aelfu had gathered white stones in her basket and was setting them down in rows on the flat ground of the yard. Benna put her hand down beside her, on the other child lying there asleep, warm and soft under her hand. "Aelfu," she said, "what beautiful stones. What are you making?"

"A picture," Aelfu said.

"A picture of what?"

Crouched over her stones, her hair in dirty wisps around her lowered head, the child shrugged up and down. "Just a picture."

Benna looked down at her hands. Her drawing was on a bit of stiff dried deerskin. She held it out, frowning, and moved her gaze from it to the real smoke, the real trees. Just a picture. She laid the hide down again before her and used the edge of the brush to make the trees leafier.

Much nearer, on this side of the water, a flock of gulls prowled and squawked over the edge of the meadow, where the family dumped their garbage. Abruptly now they whirled up into the air, a vortex of wings, and through them she saw Corban coming, walking up from the beach, a string of fish in his hand. He walked straight through the screeching fluttering gulls, driving them up and away, and they spun around him, drawn back by the fish dangling from his hand. Surrounded by the wild noisy birds, he came striding up the trampled grass toward her.

She was up before she knew it, and walking toward him. The gulls flew up and away and she went into his arms. They stood together a while, their arms around one another. Benna laid her head on his chest. Aelfu called out to him and he started over to look at what she made, and Benna went back to her place by Miru.

He took the fish inside. She could hear him in there stamping around, and when he came out he was carrying a sack in one hand. He sat down next to her and dumped the sack down. Inside it, she knew, were clamshells, which the boys had brought yesterday; they clicked and tocked together in the sack.

"Let me see," he said.

She showed him the picture, and he did what she had done, looked from the deerskin to the far shore, and the smoke. He said, "The water doesn't look right."

"I'm not done with it," she said. "I wonder how I could make colors."

"You could use berries."

"That color fades."

"I thought you didn't care about keeping them."

She said nothing, but took the deerskin back and reached for her brush. It wasn't to keep them, but to make them better. She didn't have to explain to him. He accepted what she did with few questions; he understood it sometimes better than she did. Beside her he sat picking fish scales off his sleeves. The seagulls had settled back down on the bank, a white scud along the green of the meadow. He smelled of the warm sun and the shore where he had stood fishing, the dried salt seaweed beach smell.

Presently he said, "The boys have not brought the boat back yet."

"Did you think they would? You said they could have it all day."

"I'll take the log. I want to go over to the mainland."

"Wait for them, and they can go, too." She stroked the brush over the water. The log boat seemed dangerous to her.

"No, the log will do fine." He stroked his hand down her back. "I'll bring you something."

"Not more berries," she said. "We have too many, they're molding." She lifted her face and he kissed her. Aelfu was setting stones on stones. She leaned her face against her husband's, smelling his salty, sandy skin. He kissed her again, then swung the sack over his shoulder and went away down toward the cove, where he kept his boats; she took the deerskin on her knee and drew the water of that stretch of the bay flat and calm, to keep him safe. But everywhere else, she drew whirlpools.

⚓

The log was a boat made of a single tree, the inside burnt hollow, the ends shaped with an axe. Corban had found it some time before, beached on the island's south side; he had patched it and carved some wooden paddles for it. Probably it had once belonged to one of Tisconum's people, who paddled around in similar boats, most of them bigger than this one. Tisconum had shown no interest in it, and no one had ever claimed it from Corban, so he kept it. It was cumbersome and leaked, and he used it mostly around the shores of the island. Now he threw the sack of clamshells into it and ran it out into the water. Getting in was always touchy, and he settled himself cautiously down in the stern and set off paddling.

The afternoon was turning hot; he could feel the coming of a thunderstorm, like a tingling in the air, and he kept his eyes on the far shore and worked hard with the paddle. He had waited until slack tide, when the strait was calmer, but the water was always tricky through these narrows, choppy under the wind. As he paddled he kept an eye out for his son and his nephew but saw nothing of them.

When the new ship was done, he would give them the old hide boat. Then he supposed they would make off with the new ship whenever they could. He meant that not to be very often.

The log boat was stiff and grudging in the water, but still he liked the work. The flat waters of the bay spread out around him, murmuring past the boat, and the paddle made silvery curlicues of bubbles in the dark green water. As he drew away from the loom of the island the farther shores appeared, hazy with mist and distance, the whole broad stretch of land and water smiling under the summer sun. His heart rose. He loved this place; he had from the first time he saw it, when in Ulf's ship they came searching for a safe harbor.

When they sailed into this bay, that long-ago time, it had been a day such as this one, not so hot, at the end rather than the beginning of the summer. At first Ulf had wanted to keep looking, because all along the shore the smokes rose of campfires, but Corban had known that if other people lived here, then he

and his wife and sister and her baby could make a home here
also, and he told Ulf to take them in and put them ashore on the
big island.

On the tree-covered slopes they had found old campfires and
the tracks of people, but no one was living there at that time, and
so Corban settled his family on the island, and he had never re-
gretted it. The waters around them were full of fish all year, and
birds nested in the trees, and deer came across the narrow strait;
they could gather wild fruit and herbs and mushrooms, eggs in
the spring, and they found fresh water in ponds among the rocks.
Up on the height of the island, something like hemp grew in
sweeping fields, and every fall they harvested sheaves of it and
made rope and nets from the fibers, and Benna talked about
building a loom, but never did.

He loved such talk of what they might do, which seemed like
a road ahead of him into days to come; he thought they would live
here forever.

Before him, against the dark hedge of the trees, the pale
shore curved out into a point and then arched away, through
marsh and sandbars, to the south. Off beyond the ragged tops of
the pine trees, the freshening wind was dragging the top of the
plume of smoke across the sky. That was Tisconum's village, on
the bank of the river a short way up from the bay. Just off the
point the water broke into a rough chop; he drove the boat
through it, leaning against the sudden rock and lurch, and lum-
bered into the quieter water beyond.

In the marsh that fringed the coast some women were stooped,
gathering rushes. When Corban approached they popped straight
up and stared at him. The front of the log crunched on the shore,
and he swung out and dragged it up onto the land. The women
watched him steadily, but he ignored them, picked up the sack of
shells, and walked away through the marsh grass toward the higher
ground beyond. Behind him, he heard the sudden babble of their
voices. He followed their own path back across the marsh, where

the white lips of old dead clamshells stuck up in clumps from the black muck, and dragonflies buzzed zigzag past him.

Where the marsh climbed up to the pine woods, he came into a cloud of biting flies and broke into a hard run to get away from them, keeping his head down. The path wound through the shadowy dark under the trees and crossed the little stream that fed the marsh, where fat smelly green leaves poked up from the rot, and birds fluttered away from him up into the branches. Beyond the stream the ground rose a little, drier. Tangles of vines swarmed up the trunks of the trees. The trail was wider here. He followed it up through the trees to the edge of the clearing where Tisconum's village stood.

There he stopped. He seldom came closer than this. Before him lay strips of gardens, the green studded with yellow blossoms and tangles of beans. Beyond, the first buildings rose, round as oven domes, sheathed in pine boughs. He could hear people yelling, somewhere, and beyond the first house he caught a glimpse of someone running—he guessed they were children playing. After a while, when he thought someone must have seen him here, he went back into the forest and followed another, fainter trail to a clearing by a pocked gray rock, taller than he was.

There he sat down, the sack by his knee, and waited, and presently Tisconum came in from another direction and sat down before him.

They were silent a while, neither moving, not even looking at each other, until Tisconum opened the pouch he carried on his belt and took out a carved wooden pipe and a clump of dried leaves, and gave himself to the task of breaking up bits of the leaves and stuffing them into the pipe.

Corban brought out his tinderbox. When Tisconum had the pipe packed, he held it out, and Corban struck sparks into the tinder in the box and blew them into a little flame and lit the pipe. Tisconum offered the pipe first to Corban, who shook his head and waved it back. All this was the way it always happened.

Tisconum sucked on the pipe for a while, trailing the fragrant smoke through his nostrils. Finally he turned and handed the pipe to Corban, who took it this time, and inhaled of it also. The strong smoke roughened his throat and made his head feel momentarily swollen. Taking the pipe back, Tisconum laid it aside. From the pouch he brought four fox furs and set them down before Corban.

The first time they had met, in these same woods, Corban had been hunting and, with a big gobbler-bird over his shoulder, was going back to his boat, when suddenly through the thin sun-lit trees he saw Tisconum standing on the path watching him.

He had stopped in his tracks, his hackles rising. A few times, some of the local people had shouted at him, and thrown things. They stayed off the island, but he was wary of them. But Tisconum made no move, nor spoke, only watched him, and when Corban watched him back, their eyes met, even across the distance, and through the trees.

Corban lifted the bird from his shoulder, laid it down on the path, and backed away. With his hand he offered it to the man in the trees before him.

That man's eyes widened. For a while he only stood there, staring at Corban, but at last he came up along the path. Corban began to back away a little, keeping a distance between them. The other man was tall and lean, with dark hair and eyes and skin, dark as if burnt. He wore clothes of hide; Corban then still had his woolen shirt from Hedeby, his Danish boots. The other man bent over the gobbler-bird, took out his knife, and cut one wing from the bird. He straightened and nodded his head to Corban, then, taking the wing, went away into the woods, moving quick and neat as a deer through the brush. Corban picked up the rest of the bird and went home.

Then a little while later he was hunting in the marsh on the shore opposite his island, and the tall burnt-skinned man came up to him, as if they were long neighbors. They sat down together and the red man showed him how to smoke the pipe, laughing when he choked and coughed, and then gave him a pouch made of squirrel fur. Corban had nothing to give in return, as he had just begun hunting, but the other man—this was when he learned his name was Tisconum—insisted that he take the pouch, smiling, looking pleased.

After that they began to meet often. Corban had always kept his family apart from the local people, but he saw good in this with Tisconum, especially now that his boys were getting bigger and going all around the bay.

Every time they met, Tisconum had something for him, a fur, or a sack of herbs, but in the beginning Corban had nothing he thought worthy. Then by accident he found that Tisconum liked the shells of the clams the boys dug up out of the muck at the bottom of the bay. Corban had been using a shell for a scraper, and it fell out of his pouch, and he saw, surprised, how the red man's eyes followed it covetously. After that, he brought Tisconum all the shells the boys gathered.

This worked out very well. Tisconum traded him a steady supply of interesting things, like these three black fox furs, and seeds, which Benna had made grow in her garden. Now Tisconum took a box made of birch bark from his pouch and held it out with a little flourish. He knew Corban loved the sweet thickened sap. Corban took it gladly.

He said, "My wife will thank you also, Tisconum."

Over the years they had learned how to talk to each other, using words and also movements of their hands.

Tisconum said, "You should keep it for yourself. Women don't need such things. It only makes them stop working."

"My wife never stops working," Corban said, thinking of her drawing.

Tisconum said, "I saw you all working. I saw you caught many fish." He made the fish with his fingers, wriggling through the water.

Tisconum stroked his chin. Corban put the little birch bark container into his sack, but he could see that the other man still wanted to talk. Corban sat still, patient. Now suddenly, though, Tisconum turned to face him and said, "There is someone watching you." He made the someone with his fingers, walking.

"Hunh," Corban said, startled. The backs of his hands prickled up. "One of your people."

"No." Tisconum hitched himself a little closer, and his voice dropped, as if he didn't even want the trees to overhear him. "He is from the Wolf People. West of here. Bad people." He shook his head; his eyes bored into Corban's, and he took his finger and drew it across his throat.

Corban stiffened, cold. He said, "We do no harm."

"No. I know. They hate, those people." Tisconum made a face. "Be careful." He was standing up now, collecting the clamshells in neat stacks. It was the thick purple hinge he really wanted, Corban knew; he had seen Tisconum break that part of the shell free and throw the rest away. He wondered what they did with it. He wondered who these Wolf People were. His back was stiff. He stood; facing Tisconum, he thrust his hand out, and they gripped hands.

"I will be careful," he said, and a thought leapt into his mind. He said, "Will they hurt you?"

Tisconum's lips pinched together. He said, "I hate them." With the clamshells in his hands he turned and went off into the woods. Corban gathered up his sack, with the furs and the birch bark syrup, and went back to the log boat.

He would not tell Benna about this. Maybe it was nothing. They hurt no one, his family; there was no reason anyone would come to attack them. But the day that had been warm was cooler now, and on the south wind he heard the mutter of thunder. He thought again of the shark, and he went quickly to the boat, to get himself home.

CHAPTER FOUR

During the summer, Mav, Corban's sister, usually lived by herself in the woods, but this day toward evening she suddenly appeared on the shore of the island. Aelfu noticed her first; she clutched at her mother's skirt, and Benna turned and saw Mav coming around the northern point of the cove.

"Mav." Gathering up Miru from the sand, she went quickly down along the curving beach to meet Corban's sister. Aelfu followed along at her heels, subdued. Benna slowed to a stop and held out her hand. "Mav." Corban's sister walked up and gripped her hand, and smiled at her.

She was Corban's image, except that he was strong and square, and she was thin as a wraith, her eyes huge in the carved hollows of her face. She wore clothes made of plants, gatherings of leaves, vines, and flowers twisted together around her. She looked into Benna's face and laughed. She never spoke anymore, but she laughed often, and wailed sometimes, and muttered. Yet in her clear gray eyes Benna thought she saw that she understood everything.

"I'm glad to see you," Benna said. "I was worried about you." Mav wandered all over the woods; she even somehow crossed the water to the far shore, and Benna often wondered how the local people took her. She said, "Raef and Conn are out in the boat, and there's a storm coming." Turning, she stared away down the bay.

The water had gone dull silver. The sun had slipped away behind the high bank of clouds building up from the south, boulders of clouds, rolling gray and dark. Lightning flickered around them, as if they struck sparks as they grumbled together. To the east the sky was still blue, but the birds were flying away over it, and the wind was picking up, turning up the leaves of the brush in pale green drifts. Still there was no sign of her son and Mav's.

She turned and cast a hard look up the hill, to where Corban was working on his boat. Wherever he had gone earlier, he had come back in a dark mood and would not speak to her. Now here was Mav come. She glanced at the taller woman, standing beside her, looking out toward the bay, her fair thin face vacant. Often when Mav came, something bad happened. Thinking that made Benna feel ashamed, and she reached out and put her arm around Mav's waist and hugged her.

Mav smiled down at her. Aelfu had drawn off a little, watching them; Mav frightened her, and now she put her thumb into her mouth. In Benna's arms Miru shifted herself around toward the side opposite Mav. Benna hoisted her up higher, her arms aching.

She stared away toward the churning water of the bay again, out past the point. Between the rumbling sky and the tossing water she saw nothing, and she aimed another angry look at Corban.

"I wish he hadn't let them go out alone. He acts as if they're grown men."

When she brought her gaze back to the running waves of the bay, a shout ripped up out of her. "There!"

Mav let out a high-pitched shriek and flung her arm up. Far down the bay, far past the point of land, like a leaf on the wind, the boat scudded along toward them.

Its sail was paler than the clouds. It slid behind a wave and almost vanished and then popped up again. Benna's heart lifted, gull-winged.

Corban said, "The new boat will hold the water a lot better than that."

Benna startled; she had not heard him come up. She turned toward him, remembering to be angry, and said, "You still should not let them go off so much by themselves."

He was watching the boat thrash toward them; he slung his arm around her, indifferent to her bad humor. "They'll do it without any word from me, anyway." His eyes sharpened, his black brows pulling down; leaning against him she felt him stiffen all over. He looked over Benna's head at his sister. "Can you hear them?"

Mav gave a wordless cry. Benna gripped his arm, standing on her toes, trying to see better. The boat was weathering the southern point of the cove now. In it she could see people— Raef's white hair—her son—and someone else.

She screamed. Beside her, Mav was muttering and waving her hands, and Corban said, under his breath, "Well, damn. Ulf's come after all." Benna pulled herself out of his arms. Her heart was thundering. She could hear them now, shrieking to her, and more, she could see who came with them.

"The ship!" Raef was shouting, waving his arms, "The ship!" and at his shoulder stood one she had left behind fifteen years before, and missed sorely every day of it. She rushed forward, into the water of the cove, wading out to meet the boat.

"Arre! Arre!"

The boat swung up before her, as she stood waist deep laughing and crying in the cove, and from the boat her sister climbed laughing and crying down into her arms.

⚓

Ulf was older, but still solid, his shoulders sloped with muscle, his legs bandied from sitting too long in ships. The hair on the top of his head was entirely gone, but his beard grew like a drapery, gray and white, beneath the shapeless bulb of his nose.

His eyes snapped with good humor. He said, "I don't mind telling you, I had thought not to come again, the crossing is so risky. I thought I had leaned a little too hard on my luck the last time."

"You have a greater ship now, though." Corban looked down at the cove, where Ulf's ship stood at anchor, a fine, fat-bellied trader, ten oars to a side, humbling the hide boat beside it.

"She's his," Ulf said, and nodded.

Corban knew without looking where he was pointing. The crew was coming in from the ship—only twelve men, in spite of the oar room, Ulf as usual cutting the edges close—but ashore with them also stepped Euan Woodwrightson, the merchant of Jorvik, Benna's sister's husband.

Even before Euan's foot trod the shore, he was looking around, as if his gaze pinned everything in its place, to be sized up, valued, stored away, and used. Corban wiped his hand over his face. What Tisconum had told him gnawed at the edge of his mind. He had thought himself safe, but they were coming at him from both sides now.

The captain was watching him steadily, his lips pursed in his grizzled beard. "Show me the new ship," Ulf said. "She looks almost finished."

Corban led him up the slope toward the boat in its cradle. Ulf tramped after him. The thunderstorm had swept past them, and the air was crystalline, sharp and bright, everything glittering wet. The sun was going down in a stream of pure pink light. Beyond the spine of the island, above the western shore, an osprey fluttered motionless, its wings beating into the wind, and then broke suddenly downward.

"Do you have enough to feed us?" Ulf said.

Corban shrugged. That was not the matter here. "I have food. There's a herd of deer down the island, we can hunt them. The woods are full of berries and fruit, this time of year. The bay always has fish."

"I have some bows and a few arrows."

"Good." They had walked past the house, to the new ship where it sat on its crutches. He laid his hand on the new gunwale. The rain had dampened the golden oak of her strakes. The sweet swelling line of her freeboard heartened him, as it always did. This he had done well, whatever else happened.

"Ah," Ulf said. "She's a beauty. She's a dragonfly if I ever saw one."

"You showed me how," Corban said, "and Benna drew the pictures," but his chest filled at the dansker captain's admiration. Seeing the boat appear under his hands had made him love it. He could feel the power in it also; he knew it was not his, but its own creature. "You showed me how to choose the wood." He had prowled the forest every winter looking for trees whose grain ran in the shapes he needed, felled and hauled them home across the water, split each piece out with his hands and his axe. "I'd never made a ship with a keel before. You showed me how to do that."

"Yes, but this is very neatly done," Ulf said. He ducked under the bow to the other side, and Corban walked around after him. "How did you sew on the strakes? Since there are no horses here." He had said the dansker people used horsehair.

"Hemp string," Corban said. "We fastened them to the ribs with treenails, see. I just put the gunwale on, yesterday and today." He rubbed his thumb over the pounded end of a treenail, bulging up from the smooth wood. "The boys helped, very much."

Lifting his eyes, he saw Euan coming toward them.

His good mood faded. A long time ago, when he and Euan had together overturned the King of Jorvik, Euan had been only a boy, not much older than Raef and Conn were now, strange and clever and inward. What they had done together, Corban still saw no way to have done otherwise. They had had to get rid of Eric Bloodaxe. Yet he brooded on it: He could not escape the truth that he had committed a murder.

Until now that truth had been old and worn and shadowy, but now here came Euan, bringing it all back with him.

Euan was a well-grown man now, stoop-shouldered, with a heavy tread. From Ulf's earlier voyages Corban had heard news of him, that he prospered in Jorvik, after Corban left, buying and selling, as he had learned to do in Corban's service, and that he had married Arre, Benna's sister. Corban knew no reason why Euan then should be turning up out here, on the edge of the world, with his wife or no.

Euan reached the boat and nodded to him. "Well met, Corban. It's been a long while."

"A long while," Corban said. "And a far distance. Was it a hard crossing? Ulf says it's much worse coming than going."

"I taught my wife to play chess," Euan said, "to pass the time." His eyes were unblinking. Above his high forehead the brim of his hat pressed down his hair. He said, "You are not especially glad to see us, are you."

"No," Corban said, "I'm not."

Ulf was looking from Euan to Corban and back again. Euan shrugged.

"No, I can understand that. You have a pleasant little place here, out of the way of things, and why share it with anybody? But things are bad in Jorvik again. They've saddled us with the Archbishop, and an ealdorman who will not leave off pressing, and we pay taxes now to the King of England." His voice grated. "We should have our own King, in Jorvik, as we always have, but they throw aside our rights, and walk over our backs. And so I thought—" His pale, watchful eyes met Corban's. "I would go find my old friend Corban Loosestrife, who saved us once before."

Corban leaned on the boat. He said, "I don't remember it that way. The taste of that undertaking's been like ashes in my mouth for fifteen years."

He tore his gaze from Euan. Beyond, Ulf's men were walking up across the meadow, carrying their gear, Conn and Raef among them; each boy hauled a carved wooden chest. Over by the door into his house, Benna stood, with her sister, their arms around one another, their faces bright as lamps. "Yet I am glad to see my wife so happy, and for that I thank you."

Euan said, "Yes, it's easy to make women happy." He sauntered off.

Corban gave a bark of a laugh. His hand was locked onto the gunwale, and he opened his fingers. Beside him, Ulf said, "The Archbishop sent men to arrest him—he had to get out of Jorvik, and he offered me much money to bring him and her here, and the use of this fine ship besides. Otherwise . . ."

Corban's gaze strayed to the ship, beached just inside the mouth of the cove, where the sand was firm enough to stand on. It was an excellent ship, carved fore and aft, its sides pierced for the oars, dwarfing this little creature of his. Otherwise, he knew, Ulf would not have come here.

His skin roughened. He felt crowded out of his own place. He said, "Keep them all on the island. I'll see to feeding you. There's not so much room in my house for this many, but the nights are fine, they can sleep outside." He walked away across the meadow.

—⚬—

Raef and Conn hung around the sailors all the day, avoiding chores, until Corban shouted them to the work of building a fire. He was unaccountably angry, Corban. Conn saw no reason for that at all—the excitement of so many visitors, new faces, new talk, made him fairly giddy.

Raef was twitchy, as always. He looked at everything out of the corners of his eyes, mumbled when the sailors spoke to him, and blushed like a sunset every few moments. Captain Ulf, to Conn's great delight, remembered him, teased him about growing so big, got him into a quick wrestling match, and let Conn overturn him onto the sand. After a quick glance at Raef, Ulf left him alone.

Raef skulked around on the edge of everything, watching. "Everybody's your friend," he said, while they built the fire.

Conn broke up kindling in his hands. "There's so much I want to ask, I don't know where to start. Jorvik, Hedeby! They've been to Hedeby!"

Raef coughed. "I wish they'd never come to our island."

"Bah," Conn said. "You're just talking now. Wait until you hear the stories." He went off to bring more firewood. Raef trailed after him, muttering.

While they built the fire, Corban harvested all their crab traps, and Benna brought in some of the big yellow gourds from her garden to roast. There was fish also, and some venison, and a drink Benna made from elderberry blossoms, sweetened with birch syrup. They all sat around the fire as the sun went down and gorged themselves.

Conn sat close by his father, wanting to hear everything that went on. For a while they only talked about the trip across the sea, and Conn's mother's sister's husband had much to say about some Archbishop somewhere, which Conn did not follow. But the night rolled over them, and the moon and the stars rose, and soon the real stories began.

They talked about heroes, Thor and Odin, Ragnar Hairypants and Sigurd Snake-in-the-Eye, Arrow-Odd and Hastein, battles and travels, encounters with gods and demons and strange magical women. Conn saw these doings as plainly as if they happened in front of him; he stared into the fire and watched ships sail through blasting storms, and swords clash like lightning.

After a while, Ulf brought out a little keg, which he unsealed and opened, and then dipped in a cup, which went around the fire. Someone was talking about a place called Miklagard, where bolts of fire hurtled through the air, and gold and silver birds sang in trees studded with jewels. Then Euan said, "I will tell the story of the death of Eric Bloodaxe."

Beside Conn, Corban stirred suddenly. "You will not." The cup came to him and he handed it on.

One of Ulf's sailors, a man with wild red hair, said, "I have heard that Eric died a hero's death in the battle of Steinmore, where five kings died. I heard he died defending Jorvik against the pagans. Is there more to it than that?"

Corban said, "No, that is all. A hero, Eric. And a Christian man, too, as they likely say, who gave to the poor and the virgins."

He was staring hard at Euan. Beside him, Conn sipped eagerly at the brew in the cup. He choked, startled, on the harsh fiery taste, and the men around him began to laugh and pound him on the back.

"Don't spill it!"

Somebody snatched at the cup. Conn clutched it. "Wait—wait—" In a storm of laughter he brought the cup back up to his lips and drank another long draught. Somewhere inside his head a star exploded. He sat blinking, while a dizzy warmth spread outward through his whole body.

Somewhere, the redheaded sailor was talking. "I have heard good of Eric Bloodaxe, yes."

"God bless him, then," Corban said. "He has nothing to do with me." He turned to Conn. "Don't drink any more of it, do you want to be a worse fool?" He took the cup and held it out to somebody else. Conn shut his eyes, glowing all over.

Euan said, "Do you think you can escape from what you did, Corban? Is that why you came all across the sea?"

Conn opened his eyes. He thought one more swig of the brew would make him utterly happy. But the cup was traveling away, around the circle.

Beside him, his father said, "Yet Eric was a Christian hero. You heard the man."

Raef dug an elbow into Conn's side; his breath warmed Conn's ear. "What are they talking about?"

"I don't know," Conn said.

His father was staring straight across the fire at Euan; Ulf, in his place on the far side of Corban from the boys, was looking from one to the other, his face washed blank of expression by the firelight.

Euan said, "Eric Bloodaxe the hero of Christian Jorvik. That is as true as what you are doing here."

"We have made a life here, fit and good," Corban said.

Euan's voice rose, edged with impatience. "What kind of a life is it, living alone like this, as if you were Adam and Eve in the first days of the world? You belong in Jorvik. What will happen to your children? Who will they marry? How will they live, here, with no one else around?"

Conn's warm merriment faded. He thought it very hard of Euan to be judging them like this. He glanced around at the rapt faces of the onlookers, all cranked up tight as a windlass with this wrangling. Raef dug his elbow into his side again.

Corban said, "If you came here to talk me into going back to Jorvik, and fighting there again, you came a long way for nothing, Euan. I will not go back. What we did there was grim and low and hard. I see no reason to repeat it. I owe a blood debt for it that weighs on me, and I will not add to it. But tell me more about Bloodaxe's heirs, and his wife. What of Gunnhild, and the Ericssons? Has she made one King of Norway yet?"

Then all around the circle the taut attention eased, as men laughed and sat back and made small jokes. The cup went back to Ulf, who filled it again.

"Harald Ericsson is King of Norway," Ulf said. "There being a great abundance now of kings called Harald, we call him Grayfur, because he traded once in squirrel pelts—that's another story. But he and Gudrod are the last of them—of Eric's sons with Gunnhild. The rest are dead—Gimle and Sigurd and the rest, fighting to become king, or stay so."

Benna said quietly, beside Corban, "I wonder if she is happy now." She leaned against Corban, her arm curling around his. The cup was traveling slowly around the circle; Conn watched it, licking his lips.

"Hear this," Ulf said, suddenly, "which will make you laugh. Harald Grayfur is a Christian."

"What?" Corban said.

"As I said. They all became Christian, one after another.

Gunnhild raged, but they cast her off and went on alone, and she sits in some tower somewhere in Denmark and broods on it, they say. An old woman already." Ulf shrugged. "She was a beauty, once."

Benna said, under her breath, "She is a beauty still, I suspect, old or no." She had Miru and Aelfu beside her. "I shall take my babies to bed."

"I'll help you." Arre rose to her feet. All around the fire, the men stirred.

Conn staggered up onto his feet, alarmed; he could see everybody was going off to bed, the stories over. "No, don't—" he began, and his legs wobbled and he sat down hard on the ground, his head swimming. All around him a roar of laughter broke out. He struggled to sit up, but it came to him that it would be just as easy to sleep here, and he found himself lying down already, and shut his eyes and waited for the world to come to rest under him.

CHAPTER FIVE

When Miska left Tisconum's country he went off into the west, through the hilly woodlands. He saw the smokes of other villages but avoided them. He ate what he found on his way, but the way was much easier, since now he was only retracing the path he had made coming out. He forded the broad river, brown and slow in its summery progress, and wound his way through the folds of the hills, until he came to hills he knew, and then out onto the little plain along the river where his people lived.

He stopped on first seeing, his heart gladdened. His hand went to the sack of charms around his neck. A surge of gratitude warmed him. His grandmother had sustained him, and brought him home alive. Burns-His-Feet on a whim had sent him off to die or fail, but he had done the task, and now he was home, which was the best reward.

The plain lay between low tree-covered hills. Already yellow in the summer heat, the grass spread off in a broad swath toward the river, and down there, along the western bank, stood the fortress of the Wolf People.

A stout fence surrounded it. In their long wanderings, the Wolf People had learned the value of strong walls. When they first came here, there were no other people living here, but others did live over the horizon, and so they made the fence strong and high. Now, throughout this country, everybody else feared the Wolves, everybody else knew not to cross their paths, and nobody else came willingly near their fortress.

He followed the deep-worn dusty path across the plain. At first shaggy woods buffalo had trampled through this meadowland, but the Wolf People had hunted them all off. The grass grew tall and strong. Along the margin of the plain, birds chattered and fluttered in the brush below the first trees. The webs of spiders hung in the brambly bushes sprouting up along the path. The tracks of small creatures dotted the thick dust under Miska's feet. By some raccoon scats, a side trail tunneled off into the high grass.

Halfway out across the plain, he crossed into the gardens of his people, the path running through a gap in a low fence of brush. Off on either side, the women stooped and straightened and stooped like birds over the green plants. He thought of what he would say tonight at the evening gathering and drew in a deep, sharp breath; they would think better of him, those women, when they knew what he had done.

Now beyond the line of the fence he could see the roofpoles of the longhouses, the brushy peaks of the lodges. The thousand other times he had seen these things, had walked home toward this close horizon of fence and roofs, rushed up from memory. Surely this was a blessed place, the center of the world. He thought a short prayer of thanks, that he had done the task demanded of him, and that he had come home.

He came to the gate, standing open; Hasei was the guard, leaning up against the wall, his eyes closed. Miska went in past him and into the village.

It was midday. The women were in the fields, the men at their business; the village seemed deserted. He went in past the Big Longhouse, its open door empty as an old man's mouth, and the potters' oven, mud-plastered, to the lodge near the fence where he lived with some other young men.

This lodge was empty, too. Usually at midday in the summer the men and boys went down to the river to cool off and cajole the women into feeding them. Probably also many had gone off to hunt, or raid other people's hunting. The lodge was dim and stuffy and smelled of rotten food. Robes, clothes, bits of food, and the pieces of a broken bow littered the floor. Someone had been trying to make a bowstring and left a snarl of hemp strands on the floor. Before he left he had rolled up his things in a robe and stuffed them in under the edge of the wall, and they were still there, crammed in between the wooden foot-planks of the wall. He shook the robe out, kicked aside the litter, and laid out his bed, to show he was back.

Reverently he took the bag of charms from around his neck and shook it out onto the robe. His grandmother's fingerbone, small and brittle and white, he took up and kissed, and put back in the bag; he always carried that. The feathers, the clear stone, and the wolf's tooth he gathered into a scrap of hide and tucked into the crevice below the wall, where he kept other things. They belonged to the place he had just come from; he would save them for the right moment.

That left only the little white stone he had picked up on the shore of the bay, back there, where the woman of the woods had stood. He took it, wondering what to do with it; idly he tossed it up into the air.

It fell back into his palm; it struck his hand with such a force and weight that it threw him entirely down, flat on the ground. Astonished, he lay there a moment, his cheek pressed to the fur of the robe. The stone lay in his outstretched palm, light as a bean. He drew it closer and saw only a small white pebble, rough-edged. He put it into the bag and hung the bag around his neck again.

"You."

He jumped. Jerking around, he saw Lasicka, the sachem's younger nephew, staring at him from the doorway.

"Yes." Miska stood up, stooping a little under the low beams of the lodge. "I am back now. I meant to come to Burns-His-Feet, as soon as—"

"You're back." Lasicka's mouth twisted. "What did you do, go off into the woods a while, until we'd think you'd really left? Who helped you? Somebody must have brought you food."

"No!" Miska threw his head back, angry, and cracked it on the beam. The lodge swayed. "I did go! I went all the way to the world-water. I—"

"You're lying. Come on, my uncle wants you, and you'd better think of a good story, Miska, sneaking back in like this."

"But I did go," Miska said. He followed Lasicka out of the
lodge and down through the village. He wished he had brought the
medicine bundle he had made, the things he had brought back
with him, as proof. At once he saw what they would make of that.
Lasicka led him in past the Gathering House and down to the river.

There in the shade of a huge old tree Burns-His-Feet and
some of the other men were lying on the ground eating nuts.
Burns-His-Feet was Miska's father's father's younger brother; he
had been sachem of the Wolves since just after they came to this
place. He was a big square man, his chest striped with ridged
scars, his arms and throat mottled like snakeskin with tattoos. One
of his knees hurt him, and he always sat with that leg stretched out
straight. In his hands the nuts cracked like little heads.

He said, "Miska! What are you doing back here—I told you
go to find those strangers, off on the salt shore."

"I did," Miska said.

Burns-His-Feet blinked at him, and then gave a harrumph of
a laugh; immediately all the men behind him began to laugh, too.
"Then where are they?" Burns-His-Feet said.

"What?" Miska gulped, feeling stupid. "You said nothing
about bringing them. I could not have brought them. There are
too many."

"You're lying," Burns-His-Feet said. "You never even saw
them." He crooked a finger at Miska. "Come to the tree this evening and I'll decide there how to punish you for coming back
when I sent you off."

Miska went hot all over. He put his hand to the amulet bag,
his mouth dry and his heart pounding. He thought of showing
them the magic stone and shied from that: They would take it
away from him, somehow. Burns-His-Feet was watching him
steadily, slit-eyed. He said, "Go away."

Turning on his heel, Miska walked off.

His head whirled. He went back through the village, hearing their laughter behind him. The delight at being home had gone cold in his belly. It was well past noon now, and the women had come in from the fields; they passed him, talking together in their little groups, and he could not lift his eyes and look at them. He crept back to his lodge and went to sleep, and did not dream.

⸺❦⸺

Burns-His-Feet ate little, although the meat was good. The chatter around him annoyed him; he tapped his fingers on his outstretched knee. Most of the people gathered around the fire before him were the women and their children, noisy, disorderly. He missed the respectful silence of his men. He wished he had gone with Anatkwa to hunt. The company of women was lowering. Now some of the younger ones were standing up to dance, and he still had this matter of Miska to deal with.

He clapped his hands, trying to call up their attention. The two old men dozing beside him straightened abruptly upright, their eyes wide, but the girls were still giggling and watching their feet, swaying in a long row on the far side of the fire. Burns-His-Feet clapped again, and one of the men shouted, and the women, abashed, went to sit down. In among them, Lasicka brought Miska toward the sachem's place.

Miska trudged along, his head down, his hair in his face. Burns-His-Feet felt a surge of anger. He had always hated this hostile, sullen boy; he had thought to have gotten rid of him the last time they argued, but now here he was back again.

"Very well, Miska," he said, before the young man had even stopped walking toward him. "Are you still going to lie and say you went all the way to the salt sea?"

"I did do it," Miska said, between his teeth. Through the shag of his hair Burns-His-Feet could see his eyes glitter, like something caged. "You told me to find the white strangers, and I did."

Burns-His-Feet leapt up. Everybody was watching now, he saw. He swelled his voice to a roar. "Bah. You say you went all the way to the land's end?" Is that what you're trying to tell me?"

"I did," Miska said. "They live on an island there. Not in the world-water, in a kind of lake of it. You said I should find Tisconum—"

Burns-His-Feet twitched. Tisconum was a great sachem, who led the councils all over the east country. "How did you? A green fool like you! Anatkwa himself said it was impossible."

"My grandmother showed me the way," Miska said, and bit his lips.

Burns-His-Feet roared, "Your grandmother! Dead three winters now! You cannot even tell good lies, boy!"

Burns-His-Feet laughed. Around him the men were laughing, also, their voices off-key. They all remembered Miska's grandmother, although they wished they didn't. The women, though, had now turned solemn. They sat in their circles, like little knots, and their eyes were fixed on Miska, hanging his head, his face dark with anger.

"How do we deal with a liar and a worthless boy?" Burns-His-Feet cried. "I say we drive you out of the village with stones!"

"No," Miska cried. "This is my home—you can't do that. Where would I go?"

The women were whispering, crowding their heads together, urging one of them up—Epashti, the young medicine woman. She seemed frightened, unwilling to speak, but finally, under the urging of the other women, she stood. "Wait," she said.

Burns-His-Feet said, "Do you doubt me? What is this, now?"

"If he has done what he says, we should know it," said Epashti, standing among the women, who all murmured and nodded and reached out to touch her, nudging her on, their eyes now steady on Burns-His-Feet, as if all together they could give him commands. Epashti walked up through the seated people and went to Miska.

She laid her hand on Miska's shoulder, and he stiffened, straightened, turned his face toward her. She touched his arms, drew his hands forward in her own and turned them over palms up, and leaned toward him and sniffed at him. All the other people stared, silent and rapt.

Burns-His-Feet clenched his teeth. "What is it? What do you think, Epashti? He's lying, isn't he."

Epashti stepped back, letting Miska's hand go. Her face rumpled with doubt. She had been medicine woman only since midsummer when her mother suddenly died; and recently her husband had died, too. She said uncertainly, "I don't know where he has been." She spoke to Burns-His-Feet, but her gaze turned to rest on Miska, and her voice strengthened. "It was nowhere any of us has ever gone, though, I'm sure of that. And he smells of salt. I think he tells the truth."

A great sigh went up, as if everybody exhaled at once. Miska lifted his head, his eyes shining and his mouth soft. Epashti went back to where she had been sitting, and the women on either side of her swayed and leaned around her, rippling like a pond when a splash of water falls back into it.

At that Miska collected himself. He stood straighter, his head high, and tossed his hair back. Burns-His-Feet sat down again, stuffing his anger down into his belly. He refused to look at Epashti. But he had to say something.

"She says you tell the truth, Miska. Maybe I've misjudged you. If so, then, tell me what they are, these people."

"Their skin is very light," Miska said. "Their eyes are strange. There are three men, two women. Little children, maybe two." His voice quickened. "I think they are evil. They have a canoe that flies, with wings. They have hair all over them."

Someone stood up, across the fire, and called, "Are they warriors?"

Miska shrugged. "They live on an island, in a lake of the

world-water, as I said. They have no wall around their lodge, but there is no way to get out there."

"You could get no boat?" Burns-His-Feet said swiftly. "Surely Tisconum has boats. Tisconum is a great man, very rich, surely he has boats."

"He did not want me to go on the water. He gave me little help," Miska said. "Someone else in his village told me he talks to one of the white ones—their sachem." His brow furrowed. "The words don't fit," he said.

Burns-His-Feet grunted at him. "You should have taken a boat out to the island. But I can see you were afraid."

At that Miska's head snapped back; he glared at Burns-His-Feet. "I—"

Burns-His-Feet held out his hand to stop him. "Tell us no more now. We must think about this. You can stay. You did what I required of you. Sit down among us, you are home now." He forced a smile onto his face.

Still high-headed, surly, Miska muttered some thanks, his eyes narrowed. He went off toward the fire, where some of the roast meat and beans remained. As he passed through the gathering, some people leaned toward him and spoke to him, but he was short even with them.

At least nobody else liked him either. Burns-His-Feet sank down on his cushions, grim; it bothered him he could not get rid of Miska. But this matter of the white people, he thought, was interesting. He shut his eyes, turning it over in his mind.

—⚬—

In the evening Anatkwa and the other men came home from their hunting.

Miska with the others ran out to greet them. In through the gates they came, singing and dancing, and carrying among them, slung upside down on poles, the many deer they had killed. The waiting people thundered up a cheer and rushed in to join them, old women and young women with babies in their arms, the children, the men and boys who had not gone on the hunt, all rejoicing. Miska with some others lifted the poles from the hunters' shoulders and carried the deer on their own backs. In a great mass, all together, they wound through the village, laughing and whooping, and the hunters made little dashes here and there, with their heads down, pretending they were the deer as they were hunted, and then falling down dead on the ground, kicking and rolling their eyes up and sticking out their tongues.

In the course of the hunt they had fought with a band of the Bear People, who had trespassed onto Wolf territory; Anatkwa had taken a prisoner, who walked along at the very end of the parade, a rope around his neck, and his head drooping.

Among his people Miska was singing and rejoicing; the deer pole wore heavy on his shoulder, but he refused to let anybody else take his place. He followed the men in front of him, and all around the village they wound their course, circling every lodge, every longhouse, to bind everyone into this luck and this meat. Finally they massed together into the gathering place, and broke up two of the deer and cooked them over the firepits, and all the night through they feasted on the fresh meat. The hunters swaggered around, talking about the hunt, and the women sang songs of praise and thanks; the little children ran from lap to lap being fed choice bits.

The prisoner of the Bear People feasted also, sitting among them as if he were one of them, eating all he wanted. He was special, they told him, he was blessed, and hearing this and with meat in his belly he seemed content and happy.

But when near midnight they laid hands on him, he began to struggle, knowing what was coming. He could not prevent it; they tied him up to the old tree at the back of the gathering place, and then, singing and laughing and giving praises and thanks, they burned him and cut him until he died. He wept and begged and pleaded, and because he was not brave, they did not accept him, they did not eat his body, but buried it the next morning in the bean field.

⸎

Epashti went through the village, looking for Miska. She had her baby in a sling before her; her hair was braided with yellow feathers, to honor her new motherhood, and sprigs of green leaves, to ward off the evil thoughts of childless, jealous women. Around her forehead she wore the headdress of the medicine woman. She carried a pack of medicines, and if people stopped her, she would listen to their complaints and help them.

At that, she knew, she was good enough; her mother had taught her herb lore and water charms and healing with her hands, and she knew everybody in the village anyway and what was wrong with them and what would work, or at least what would make them happier. That small magic was within her power.

It was the rest of it she could not grasp. It astonished her still that she had stood up before them all and spoken on Miska's side. She wondered where that understanding had come from— little as it was; no matter what anybody said, she had understood nothing significant.

In front of a shabby little lodge full of young men she found him, sitting on the ground, alone.

She stopped, keeping her distance a moment, studying him. He seemed deep in thought, his hair loose around his shoulders, his arms on his knees. His father had been her uncle, his mother her cousin. He should have seemed familiar to her, and yet whenever she saw him he seemed utterly new, like a stranger.

His parents had died in the terrible winter when they were trapped in the mountains, on the long trek away from their homeland. Epashti then had been only a child herself and remembered it more from the stories she heard of it—the endless snow, the hunger, the fighting, the cold blue darkness shutting down over them.

Miska would remember it better. And after that, with his parents dead, he had clung to his grandmother, and she to him, the two of them close as mother and child. He had carried her on their path, over hills and rivers, fed her and kept her warm and protected her, as much as she needed that, since everybody went in complete fear of her. Everybody but Miska.

Thinking of Miska's grandmother, Epashti shivered; that was the power, she thought, the true power, of which she had none. Another thing she knew about Miska's grandmother, from story, not from seeing but from women's talk, was how in his green reckless youth Burns-His-Feet had mocked the old woman, and she had caused his feet to blister and curl up, so that for two days he could hardly walk. That had earned him the name he carried now, and so every day he must hate her. Yet Miska clung to her, and from beyond the grave she gave him strength and wisdom. Epashti made herself go forward, toward him, to gather some of what he knew.

He looked surprised to see her. They exchanged the formal greetings of people related in the middle degree, and Epashti sat down beside him. She said, "Tell me where you went, Miska."

He said, "I'll show you something." He took the little deer-skin bag from around his neck and fished a small stone from it. "What's this?"

She took it from his open palm. When she touched it the stone seemed suddenly heavy, as if it would not leave him. She laid it on her hand and looked it over, just a small sharp-edged white stone, not even pretty.

"Where did you find it?"

He was staring away across the village, his gaze vacant. His mouth twisted. For a while he said nothing. Then finally he faced her and said, "I cannot tell you."

"Ah," she said, startled.

He shrugged and stared away again. "There are no good words," he said. "I saw the white people. I tasted the salt water, I fought against a strange magic that stirred the sea up—"

She gulped; she saw, in a flash, a long barbeled fish leaping, plated with armor, its eyes red, its eyes like a man's eyes, red. She made a charm with her fingers, trying to stave it off, and it was gone.

"And I found that stone," Miska said. He reached out and took it from her. "There was a woman—" He bit his lips.

She said, "I want you to tell me—" And then Burns-His-Feet was walking toward them.

The sachem strutted across the open ground, his tall feathered headdress waving. Behind him came Anatkwa, his sister's son, who was the bravest man in the village, and would be sachem when he was gone. Epashti stood up, a little flustered; her husband had often hunted with Anatkwa, but she did not know him well. Miska also stood.

"What's that?" Burns-His-Feet said, and nodded at Miska's hand.

Miska held out the little stone. "I found this, near the world-water."

"Pah." Burns-His-Feet struck out with one hand, knocking Miska's hand up, and the stone went flying off into the dust. "Can it talk? Can it prove you're telling the truth?"

Miska's teeth were gritted together. Epashti drew off to one side, where she could watch this; she saw Miska cast a quick look around, after the lost stone, and then wheel back to face Burns-His-Feet.

"Stop calling me a liar. I did what I said—what you ordered me to do."

Anatkwa stood up beside Burns-His-Feet. "Speak with some respect to the sachem, boy. You aren't even topped yet."

Miska said nothing, his face set in an ugly, sullen silence. Burns-His-Feet poked his finger at him.

"I've decided to find out for myself. We will take some of the men and go down there and see." His voice got oily. "If, as you say, these people are evil, why, then, we should deal with them. Since Tisconum won't." The poking finger turned into an open hand that palmed Miska's shoulder. "Can you lead us back there?"

Miska's face had smoothed out suddenly. He lifted his right hand up, still fisted, as if he wanted to look at it. But his gaze stayed on Burns-His-Feet. "A war party?" he said.

The sachem laughed. "Call it what you want. Can you take us?"

"Yes!" Miska seemed suddenly to grow taller, his eyes flashing. Epashti blinked, startled, at some sudden haze around him. But then it was gone. She had imagined it. He was just an eager boy, not even topped, gaping at his sachem.

"Good," Burns-His-Feet said. "We will talk at the gathering tonight." He nudged Miska with his fist and went off, Anatkwa on his heels.

Miska let out his breath in a whoosh. He turned, smiling, and saw Epashti, startling, as if he had forgotten she was there.

He said, "Well. They keep saying I am not topped—they will have to take me now, won't they. One lodge or another."

"I think so," Epashti said, although it was not women's doings. The lodges chose whom they would take in, when the boys' hair was topped. Miska should have gone to one or the other years ago, but no one would take him. She nodded toward his fist. "What do you have in your hand?"

He opened his fist, and on his palm was the little white stone. "I felt it come back," he said. "It struck my hand."

Epashti said, "I don't understand." Her cheeks felt warm. This was what she should know, this was what she did not have.

Miska said, "I don't either." He stooped and went back into the lodge.

⸻

During the evening gathering the men, after eating, collected together and sat under the big oak by the river with a pipe going around. Burns-His-Feet sat at the middle; Miska sat out along the edge of the cluster of men, and the pipe never came to him. But that would change, soon.

The pipe smoke rose up into the dark air, and the men murmured, and one said, "Someday we will go back, I know it."

All the others grunted out agreement. Someday they would travel back across the forest, over the mountains, and come again to the inland waters, their true home. Miska lowered his eyes, silent. This talk rankled him. His grandmother had said that he would make his people great someday, but in this place, here, by the Great River.

"When we go back, the sun chief will learn what true men are!" said someone else, and everybody gave another low cry, "hoooo-aaah," as if they could see this before them, almost in their hands, even now. They began to sway back and forth, and some clapped their hands together softly in an even beat. "We will cast down his four-sided hill and make the blood run through his villages."

"We'll hunt the bison again, and have plenty of meat."

"Hoooo-aaah." The clapping spread. The pipe went from mouth to mouth in the golden firelight, mouths eagerly rounded for the pipestem, eyes glazed with the light.

"We will make the sun chief eat his own heart! We, the People of the Wolf!"

"Hoooo-aaah!"

They clapped and spoke a while longer. Miska got enough of the pipesmoke through the air to make his head muzzy. Then through the fog came the piercing voice of Burns-His-Feet, saying, "There is this matter of these white people."

Miska jerked his head up. The other men quieted.

"Kill them," Anatkwa said, behind Burns-His-Feet. "They are cursed."

Burns-His-Feet lifted his hands, and his voice deepened and swelled. "They live by the world-water, on an island. There are only a few of them. Tisconum, the great Tisconum, is afraid of them! But we can conquer them."

"Hoooo-aaahhh!"

"Then we will be greater than Tisconum and his people. Then we will be the only men!"

Around him his warriors let out a roar that shook the branches of the oak tree. Up the gathering ground, in the deepening twilight gloom, the women all turned to look at them.

Burns-His-Feet said, "Your hearts are full of fire, I laugh to see it. When the other people around here see how we sweep to our victory, they will rush to join us."

"Hoooo-aaahhh!"

"Then in such numbers we shall fall on the sun chief and destroy him."

The men roared out again. Miska turned to glance at the women and saw them watching, in the darkness. Around him now the other men were clapping and singing out a pounding rhythmic chant, their voices buoyant. The pipe went from hand to hand. Miska wondered how all this had been talked over, and yet Burns-His-Feet had never mentioned his name. His belly turned. His skin thrummed with warning. He remembered the water whirling and whirling around, swallowing him down, and tilted up his face, suddenly hot, to the cool dark night. All around him, and yet apart from him, the men made songs of war.

CHAPTER SIX

Benna went up with Arre to the slope beside their house, above the point of the island. On one side of them lay the cove, where the men were floating the new ship for the first time. They had hauled it down to the shore; most of the cove's edge was reedy marsh, but at a good approach below the slope from the house Corban over the years had built up a ramp of rushes and sticks. With the boys and several of Ulf's crew, he was drawing the ship down this easy way into the water. On the grass above them, Benna spread out a blanket, and she and Arre sat down on it.

Benna was still amazed to find her sister there with her, after so many years; she kept her gaze on her, and every sound she made seemed like an oracle. She had changed, Arre. Over the past many years Benna had drawn her, over and again, but always as she remembered her, a carefree, great-hearted girl in a muddy apron. Now here beside her was that girl, but grown into another person, a woman in her years, steadier, calmer, carefree no more.

Benna said, "You must miss your children." Arre had left her two sons with Euan's mother when they fled.

Arre's head bobbed. She was watching the men, her eyes narrowed; she had brought some needlework to do while Benna drew, but it lay idle in her lap. "Look, they are putting up the mast. It's a pretty little ship, like a dragonfly, as they say." Her voice dropped a notch. "I miss them, very much, but I wanted to see you, and Euan had to leave. The boys were safer left behind. His mother dotes on them." She laid her hands together— smooth, pale hands, sunburnt from the sea voyage, but not the hands of a gardener anymore. Needlework was her craft now. And following her husband into exile.

Arre said, "You've changed, too, you know."

"I'm certain I have," Benna said. That was the old Arre: understanding other people's thoughts. "I'd like to draw you."

"Go ahead, then," Arre said. She leaned forward suddenly, keen, her face shining. "See! Now they're raising the sail! How beautiful!"

Benna glanced down toward the sheet of quiet water, ringed in cattails. A thin gray path ran down through the grass to the mucky shoreline. Down on the cove Corban and Ulf, at either end of the new boat, were hauling on ropes, and the new sail mounted up the mast, an empty sack of red and white stripes, drawn upward on its yard above the trim sweep of the hull. The sail hung flat against the mast. The men on the shore gave up a cheer.

Arre crossed herself. Benna was taking a flat stone and one of her brushes out of her bag; she mixed water into a pot of ink. Aelfu and Miru came down the slope from the direction of the house. Raef had brought them a baby rabbit, and Aelfu had the little thing in her hands; she squatted down near Benna and Arre to set it on the ground. The rabbit hunched down, looking dazed, its ears flat against its back. Miru, crouched next to it, poked it with her finger.

The men around the boat hushed for a moment, bent on some work; the long flat water of the cove reflected the sky, perfectly clear above and below, as if they floated on the island like a cloud in the blue vault.

Arre gave a little, uncertain laugh. "There are no church bells. How do you know when to pray?"

Without thinking, Benna said, "I don't pray anymore."

Arre's jaw dropped. She signed herself again and pressed her hands together. "Mercy of God on you, what have you done, Benna?"

Benna lowered her eyes to the stone, and drew. "I suppose it sounds ungodly. Yet I see god everywhere here, or what I think is god—god is here and sees me. I don't have to pray. Whatever I do, god will know, and that is my prayer."

Arre was still looking hard at her, her mouth drooping.

"How can you do good, when there are so few other people?"

On the stone, Benna made her sister's broad forehead, the strong arched bones of her face. "I can't answer that. It seems the wrong question to me. I don't know why."

Her sister looked away, toward the cove. After a moment, she said, in a tentative voice, "See, they are sailing."

Benna turned her head. Down there, the men had the boat with the wind, and the sail was filling. It swelled out; for a moment the boat seemed stuck where it was, standing on its upside-down reflection. Then imperceptibly it was gliding off, the red and white sail like a bloodstain above the water.

Arre said, "I don't mean to judge you."

"No," Benna said, startled. "I didn't think you were." She wondered where this crosscurrent had suddenly arisen from. She searched for something easier to talk about. "Where is Gifu? I wonder she didn't come with you." Gifu was their younger sister.

Arre's head swung toward her. "She married. Did you not hear that? Years ago, she married a man of the new ealdorman's."

Some undertone in her voice told Benna that Arre had fewer qualms about judging Gifu. "Married. That's amazing. I thought she would run wild, without me. Is he then an Englishman?" The English were Euan's enemies.

"No—he's a stranger. Richard is his name, they call him Longsword. He's some kind of Frank. He served the ealdorman for money; Waltheof—that's the ealdorman—is very loath to do much on his own. He sent Richard to Jorvik when Euan—when the first trouble happened." Her lips pressed together a moment. Benna thought suddenly: Things have gone wrong for her, that's why she's unhappy. Euan has gone wrong for her. She contemplated herself, judging. Arre was staring away toward the cove. Her voice came again, quiet, almost idle.

"Then one day he saw Gifu riding over the moor, and he chased her and couldn't catch her." She laughed and was lively again, her good self, unburdened. Now her eyes sparkled; she looked Benna in the face. "She took him on a wild chase, so I hear, and distanced him—she would not speak of it, I know this by gossip. By then she was living as she wished, with her horses and her hunting; I saw her very seldom. But he kept looking for her, and finally, after much chasing, he caught her, and brought her back to Jorvik and married her, that same day. I hear they are very pleased with each other. They have several children."

"In Jorvik," Benna said, amazed. Her youngest sister had always startled her; she remembered her wild nimbus of fair hair and her blazing blue eyes.

"No, no," Arre said, as if Benna should know all this. "Richard and the ealdorman got across each other, somehow, and Waltheof threw them out. Now her husband serves the English king."

"But he is not English."

"No," Arre said. "He is Norman, I think." She cast her eyes around them, toward the water.

On the slope below them, Aelfu and Miru were chasing the rabbit, which was eating the grass; it let Aelfu come close, but when she bent over to pick it up, the little thing hopped away again, just enough to get away from her. This happened over and over, the children and the rabbit turning a slow circle around the grass. Arre turned to look up the rise, toward where the house stood, in the lee of the great rock.

"You live very well here. I have seen, Corban has no difficulty finding meat for all these men."

"It will not go on so," Benna said. "He will send Ulf away as soon as he can. This is a time of plenty, but in the winter it's very hard. And he will fret over losing so many of the deer. The people over there"—she gave a jerk of the head toward the shore—"they go away, even, it is so hard, in the winter."

"Who are they?" Arre asked, swiftly. "I saw the smoke—are there villages out there?"

"Several villages, around the water here. The people there

are not like us. They're much darker, and of very strange customs. We stay away from them, and them from us."

"Christian people."

"No." Benna laughed; she saw her sister had no understanding of it. She said, "They have their own ways. They manage well enough. There are many of them, not as many as at Jorvik, but a good number, men and women and children. Sometimes I think they aren't as different from us as they seem. In the winter, Corban says they go north, to hidden camps."

"Ah. And what do you do?"

"We stay here. It snows, sometimes, days on end, and so high it piles above the eaves and we have to dig a tunnel through it out of the house."

Arre's dark eyes were wide. "But how do you live then?"

"All summer we store up food and wood," Benna said. "We have some warning before the storms come, and everybody has a task to hand, and we keep the fire going and tell stories."

"How do you have warning?"

Benna looked up toward the great gray rock crowning the ridge above them. Brush overgrew its foot, a dense skirt of green blotched with red. There among the tangled leaves she could just make out Mav, sitting wrapped in Corban's old red and blue cloak, in spite of the summer heat.

Some of the men of the crew had already approached her. She had dealt with them hard, and they would not try again. Benna wondered what she made of this, and thought she was probably angry.

"Corban's sister tells us."

Arre was silent for a while. Benna went back to the drawing, trying to capture the shadow in her sister's eyes. Under her breath, Arre said, "I didn't realize how far from home you had come."

Benna leaned out and put her arm around her, and Arre bent toward her and hugged her. The girls were following the rabbit hopping slowly across the sunny slope. On the cove, the little ship was running before the wind now, swift and light; over Arre's shoulder, Benna watched it sail away across the sky-blue water. Arre was warm in her arms, and yet there seemed so much between them now. Still her heart rose, to have her sister beside her again, and she cast away the rest and hugged her tightly back.

⚓

Burns-His-Feet took the pipe from Tisconum and smoked of it; behind him, ignored, Miska sniffed the burning leaf and suffered a hot stroke of longing. He would get nothing of this pipe, even though he had led them here, even though they could not do this without him. Burns-His-Feet held the pipe in his hand and gave it to none of the other Wolves at all. He lifted it to his lips again.

Tisconum was still angry, his lips pressed together and his eyes narrow almost to slits. They had sent Lasicka to him when they arrived here, just before sundown, and he had come straight back to meet them, striding out of the woods with just a few of his own men, to show how little Burns-His-Feet scared him, Miska thought. And also to show he was angry and would do the Wolf sachem no honor. Now, sitting straight up in the deep hue of the firelight, he spoke in a harsh voice.

"There are more of them now. I think you should turn around and go back where you came from."

Lasicka, sitting to the left of Burns-His-Feet, let out a startled hiss. He turned quickly to look at his sachem, who sat unmoving, unmoved, the pipe to his lips, taking in the smoke. Burns-His-Feet lowered the pipe; after a moment he let out the smoke in a stream that boiled in the orange light above the fire.

"How many?"

Tisconum's gaze did not waver, but he swallowed, and his mouth twisted. His eyes scanned the crowd of the Wolves. "Not as many as you."

All the Wolves stirred at that, turning to one another, nodding; Miska, behind them all, kept still. He had brought them here as straight as if to his home fire, and with each step of it the feeling had grown heavier in him that he was doing something wrong. He thought of the heaving water, and the whirlpool, but he had no way to speak of these things to Burns-His-Feet and the others; no one gave him the opening. He watched as Burns-His-Feet handed the pipe back to Tisconum.

"Where are they coming from?" Burns-His-Feet asked.

"From the world-water," Tisconum said.

"That is impossible. We have to get rid of them. We will surprise them in a rush, and destroy them. Come with us. We shall do it together, and do honor to our people."

Tisconum sat straight in the copper light, his eyes gleaming, and the corners of his mouth curled down. "I will not do so. He has become my friend."

"You are afraid," said Burns-His-Feet, and the Wolves all gave a low laugh. Miska twitched suddenly, a ripple in his gut, like a fish tail.

Tisconum stiffened and got up onto his feet. "I came here as one who belongs here," he said. "To speak to you, and to offer you some guidance. But I see it is wasted. You are a fool, Burnt Feet"—he said the name oddly, in his own twisted speech—"and you shall suffer for it if you try to attack him."

Burns-His-Feet said steadily, "You're afraid. We will show you how to be men."

Tisconum turned without a word and went off into the darkness of the forest. The three young men who had accompanied him went silently away after him. Miska got to his feet, his chest tight. He thought of the island; he tried to think how to attack it, and always as he thought about it the dark green water rose up before him like a wall.

Tisconum was gone. Around the little fire the Wolves gathered close, all but Miska. Burns-His-Feet leaned in among them.

"Lasicka! You went into the village, when you told Tisconum we were here. What did you see there?"

Lasicka rubbed his hands together, his eyes glittering. "They have no wall. Their houses are spread out. They have much food, and many women." His hands crossed and gripped each other.

Some of the other men grunted. Miska sank down on his heels behind them, where he could follow everything that happened. Over Lasicka's shoulder he saw Burns-His-Feet cock his head back.

"That would be good to know if we were attacking Tisconum. We have to get out to that island. Did you see any boats?"

Lasicka looked confused, but on Burns-His-Feet's other hand, Anatkwa said, "Yes, not good ones. Just dugouts." He turned toward the others, laughing. "They can't even make a good boat." Everybody else laughed, too. In the firelight they were a shifting circle of faces, turning this way and that, leaning forward, ducking back, appearing and disappearing, one after another.

Miska put his hand to the amulet bag, with its charms and powers. He said, as loud as he could, "The water is not passable."

Here and there, in the mass of men around the fire, a head turned abruptly, and eyes poked at him. He waited for one to answer, so that he could speak more. Two by two, the staring eyes turned toward Burns-His-Feet.

The sachem said, unperturbed, "Where are these boats?"

Miska said, "No, listen to me—"

Directly in front of him, Lasicka turned and struck him hard across the face. Miska went down, even more from surprise than the blow. He heard, through the roar in his ears, "Speak when you are spoken to!" He cringed against the damp ground, sure they would all now leap on him.

Nobody else struck. He heard, as his ears cleared, Anatkwa's voice.

"The boats are drawn up on the riverbank, this side of the village." Anatkwa's tone smoothed out, moving on into the next bend of this. "We can take them easily enough. Just walk down through the trees there, along the riverbank."

"Then let's go," said Burns-His-Feet.

—⚬—

Euan said, "What is of value here? The timber, surely, if it could be gotten to Iceland—they have much need of timber in Iceland. Hides, from your hunting."

"Furs," Corban said. Clamshells, he thought. Birch syrup. He saw what Euan wanted, things of trade; he saw these things stretching like a chain between here and Jorvik, and he looked away, furious.

Euan was watching him steadily. "You mean to stay here forever."

"I had some thought of that." Corban moved on down the shore, the soggy ground squelching under his feet. They had brought Ulf's ship down to the more sheltered anchorage deep inside the cove; beside it the little hide boat bobbed like a seed. The boys had taken the new ship off down the strait.

With the awnings off his big merchant ship, Ulf's crew had made tents on the open slope, spreading out below the flat bench at the foot of the rock where Corban had his house. Most of them had gone back into the forest to hunt, and two or three were fishing down in the cove. Corban pulled his gaze away from them. Every place now seemed crowded, trampled on, not his anymore.

Euan followed him like a tracker after a deer. "But there is nothing here. How can you live in a place with no other people?"

"There are other people." Corban was still walking, as if he could escape.

Euan dogged him. "What? These creatures who live in the woods? They are nothing to you. You were a great man, in Jorvik." Euan caught up with him, peering into his face. "You saved us from Eric Bloodaxe."

Corban laughed, not happily. Every mention of Eric jarred him farther along on some course he recoiled even from thinking about. Eric had been a wicked man, he thought, a wicked man. A walking proof that murder never went unpunished. Corban saw no reason why he himself should be different, and his murder.

Euan said, "What about your family? Your sons? Your daughters? Do you expect them to stay here, too?"

He had thought about this, coming to no certain answer. He stopped at the top of the rise between the cove on the right and the tilted stretch of grass below the rock, where his house stood, dug into the ground. As he always did there, he looked out over the strait, reaching out his eyes into the indefinable distance. The sky was clouding over, and the lapping water looked cold and uneasy. From here the opposite coast stretched away, green with cattails, into the north; the island's shore bent away south, so that the western bay widened out before him, its myriad small islands breaking the flat water.

Euan said, "How can you live by yourself, like some kind of hermit?"

"I'm Irish." Corban was looking at the coast just across the narrow neck of water here, where a gathering of people seemed to be doing something. He frowned. He thought they were pushing boats out into the water.

"Bah." Euan's voice ground remorselessly on. "A man is nothing except in the society of other men. You are wasting yourself here."

"I was nothing there," Corban said. He turned suddenly, scanning the grassy slope by his house. "Where is my sister?"

"Ah, that one," Euan said. "She's mad enough, she could live here by herself. Talk about Irish."

Corban wheeled back, squinting to see that far shore. He said, "They are coming here." He remembered suddenly what Tisconum had said: Someone is watching you.

"Who?" Now Euan pushed up beside him and stared away. "I see nothing."

Corban strode up higher on the slope, his gaze pinned to that far shore, where now he could see boats in a swarm, pushing out over the water. Euan was following him, still talking, and Corban grabbed him by the arm and shook him.

"See—out there—many boats. I don't like this. They have never done this before. Go get your men, with their bows."

Euan's face went long, and his mouth dropped open. He gave a single glance out over his shoulder at the bay and ran off, around the western edge of the rock, toward the woods. Corban thought of the boys out sailing, of Benna who had gone with the children to pick berries. Of Mav. He broke into a run, heading toward the great rock that rose above the long grassy roofline of his house.

⸺⸮⸺

Burns-His-Feet had painted his face with streaks of white clay, and his eyes gleamed as if through a mask. "There don't seem so many people there at all, to me. This will be easy." He brandished his warclub in one hand. "Let's go. Move! Into the water!"

A yell went up. Around them the Wolves grabbed the dugout boats and hauled them into the bay. Miska grabbed one end of his boat and Lasicka took the other, and they ran out through the shallows. Dropping the boat into the water, they straddled it and began to paddle it forward. Miska's heart began to pound; all around him were other boats, other Wolves, swarming out onto the bay, driving swift and potent through the water. In their midst, one of them, he could do anything. He flung himself into the work, whining under his breath.

On either side of him the rough-barked logs surged forward. The paddles lashed the shallow choppy water to a foam. Miska stroked with all his strength; the dugout rolled like an egg in the little waves. Part of them all, he shouted and whooped and dug his paddle down into the water.

The other boats were crowding up around him, all racing, all wanting to be first. Burns-His-Feet waved his warclub again and nearly dumped his boat. Miska could see people on the island, turning now, seeing them come, and one ran off, already frightened. He screeched. He would frighten them all, one by one, before he killed them. He strained with the rude paddle, forcing the boat on. Burns-His-Feet was so close to him their boats banged together.

Suddenly, directly in front of them, a great fish leapt, an arc of spiny gray, that hung in the air before them for a long heartbeat before it plunged back. Miska froze, startled; a yell went up from the other Wolves. The fish splashed into the bay and vanished. The wave of its passage rose up, and up. Burns-His-Feet shouted, flailing out with his club, and his boat tipped and he went into the water. The wave came on, rising, higher, whitecapped. Burns-His-Feet was trying to get back onto his boat; the other dugouts were banging together, no longer moving forward, the men confused, unsure, and the wave mounted, climbing up before them, curling over.

Miska screamed, "Get back!" He swung his paddle around to the other side, trying to keep the dugout straight across the oncoming wave, and then the water was rising under him, the boat was tipping upright on its butt end, he was falling. Someone crashed against him, driving him down under the water. He slid past another desperate thrashing body, scrabbled out with his hands, trying to catch hold. His foot touched the rocky bottom and he strove upward again and his head hit something and he gasped and sucked in salty water.

Desperately he floundered toward the shore. Around him men shrieked and wailed. A hand seized his arm and dragged him down. He kicked out, trying to free himself. His knee scraped on gravel. On hands and knees he scrambled up through the shallows and back to the shore.

Sobbing and gasping, the rest of the Wolves were struggling up around him, crawling out of the water onto the slick muddy shore. Lasicka sat down abruptly on the mud, his mouth agape, staring out at the bay.

"That fish," he said. "It had a man's face. I saw it."

"Help," someone called. "Help—" Miska leapt up and rushed back into the bay and helped Anatkwa drag Burns-His-Feet, half conscious, in through the shallows to the shore.

The other men lay or sat on the mud, panting. Miska sat down with a thud, his heart racing. He put his hand to the medicine bag around his neck and looked over toward the invulnerable island. Someone was watching them from the top of a big rock above the shore. He shut his eyes, humiliated.

Burns-His-Feet coughed up water. Braced on his arms, his head hanging, he got his breath back, while Anatkwa and the others crowded together in silence. The boats were drifting away.

Burns-His-Feet pushed himself up on his arms and sat heavily, the smeared white color flowing down along his cheek and his throat, and his hair plastered sodden to his head. His breath sucked up under his ribs; he looked like an old man suddenly. Everybody was staring at him. Miska felt the first ripple of the feeling that Burns-His-Feet had done this to them, that Burns-His-Feet should suffer.

The sachem's eyes gleamed through the drying muck. He said, "Lasicka, you said Tisconum's people had no wall around their village?"

"No," Lasicka said. "We can walk right in."

"Then let's go," Burns-His-Feet said. "Or do we want them laughing at us tomorrow?"

From the other Wolves a harsh growl went up, a gritty edge, as if they had been cheated. They shuffled to their feet, collecting their weapons. Miska had no warclub yet, but he had his knife. He thought of Tisconum, and his heart beat heavily in his chest. That old dread came back to him, that he was doing something wrong. It was not Tisconum's fault they had been humiliated. Yet with the rest of them he moved forward, back through the trees, following Burns-His-Feet back toward Tisconum's village.

Corban shaded his eyes with his hand, his heart racing; he saw the people there on the shore get up and start off, not back into the water, not to attack the island again, but along the shore, and toward the river. In the distance, he heard their yells.

He scrambled down the side of the rock, slipping from foothold to foothold, down to the tangled brushy ground. Mav stood there, wrapped in his red and blue cloak, staring away toward the shore; her face was gaunt and taut and fierce.

He said, "What is it?" Fifty yards away, in the sunlight, Euan came up the rise toward him, his hands loose at his sides.

Mav gave Corban a single intense look and thrust her arm out, pointing to the far shore, then fixed her gaze there again. Corban went on toward Euan. He stopped, in the warmth of the sunlight, and looked down toward the shore again. Those running, shouting men were certainly making for Tisconum's village.

He wheeled toward Euan. "Where are the others? Call them—have them bring their bows—"

"What?" Euan said. "They have turned aside, look." He pointed out over the narrow neck of the water. "They are no harm, after all."

"Get your men!" Corban ran on, down toward his house, cupped in the rise of the land and the sheer of the rock. He had nothing to fight with save his axe, and he plucked it out of the stump by the front door and went back, down the slope, toward the shore.

Across the narrow water the running pack had gone out of sight, into the woods, but now suddenly from that distance, from the thick green of the trees, a great many-voiced howl went up, like a smoke of fearful noise.

He had to cross the water. He thought of the hide boat, over in the cove. Euan's men were still gone, off hunting, Euan himself stood on the rise above him and watched and did nothing. Then, around the lower point of the cove, the red and white sail burst into view, fat with the wind.

He yelled. Carrying the axe on his shoulder, he rushed out into the water, out into the current, and waved his free arm. On the little ship his boys had seen him. Running before the afternoon wind, the red-streaked sail swelled toward him. They had no weapons. The oars. He waved his arm, shouting to them, and the ship veered toward him.

—⁂—

Raef saw, first, not his uncle wading out from the island, but a little plume of dark smoke poking up into the sky, beyond the first trees on the mainland side of the water. Then Conn yelled, and he jerked his gaze around and saw Corban there, to his waist in the swift moving current, his mouth open shouting, and the axe on his shoulder.

Raef gave a great shiver, as if he were putting on another skin. Half sick, he looked back toward the smoke, wondering what was happening; the smoke was billowing up, much more now, thick and black and swollen. Behind him Conn shouted again, sharper, and he reached out for the sail's foot and pulled it back, and the ship slid softly over to meet Corban.

His uncle hauled himself up over the gunwale. He was speaking even before he was aboard. "We have to get to Tisconum's

village—someone is attacking him." He went to the stern, with
Conn scrambling out of his way, and took the steerboard and laid
it over. "Row. The wind's foul."

Conn and Raef pulled out the oars; the sail slatted against
the mast. The sting of hot smoke itching in his nose, Raef
brought his oar across the gunwale and bent his back down to the
rowing. He had a sudden sense of distance from what went on
around him, as if the space around him bulged, separating him
from everything else. When the hull grated in on the pebbles of
the beach, embers were drifting down like black snow falling,
hissing when they struck the water.

Raef's hands and feet felt swollen. His head was throbbing.
The world around him seemed to be falling to pieces. Everything
was happening at once. Somehow they were on the shore now.
Corban thrust his oar into his hands and pushed him along, back
through the soggy marsh, into the trees. He fought the awkward
weight of the oar, trying to carry it over his shoulder, but the
trees kept hitting it with their branches. He heard Conn behind
him calling sharp questions, and Corban answering, but Raef
made no sense of it; he wondered how they could talk when
around them everything was crumbling apart.

They burst out of the trees toward the blazing village, and it
was as if the light and heat filled up his eyes and there was just
too much to see. The horrible noise of the fire rumbled in his
ears, and his throat ached with the smoke. People were suddenly
running toward him, screaming, wild-eyed. He gripped his oar
with both hands. Should he hit them, should he attack them?
Corban grabbed him by the arm and pulled him forward, in
among burning heaps of coals that gave off buffets of heat,
where hidden in the glare men fought like shadows in the rolling
smoke. His eyes felt boiled. Then before him Corban reared
back, the axe-whirled above his head, his body twisted to swing.

Suddenly a naked brown chest rose up right between them, a
head of flopping hair. Raef flailed wildly with the oar. The wood

shivered in his hands, striking something, too twitchy to keep hold of, and he dropped it. Empty-handed he goggled around him. The wild swirl of the burning light made everything blend together, a churning of bodies, a cauldron. He snatched up the oar again and swung it around him, trying to keep all the whirling colors away from him. Before him he saw Corban, fighting axe against club with a bigger man whose face and chest were streaked with white.

Then Conn rushed up beside him, and in Raef's mind suddenly an order appeared, of himself, Conn, and Corban, where he stood at one point, and they at two others. Abruptly everything seemed easy, even with the whole world spinning wildly around him; now nobody could come at him from behind, and when a man rushed at him from the front Raef jabbed the oar into his belly, and knocked him flat. Then behind him somebody screamed, and he spun around, to see Corban ducking under a sweep of the club, and rising to chop the white-streaked man off at the waist with the axe.

A great screech went up from the men they were fighting. Raef felt them flinch back, their voices keen with fear, higher, edged with a strident restlessness, falling away. Corban rushed forward, and Raef knew to keep with him, at his point of the three-pointed figure. Still the spinning colors and sounds around him drowned him, fragmented, terrifying. His belly felt sick. He stepped on something soft and his guts heaved.

Before him was a soothing darkness. They were among trees now more than people. The smoke stung his eyes. He gasped for breath, hearing the fading yells and screams ahead of them, disappearing into the forest. He dropped the oar again. Corban stood before him, his mouth open, breathing hard. The older man turned; his gaze ran slippery over Raef.

"You're all right?"

Raef opened his mouth; no words would come out. His uncle smiled at him, and bent and picked up the oar and put it back into his hands. Palming the boy's shoulder, he nudged him softly back.

"Go. It's over. They've gone." His hand rested gently on Raef's shoulder.

Raef turned, his legs shaking. Conn came up beside him and slung one arm around him.

"We fought a battle! Do you realize that? We have fought in a battle together!" Conn yelled. His eyes glittered; he was smiling. He held up something in his other hand, a long stout painted stick, curved at one end; the curve like a fist of wood held a round stone. "See what I won? Ulf and the others are just getting here. They missed it."

Raef blinked; a battle: He supposed that was what had happened. The club in Conn's hand held his eyes, the curious carving and painting of it, the stone locked solidly in its grip. He heard a loud dansker voice, over across the ruins of the village, and Corban beside him shouted, "Ulf! Over here!"

Raef took in a deep breath. He felt as if he had not breathed in days. Blinking, he looked around him, startled. The village was all burned, no houses left, only heaps of smoking charred ruins as high as Raef's head. The light was bad—the sun was going down. All around, like tendrils of smoke, the wails of the people rose. Before him an old woman knelt above an outstretched body and struck it over and over with a stick, wailing and screaming. The deep orange light of the burning village flickered over her face.

Corban stood before him; Raef moved closer to him, afraid, and suddenly Corban reached out his arm and gripped him tight. "You did a good job of it, Raef."

Raef said, "What—what—" He wondered what he had done. He remembered nothing. He wondered if he had killed anybody. The white-streaked body of the man Corban had killed lay just off to his right, in the red flickering light of a burning hut. As he watched, the villagers, weeping and screaming, gathered around it and began to hack it to pieces. Raef's belly jerked up into his throat.

Corban said, "Oh, no."

From the darkness Tisconum walked toward them. The tall man held a body in his arms. Conn's hold tightened on Raef's arm. Tisconum's face was slimed with tears. He walked up to Corban and held out the body in his arms, a boy, a boy that Raef had known, the long-jawed scornful boy that Conn had beaten on the ocean shore. Raef sobbed; he broke away, running, heading for the woods, and in the shadowy dark and the broken brush he dropped to his knees and threw up.

CHAPTER SEVEN

Lasicka wiped his hand over his face. Still dazed from that fighting, he was slumped against a tree, his throbbing leg stretched out before him; the other men stumbled in through the trees and sank down around him. He heard them moan in pain, he saw them clutching wounds, he smelled clotting blood. He smelled the sick sweat of frightened men. He gasped, his leg a fiery ache, and looked around him at the others, and his chest contracted at what he saw.

Every one of them was hurt, one with an arm dangling, another gashed across the face, over there a man doubled up on the ground, knees to his chest, his breath slobbering through his lips. Mostly there were too few of them. Burns-His-Feet was dead, and Anatkwa, and three others, and these their living brothers had left them behind; their bodies lay in the hands of their enemies.

Miska came in among them, with their packs and camp goods, and Epashti.

Miska alone bore no wounds. Lasicka searched him with his gaze, amazed again at that. Miska had fought at the front of them, had taken and given more blows than anybody, yet he was untouched.

The memory swamped Lasicka again. At first they had been winning, but then the whites had come, and more and more of them, as if they would never stop coming. Like a wave shoving them back, breaking them up and shoving them back. Lasicka had fallen, his leg crumpling, and Miska had hoisted him up on his shoulder and hauled him away. Even now, through the daze of his pain, he remembered that sure hard touch on him, Miska lifting him up.

Epashti brought him some infusion of elderberries. Night

was falling but there was no fire. In the damp gloom they huddled together on the floor of the forest like mice, afraid. The dark
around him hummed with the whimpers of the other men. Some
were hurt enough to die. Many might die. Lasicka himself could
die, his leg a useless sack of flesh and bone. Epashti went tire-
lessly among them all, murmured gentle words and charms, gave
them what she could, her hands a momentary comfort.

Worse than hurting, worse than maybe dying, was that they
had lost. Lasicka closed his eyes, heartsore. He wondered how
they could even dare go back to their home. Everything in him
was gone, hollowed out and eaten by their enemies. Burns-His-
Feet. Anatkwa. His leg throbbed with overwhelming hurt; his
mind throbbed, too hurt to think.

Beside him, Miska said, "We have to get moving."

Lasicka's head bobbled on his weakling's neck. He felt the
current of this carrying him away down into a deeper dark.
"What's the use?"

Something struck him, hard. He lifted his head, amazed.
This topless boy, this green shoot, had hit him. A spurt of out-
rage stiffened him. He stared into Miska's eyes, inches away.
"Don't you touch me, you whelp."

Miska smiled, his eyes unblinking, staring into Lasicka's.
"Remember last night? I told you the water was unpassable, and
you hit me then. Remember? I'll hit you more, if you quit. We
are going home. Find something to lean on so you can walk."

"We can't go home," Lasicka said bitterly. "We lost."

This time he saw it coming, even in the dark, the hard slap
toward his head; he ducked, but it hit him anyway. He gaped at
Miska, who dared this.

Looming over him, in the dark, Miska seemed much bigger.
Unwounded. The whites could not hurt him. He said, "We
haven't lost. If you had listened to me we would not have lost. I
will find some better way, and then we will win. But you must
not give up now."

Lasicka laid one hand against his swollen leg. Everything had fallen apart, if this could happen. A topless boy, whom he had beaten yesterday, beat him today. He said, "Who are you to say this, Miska?"

"When it happens," Miska said, "you will know. Now, come on, help me, we have to get moving."

He went off through the dark. Lasicka saw him talking to Epashti, and soon the other men were up, complaining and whining, cursing Miska under their breaths. But they were all up, all moving. Going home. Lasicka hoisted himself onto his good leg and leaned against a tree. Going home. Carefully he edged his way on to the next tree.

Ulf said, "You haven't asked me, but as an old friend I think we all ought to get out of here, now."

"No," Benna said.

Corban turned toward her voice, and their eyes met. She sat small among all these strangers, penned up, her shoulders hunched, her mouth curled down. Beside her, Conn raised his head, and his voice rang out loud around the fire.

"No! My mother is right. This is our land, and we won! We beat them. So we don't leave."

Corban turned his gaze back to Ulf, across the fire from him. "You hear them." He knew they had only begun this.

The old sailor grunted. The firelight shadowed the deep prickled seams of his face. "I think you're all mad." He and most of his crew had come back from hunting with a fine deer, sometime before dark, and Benna had harried them on over the narrow water in the hide boat. Their sudden rush had broken the strangers, sent them scurrying away into the forest, leaving behind their dead. Corban locked his hands together; he had done death again, inescapable.

Euan said, "Well, if you won't leave, Corban, someone must go back to Jorvik and bring help."

Angry, Corban jerked his gaze toward him. Euan had not come across the water to fight; Euan did nothing but complain. "What help do you think you could raise, Euan? Who would come out here, to the edge of nowhere?"

Euan leaned forward, his face like a wedge, forcing his purposes on. "For me, no one. But they would come for you."

"Pagh," Corban said. "I don't believe it." He turned away, not liking where this was going.

Ulf nodded solemnly at him. "Many a man would follow Corban Loosestrife, even all across the sea." Behind him, his crewmen, listening, raised a general murmur of agreement.

Away beyond his mother, Conn was watching his father with shining eyes. Corban lifted his hand up between them; he wanted nothing of that kind of look. He said, "I would sooner go back to Jorvik myself, with all my family, than bring such as Eric Bloodaxe here."

"Bloodaxe is dead."

"None of the Ericssons. Or Bluetooth. Is he not still the King of Denmark?"

"No, not Bluetooth either," Euan said. He sat motionless, canted forward, his hands on his knees, his eyes direct, his voice steady, even mild, a man who turned other men by his will, and not his strength of arm. "But there are still free men in Denmark. There's Hakon of Lade. There's Palnatoki."

Ulf burst out, "That's the truth." He turned around, looking over his shoulder, and his sailors nodded and muttered, excited. Corban lowered his hand to his side. Euan sat still a moment, letting them talk around him, building up a little wave of agreement. His gaze met Corban's, and they stared at one another.

Beyond Euan, Arre was looking somberly in another direction. Corban followed her gaze and saw Benna's heart-shaped face there, pale as a moon.

Off in the dark, suddenly, another voice rose, a sharp, alert bird-cry. Still under Corban's gaze, Benna startled; she got to her feet. Corban stood up, turning toward the noise.

Out of the darkness, Mav came walking, the firelight washing up over her as she approached, and by the hand she led Tisconum.

A great shout of alarm went up from Ulf's men. Many of them reached for their weapons. Corban went quickly out to meet his sister and the native lord, calling, as he did, "Stay where you are. I know him, he is a friend." He gave one quick look into Tisconum's face, set and hard, and turned to shield him from the others.

Ulf and Euan had risen up to their feet; Ulf clutched a long knife. At Corban's look he sank down at once on his heels. Euan sat back by the fire, and the sailors quieted behind them, and there was silence.

Corban faced Tisconum. The other man looked all undone, his hair hanging ragged around his shoulders, his face smeared with mud. His sunken cheeks were seamed with bleeding scratches, as if he had torn himself with grief. He raised his hands and spoke in the language they had made between them, half words and half gesture.

"You came to us. You came and fought for us. We thank you. If not for you they would have killed us all."

Corban glanced at the others of his camp, hunched around by the fire, every face turned on him, watching him. He wiped his hand over his mouth. To Tisconum, he said, "There are many dead. I am sorry." He had no way to say that he thought he had brought it all down on them. "Was that your son?"

"My sister's son." Tisconum's eyes burned in the bloody ruin of his face. "The hope of all my people. He would have been headman after me. We all loved him." He blinked. "We didn't kill them all. Those others—they will come back."

"Who are they?"

The other man's face twisted, until in the firelight he seemed like a wild beast snarling. "They are the Wolves. They came from the west, not long ago, dragging their feet, their tails down, yes, they were running away from something when they came here, not so fine then, grateful for a little peace. Now they have licked their wounds and think themselves strong again, and they hate us, because we have the waterland, which is the best and richest country in the world." He blinked at Corban, an eddy in the spill of words. "You know that. That's why you came here to live. They want it, and they will come back again to try to take it from us."

Corban said, "Then we will fight them again. I'll help you."

Tisconum lunged toward him, and by the fire everybody leapt forward; Corban thrust his arm out, holding them back. Tisconum lifted his two fists between them.

"Your help is what I need! These are what I have to fight with! But you—" His hand shot out to snatch Corban's knife from his belt. He jerked the blade up between them, so that the firelight glanced off the steel.

"You have this. And other things of magic shape and power. I have seen them. I saw you strike down Burnt Feet with one such." He swung his arm out wide toward the other men. "There are many of you now. Let more of you come. We will let you have the whole of this island, and every other island in the waterland, if you will destroy the Wolves."

Corban bit his teeth together. He looked over at Euan and Ulf and the others, and saw that Benna had gone, and Arre also. Nobody else could understand this, he realized, but everybody was staring at him, waiting for some conclusion.

Tisconum gripped his arm. His voice hissed in Corban's ears; his free hand made shapes in the air. "I want to tear them. I want to find their villages and burn them down, and kill them all, and drag their women and babies away here to work for us, to live on the leavings of our children." He cupped his hand to Corban. "I beg you this. You can give me this."

Corban swallowed; he could not keep his mind off the idea that if he had never come here, none of this would have happened. He met Tisconum's eyes, and touched his own head. "I will think on it. My son—" Conn was sitting on the ground, just behind him, and at a nod came leaping up onto his feet. "My son will serve you. I need to think about all this."

Conn said, "Pap, what should I do?"

"See he has the best meats to eat, and something good to drink. Stay with him, keep these others off." Corban nodded to the headman and waved to his son, then turned and went off away from the fire.

In the cool darkness he turned his steps up toward the ridge. After the glare of the fire and the insistent looks of all those people, he was glad to be alone and in the dark. He went up through the trodden grass toward the foot of the great rock.

In the space of a few days his life here had come apart in his hands. Yet in the very disassembling he saw some order. It was his fault, all of it. He thought again of the shark, rising from the sea to take him.

Maybe not a warning. Maybe a summons.

Before he had gone past the side of his house, Benna had joined him, walking along beside him; her hand touched his, and he took hold of it. She said, "Did you think I would let you decide this by yourself?"

"You never have before," he said. He squeezed her hand. "What does Euan want? Tisconum is asking me for revenge."

"Ah, please," she said. "Against what? Who are these enemies?"

"Some people to the west he calls the Wolves." He caught himself making the gesture Tisconum had used, two pointing fingers and a cocked thumb, a wolf's head.

They climbed to the rock and sat down with their backs to it, looking south and east over the narrow water. Benna beside him was silent. He put his arm around her and she snuggled in against him, her head against his shoulder. Some of the heat of the day still lingered in the stone against his back. The grass around him was just blooming. Out there beyond the low dark shape of the land, the stars were pricking through the darkness. The moon, almost full, stood a couple of fists above the horizon; lower, away to the left of it, was a brilliant blazing blue star that he thought was one of the wanderers.

She said, "I will not go back to Jorvik. I'm happy here. Or was, until these people came. But—"

She stopped. He thought, again, if he had not come here, none of this would have happened. None of the good either, but the good seemed so frail, so uncertain, against the spreading evil.

She was holding his hand; he could feel the thin bones of her fingers that made the world around him.

He said, "What if I went back? Just for a while."

"What," she said, pushing away from him. "To bring back a few ships full of Vikings? No." Her eyes searched his face. "What is it?"

He said, "Well, I think I have something still to do back there."

"Ah."

"This is all happening because of what I did back there. It's followed us, it will forever follow us, until I make it better. Pay what I owe, level things with those whom I hurt. Then we will be free."

She said nothing. Finally, she said, "I did it also."

"You did only good, as you ever do, and you did it for my sake." He gave her what he knew would bend her to him.

"I will bring no Vikings back, Benna. Maybe some more food, to keep these people here through the winter, but then in the spring your sister and Euan, damn him, can go home again, and everything will be as it was. You and I will help Tisconum defend himself."

Her breath hissed between her teeth. She said, "There's no other way?"

"We could go back with them, all of us, now. Leave Tisconum to his fate. He says they'll come back."

She rubbed her face against him. Her hand was cool in his fingers. Eventually, she said, "No."

"Then what else?"

"You could stay here."

"Then I think she will follow me, everywhere. Everything I try to do will come apart in my hands."

"She."

"You know who I mean."

She was quiet again, and he waited, letting her sort it all out; she often saw things clearer than he did, but this time he knew he was right.

She said, "How could you go?"

"In the new ship," he said.

"Alone," she said. Her fingers curled around his hand.

He laid his cheek down against her hair. The stars twinkled at him. In the evenings he often sat here and watched them, his mind struggling with their order, startled at their waywardness; surely there was some symmetry in them, some gigantic way of knowing, but he had never found it.

All he had was his plodding inadequate wit. He said, "I could take the boys. It's not such a hard trip, going east."

He felt her move slightly against him and tightened his arm around her. She was silent a while. He guessed she was far ahead of him, had seen this coming before he said it, before he himself reached it; he thought of Mav.

As if she heard him, she said, "Mav may not let you take him."

"I'll ask her," he said. He brushed his lips over her hair. "Euan and Ulf can do the men's work here until I get back. Hunt, and fish, and keep guard. And with the big ship, and Ulf and his crew here, if anything happens—" He stopped. He knew she would never board the big ship to sail back to Jorvik. He said anyway, uselessly, "You could escape."

She said nothing for a moment. In the black of the sky the wandering star shone blue-white, steady as a beacon.

"Conn wants to go," she said. "He would have left with Ulf, when Ulf went back, if you let him, even if this had not happened. And taken Raef with him. But she will not let Raef go, unless . . ."

He sat still, holding her, his eyes filled with the erratic light of the stars, waiting. At last she went on. "Unless she thinks it should be. She will know. If she agrees, then let it be."

He sighed. He was holding her tight against him, and now she laughed, a little breathless, and stirred, and he eased his grip. He kissed her hair again. He said, "I can't live long without you, Benna. I'll be back before the first snow."

"If she says . . ."

Her voice faded. Warm and strong in his arms, she laid her head against his chest and was still. Down along the rumpled horizon another bright little dot was poking up into the sky; he recognized one more of the wanderers, fainter, red like an old fire. The wanderers seldom came so close together; he wondered if that meant something. He had spent a lifetime wondering what things meant.

The stars would be the same in Jorvik. He had taken comfort from that, when they first came here, that the stars were the same, the sky. Now that he was going back, they gave him comfort again. He held his wife close against him, his face against her hair, and gathered himself for what was to come.

⚊⚬⚊

Tisconum sat beside Corban's son, whom he had seen often before, a chunky, muscular boy who smiled too much. The boy gave him a piece of meat from the deer—the best part, from along the spine—but as the boy sat beside him at the fire, every now and then he gave him a sideways look, and the look was not as good as the meat.

Anyway Tisconum could barely eat. The weight of what had happened lay over him like a fall of earth. He drew his deerskin coat around him. Slowly he grew aware of the other men around him.

Like Corban's son they were watching him, not steadily, but from the corners of their eyes, and over their hands, and through their hair. All the while, they chattered to one another, and some of them were wrestling. The boy, Corban's son, stood up once, eager to join that, but then looked down at Tisconum and sat down quietly again.

Tisconum looked sideways back at these strangers. He could not understand their words, but he understood what their bodies said. They shoved back and forth at each other, laughing. Those shaggy faces, like animals. A creeping fear edged its way over him. The meat was like charcoal in his mouth. He gathered his deerskin up close around him.

The boy turned and held out a cup to him, a hollow carved of wood. He took it, saw them all watching him, all of their eyes like arrow points glinting in the firelight, and was warned, and let his lips only touch the water in the cup.

The stuff burned. He thrust the cup away so hard it flew from his hand and the liquid splashed into the fire, which whooshed up; Tisconum's hair stood on end at that sight. Some of the men burst out laughing, openly, not hiding their mirth behind their hands even before him, a chief of his people. Rigid, only half breathing, he saw how some of them growled, angry that he had thrown aside their offering.

He knew it was poison. He sat straight, sure they were about to kill him, and the boy sat beside him and said something, and the whole mob laughed and went to something else.

The cup came back, filled again, and he watched the strange white men drinking of it. They paid less attention to him, except now and then to yell something at him, as if he would understand what they said if they only made it loud enough. They staggered when they stood up, and fell flat, and fell asleep on the ground.

All the while, they thrust and struck at each other, and wrestled, and fought.

He thought, they are like the Wolves. I have given the heartland of the world to people like wolves.

He stood up, his knees shaking. Corban's son stood with him, watching him, and Tisconum turned and went stiffly away, down toward the shore.

—⊶—

The fire was banked down, glinting red eyes under the dark ash; the men had fallen asleep by the fire or gone to their beds in the striped tents on the grass. Tisconum was gone. Corban went to the door of his house and looked in; a pine knot burned in the little lane between the rooms, and he could see the boys in their side, pretending to sleep, and on the other side, in his bed, Arre, lying on her back, with Aelfu wrapped in one arm and Miru in the other.

He went out again, on down toward the water. The wind rumpled the striped cloth over Ulf's men; their feet stuck out under the edges of the makeshift tents.

He had walked along this land for years and yet now it suddenly seemed new to him, new and strange. Mav was nowhere. He went down to the bank above the shore, thinking how he would talk to her. She no longer bothered with the speech of ordinary people, but he always managed somehow to talk to her. He was thinking what he should do, if she refused to let Raef go, and then, as if she condensed out of the air, she was walking along beside him, his old red and blue cloak wrapped around her.

He drew in a deep ragged breath. They went along the shore together, not speaking, up to the point where the island bent away sharply south again, and there he stopped. He could still smell the smoke of the burnt village. The night lay cool around them, murmurous with the wind.

He faced her, collecting words. In spite of the dark he saw her clearly; the wind blew her hair wild around her, a great cloud, and her eyes were like skies. She smiled at him. Reaching out she took hold of his hands. Her hands were hard and cold, and she gripped him tight.

"Take him," she said. Her voice was harsh and low. She smiled at him. "Come back. You and Raef." Her hands tightened painfully on his a moment before she let him go. She swung the red and blue cloak from her shoulders and put it around him, and kissed him, her cheek against his, and looked deeply into his eyes for a moment. Then she let him go, and turned, and walked away.

"Mav," he said.

She ignored him, walking on. He watched her go down along the shore, her feet silent on the pebbles. He wondered how she crossed the water. Aelfu had said once she had seen her fly. He did not doubt it. His heart wrenched in his chest, wanting to follow her; all their lives, she had led him, but now she had grown too strong and wild for him, leaving him always farther behind. His eyes ached, trying to see her in the dark, but she was gone.

He was alone. He gripped the cloak in his fists, glad of it, and went back up to his house, to his bed, to his wife and children.

⚊⚬⚊

Ulf took Conn off to one side and gave him a cloak of red wool. "Here. You're going to be laughed at enough, you should have something respectable." The old captain put his hands on the boy's shoulders and looked into his face. Conn flushed under the look, wondering. Then Ulf sighed.

"Ah, you're going off to see the world, off to a hero's life. Well, it's on me to give you advice, since you have no uncle." Ulf nodded gravely at him, his lips pursed. Conn waited. He gave a quick glance down the shore, where Raef and Corban were standing by the little ship, and faced Ulf again. Finally the old man shook his head.

"Damn it, how can this be, that after all these years, I really don't know much? I'll tell you this, though, Conn—never back down from a fight. And make sure you follow the right man." He clasped Conn's shoulder tight. "Go on, then, son." Quickly he turned away.

"Conn!"

"Thanks, Ulf. I'll remember." He waited a moment, thinking there should be more to this, and then tucked the cloak under his arm. "Good-bye."

He went on down toward the shore. His mother was there, his sisters, his aunt, the whole crew. His father and Raef were already pushing the little ship out onto the glittering water. The tide was ebbing fast, dragging him off, away from the island, out into the world. He could not walk; he broke into a run down the slope, kissed his mother almost without stopping, called to the rest of them, and ran out into the shallow water after the ship.

⟶

Miru was crying, and Arre stooped and lifted her up into her arms. Aelfu pressed against her. Their own mother could not comfort them; she stood down at the edge of the water, not crying, not wailing, not even moving, except her eyes, following the little ship away.

Ulf and his men had long since gone up the hill, to do their daily round of ordinary things. Euan was shouting at them; Arre could hear him behind her, bellowing orders.

Her eyes burned. The child nestled warm and heavy in her

arms, and she hugged her tight against her. Down on the shore her sister stood rigid, watching the little ship take her husband and her sons away, and now the tiny red and white sail was skirting the tree-covered headland; in a moment it would be gone entirely.

"Benna," Arre said.

Benna did not turn. Arre licked her lips. The sail was gone now, nothing under her eyes but the rumpled blue water and the green slope of the headland. She turned and swept her gaze across the little house yard, the sloppy tents, the dead fire, the men clustered around Euan who would give them orders, who would make everything neat and bustling.

Corban would walk here again, she felt that certainly. Yet her mind quaked, thinking it, thinking of Benna.

Down there, at last, her sister turned. Her face was long and thin, her mouth sad. Her eyes were dull. She came up toward Arre, and Aelfu ran to her and Benna stooped and put her arms around the little girl and kissed her.

Arre said, "They will come back."

Benna wiped her wrist over her face. "What if something happens to him?" She stopped, her lips trembling. Miru in Arre's arms stretched out her hands to her mother. Arre brought them all together, one arm around Benna's shoulders. Under her arm she felt Benna quivering, as if she longed so to go with Corban her body tried to lift itself across the space between them. Benna whispered, "I should have gone with him."

Arre gave a little unhappy laugh. "But your girls are here. And I'm here." She held her tighter. "I love you." And now they had to make a life in this wild place, with nothing but stones and sand and wind. Benna stumbled, walking beside her, and she held her sister on her feet. They went up the slope, toward the snug little house.

⁓

Tisconum stood on the shore where the bay met the edge of the world-water; he could still see the red stripes of Corban's sail, far down the waves to the east. His belly twisted. This had begun so simply, and now it was spreading away from him like a bad fire.

Everybody in his village was saying he had brought this on them. They said he should have killed Corban, the first time he saw him, and then none of this would have happened, the fighting, his nephew's death, the deaths of so many others of his village, still dying, a few more every day, as they gave in to their wounds. Worse, they were leaving. That morning, two of the lodges had collected their tools and hides and baskets and children and walked out, to go with the Turtle People on the far side of the bay, who were of a kindred lineage.

Those who stayed behind were huddled in the ruins of their houses. Nobody tried to rebuild anything. Nobody went hunting, and he himself had not the heart to bring the hunt together. They were eating up their stores. Soon they would have nothing left. His mind flinched from imagining what would happen then.

Tisconum, their headman, walked along the shore, wishing for wisdom. The sea was calm, and the waves broke tamely along the white rim of the land. Out there a billowing cloud rose enormously into the sky, its upper reaches blazing white. Below its gray underbelly the sail was a speck of red, and then gone.

Curse you, Corban, Tisconum thought, and felt something clench in his heart. Corban had done nothing, had asked nothing, had come to help him fight off Burnt Feet. Had instead cleaved him apart, his people falling apart, dead, dying, or leaving, and all hating him. There was some terrible import in that, which Tisconum did not care to fathom. He felt as if he had walked down a path all his life, every day, and then one day it took him to some utterly new and terrible place, which all innocently he had entered into before he saw what he had done. New and evil and out of his grasp. His gaze pinned to the place where the red sail had gone, he wished bitterly that Burnt Feet had won.

CHAPTER EIGHT

With Corban gone, everything seemed easier to Euan. He was thinking differently about this place, anyway; he could see now why Corban liked it here.

The house was good enough, set well down into the sod, with stout walls and a deep, solid roof. A narrow passageway separated the two rooms and kept the wind out. He and Arre slept in the lower room, where the two boys had slept. Benna and the little girls had the upper room, which was bigger and had a small window to let in some light; Euan liked this room better, although it was crowded with Benna's drawings, which annoyed him.

The only other building was the storeroom, hunched down into the ground beneath its hairy roof of sod. Euan had been loath to search around in it when Corban was there, but now that he was gone, he felt free.

Mostly, he discovered quickly, the storeroom was full of dried fish, of which there was a great quantity, even after Corban took a lot of it with him for the sea voyage. Behind the strings and baskets of the fish, he came on other food, tiny sour apples and nuts, little bark containers of the delicious sweet stuff that flavored Benna's potions, baskets of dried herbs, a pile of excellently worked hides, and, in the very back, two wooden chests of dansker make, full of furs.

Euan sank down, lifting out the top layer: Even in the dark he could see these were thick, deep-piled stoat pelts, brown spotted with white, furs to adorn the robes of kings. Just touching them made his mind whirl.

He buried his hands in the softness of the fur and considered all this. Corban's land was full of riches. Besides the game, the fur, the fish, there was timber here such as was no longer seen in

England. And no one ruled here. In all his years here Corban had seen no other men save the dark creatures on the coast, who were hardly men at all. Euan's fingers curled into the dense silk of the fur. Corban didn't know what he had.

Corban should not have it.

He sank down in the dark, crushing and stroking the fur in his hands. Everything seemed different suddenly. He saw a real danger now that Corban might get one of the kings involved—or worse, some adventurer who had no land of his own. Once someone else saw this place—anyone else, Corban being as mild as he was—

Or Corban could fail. Die, perhaps, at sea.

Euan's mind leapt past that, to a time when he, Euan Woodwrightsson, ruled here. He could bring in some people from Jorvik—he knew who might come—not many, enough to work a farm or two. Haul some sheep across the water, some horses and cows.

His mind skipped lightly over the sea, which now seemed narrow as a little stream, and the people he might get from England. He lifted the fur to his cheek. Actually, he thought, if he could master them, these dark native people would be happy enough to give him tribute and do the necessary work. He would build a hall, not here, this place was too cramped, but perhaps somewhere inland, on a hill. There, far from the troubles in England and the greed of the Norse and Danish kings and the ships and swords of Vikings, he would be master. Lord of everything, with power over everybody.

His head swam. He wondered how far the land went on from here.

A sharp prickle along his neck jarred him. Somebody was watching him. He turned, looking, his fingers still buried in the long dark fur, and saw, his eyes now open to the dimness, over by the foot of the wall there, Corban looking at him.

His skin heated in a sudden rash of guilt. His belly heaved. But it was only one of Benna's infernal images, painted on a stone. He tore his gaze away from it and threw the fur back into the chest. Quickly he stumbled back into the front of the room, where some light came through the door.

—⚬—

Benna could not draw. Everything that she had looked upon was gone, lost under the clutter of new feet, new faces.

She had made a mistake, letting Corban go. He was part of everything she did. She had thought it would be enough to be here, in her home, on the island, but it wasn't. His absence was like being unable to breathe.

And he was going into danger, although he seemed not to think so, yet everything in her prickled and tingled with it. She had let him go alone into some terrible danger. He needed her, and she was not there.

She couldn't even busy herself with the little girls, although Arre, missing her own children, delighted in caring for them, and they loved Arre very well and didn't seem to mind that their mother was so low.

But there was Euan.

She had known from the beginning why Euan loved her sister. Arre had enough deep feeling for both of them, while Euan had none of his own. Where his feeling should have been there was a great hole, which he filled with schemes.

Now Euan walked around shouting at them all to work, and thought he worked; he had bitter words for everybody.

"Why do you sit here doing nothing, when we must build the wall?" He himself did not build, only harried all the rest of them to it, driving them to haul rocks and place them one on the other in a ring around the house and yard, a ring growing higher every day, shutting out the water and the shore opposite. In this wall was an opening, where everybody had to go in and out, and there Euan stood guard.

Every day the rocks were harder to find, had to be hauled from farther away. Benna's hands were bruised and raw. She went to Arre, who said, "He'll fret himself to rags if he has nothing to do."

"He could hunt," Benna said, thinking of Corban. "He could fish." Thinking of Corban and her son and Raef, her heart aching.

She should have gone. She had done it, too, what he had gone to make amends for. Maybe that was why she felt so bad.

"Euan?" Arre said. "Hunt and fish?" She laughed. "Well, we need the wall, you know. Those people could come back."

So the wall grew higher and higher around her. Euan made her work, shouting at her until she got up and dragged herself over to lift stones. When he was gone she stopped. She went into the house, to the far corner of her room, where in a hole in the wall she kept her charms, and found the looking glass.

Its face was dirty, and she cleaned it with the edge of her skirt until it shone again. Corban had given it to her, long before, in Jorvik. Then she had not known its true worth, and it looked like nothing much now, grimy and chipped. She hung it by its string around her neck, found a flat rock by the door, and went off behind the house, to a quiet place where Euan would not find her.

Sitting on the ground, she drew Corban, as she had drawn him a thousand times before, the flare of his cheekbones, his clear pale eyes. She made no shoreline behind him, no place for him, because she had no knowledge of the place he was. Then beside him she drew herself, using the looking glass.

This comforted her at once. She sat looking at the two of them together, and a deep peace stole over her. Somewhere beyond the house Euan shouted in a cracked voice. Suddenly he seemed somewhere else entirely, inside his own wall. Carefully she laid the rock against the side of the house, and went back to work.

The trouble was, Euan thought, he had not enough hands. Making the wall was going very slowly, because so many of the men had to be off hunting or curing the meat or hauling in the fish or doing some other necessary chore. He began to think hard about making the people across the water, whose village they had, after all, saved, bring them the food they needed, so that he could put all Ulf's men to finishing the wall.

He had not gone to fight, when Corban called them across the water to rescue those others. He talked to some of Ulf's crew who had, and what they said heartened him. He thought those people were probably just waiting for him to come over there and give them his protection.

He got most of the men together and told his wife, "I will go over to the village, where those other people live."

Arre gave him a sharp look, but said only, "See if they have some sort of bread—I am starving for bread." She was plucking out the feathers from a duck; a great flock had arrived that morning to settle down on the cove and feed in the marshes and devil everybody with their constant uproar. Euan watched her a moment, the quick hard motions of her hand with the clumps of wet feathers; he wanted to say something, to bind her while he was gone, but she was already busy, and she would not look at him. He took his men and went down to the water's edge.

The tide was slack and the water very low; they crossed in the wretched leaky hide boat and a strange thing made of an old log that floated, nonetheless, and so got men over to the mainland. They reached the shore just above the mouth of the river, clogged with rocks and driftwood, and made their way back through the wood toward the village.

Euan saw the trail at once and led the way. The men following him were silent and kept close; he could smell old smoke in the air still. They skirted a marsh, also overrun with ducks in a flapping, quacking swarm. Where the trees began another swarm attacked them: thousands of biting flies. Euan gasped and clamped his lips shut and, blindly windmilling his arms, barged through them, stumbled on a root, and nearly fell.

Ulf caught him by the arm and held him. "Move, come on, keep moving," he said, and shoved him, and they rushed and staggered along until they had escaped the insects. Euan's neck and hands itched. Now Ulf was leading them, and he followed grimly along on the old captain's heels and wished he had bade Arre make a salve against stings.

They thrashed on up through spiny dark woods and into a broad meadow. Euan reached out and caught Ulf's shoulder and held him, and stood looking around him, seeing the overgrown gardens here, the plants heavy with long pods, and then, ahead, a great burnt-out place, a black hollow in the green wood. He went a few steps on and realized that this devastated place was the village.

He grunted. Somehow in the back of his mind he had imagined these people would have real houses, with daubed withy walls and thatched roofs, like the ones at home. As if he could just walk over the hill and be in Jorvik. A premonition washed over him; he wondered if he could trust what his eyes saw. With the other men on his heels, he went out across the fields toward the burnt place.

The fire had destroyed much of the village, but some round huts were left, near the far end of the meadow. Before these a few people sat on the ground, glowering at him. They wore shawls of hide and kept their black hair all gathered up on top of their heads; their skin was dark, almost coppery. They were barefoot and filthy. As he stared around more people came crawling out of the huts, and one was the tall man who was Corban's friend, all but naked, around his neck a chain of white beads.

Euan straightened, glad to see him; if Corban had talked to this man, surely he could. He had prepared several different speeches to begin this, and now he chose the most cautious. He said, "Good day, fellow. I am Euan, I am in charge here now, and I have come to help you."

The dark man standing before him showed no signs of comprehension. He frowned at Euan, gave a long look at the men following him, and then said something and made motions with his hands, and there was the rising note of a question in his voice, and Corban's name.

Euan fumbled with his hands; he remembered Corban doing this, but he had paid no heed, thinking it only some nervousness. He said, more loudly, "We will help you rebuild your village here, and then you will help us, as is only right." The perfect logic of this gave him confidence; he nodded at the tall man, and smiled.

From behind the tall man, suddenly another of the strange creatures burst up off the ground. Startled, Euan realized this was a woman—her naked dugs hug down like empty purses—and she was screeching like a cat with its tail caught. She screamed at the tall man, who drew back, frowning, and then she wheeled and shrieked at Euan, full in his face, only a few feet away.

Ulf rushed up beside him, a knife in his hand. "Here, you hag—" Euan flung his arm out to hold him back.

"No—wait—"

But now everybody was shouting. The tall man had turned and was calling out to his people, but nobody heeded him. All the other villagers were crowding up toward him, their voices high and sharp. Euan stepped back, away from the harridan, whose ruddled cheeks were seamed with fresh scars. Then from somewhere a stone struck him on the arm.

He yelled. Instantly Ulf sprang past him, slashing with his knife, and the old woman went down. "No," Euan cried; he stooped down, his hands out to protect her, but the others rushed forward, armed with sticks and rocks, and Ulf's men lunged to meet them. Caught in the middle, Euan hunched down, his hands raised to ward off blows. The old woman who had started it all huddled whimpering at his feet. People banged into him from all sides. A bare foot stepped down hard on his toes. He shoved back at a great panicky blur of colliding bodies, and then abruptly the squeeze around him eased. The others were running off. He stood up, by himself, gasping for air; the old woman, blood all over one arm, lurched to her feet and paddled away after the rest of them, wailing, and Ulf's men, belling like hounds, gave chase down through the burnt village.

"Come back, you idiots!" Euan took a step after them, watching their backs rush away from him as they ran away into the unknown forest, and this time they heard him. Ulf turned, and the rest of his men, and they all came jogging back through the ruins. Euan looked around again for something to take back to Arre. There was nothing. Certainly no bread. He barked a laugh. He saw now how stupid that was. He lifted his eyes toward the dark trees looming all around. Those dark devils owned that forest. In there, how many of them lurked? His scalp tingled. Nothing was as he had expected. Suddenly he knew this place enormous, beyond comprehension, and full of evil. He licked his lips and turned to Ulf and said, "Come on—let's get back to the island, now."

<hr />

One morning, when Corban had been gone a whole month or more, while Arre was outside in the dooryard stirring up the fire, Aelfu came to her and said, "My mam is gone."

Startled, and seeing the fear in the child's face, Arre went swiftly after her into the house. Benna was not gone, she was there, in the bed, but she lay still, her eyes shut, her face glistening with sweat.

Arre's heart leapt into her throat. She sank down beside her sister and laid one hand to her cheek. Benna did not stir.

Aelfu leaned on Arre, her gaze on her mother. "Is she all right?"

Arre put one arm around her. "Yes. Yes. Go out and play with Miru." A low terror gathered in her belly like a lump of ice. She wrapped her sister up in warm blankets and gave her sips of broth; Benna would not waken enough to drink, and her hands were cold even under the blankets. Arre knelt by the bedside and prayed to Jesus and his Holy Mother for help. All around her, ranged along the foot of the wall and in the chinks and corners, were Benna's drawings; she saw Corban's face there, over and over, and she thought of what Benna had said when he left and was briefly jealous of such a love as that.

Aelfu came back in, cast a single look at her mother, and turned to Arre. "Will she come back?"

"Yes," Arre said, stout as she could say it. "Yes." She stroked the little girl's face and sent her out again.

She did everything she could. She stroked Benna's hair back, bathed her face, made a tea of herbs she had brought with her from Jorvik, and slipped it drop by drop onto Benna's tongue, but Benna never moved. Arre could not see that her sister swallowed anything. She prayed. She wondered if Jesus and Mary even heard her, so far from home and the church and the priest, but she begged them anyway to help her sister.

Outside she could hear the men moving back and forth, the distant careless sound of voices, the clump and thump of their work. She made a little cross of twigs and put it by her sister's head. Remembering what Benna had said, that she did not pray anymore. Thinking this place might be beyond the reach somehow even of Jesus. Yet God was everywhere; she pushed herself toward that, pleading for her sister's life.

Aelfu hung in the doorway. "When will she come back?"

"Soon," Arre said. "I hope." She wiped the tears from her cheeks with the hem of her apron. She had journeyed so far, and they had had only this short time together, and now Benna was sinking away from her. She laid her head down on the bed and sobbed.

The sun vanished down over the hill; the men roasted meat over the fire, and ate the last of Benna's little patchy garden; she had never been good with a garden. Aelfu came to the doorway, her face crumpled and gray, and said, "I want my mam."

Arre held Benna's cold hands and looked into her face, and could not speak. Behind her the little girl began to cry miserably. Arre reached out blindly, for comfort and to comfort, and gathered Aelfu into her embrace. The child understood, and wailed and shrieked, and the men came running, and Arre had to tell them all that Benna was dead.

—⚬—

Aelfu went wild when they took Benna's body to bury, crying over and over that Benna would have no place to come back tő, and Arre bundled her up and took the sobbing baby and carried them off into the forest. When they got under the trees, Aelfu squirmed to the ground and went ahead of Arre on the path, leading the way.

Arre's heart was numb in her breast; she carried little Miru even when she stopped crying, as much for her own sake as the tiny girl's. Aelfu took them on a winding way through the woods, stopping here and there. Finally she came out on an outcrop of rock and stopped.

Arre was out of breath. She stood on the rock, looking out over the trees, and saw the water gleaming in the distance, and the wind rushed over her and she saw the clouds scudding over the sky, and the wildness of this place overcame her. She sat down and hugged the baby in her arms, looking east, toward Jorvik and her home. Aelfu sat by her feet and put her thumb in her mouth, and her eyes began to move, traveling from side to side, and Arre realized she was looking for her mother. An unbearable ache began in Arre's breast, and a low moan escaped her.

Then from the trees the madwoman came, Corban's sister. She walked down the steep short slope toward them. At Arre's feet Aelfu reached up and took hold of her skirt. Arre clutched the baby, thinking what she might do if this woman attacked her. The woman's eyes held her, clear as water, deep as wells. Arre sighed, her muscles loosening. Corban's sister sat down beside her and put her arm around her shoulders. Arre turned her gaze toward the water again, feeling suddenly warmer and easier. But she wanted to go home. She wanted more than anything now to go home. She leaned on Corban's sister and fixed her gaze on the water.

⸺

Miska woke suddenly, sharply, his skin tingling; the dream still flowed through his mind. He saw the island, as if he were standing there on Tisconum's shore, and he saw the water between him and the island sucked away, every drop, drawn up out of his way, and he walked across the dry ground to the island, untouched.

He knew his grandmother had sent him this dream; he could almost hear her voice in his mind. He felt the truth of it down to the soles of his feet. The blood pulsed hot in his veins. He could take the island now. He could lead the Wolves to their revenge and, leading them, rise up where he belonged.

He could not sleep, or even lie down anymore. Untangling himself from his bedding, he groped his way out of the lodge, past young men still rumbling in the dark, and to the open air.

The night hung over everything. The ground was damp with dew; after the closeness and stinks of the lodge, the air was fresh and clean, and he gulped it down, trying to cool his excitement. The village was silent. He stood a moment looking around, at the dim shapes of the other lodges, the even line of the wall, the overarching sky, all pricked out with stars. The moon was setting. The sun would rise soon. He went down the path through the lodges to the meeting ground, in the center of the village.

The firepit was cold. They had not danced for a long time,

not since the men had followed Burns-His-Feet to the disaster at the world-water, but the ground was still soft from years of pounding. Groping in the darkness around the foot of the oak tree, he found a drum, and he sat down beside the dead fire and began to beat on the drum. He knew no music, he had no art for this; his hands felt awkward on the taut hide. He made a steady beat like walking. In his mind the dream hovered like a mist over everything he saw and thought.

Soon the others came, one by one, creeping out from the lodges, walking down to the meeting ground.

Lasicka came first, Burns-His-Feet's youngest nephew; his left leg still didn't work right, but he had healed, at least, when so many others had died. Seeing it was Miska with the drum, he stopped and stood staring at him. Maybe he remembered what Miska had said to him after the terrible defeat, when Miska had struck him, over and over, enjoying it. In any case Lasicka came now and sat down before him, and after him the others gathered around and sat down.

They made a smaller circle now than before. Besides Burns-His-Feet and Anatkwa and the others dead in the battle, three more had died in the long hard walk home. They sat before him with their heads down, not looking him in the eyes. With Burns-His-Feet and Anatkwa, his sister's son, both gone, they had not asked the women to choose a new sachem; nor had the women given them one.

Quietly, near the edges of their pack, others came, untopped boys even younger than Miska. And these watched Miska, their heads up, their faces smooth with hope.

Miska's hand pattered on the drum. He had no pipe to pass among them, to draw them together; the drum had to do. He said, "It is time to avenge Burns-His-Feet. We can take the island now. I had a dream."

At the core of the pack, the older men stirred, turning to look at one another. Lasicka frowned and leaned forward.

"You are no one, Miska. Nobody. Why should a true dream come to you?"

"My grandmother sent it to me," Miska said.

They stirred, crowding together, uneasy at the mention of his grandmother. The sun was rising and he could see their faces, the planes of their cheeks, the wary suspicion in their eyes, and the fear that crimped their mouths shut. Only one or two of the untopped boys nudged each other and turned their gaze steadily on him. He made the walking beat on the drum, but none of them spoke. The grown men huddled together, as they had on the long way back home, and said nothing. Around them, the boys waited, taut.

In the village, the women were coming out of the lodges, as if they waked up to some ordinary day. Someone among them gave up a stream of song, welcoming the sun, and a child cried. Bark buckets in their hands, three women walked down toward the river for water and looked over curiously at the men in their pack. The first tang of smoke rose from fires stirred back to life. A fat thrush perched on the fence began to sing.

Desperate, Miska laid his hands flat to the drum, walking. "We can take the island now," he said. "We can win now. We can get back what we lost there."

In front of him Lasicka lowered his eyes to stare at the ground. The men leaned on one another. The long death walk home had gotten into their bones like a poison. They sat motionless with their heads hanging and said nothing.

Miska flung the drum away. "You are all cowards," he said. "You are not my people. You are not Wolves." He rose up onto his feet, his skin tingling with the force of what he felt. He said, "I am going. I shall avenge Burns-His-Feet and our honor, I alone. I spit on you." He turned and walked away, off through the village.

Behind him, he heard a great shuffling. He did not look back; he walked faster, his eyes already on the path.

Squatting by the fires, sitting with their babies, the women stopped to watch him pass. Epashti was one of them, standing before her lodge. As he went by, she called, "Miska! Where are you going?"

"To avenge the Wolves," he said, and walked on.

"I am going," she said. "Wait for me."

He did not wait. He walked out between the lodges to the gate in the wall, where already some of the women were picking up their hoes and rakes. As he went out the gate, Epashti caught up with him, carrying a bundle and with her baby on her back.

He did not look at her; he kept his gaze aimed straight ahead, but he smiled. Now he heard other feet, following him. He did not have to turn to see. He knew the men were coming, after all—he had drawn them, he was leading them. Smiling, his eyes straight ahead, he went on down the path between the fields, back to the east, and their enemy.

$$\Longleftarrow$$

A few days after Benna's death, Arre came into the house and found Euan in the upper room, and he was gathering up all Benna's drawings.

"What are you doing?" Arre cried. She came into the room, reached out her hand, and took hold of his arm.

He turned, shrugging her off, a pile of flat stones and planks in his hands. "Take these away," he said. "We should sleep in here now, but I can't stand all these faces looking at me."

She took the drawings from him. They seemed warm to her, warm and heavy. She sat down on the bed with them in her lap. The topmost was a dark stone with an image of a newborn baby, sleeping curled up, perfect down to his toes, his ears. Every tiny curve was an echo of the curve of his body, the memory of the womb. She lifted her eyes again to Euan.

"Can't you leave them where they are?"

"I hate them," he said, as if that were all that mattered. He kept his back to her and bent for another stone, groaning with effort. "I don't understand why it's so hard to take these up. It's as if they have roots down into the wall."

She looked down at the baby on the stone in her lap and gave a little start: Its eyes were wide open; it was looking back at her, so real its eyes seemed aware. She was sure its eyes had been closed, before. Then, as she watched, the baby faded away. The lines vanished into the gray of the rock. The wide dark eyes paled away into blank stone, and it was gone.

"No," she cried, and reached for the slab of wood below, but it was the same: a blank space. In her lap was only a clutter of rocks and wood. "No," she said. She looked back to Euan, who had torn the last drawing from the wall.

"What is it?" he said, his face bland. When he had no argument but meant to get his way, he gave her this same stone face. She lowered her eyes to the rock in her hands, her heart torn.

"Nothing," she said, and rose, gathering the clutter up in her skirt. "I'll take these away."

A few days later, though, as she was roaming the compound thinking of Benna, she came on another stone, just behind the house, with a drawing on it.

It was tilted up against the back wall of the house. Careful not to touch it, she sank down on her hams to look at it. It startled her: There on the flat surface a man and a woman lay side by side with their arms around one another. She could not entirely see their faces, which were turned close together, but she thought the people were Corban and Benna.

Her skin crept; she thought instantly of her and Euan, in their bed at night, and felt a wash of heat rise up her arms and throat. Her mind tumbled in confusion. This was surely sin. Such things should never be made into pictures. Benna should not have done this one.

But she had done it. Arre put her hand to her breast, where her heart was beating at the gallop, and made herself look at the drawing again. She was sure the two people were Corban and Benna, lying in one another's arms.

She should not be seeing this, her sister's intimate thought. Yet it was beautiful, as everything Benna made was beautiful. She put her hand out to the stone; it seemed warm against her fingertips. After some while she laid both hands on the stone and tried it gently. It came up easily. She went around the house, over to the height under the rock, where her sister lay in her windy grave. Miru and Aelfu, playing in the dooryard of the house, saw her and came over to her.

She laid the stone down on Benna's grave and sat there and prayed a while, with the two little girls sitting in her lap. Miru laid her head against Arre's breast and fell asleep, and Aelfu sucked her thumb and fingered Arre's sleeve with her free hand, her eyes aimed steadily at nothing. Arre crossed herself.

She thought of what Benna had said about God, and how she had flinched from that, how she had been horrified. Now she struggled to see what Benna had known and seen, which seemed somehow all around her, and yet out of reach. She longed bitterly for Benna, to help her understand. She cursed herself for not listening more when her sister was alive.

Her heart rolled over in her breast. Words rose unbidden in her throat.

"I think by now, sister, you must wish we had never come here, and I, too, wish that so heartily. And yet to see you again— to see you—I would have come twice as far, if only—"

Her eyes swelled with hot tears. In her lap, Aelfu turned, her eyes wide and distant, and laid her hand on Arre's lips. Arre closed her arms around the girls, their hair against her face smelling of seaweed. The wind roared in the trees; she felt again that vast, hostile stirring.

CHAPTER NINE

Lasicka swung his hatchet-face toward Miska. The journey here had wearied the older man, and he leaned heavily on his good leg. He spoke in a voice of great sadness. "So, here we are, Miska. And it is as it was, there is the island, here is the water, what can we do now, where we failed before?" He shrugged, answering himself.

Miska rubbed his hand over his mouth. Before him lay the great water's rumpled uneasy edge; out there, on the slope of the island facing him, was the strange dwelling of the pale-skinned strangers. But it had changed since he had seen it last. Now a ring of stones surrounded it and a wide dusty swath of the ground around it, and inside this ring he could see people gathered. Even outside the ring, the grass was beaten down. He saw some men leave the ring and tramp off along the foot of the great rock, reach the end, and turn into the edge of the forest.

He sank down on his hams, thinking about this. The place looked much more formidable now. The dream faded in his mind. Behind him Lasicka stood with his mouth pursed, waiting, Lasicka, who crippled or not was of the blood of the sachems; for an instant Miska's spirit quailed.

Faced with the uneasy water again, he remembered the great fish, the salt wave rising up, and he shrank from trying. If he could not do it, he could never drive these other men to do it. All the way here he had studied them; he knew which was strong, and which was fast, and which was worth listening to, but he had learned no way he could force them to go willingly into this water.

He realized he was clutching the amulet bag that hung around his neck—where he kept, now, only two objects: his grandmother's fingerbone and the little white stone.

He had sent one of the boys on ahead of them, to see where Tisconum was—to make sure Tisconum had not caught wind of them yet. Most of the other men were wandering around the shore looking for something to eat. Above a broad band of slick stinking weeds and driftwood and shells that coated the top of the shore, the land shelved up toward some trees. Epashti had left the men and gone back there to the shelter of a shallow bank, where she was making a camp. Her baby gave a wail, and she stopped to comfort it.

Miska turned back toward the island again. The encampment on it looked like a big scar in the slope of the hill. A worm of rage stirred in his gut. There had to be a way to root these people up. He stood, went into the water to his knees, and bent down and put his hand on the flopping, tumbling surface. It was colder than he expected. Behind him, somebody called his name.

He turned; the boy was jogging down past the stretch of weeds and wood toward him.

He said, "I found nobody, Miska. And no village, either—a burnt-out place, but nobody is living there anymore."

Lasicka was ambling up to them, his head turned a little, as if he did not really want to be there but something drew him on. He said, "Are there more of them?" His head jerked toward the island.

Miska rubbed his hands together. That thought had just occurred to him, too. Maybe more of the white people had come, maybe a lot more, the whole tribe. He squinted toward the island. Yet there were no more boats, and he could make out no people at all. He turned to the boy, whose name was Ellioh. "Were there any boats at the burnt-out place?"

"Boats?" the boy said, startled.

Lasicka swung toward Miska, his eyes narrow. "We tried that. I remember what happened."

Miska's chest hurt suddenly, as if some big fist clenched around him. The smell of Lasicka's fear made his hackles rise. But he saw suddenly a way of forcing this.

He said, "I will go, tonight, myself, to show you it can be done. And come back. And then we will all go."

Lasicka hissed between his teeth. Miska watched him steadily, aware of his own long hair, his boyhood, in front of this warrior, and the insult in what he said. Lasicka gripped his hands together, gave a long stare toward the island, and turned back to face him.

"I should let you go alone, and be destroyed. It's what you deserve, Miska."

Miska fought against a smile. "I said I would."

Lasicka pressed his lips together; Miska saw the fear in him fighting with his pride, and he saw the pride win. The sachem's nephew said, "I cannot let you do that. You and I will try. If we reach the island"—he shrugged, looking out over the water a moment—"we will signal to the others to come. But if we fail, we will all go back home."

Miska snorted. "You will have to keep up with me. I won't wait for you, Lasicka," he said. But when Lasicka's head jerked up, his eyes angry, Miska looked loftily off, his chin in the air. "Good, we will do it your way."

⸻

"In the dark?" Ellioh said, his eyes popping. He was only a boy, and should not be speaking up, but with untopped Miska there in front of him he was bold enough. "You'd try to cross the water in the dark?" Behind him, Epashti looked up; she was pounding seeds and nuts in her wooden grinding bowl.

Miska said, "Otherwise they'll see us coming. I will go first, and signal you with a torch when I get to the shore."

Beside him, Lasicka grunted at him, and he nodded, not looking around. "Yes; Lasicka and I. Anyway, when we have proven it can be done, you will come after us."

Ellioh swiveled his shocked gaze toward Lasicka. Beyond

him one of the other men stirred, Hasei, whose brother had died with Burns-His-Feet in Tisconum's village.

"If two of you can go, I can go. I'm not letting someone else go before me." Beside him, another of the boys, Tiko, muttered and bobbed his head.

"Me either."

Miska straightened, startled. They were all pushing toward him. Their voices rose, clamoring together, each trying to out-shout the other. "You can't go without me!" Only Lasicka sat silent in the midst of them, his head sunk down and his eyes gleaming.

Finally, he said, "So it is, Miska. We will go. We will see what becomes of it."

⸻

In the night Arre heard shouts and screams and was instantly awake. Euan struggled up beside her on the broad bed platform. "What is it? What is it?" He cast back the thin ragged blanket. Outside Ulf's voice rose clear and loud against the general uproar.

"Up! Everybody up!"

Arre turned and gathered the two little girls into her arms. "Somebody's attacking us."

Euan let out a burst of oaths. Flinging a cloak around him, he plunged through the door into the little aisle between the rooms. Arre pulled the rag of the blanket around the little girls and bent over them and kissed their faces.

"Now, you must be brave, and stay right here, and not make me worry about where you are," she said. Her skin tingled; she knew she had to do something. She got out of the bed, pulling her gown on over her shift. In the passageway, the torch sud-denly crackled up alive, and the red-orange light swam in and she saw the two girls sitting swathed in the blanket, their eyes wide with terror.

She heard Ulf's throaty bellow outside again, shouting names. Euan called some answer and plunged out, taking the torch with him.

He had left behind his belt knife, which Arre found easily, even in the dark. She went into the doorway, the knife in her hand, and looked out.

The moon was full and bright; the house yard lay before her washed in its brilliance, the sky gleaming like a looking glass, the black shadow along the foot of the wall like an opening into the abyss. Through this radiance ran Euan, with some of Ulf's men, heading down toward the wall, where already people rose up fighting, a thrashing shadowy mass.

Arre went a step outside the house, the knife gripped in her hand. She forced her pounding heart to slow; she calmed herself, seeing what was going on. Down there the wall swarmed with men. Their confused voices rose unintelligibly, like the crackling of a fire. The moonlight made everything strange, only half visible. A dark figure climbed up onto the top of the wall, a club in his upraised hand, and struck downward—struck toward her, he was facing her, he was an enemy. She flinched back, casting quickly around her, the knife no longer seeming much.

There beside the door, where Corban had cut wood for the fire, the axe stuck up from an old gray stump. She seized the haft, twisted the iron head up out of the hard wood, and backed into the doorway and waited.

Near the fire ring in the center of the yard, halfway between her and the wall, Ulf stood, a bow in his hands, nocking an arrow. Two others of his crew rushed up beside him with bows. Down along the wall more men were climbing over into the compound. Arre saw Euan down there, by the wall, wrestle one of the invaders to the ground.

Ulf shouted, his voice ringing clear, and shot.

On the wall one of the attackers stood straight up, hung a moment as if the arrow pinned him to the dark, and flopped back. Still they were scrambling over, and now Euan was staggering back away from them, one arm raised. The defenders around him were already running. The wall swarmed with attackers, who scrambled over and rushed straight across the yard at Ulf and the other bowmen.

Arre started forward, a scream mounting in her chest; she saw Euan go down in the first charge, and then suddenly two of the enemy were running straight toward her.

She saw them, in the moonlight, tilted forward toward her, their teeth bared, their faces streaked with white, and she saw them in that moment as completely as if she had stared at them for years—their skin polished with sweat, their arms pumping, their eyes already seizing on her, their hands grasping for her. She sprang backward, into the protection of the doorway; the first one, two steps ahead of the other, bounded toward her, and she swung up the axe and caught him hard across the knees.

He went down, the axe tangled in his legs, and she lost her balance and fell back into the low doorway behind her. The other man loomed over her. He shut out the moonlight. She smelled him, rank and hot. She scrabbled frantically for her footing, trying to get up, the axe heavy in her grip. The white-streaked face loomed above her, and he swung his club at her head.

She flinched down, but the club struck the top of the doorway. Arre stopped trying to get up. She crouched in the doorway and swung the axe again, aiming at his legs, and he dodged away, back out of the confines of the doorway.

The moonlight swept over her again. She leapt to her feet, gasping for breath, clutching the axe. The man she had struck down lay sprawled motionless on the ground; beyond him, the other attacker was fighting with Euan, who had come up behind him, the two of them locked together, their arms entwined, face to face, and then the dark man kicked out and Euan went down hard.

Arre screamed her husband's name, scrambled up to her feet, hoisting the axe in her hands. The white-streaked dark face swiveled toward her, two blazing eyes met hers, and lunging toward him she launched the axe at his head. He dodged the awkward blow easily, but he darted away, out from between her and Euan. From his knees, Euan dove at him, grabbing for his ankles, and the dark man kicked him savagely in the head, knocking him back again.

"Euan!" Arre flung herself on her husband, to protect him, but the other man was no longer fighting. He bent over his fallen friend and hauled him up by the arm and dragged him away, the body dangling in his grasp.

Somewhere Ulf was shouting, hoarse, greedy, "Get them! Get them!" Arre wrapped her arms around Euan, panting and groaning on the ground.

"Jesus," he said. "Sweet Jesus. I'm hurt."

She sank down on her knees beside him, her breath like a bellows, her chest furnace hot. There was an immense pool of blood on the ground, not Euan's. The man she had struck. A wave of nausea passed through her. She was still clutching the axe, but the fighting seemed over. Out there near the center of the compound, Ulf stood with his bow in his hand, shouting and waving his arms. The other men were all along the wall, yelling. The attackers had run off.

She laid the axe down and turned back to Euan, half sitting on the ground braced on his arms, his head hanging. She put her hands on his head and he twitched, moaning.

"Ssshhh." She felt carefully along his head, feeling sticky blood in his hair. He gasped once, but to her relief he lifted his head and pushed himself to sit upright.

"Where else does it hurt?" She turned toward him, reaching for his hand. "You were so brave. You were wonderful, Euan."

He put one hand to his head. "I am no fighter. When they came at us like that—what's Ulf doing?" He began to try to get to his feet, pushing with his hands on the cold ground. "How many did we lose, Jesus have mercy—"

She stood and helped him up. She looked around the yard for bodies, for hurt people—saw something lying motionless just at the foot of the wall, and two men sitting down slumped near the fire ring, where Ulf still roared and waved his arms. Behind her, in the house, then, Miru wailed. She turned and went in to the children.

⚊

Getting Ellioh's body back across the water had cost Miska the last of his strength. With the dead boy over his shoulder he staggered up through the shallows, toward the glimmer of the fire on the beach. Epashti came to him at once, with a gourd of sweet water. Before he drank he lowered Ellioh down onto the ground and straightened the body; one of Ellioh's legs was all but cut off at the knee, and Miska pushed the limb together again. Until Ellioh was properly buried he was like a living man, and Miska tipped a little of the water over him.

The rest of the men began to splash up from the water. Miska kept his back to them, drinking the water in the gourd. The muscles of his arms and legs shuddered with weakness. The other men clustered around the fire, bent over the flames, their heads down. Epashti went among them, speaking softly to them, giving them water, and nursing them.

They would not look at him. His heart contracted in his chest. He felt their anger like a hard wind that would blow him down. They had come all this way, enduring his scorns and prods, because he had promised them revenge, and now he had only given them another failure.

Even in his weariness, the fighting still buzzed in the back of his mind; if he gave himself to it, he could bring it all back, as if it were there before him again, the white glare of the moonlight and the howl of men fighting, howling himself, the feel of a man going down under his club. He sat beside Ellioh and watched

Epashti going from one man to the next, speaking their names, touching them, and in spite of his cold dread of the other men, his soul rose up, swelling stronger on the memory of the fight.

He had nearly taken a woman—not the one he wanted, but another light-skinned woman. A woman of power, who had struck down Ellioh: Miska had almost taken her. He pressed the heels of his hands against his eyes. Not over, he thought. He felt that, very strong, like a hand on his shoulder. This was not over.

He got up and went around the fire. The other men watched him sullenly. He stiffened himself against them. He sat in the fire's warm hold, ignoring their stares, and found roasted meat there on a flat rock: Epashti had not been idle while they were gone. His belly growled, and he began to eat. Under their stares like knives aimed at him, he tore at the meat with his teeth.

Lasicka thrust his face forward, his eyes bright in the fire. "You see what you've done, Miska. Poor Ellioh dead, who trusted you, Tiko dead, Hacoka—and we lost again. You and your revenge!" He lifted his hands and let them fall limp to his knees. From the others came a murmur of pain and self-pity.

Miska wiped his fingers across his mouth. "Bah. Don't talk to me. You want to lose."

Lasicka's hand went to the knife in his belt. Miska fixed him with a steady stare. For a moment he said nothing, only put all his strength into the look. Lasicka stared back at him, through the smoke and rippling light of the fire. Miska remembered the fighting; he touched the medicine bag around his neck, and after a moment Lasicka looked down.

Miska said, "Did you think this would be easy? If it were easy, would not some lesser men have already done it?" He swept them with a look. "We were in their village. If we had taken down the men with the bows we would have beaten them." He could not remember exactly why he had run, only that suddenly he had been alone, facing two enemies, with Ellioh dead at his feet, the rest of them running like deer in the moonlight. "The next time, we will do it."

"The next time!" Lasicka turned his head from side to side, drawing in the others. "Are we going to let him do this? Kill us all, for some wild dream?" He faced Miska again. "You have Burns-His-Feet's sickness. You want more than we can do. We are only ordinary men. We should go home, where we belong. Protect our hunting, and fight our enemies there."

They murmured, watching Miska, their eyes dark as pits in the flickering shadowy light. Epashti came in by the fire and knelt down, her hands on her knees. Lasicka, the sachem's nephew, the real sachem, faced Miska again with a sad face that barely concealed a sneer. "If you will not lead us, Miska, I will. I will take us home. You stay here. You kill the strangers."

Miska put his hand to his amulet bag. His body rippled with exhaustion, and he could not think. He said, "Go, then. I don't care." He could feel the sharp edge of the little stone through the deerskin bag. He stared around him, to force them again to his will.

The others would not look at him. His stare glanced off their shoulders, the backs of their heads. They were already starting to lie down, going to sleep, Epashti moving among them bringing water and food and the consolation of her voice and touch. A lump of grief and fear and rage filled his throat. They were the Wolves. They could not lose. But they were giving up. He went down to the water's edge, sat down on the sand, and turned his gaze out across the water at the island.

⁓

Ulf said, harsh, "You do what you want, Euan. I'm getting out of here."

Euan was slumped on the ground, Arre beside him; his head was throbbing with pain so intense it was hard to think. He said,

"We ran them off. We can build fires at night, to see them coming. Post better guards." Send out scouts. Find out what was really out there. His head felt swollen, too full to think.

Ulf grunted at him. The sun was rising, and the feeble light showed the old captain's face seamed and wrinkled as an old apple beneath the shiny dome of his head. He said, "We lost three men this time. There's two more hurt, and may die. That leaves seven of us, with you and her and the babies. If we lose any more, we won't be able to sail the ship. We'll be stuck here forever."

"Until Corban comes back," Euan said stubbornly. "We said we'd protect his home here."

"Corban may never come back."

Euan wiped his hand over his face. The vicious pounding in his head overwhelmed everything. Rich, he thought. This place, so rich. I could be master. And thinking that he saw himself in the center of a store of wealth. But then in his mind the place around him grew, and grew, and he himself shrank away in the middle of it, until he was just a little stone in the center of a vast unknown.

He faced his wife, sitting beside him with the baby in her arms, the little girl clinging to her side. He said, "Arre." Pleading with her, who had always been by him.

She turned her face toward him, pale as a full moon. "I want to go home, Euan."

He shut his mouth. He could feel it all slipping away from him. His gaze rose, away from the frightened weakling people; he looked around him, the trees of the island appearing now like spikes against the brightening sky, the narrow water rushing with the incoming tide.

Ulf pressed him, merciless. "There's a lot of food in the storehouse. We have casks for water. The ship's sound. We can load it in a day. In a morning. We can go out when the tide ebbs."

Arre said, "Euan, please."

He sighed. It was his ship. But he had no strength to argue anymore. His head hurt like torture, and Arre was against him;

the last of his resolve went out of him with the breath in his lungs. He said, "Very well."

They stirred, suddenly vigorous again. The men all rose at once, in a babble of voices, and Ulf gave them a string of orders. Excited, eager, they hurried around, but Euan sat there on the ground and hung his head, defeated, until Arre came and led him like a child back to the house to rest.

—⚬—

Miska woke up with the sun bright in his eyes; he had fallen asleep on the beach. Epashti sat nearby him, suckling her baby, but none of the other men was anywhere in sight.

He looked out at the water, which had crawled down the beach away from him, uncovering low flat rocks furry with weed. He said, "Did they go?"

She smiled, her round face placid; with the baby in her arms, she was her own world, complete. She said, "Not yet—they will not leave without you, no matter what Lasicka says, Miska. They're off hunting. But when they come back they will want to go."

He stood up, stretching his arms over his head. His legs ached. He said, testing her, "Maybe we should."

She only smiled again, her eyes narrowing. He turned to look at the island.

The breath stopped in his throat. "Did you see that?"

"What?"

"A light—I saw a light—" Then, against his chest, something thumped like a drum.

He gasped. He put his hand to the amulet bag, and the rock inside jumped against his palm. He stretched his gaze out to the island again, and saw, again, on that far shore, the brief flash of a light, bright as a star, and then gone.

"It's her," he said. The stone was banging against his chest.

His belly churned with a sudden mad excitement. "It's her, out there, calling me—"

Epashti's face fell open, and she plucked the baby from her breast and rose up to her feet. "What do you mean? Who?" She came toward him, her tongue licking her lips. "Where are you going?"

He started down toward the log boats on the shore. "She's calling me—the woman I saw—once—"

Epashti said, "Wait—Miska—maybe this is a trick—what woman?"

He said, "She's calling me." He pushed the first of the logs out onto the water, wading in up to his thighs on the slippery hairy rocks.

"Miska! What about the others—"

"Send them after me," he shouted, and lay down on the log, and with hands and feet paddled his way out onto the shifting water of the bay.

The water tugged him along toward the island. He paddled like a turtle, the log rolling and slipping under him, as if it would tip him off. He fixed his gaze on the island but saw no more of the light. But against his chest the stone was jumping so hard it hurt.

The water was uncertain; sometimes it drew him on, but sometimes it churned, and broke into contrary little waves that jerked and tumbled the log around. He rolled off once and climbed back on again. No fish rose. No high overwhelming surge. He kept his gaze pinned steadily on that far shore. The contrary tugging of the currents was dragging him down toward the point of land; he would come ashore there almost at the feet of his enemies. He could not stop; he strained to kick harder, to paddle more strongly with his arms.

The log crunched against the shore, and he stood. His gaze swept the beach and the rising ground before him. No sign of her.

No sign of anybody.

His hair tingled up on his head. He walked up the shore, up the steep rise toward the rock wall, the strange huts. There was nobody here. Like the great fish leaping, his heart rose in his chest. He climbed over the rock wall where the night before the pale-skinned men had met them with arrows and slashing knives and this time no one stopped him. The circle inside the wall was empty. The strangers had gone.

He walked up toward the house, its tilted overgrown roof spangled with flowers, and stopped, and looked all around. A harsh laugh broke from him. He stood sweeping the whole place with his gaze, conquering it with his eyes. He had won. His chest swelled so tight with triumph that for a moment he could not draw a breath.

Off toward the trees there were four long humps of earth on the ground. He went that way and saw they were fresh-dug graves—three very new, within the day, and one older.

On the older one lay a flat rock with lines on it in black, smudged from the dew. He stooped, curious, and put his hand out to the rock. It was warm to his touch. The dew-washed lines melted when he drew his finger through them.

When he took his hand away, the black lines formed again, and he twitched, unnerved, seeing there somehow both the rock and a man and a woman, side by side.

He shrank away. This was an altar, he thought. Maybe they were still here. Something was still here. He stood, wary, looking around, and there, across the water, he saw the others coming, a stream of log boats, gliding toward him on the shining surface of the bay.

He laughed. He raised his hands over his head, not to signal them. He would never have to signal them again, or call to them, or wheedle or beg for their attention. When they saw this they would know, once and for all, what he himself had not quite dared to know until now, that he was their sachem, that they belonged to him.

She came out of the trees toward him.

He stood still, astonished, under the force of her look. She was pale as sunlight. Her hair floated around her like a gray mist. She wore leaves and flowers like a veil around her white body. Around her neck on a string hung a flat glistening bead the size of his palm. Her bright eyes held him. Her lips curved into a smile. His loins fluttered. He had never been with a woman, but he knew he would be with her. Yet he had no power to move. She came up to him, smiling, and reaching out took his wrists and lowered his hands to his sides. She took hold of the amulet bag, opened it, and shook the pebble out of it. He trembled with a rushing excitement. Her wild scent enveloped him. Under his loincloth his manhood was stiff and hot and aching. She stooped to lay the pebble on the altar mound. She took the shining circular bead from around her neck and laid it down there, too. Then she straightened, and reached to take him by the hands, and rough with her own hunger she drew him down onto the ground.

King Forever

CHAPTER TEN

Corban lost track of the time at sea. Day after day went by the same. The little ship was true as an arrow, and the weather stayed fair almost all the way. Rowing sometimes, sailing much, they ran to the east over a sea lively with fish, great cod whose schools stretched over the horizon, whales dozing like black blisters on the water's surface, flickers of flying fish, sharks weaving through the sea coursing for blood.

After a while there rose ahead of them a mountain range of clouds, towering into the sky in white billows. Sailing eastward, countersunwise, they slid beneath the cloud mountains, looking up through the white mass, and entered the broad warm blue river of the midocean, where there were no fish.

Here nearly every day storms blew up suddenly from nowhere; after a sudden gust laid the ship over, they took down the sail and put the oars out. Rowing hard along the ocean stream, they were borne far northward before they could slip free and raise the sail again in kinder water.

They sailed over the drowned mountains, and beyond that the land began to rise again, and poke here and there out of the watery surface, flecks of sand and cliff and rock, then larger massy chunks, Skye, Orkney, Mainland, England, until they came to the broad shelving edge, no thicker than their heels, where the ocean at last ended at the edge of the world island.

Following what he remembered of Ulf's lore, and more and more what he knew to be some strange gift of Raef's, Corban fought through the narrow channel in between Denmark and Norway, where the seas rushed together in rips and rogue waves and sudden eddies. Beyond, in calmer, closer water, with Raef at the helm, they followed a stream of other ships southward through a clutter of low green islands. To the west lay the long hilly shoreline, fringed with white beaches. Finally that shoreline broke, and among a vast solemn parade of other ships they rowed up a briny river and into some lakes strung together like jewels in the green land, and in the farthest lake they came at last, nested in its wooden walls and pathways, noisy with the trade of a thousand nations, to Hedeby.

⚬

The boys' eyes were wide and round as eggs even before they landed. Corban steered the ship to a place at the very end of the long curving beach, where he found a mucky shelf of shoreline too narrow for a larger craft. While he got the ship up on the land and stowed the gear, the boys stood knee deep in the water, goggling open-mouthed at the great city before them, the stacks of its buildings, the thick clog of traffic along the waterfront, the steady uproarious smoky smelly din that overhung it all.

Corban remembered how Hedeby had amazed him when he first came here—it had seemed then an enchanted city, where anything could happen, where he could find anything he could imagine. Now, compared to his island, the enormous sky, the silence under the great trees, the cool salt wind, the city seemed cluttered and crowded and dirty.

When he thought back, all he remembered was happiness, Benna's smile, Benna's hands, Benna's voice, his and Benna's children, and all around them the peace and sweet beauty of the island. He could bring to mind the terrible snowstorms and the awful grating hunger and the deaths of the two little boys, born between Conn and Aelfu, but it was the summer happiness of his life there that endured in him.

All the way coming here, he had thought how he could get back there, get that place back again, and free his home of the evils that had somehow followed him. What he had left here unfinished and unanswered had poisoned his life, even the new life he had tried to make so far away. He had to make amends, settle his debts, bring what he had done here to some end. Then he could go home to Benna and the island, and everything would be as it had been.

The boys swayed dreamily from side to side as they gaped around them. Corban laughed, feeling the land rocking under him, too; they would get solid on their feet soon enough. Leaning down into the ship, he reached deep into the close space under the prow and got out the money pouch that Ulf had given him and the sealskin bag with the furs, and slung that over his shoulder.

"Come along." He beckoned to Conn, still standing in the water where he had stepped out of the ship. "Get your boots on, and whatever else you need, and let's go."

The boys twitched out of their startled amazed stillness. They rummaged around in the ship for their tall bear-paw boots; Conn had the cloak Ulf had given him, but Raef wore a tunic of deerskin. Corban followed them up the short rise to the boardwalk that ran along the edge of the harbor and saw them already drawing curious looks from the passers-by.

Conn was still gaping at everything. On the boardwalk, he slowed down and drifted over to stare at an enormous dragon that was drawn up on the shore, its high coiled prow carved into patterns of snakes, and doing so he almost ran head-on into a man walking the other way, who thrust him off and strode on without a word or even much interest. Corban came up behind him and herded him along. Raef had his head down, his shoulders hunched; he had seen the people staring and smiling. Even here in Hedeby they looked strange.

They swung out to pass a crowd of people in front of a merchant ship, much like Euan's ship, where naked men roped together in lines were unloading bales of wool. On the other side of the boardwalk, for a hundred yards in either direction, stood

great stacks of wool, barrels one on the other, sacks in mountains, and, in pens made of poles, men and women.

Corban bit his teeth together. He had forgotten the evils of
this place. One hand on Conn's back, he pushed his son ahead of
him past the steady stream of walking people coming the other
way. Ahead the wooden path widened into the open square
where the big road from the west reached the harbor.

"Straight down this way, here. Stay to the one side, follow
the people."

He turned the corner, looking down the broad western road,
his eyes filled with the rhythmic bobbing of the crowd walking
away from him, the parallel stream walking toward, the orderly
confusion of the city, like one vast beast crawling all through
Hedeby. For a moment it overwhelmed him, and he could not
think even how to take another step.

Straight ahead, he thought. Do what you can find to do.
Herding the boys before him, he plunged down the boardwalk
into the crowd.

⸺⸻⸺

Conn strode along, laughing and pointing, his eyes sparkling, but
Raef hated this place immediately. The smell turned his stomach
and the constant racket hurt his ears, and he felt the people around
him like a coil of brambles, poking and scratching and catching on
him, their looks like snags, their voices like a net of sound.

It made no sense, anyway, from the wooden walkways that
made you walk in lines to the jostling hundreds in their lines to
the awful smell of rot. He knew nothing good could happen
here. He trudged along after his uncle and his cousin, while
Conn cried out joyfully at every new sight, and Corban walked
along easy as if on their own island.

Not easy. Corban was changing with every step, it seemed
to Raef, who skulking after him had him always under his eyes.

Corban seemed to be growing taller, and yet he walked with shorter, harder steps; he carried himself closer, as if he put on some bony armor. There was a little frown constantly on his face, always figuring something out. He seemed taut, not watchful so much as waiting for something he could not watch for.

They walked inland up a long boardwalk crowded with people, and with the most amazing array of things among the ordinary piles of bowls and cloth—odd tools, little boxes full of sparkling stones, strange figures and shapes, like something his aunt might have made, beautiful and tantalizing, figures as real as life, like nothing living he had ever seen.

He thought he had seen nothing, until now.

Through the awful stench a sudden mouthwatering flavor tickled his nose. Then they were walking by heaps of some golden brown stuff, made in different shapes, giving off a lovely warm aroma that stopped him in his tracks, enveloped.

"Bread," Corban said to him, and pulled him on. "Remember? Ulf brought some once." His uncle turned them into a narrower way, a strip of wooden boards flat on the ground between walls of twisted tree branches. Now in the rows of boxy wooden fences, square-cornered houses, they came suddenly to a gap, and there Corban stopped short.

Raef took one look into this empty place and recoiled. The strip of land ran away from him between two fences, with houses on either side, but even those fences and houses seemed to lean away from this plot of ground. Once a building had stood here, but only two cornerposts and a piece of the wall were left. Brambles and weeds grew up over it all, thickets of thorny berry vines, vines scrambling up over the ruin of the house, some spindling new trees struggling above the brush, their branches already dying.

The place was cold, and dark—even now, in the height of the day, with the sun shining down—and it was silent. No bird sang here, no butterflies skittered over the brambles, no mice nibbled at the seeding grass. Raef glanced at Corban, startled, and saw him studying the place, his lips tight, the frown deeper between his eyes. People hurried up and down the boardwalk past them, and Raef saw that they who lived here went as quickly and as far away as they could by the gap in the fences.

Corban wheeled. With Conn and Raef at his heels he plunged into the passing crowd, and after only a few strides he caught up with a lanky boy, years younger than Conn, striding along carrying a bucket in either hand. Corban swung around in front of this boy and stopped him.

"Wait, here—" Corban fingered up something from his belt, something small and glinting, and held it out to the boy. "Let me ask you a few questions."

The boy plucked the bit away. "What? I have to go."

"That spot back there, that empty ground—why has no one built anything there?"

The boy's eyes widened, alarmed; he cast a look down the boardwalk. "That place. Who would build there? Everybody knows it's haunted." He made to run off, but Corban caught his arm.

"Haunted. How?"

"By a witch. I don't know much. Lights at night, people say. Noises. Please." The boy leaned against Corban's grip, his eyes sleek with fear. "Let me go."

Corban opened his hand, and the boy sped off. Raef wrapped his arms around himself, wondering what Corban was doing. Corban turned, looking back down the boardwalk at the gap; then he turned his gaze first to Conn and then to Raef, studying them as if he had just noticed them there.

"Pap," Conn said, "what are we doing here? What's this place got to do with anything?"

Corban's face kinked with annoyance. He had a little pouch in his hand, which jingled when he pushed it into his belt. "Well," he said, "we have to start somewhere."

Then he threw his head back, his eyes wide. "Watch out!" He grabbed Conn by the arm and pulled him around, and swung to put Raef behind him, too.

Raef gasped. Up the boardwalk a man was striding toward them, drawing his sword as he came.

"Corban!" this man yelled. He was tall, rawboned, older than Corban, with a wild grizzled shock of red hair; there was something wrong with his mouth, and Raef could barely understand his sputtered, shouted words. "How dare you come back here! Did you think I would forget?"

"I'm unarmed, Eelmouth!" Corban shouted. "These boys are unarmed!"

"Ah," Eelmouth shouted, slobber flying from his lips. He had no teeth, Raef saw, that was it, his mouth just a hole in his face, through which words volleyed. He stopped square in front of Corban, his sword raised. "But you can kill a man with his own weapon, can't you?"

"Hold on, here."

This voice came from behind Raef, who turned, trying to get out of the way. A man taller than he was by a foot went by him and pushed between Corban and the furious Eelmouth. Conn started forward and Raef grabbed his arm. A crowd of other men surrounded them all, each carrying a sword or an axe in his belt; clearly they were followers of the tall man.

They all wore cloth shirts and leggings and leather shoes. Raef felt again the shame of his boots of bear fur, his deerskin shirt; he went hot all over, as if he were sick.

"Damn you, Palnatoki," Eelmouth said. "I've got a right to kill him—he betrayed me."

"There's no feuding in Hedeby," the tall man said. "You know that."

"I did nothing to you, Eelmouth," Corban said. "You know why I did what I did."

"You set us up," Eelmouth shouted, lunging forward, and the

tall man Palnatoki gripped his shirt and straight-armed him away.

"I said no feuding."

The redheaded man tore his angry gaze from Corban and aimed it at the tall man. "And who are you to command me, hah, old man?" But he thrust his sword into its scabbard on his belt. He jerked his chin at Corban. "I'll see you later, Irish." High-shouldered, he sauntered off down the boardwalk; the crowd of men surrounding them parted to let him pass through their midst, but their gazes trailed after him, and they muttered his name.

Palnatoki watched him go a moment, then swung around toward Corban. "You are Corban Loosestrife," he said.

Conn's elbow dug into Raef's side; Raef jumped. Corban said, "Yes, I am."

The tall man grunted. He was homely, with a broad, dished face, a wide nose, and pale hair in two hanks by his ears. He said, "Well, then, I think you should come with me."

Corban was starting down after Eelmouth, rapidly vanishing into the crowd. He said, "I have something to do. And I am not what you think I am."

"Pap," Conn said.

Palnatoki smiled, putting his head a little to one side. He said, "I know who you are. You should come with me. Eelmouth is a bad enemy."

"I can deal with Eelmouth," Corban said.

Palnatoki's smile widened, like a crack opening. "I am offering you my protection. Don't make me use a strong arm."

Raef's throat tightened. Corban turned from staring after Eelmouth to look at Palnatoki, and then at the men surrounding them, as if he had only now noticed them. "Well, since you put it so," he said mildly. "We'll come."

Palnatoki clapped a companionable hand to Corban's shoulder. The threat faded from him; Raef felt easier at once, and wondered if he had imagined it. The tall man said, "Very good, then. Let me make you welcome to Hedeby. I keep a great hall here. You will be my honored guest. And your sons, here, also." Corban snorted. "As you say, sir. Lead on."

—⁂—

Conn's legs had been shaky at first, almost threatening to throw him down, but now he felt good, walking again, glad to be on land. Glad to be here. He could not keep from smiling, looking all around him at Hedeby.

He knew this place already. He had been here all his life. In his mother's stories and pictures, in his parents' casual talk, in Ulf's visits, surely he had heard these names and caught glimpses of these places since he could remember, and all of it tinged with a haze of glory.

Now it was real. Now it was around him, the faces of the other people, light-skinned like him, with pale eyes like his. Here were the buildings that Corban had copied, back on the island. Here he heard his own language all around him. Back on the island they had been strangers, different from everybody else, everybody else's enemies. But this place, here, this was where he belonged.

So he followed his father with a light step, in spite of Raef's glooms and the crowd of strangers and Palnatoki's velvety threat. Whatever happened here, he would understand, he would be able to deal with it. He thought, I have been waiting my whole life for this.

The crowds of people passing by them were almost all men, but then suddenly coming down the wooden pathway toward them were some girls, carrying buckets. They were young, like him, with long pale hair twined with colored cloth; he could not take his eyes from them, from the soft shape of their bodies in their long embroidered gowns, and their cheeks pale as his mother's. His blood sang. They burst into giggles; one of them started boldly back at him, smiling, and they darted past, laughing, tossing their heads, leaving behind them a stray fragrance, and a curious ache all through him.

Looking around, he saw Palnatoki's men laughing at him, and his spirits sagged a little. Just looking at them, he knew how rude his clothes looked—at least he had the good cloth shirt that Ulf had given him, although it was stiff with salt and sweat, but his legs were bare, except for his bear-paw boots, which he had begged his mother to make for him, but now wished on anybody else's feet save his. Everybody else, he saw, wore low-topped shoes, leggings smooth over their knees, bright woven shirts, and gold rings on their arms, and gold chains around their necks, everybody but him.

They knew Corban here, though, and in spite of the little threat Palnatoki had made, Conn could see that he honored his father, who certainly wore no gold. Still Conn chafed over his lack of rings and chains. They came to a high wall of earth and sod and passed through a hole in it, and then were outside the city. He turned to look back, seeing the wall snake away from them, the jumble of roofs beyond.

Outside the wall, the land rolled away from them, the low hills buried in trees. Along the outer course of the wall the trees were cleared away in a wide band, but just south of where they stood now, sprouting out of the side of the earthen wall around the city, another earthworks ran off from Hedeby into the west. Rocks cobbled its foot. A little way down its flank from where it joined the city wall, a young tree grew up out of it like a stray hair on a bald man. Just above, a ledge made of wood stuck out of the top of the earthworks, and there someone stood watching them.

"The Danewirk," said the young man walking beside him, one of Palnatoki's warriors. He was taller than Conn, wide-chested, with bright red-yellow hair. "Where did you come from, that you are so green?" Around him the other men, watching, chuckled a little.

Conn said, "Wherever I am from, at least I am here now, and seeing all these wonders for myself. You can make me wiser— what is this Danewirk, then?"

"You are well spoken, for a country lout. It's a great wall, as you see, that stretches all across Denmark, from sea to sea, and keeps the Germans out." The other boy puffed his chest out suddenly. His beard was already sprouting thick along his chin, lighter red than his hair. "It's King's work. My father built a lot of it."

"Sweyn!" Palnatoki called. "Come here."

The boy mumbled something and went trotting up toward the older men. Conn looked around. They were walking along a little lane into the woods, and after only a few steps they came to a clearing, where stood a hall, built the way his own home was built: the heavy posts at the corners, the woven walls.

Unlike his home, this was a grand place. Other, smaller buildings clustered around it; the land fell away a little past it, and he could see more sheds down there, with fences around them. In the yard before the door several men were gathered, and some great beasts, and at the sight of these his breath left him and he reached out and grabbed Raef by the arm.

"Horses. She was right, my mother."

Raef grunted at him. Raef's head was sunk down into his shoulders and his arms were clutched tight against him. Conn laughed at him, slapped him on the arm, and pulled him on.

"What now, scared again—come on! We're home, Raef!" He laughed again, buoyant. Corban cast him a sideways look. They walked up to the crowd of people in the yard of the hall; Raef and Corban hung back a little, looking around, but Conn moved in among the strangers, toward the horses.

There were three of them, great dark brutes, bigger than deer, their heads tied with straps and their backs draped in cloth; they carried the men on their backs comfortably enough, stamping their feet and snorting and shaking their long rippled manes.

Conn licked his lips. He wanted to touch one, to ride one. Their great liquid eyes seemed full of wisdom.

The men on the horses slipped down to the ground and went to greet Palnatoki, clasping hands and paying each other praises. The tall man stood with his head stooped slightly listening to them, and then sent them off with a wave. Sadly Conn watched them lead the horses off.

But Palnatoki was speaking now to Corban, and about Conn. "Welcome to my hall. Come in and we'll have some talk and some ale. Sweyn—" The tall chieftain cocked a finger at the boy with the red-gold hair, who stood waiting like a servant a few steps away. "Take these two young men into your company— they being, of course—" He turned toward Corban.

"Conn and Raef," Corban said, nodding from one to the other.

"Good enough," Palnatoki said. "Conn Corbansson and Raef Corbansson. Take them, Sweyn, and treat them as befits the honor of my hall."

CHAPTER ELEVEN

Corban sat back, his belly full of the first good meat he had eaten since he left the island, and took another deep draught of the first ale he had drunk in more than fifteen years. A girl came at once to fill his cup again, and smiled at him, her eyes sideways. He was still getting his mind around the way his name had thrived here, with him gone, and somehow grown into a monster.

He said, "I am very grateful to you for your welcome, sir. I'm sure I don't deserve all this honor. But in any case I have something else to do, and I can't stay long."

The tall man in the high seat to his left swung toward him, leaning one arm on the arm of the chair. "In truth I was just thinking how poor a greeting I had made for such as you." His pale blue eyes, housed in wrinkles, were mild as a woman's; Corban felt himself warming to his kindliness. "All know you for a great wizard. You have been long gone from Hedeby, though; no man has seen you since the day you slew the witch."

"Aaah," Corban said, thinking of the cold dark space, back there in Hedeby, where the Lady's house had stood. "I think you give me too much."

"Is that not true? You destroyed her in mind-war, and freed Hedeby from her. Yet none has seen you since. Where have you been, although I am bold to ask?"

Corban said, "In the west."

"Orkney? We would have heard that here. Or Iceland?"

"No—in the west, that is all I can tell you."

The tall man pursed his lips, sorrowful. "Why do you put me off?"

Corban laughed. He drank more of the ale, which he realized he had missed more than he knew. "No, I am telling you only what I can. There is no name to that place you would recognize. I mean no harm. And I have no power. I can give you nothing. You have no reason to keep me here."

Palnatoki blinked at him. His voice came slowly, as if he dragged the words up from some deep fund. "I wonder you think I need any reason but the honor of having such a guest." He made a little putting-off gesture with one hand. "Yet now you tell me you have come back from a far country. For this council?"

"I had no knowledge of any council." But that explained much, Corban thought. He said, "Is Gunnhild Kingsmother at this council?"

"You have business with her?"

"Some, yes."

"Eelmouth seemed liable to kill you, if he could have. Eelmouth is still her man."

Corban said nothing. Under Palnatoki's curious probing look he turned his gaze away, watching down the hall, where Conn and Raef sat at a table digging their way through roast meat and bread. Raef sat rigid, stuffing his mouth while his eyes darted everywhere, but Conn was already the middle of a cluster of other young men, half hostile, half fascinated, babbling questions and jibes at him. Leader of them was the handsome red-headed boy Palnatoki had made so much of. He and Conn sat face to face, tossing off questions and jibes that set the others now and then into roars of laughter.

Corban scanned the rest of the hall. Palnatoki had a good crew with him, thirty or thirty-five men at least. He said, "A war council, is it?"

"Is it?" Palnatoki said swiftly. "What do you know?"

Corban laughed "Nothing, I promise you. I am ignorant of it all. I could not name the King of Norway to you."

Palnatoki's face contracted in a grimace. "You dissemble too much." He nodded to the serving girl, who poured more ale into Corban's cup. "I am just a simple farmer, you understand—I know very little of these intrigues and alliances. Were you summoned here? Not by Bluetooth. I guarantee you he does not know you are here."

Corban said, "What is the business of this council?"

Palnatoki twisted in the high seat to face him better. His arms folded over his chest. "On the face of it, it is to divide up Denmark."

"Really. Bluetooth is still King here, is he not?"

"Yes, of course, which is why I doubt the whole issue. In the generations he has been King, Bluetooth has given up nothing, shared nothing, brooked no rival. Yet here is this big council for giving away all his kingdom."

"To whom?"

Palnatoki stroked his shaven chin. "First is his nephew, another Harald. There are many Haralds in this, all of which calls for a pruning, if you ask me, husbandman that I am. Harald Bluetooth's brother Knut had a son, Harald, who has been aviking, and now comes home, with much gold, and much talk of how he will now share the throne with his uncle, as is the custom of our people."

"Is it?"

Palnatoki gave a little chuckle. "There are many customs we Danes honor by keeping their observance very rare, you know. Anyway, this Harald, whom we all call Gold-Harald, because he is so burdened down with wealth, wants half of Norway, and Bluetooth pretends he will give it him."

"Pretends how?"

"Calling this council. And also he has summoned here Harald Grayfur, who is King of Norway, so you know, to give to him lands that have by custom"—he made a little gesture with his hand at that word, and laughed—"belonged to the Ericssons. And that, too, goes against this rule: that Bluetooth gives up nothing. So I am suspicious."

Corban put his cup down on the table and laid his hand over

the top before the girl could fill it again. "This Grayfur is Harald Ericsson," Corban said. "Bloodaxe's son, and Gunnhild's."

"Yes."

"Where does she stand in this?"

Palnatoki waited a moment. Behind the wedge of his nose his eyes drooped, pensive. Finally he said, "It's odd that she is coming down to this council, too. The word is, she has cut herself off from Grayfur, for being too enthusiastically Christian. And she and Bluetooth despise each other. It's unwise of her to put herself within his reach like this."

"I thought never to care about such matters again," Corban said.

He glanced down toward his boys once more, remembering something long unheeded about Raef, something that maybe now was important.

Palnatoki was scratching his stubbled chin. "Now you are come here, too. Something is going on."

Corban said nothing; Palnatoki, simple farmer, had his own oar in this somewhere. He thought of Eelmouth, storming toward him with his sword, and wondered how he could get face to face with Gunnhild without being killed.

A roar went up. Down there around Conn several of the strange boys had leapt to their feet, shouting. Corban wrenched around, alarmed, until he saw they were not fighting, not yet. The redheaded boy was going around the others shaking hands and slapping shoulders, while Conn climbed over the table into the space in the middle of the hall.

"Hunh," Palnatoki said. "A little entertainment. Fortunate: I brought no skalds." He gave Corban a sideways look.

Corban sat back, saying nothing, and shot a glance at Raef, who still sat on the bench, hunched over his food. In the middle of the hall Conn and the other boy, taller, with longer arms, sidled around each other, their hands out. Sweyn, his name was, the other boy, Corban remembered, and a princeling, by his clothes and Palnatoki's favor. His friends drew back, grinning, nudging one another in the ribs. Corban set his teeth together; he thought, They have trapped him.

Sweyn lunged, his hands out, reaching for Conn, and Conn met him straight on. Their arms wound together, their faces went nose to nose, and they locked, each one straining so fiercely the veins stood out on their faces.

Each one was unable to budge the other. Corban saw Conn gather himself and improve his stance slightly, but Sweyn at the same time stiffened and lowered his shoulders and they remained locked together, straining, fierce, and immobile as stones.

Then suddenly Conn moved, too fast to see, falling backward, and lifting the other boy forward up on his toes. With Sweyn off balance, Conn surged up again, his shoulder driving into Sweyn's midsection, and the redheaded boy left the ground, arched neatly over Conn's shoulder, and landed flat on his back on the floor. Conn drew away, his chest heaving for breath, his hands spread wide.

In the sudden, shocked silence, Corban unkinked his muscles and sat up straight, relieved. From the benches where the warriors sat there rose a low, amused cheer. Sweyn sat up, looking dazed, his hair full of straw. Conn went over and held out his hand to him, to help him to his feet.

The murmurous cheer turned to a ripple of applause. Corban lifted up with pride. He thought, This is a man I brought here. Around the hall all the other men leaned forward, watching. Sweyn reached up, got Conn by the hand, and surged up again, and at once, again, they were locked together, nose to nose.

So they stood only for a moment. Then Sweyn laughed and broke his grip off. He thrust out his hand to Conn and said something nobody else could hear.

Conn straightened, smiling. He took the other boy's hand, like some kind of pledge. Corban grunted; he could see something was growing between these two, just in these moments. The two young men went back to their places on the bench, while all the warriors called out and beat their hands together. Corban sat back, reaching for his cup, which was full again. Palnatoki was grinning at him.

The applause died off. The tall man turned and beckoned to someone behind him, and when that person came up, Palnatoki took one of the gold rings from his arm. "Take this to Conn Corbansson."

The servant went scampering. Not a servant. Corban watched the skinny little boy run down the hall with the gold ring in his hand. He rubbed his hands together, uneasy. Somewhere beneath the calm of Palnatoki's welcome, the rough edges of this place ground together like broken bones.

Down there, Conn took the ring with a yell. He looked up at Palnatoki, and stood, and flung his right arm up in an outlandish salute.

The onlookers murmured, laughing, but Palnatoki only leaned back in the high seat and cast up his own arm, in the same salute. A swell of laughter filled the hall. The tall man settled down again, smiling.

"Your son is a good fighter."

Corban said, "Conn is who he is. Is that your son, there, Sweyn?"

"Not *my* son," Palnatoki said, grinning.

Corban looked down toward that lower bench again, where Conn sat pushing the gold ring up onto his upper left arm. Conn glanced up toward him and their eyes met, and when Corban smiled Conn flushed dark as a beet, lowering his eyes, smiling, too. Raef was still eating, having paid little heed at all to the wrestling. Certainly none to the gold ring.

Palnatoki's gaze remained steady on Corban. He said, "Tell me what could bring you back across the whole world, then, if not a summons. Is it from Gunnhild?"

"No, no," Corban said. "Matters of my own, only." He was

looking back over the summer, seeing things differently now; he wondered again about the shark. He said, "Sometimes, though, you never know about these things until much later." He ran his fingertip around the gold rim of the cup, hunting the right question. His gaze drifted down the hall again, toward the red-gold hair of the boy who was not Palnatoki's son.

"If not yours, whose?"

Palnatoki fingered his chin again. The kindly blue eyes watched Corban steadily. "That depends on who you talk to."

Corban said, "I'm talking to you, now."

"I say he is Bluetooth's son."

"Ah. And Bluetooth—"

"Says he is not."

Corban sat back, the pieces falling into place now. "How many sons does Bluetooth have?"

"None," said Palnatoki. "Except this one. Which he got on a maidservant in my hall in Funen, when he was staying with me once. Oh, yes." He nodded at Corban. "We have long years behind us, Bluetooth and I, and some of it not pleasant." He put his finger against his nose, his smile rigid. "Much of that involving sons. That is all settled and over, but this, that he will not acknowledge this stout, brave, good-headed boy as his own, is the worst."

"You're sure."

"I know the maid, and trust her. You know—some said the Lady cursed him, that he should have no heirs, when he turned Christian, but that of this pure maid he managed one, curse or no." Palnatoki's eyes poked at him. "You would know nothing of that, I suppose."

"I think he turned Christian long after you claim I killed her."

"She knew much."

"That's true," Corban said. "But a lot is true, and still means nothing." He was getting drunk. It occurred to him that at least now he had a bed to sleep in. He looked away down the benches again, toward the boys; they seemed farther away than before.

He was losing them, he knew, their courses splitting off from his, their lives carrying them unknowably away. That he could not stop, nor even wished he could. What held his mind now was something else, something long and old and deep going on, of which they were all only little whirling parts. He thought of the shark, of the great maw of the shark, reaching for him.

"The council is here, in Hedeby?"

Palnatoki sat back. "No. It's in Jelling, to the north. In a few days' time I must go there, and I hope you will go with me."

Corban pushed the ale away. In Hedeby, everything was bought and sold. He wondered what Palnatoki might consider the value of an ignorant Irish wizard, and who he thought would pay it. Nonetheless, whatever was going on was bringing within his reach those people he had the most interest in finding: Gunnhild, and the Lady of Hedeby, whose way of being dead might be something other than most people's.

He said, "I will go, but I am warning you, again, I have matters of my own."

Palnatoki chuckled. "I consider myself to be warned, then. Drink deep, now. I shall not have it said any guest of mine went to bed sober."

—⚬—

Sweyn said, "Are you Christian? If so, you still have our respect, but we are Thor's men here."

Behind them, higher on the slope, Palnatoki's hall still rang with noise. As Sweyn talked he led them down the long slope toward the sheds where they kept their horses. The long shape of the Danewirk rose behind the sheds, silvery in the moonlight. Then at the corner of the bigger of the sheds Sweyn turned and put this to Conn about God.

"Are you Christian or no?"

Conn laughed. Sweyn said sharply, "What, this is a joke

with you?" He put out his hand to his friends, who had followed them, eight or nine young men their own age.

Conn faced him easily, boldly, with a smile. Raef thought he had never seen Conn so happy before, and certainly he answered as if he had nothing to fear. "No, not at all. But a mystery. At home, sometimes, my father would go into a fury, and tell us that god was everywhere, in the trees and the rocks and in us, too, and that to pray, and put up altars, that was madness, because it meant the opposite, it meant you believed that god who was of you didn't know you were there and had to be reminded, or that god that is the world might not do best with all the world, so why pray, as if god were someone else than you yourself, who could be haggled with and argued with and won over? And Raef and I never understood it, until now." His face settled now, his eyes direct. "We are not Christian. We don't know Thor. God is what is, that's all, to us."

Sweyn gave a shake of his head. "That sounds like wizard's talk to me. Odin holds sway over wizards, and he's beyond my grasp." He put out his hand again. "I would have you in our brotherhood. I like your way of speaking, and I have never felt such a strength in a man as I just did wrestling you, and I see your heart is sound to the core."

Conn looked around him, at the other young men, and they rose up a rumble of agreement. Turning back to Sweyn, he gripped his hand in a strong clasp. "What about Raef?"

Sweyn gave a brief, piercing look at Raef, standing on Conn's right side. "Your brother is one of us, too, if he agrees, although all I've seen him do is eat and stare. But he's impressive at both of those, and I see he's stout enough, and in his time he may come up to Palnatoki himself for height. If he will take my hand, he's one of us."

He shook Conn's hand first, and then reached out to Raef. Raef saw no other course, since he would not leave Conn; he took hold of Sweyn's hand. Then Sweyn turned and said the names of the other men, and Raef understood that this was the brotherhood they entered into, and he shook their hands, too. But he could not remember their names a moment after he heard them, and their hands in his grasp felt cold and dead.

⁓

Sweyn said, "Palnatoki says I should be King of Denmark when my father dies. He's a good man, he raised me faithfully and he's been my truest friend since, so I do as he bids. But I am gathering a company of my own around me, as you know now, being one."

"You mean, you don't want to be King?" Conn asked.

They were sitting back on the corner bench. Everyone else had gone to sleep around them. The hall was a deep hollow full of murmurous snores and breathing. The fire was banked and gave off no glow, and only one torch burned still, by the empty high seat. Sweyn spoke in a murmur, barely audible.

"Do I look like someone else's subject? Of course I must be King. But I have a little more in mind than my foster-father can comprehend. He's a good man, but he's nothing but a farmer, as he himself will say."

Conn grunted, startled, and pleased. "Tell me what you want."

"So I will; you are apt as I am, I see that." In the dark Sweyn's eyes caught the distant gleam of the torch. His voice sank to a whisper. "Have you ever heard of the great work?"

"What? No."

"It is to bring under one crown the whole of Midgard. Denmark and Norway and England, the lands that bound the sea."

"The whole world," Conn muttered. Except, he thought, his father's island.

"Well, not all, but all that matters." Sweyn was smiling in the darkness. "The King who ruled it all would have no fear of German Otto or Frankish Charles, certainly."

"Who are they?" Conn said.

"Nobodies. So you are with me?"

"I am."

They gripped hands together. Conn was remembering what Ulf had told him, to find a great chief to follow, and thought he had done that. Soon after they, too, lay down to sleep, but he did not sleep; he imagined himself storming cities and leading ships into battle, with Sweyn beside him—often, just behind.

Unwillingly he thought about Raef. Thus far Raef had been like a wet rag thrown over all of this, mumbling and groaning and staring at his shoes. Maybe Raef would not fit into Sweyn's company. Maybe Conn would have to make a choice between Sweyn's company and his cousin. Like a chilly draft, that crept into his sweet warm daydream, and he lay down on the bench with a fur rug over him and tried to sleep.

⚬

Wrapped in a robe of marten fur, Corban slept in Palnatoki's hall, on a bench near the fire. Around him the rest of Palnatoki's men slept, and the fire died down, so that the hall was quiet and dark.

He dreamt that he woke, and the hall was still around him, dark and quiet, the air breathy. He dreamt that he saw the door open, and that Benna came in.

His heart leapt. He saw her little heart-shaped face in the darkness, and he sat up in the bed—in the dream—and stretched out his arms to her, his throat tight with all his feeling, and his eyes brimming. She came to him, she came into his arms, and they embraced, and she was warm and soft in his arms—in the dream. And they lay down together, in each other's arms, and he drew the marten fur around them, and kissed her, and they slept in one another's arms.

In the morning, when he woke, he was alone. He shut his eyes again, a great crushing ache in his chest, and hugged his empty arms against himself.

CHAPTER TWELVE

They went north to Jelling in two of Palnatoki's great dragons, coasting up the narrow channels between the Danish mainland and the islands, past villages built out over the water on wooden stilts, broad lowland meadows gilded in the fall sun, where people worked back and forth, back and forth, their blade arms sweeping down the hay into long serpentine heaps. They turned into a narrow vik on a waterway that took them some way up a steep-sided valley. Up the river, where a mass of other ships clogged the way, they left Palnatoki's dragons and followed a wooden causeway off across the valley. The fenland on either side buzzed with insects, and the stalky reeds clacked together in the wind. The causeway shook under their feet. After them came Palnatoki's men, hauling along crates and benches.

The causeway ended at the foot of the north bank of the valley. A worn road led steeply up through a rain gully in the bank; coming to the top of that, Corban stepped onto a wide flatland, stretching away north and west to the limits of his sight.

Ahead of him, across the tableland, a spread of bright-colored tents stained the pale stubble of the fields. At the center of the tent stood two hillocks, perfectly even, like two breasts rising out of the flat countryside. Palnatoki, walking that way, called his name, and Corban followed him.

He wondered if the two hills were the work of men: There were such barrows in Ireland, even bigger, some of them, and many of them hollow; Christian monks had taken some of them over. Lines of well-spaced standing stones connected these two. A little old wooden church squatted between them, but it sat ill at ease and out of place between the barrows and the lines of stones.

He said, "What is this place?"

Palnatoki said, "It used to be one of the holiest places in Denmark, until Bluetooth—" He broke off, and his hand chopped the air. "See that stone?" He changed course suddenly, striding in between the two barrows, to one side of the church.

There at the true center of the place stood a fist-shaped boulder, taller than a man. The deep grainy gray stone was trickled through with streaks of pink, like flesh turned to rock. Its flat even sides were painted bright blue and yellow and russet like dried blood. Some sheaves of wheat lay at its foot.

Lines and images covered the painted sides of the stone. Corban frowned, puzzled; used as he was to seeing Benna's drawings, he could not fathom these. The lines were only lines, and the images were so rude he could hardly make out their meaning. He said, "This is no more holy than anything else, this rock."

Palnatoki gave a sharp grunt of surprise. After a moment, he said, "In older times this stone was sacred to the harvest mother, Freya, and people brought her first cuttings here; as you see, some still do." He laid his hand on the stone and leaned on it, as if he might be able to push it away. A spasm of hatred crossed his face. "But Bluetooth has cased up this stone with writing and Christian signs, as you see—driven her out, and given us this instead."

"Unh." Corban moved around the stone, understanding it better; the splayed figure on the other side, he realized, was an image of the god Christ. His hand moved a little, in spite of himself. In his childhood his father had worshiped Christ, although the family had gone seldom to the church, the nearest one being days away, but they had signed themselves everyday. He turned and looked from one of the smooth grassy barrows to the other, and now he saw that the two lines of stones running between them were like the gunwales of a great boat, with one barrow at the bow and the other at the stern.

He imagined those piercing lines of power singing in the air around him. Here, at the center, at this stone, netted around with

Christian words and signs, nothing. But he looked down at the Christ again, and again, to his surprise, his hand began to move to sign himself, and he knew that Christ was winning.

He thought, I make up worse stories than Benna's. He said, "Is someone buried here?"

Palnatoki said, "That is Gorm's howe, there, who was Bluetooth's father. And that is Thyra's howe, his Queen." His voice dropped. "What do you make of it?"

Corban laughed. "What does that matter? I know much less than you do. What do you make of it?" He turned away from the baffled anger on Palnatoki's face. The simple farmer. Through the corner of his eye he saw Palnatoki smooth his features kind again. Corban looked around, seeing nothing of his son and his nephew, only crowds of people pushing out onto the broad flat highland plain around these monuments. Red and blue, striped and solid, flapping tent cloths patterned the yellow stubble of the fields on either side.

Someone was walking toward them, coming in between the stones. Palnatoki said, low-voiced, "Here is one to make something of it."

The man coming toward them dragged after him a trail of lesser men. At their head he tramped along with an air of great confidence, as if nothing could withstand him. On his arms and ears, in his yellow beard, and all over his chest, gold glimmered, flashing here and there when the sun struck it, so that Corban knew at once who this was.

He stepped back, off to one side. Palnatoki squared himself up, his hands on his belt, and said, "Well, Harald Knutsson, are you looking for me?"

Gold-Harald planted himself before them. He wore a shirt of fine workmanship, stitched all over with designs. Gold chains hung around his neck, some with crosses on them, two or three with the little iron emblems that looked like crosses but were really Thor's hammers. The men trailing after him came up close behind him. He said, "Well, here you are again, Palnatoki—still haven't given up, have you?"

Palnatoki's long shaven jaw clenched tight. He said, in a measured voice, "I have some rights left here, one of which is that the King must listen to me. And the King must do justice, someday, to his son."

"His son! Your son, more likely, as everybody thinks."

Palnatoki was rigid, his hands flexed, but his voice was steady. "The boy is of your blood, Gold-Harald, as anybody looking at you both knows."

Gold-Harald sneered at him. "When I am King of Denmark, neither you nor he will be anything to anybody, Palnatoki." He puffed himself up, his eyes pale and empty as bits of glass. Abruptly he poked his gaze at Corban. "Who is this?"

"That," said Palnatoki, "is Corban Loosestrife."

Gold-Harald looked Corban up and down and dismissed him with a shake of his head. "I've never heard of him." From among the men attending him somebody stepped forward, but Gold-Harald thrust out a hand and shoved him back. "You tell that boy of yours, Toki, not to be putting himself around too much. Hah?" He smiled suddenly, showing gappy peg teeth, yellow as gold. "Then maybe you and he will get through this alive." He turned and walked away, and his crew split neatly down the middle to let him through and followed after. Each of them wore gold on his arms and his belt, gold on his sword scabbard.

Palnatoki muttered something under his breath. His eyes glittered. He jerked his head at Corban. "Come on, let's get out of here."

They walked out past the larger of the two howes. Palnatoki spoke in a low harsh voice. "You see what Denmark's come to. Gold rules even the King. Nobody thinks what the right or wrong is. People have forgotten that it even matters."

They came around the foot of the howe and saw spread out before them the broad fields, with their clustered tents like huge flowers shaking in the wind. Corban said, "There are a lot of people here."

Palnatoki spoke in a low, intense voice. "When I was a boy there were gods in everything. Every village had its altars. Every stone had a name, a story, every tree. But this was the holiest, Jelling, these stones, this place. When I was a boy, this harvest gifting was a great festival. There were sacrifices every day for nine days. People came from every farm and village, it seemed, to lay the first sheaves of their harvest at the foot of the sacred stone. There were constant feastings, everyone danced, there was always a lot of fighting, men made plans for voyages, there were marriages agreed—they said a marriage arranged at Freya's Gifting would be lucky and long."

Corban said, "It seems a great festival now." They had gone past the round shoulder of the howe, out onto the plain. The flat fields all around were choked with streams of people and little makeshift buildings, stalls, and awnings. All around him the hubbub rose of voices and banging laughter and stamping feet; somewhere out there a sudden whoosh of a cheer went up like smoke, and then a rush of laughter. A stream of girls went by him, all in bright gowns and stiff white headcloths, each carrying a sprig of some dead plant. Every few steps somebody shouted Palnatoki's name, and he called some name in answer.

Corban watched the crowds for his boys, remembering Gold-Harald. Palnatoki was right; something was going on. Gold-Harald himself seemed like a long brass horn, loud with somebody else's wind. Yet that wind blew in from somewhere. They loved to plot, these people, and as Palnatoki said, right or wrong had nothing to do with it.

Beside him Palnatoki called out to someone, and waved, and Corban wondered where in this plot Palnatoki stood, and which threads he pulled, and why.

His heart pricked him. Palnatoki had treated him no other way than well; it seemed shameful to suspect him of an underhanded purpose. Yet the tall man had brought him here, was pushing him into this. He felt a sudden overwhelming urge to sleep, to let this all drop away, to sleep and dream of Benna.

They came to an open space, near the middle of the field, where Palnatoki's men were raising the awnings up to make a flimsy shelter. Conn and Raef were nowhere. Corban had no idea what he would say to them if he did see them. Under the center of the awning, Palnatoki's crew had brought a bench up, and a tub of ale, and at once people appeared from all sides to drink, and hail Palnatoki with their dripping cups.

Across the broad meadow toward the howes, a thunderous shout went up, a clatter of hands beating together, and whistling. "What's going on over there?" Corban said.

"Throwing hammers, or stones, or spears, or each other." Palnatoki settled himself on the bench; a slave brought him a cup with the foam still rising above its edge. A big curly-bearded man came up out of the passing crowd and greeted him boisterously, and Palnatoki bellowed back, clasping the other man's hand. Corban drifted away. The awning shuddered in the wind, loud in his ears.

Behind him the curly-beard's voice brayed out. "Are you going to this council, when Grayfur gets here?"

"Grayfur's not here yet?"

"No, he was supposed to get up yesterday, and now today, and now tomorrow, so you know how that goes. But you have to sit on the council, certainly—there's talk the King will settle the succession then. That priest is here."

"Poppo," Palnatoki said. "Is he giving his sermons away or selling them?"

Corban had moved a little away from them. By the edge of the awning's shadow he saw a tuft of grass, wound together, and he went to pick it up. Someone had made a little doll out of the grass stem and the blown seedhead, comical splayed legs frayed out into feet, the wild awn for hair. He tucked it into his sleeve. Palnatoki was deep in talk with a steadily increasing number of men, and Corban turned his back on them and went off into the fair.

———

Sweyn had seen the wizard go, but he said nothing to his foster-father; Palnatoki anyway was dealing with some men of Funen, who had come up to him with a dispute to settle. Sweyn stayed away from them, wary of being sent on some errand. He stood drinking ale at the center of the tent, talking with his friends about going viking.

"We can leave as soon as I get the ships," Sweyn said. "We should gather in Hedeby, I think—from there we can go either east or west."

They gave a great whoop, and then quieted suddenly, wary of drawing the looks of the older men. They crowded closer, their voices low and eager.

"I say we go east," said one. "There's places all along the coast we can hide out and watch for traders."

"That's small talk," another said. "Let's take one of the big market towns on the German coast."

Sweyn laughed; he loved such talk as this, the planning, and then the proof of the plan, and the fitting of that triumph into another, larger plan, but he had his own ideas where they would go, when he got his ships. Once he got away from Palnatoki, nobody was going to tell him what to do. He marked that Conn and Raef were talking together, a little apart from the rest, and seeing his notice fall on them they came up on either side of him.

"We are going out—" Conn's face was vivid with yearning; he waved his hand vaguely toward the fair. "Out there. Have you seen my father?"

Sweyn said, "He went—hold." Slim-Odd, one of his foster-father's men, was sidling up to him. He said, "Go, Conn. I'll see you later."

The two outlanders went off. Slim-Odd blurted out, "Gold-Harald was just here. Damn him, you should have heard him—threatening Toki and you both, he was!"

"Let him say it to me." Sweyn went back toward the rapidly draining ale tub. He wondered if Palnatoki had brought more ale and doubted it; his foster-father was no more generous at these things than he had to be. "Where is he now, for instance?"

Slim-Odd shrugged. "No fighting at the festival."

"Ah, sure," Sweyn said. Then Palnatoki was calling to him.

Sweyn hesitated, looking for some way to avoid this; Palnatoki ordered him around like a slave, or a baby. But he remembered that he owed his foster-father everything, and when the older man called a second time Sweyn went over to where he sat on a big carved bench out of one of the ships.

A cup in one hand, the other fisted on his hip, Palnatoki was looking keenly around the tent. "Where's that Irishman?"

"He went out," Sweyn said.

"Damn him, I want him with me." Palnatoki lifted the ivy-wood cup in his hand and drank from it. Sweyn reached for it, to take it back to the table to fill, which would also get him out of here. Sometimes he could not tolerate Palnatoki. The Irishman and his boys were good men, Sweyn saw that more and more, and it rubbed him like a burr to see Palnatoki weaving them into his endless schemes. That the schemes were made for Sweyn's own benefit lay like a cold hand on his heart. So he reached for the cup, to have the excuse to get away.

"No," Palnatoki said, and set the cup down, and gripped his arm. "I need to talk to you. Gold-Harald was here."

"I heard," Sweyn said.

"Now, heed me. If he comes on you, there will be trouble. But unless the King has given his word for it he will not attack you. You must not attack him. Do you hear me?" Palnatoki shook Sweyn's arm, like an old woman with a mop. "You must not strike the first blow, no matter what happens."

"Bah," Sweyn said. "I'll knock his damned head off."

Palnatoki snorted at him, his face red, and thrust him off. "Ah, you colt. Don't attack him. But if he attacks you, fight for your life, because that's what he's after."

Sweyn straightened his sleeve, which Palnatoki had pulled crooked. "I'll do what I have to do, Foster-Father." He bowed his head, trying to be courteous. "I won't strike first."

"Good. Now, go find that Irishman and get him back here."

"Yes, sir." Sweyn kept his head bowed still, for fear Palnatoki would read in his eyes that he would do nothing of the sort, and went away, back to his friends.

"Come on," he said to them; the tub was all but empty anyway. "Let's go find Conn and Raef and make something happen." He laid his hand a moment on the knife in his belt. Let Gold-Harald try anything with him, he'd show him real metal. And when it was over, he knew, the winner would decide who had struck first. With his friends at his back, he plunged into the churning traffic of the fair.

⟶⟵

Corban went along through the fair. Gunnhild was supposed to be here, and he kept a watch out for Eelmouth, in the flow of people in the meadow, the bodies clumped around the peddlers' stalls, the bigger clumps gathered beneath awnings like Palnatoki's. At the center of every tent, he knew, was a keg of ale, a little whirl of gossip and scheming.

There were some dozen of these awnings, most bigger and gaudier than Palnatoki's. He went into the largest, moving in through the crowd toward the center, hoping to see King Bluetooth himself. In the middle was not one but three great tubs of ale, which huge-breasted women constantly ladled into a perpetual ring of cups bobbing up and down around them like the mouths of baby birds. Behind them was a cross-legged bench covered with half-eaten loaves of bread and wheels of gnawed cheese. Crumbs and bits of cheese littered the ground, and little birds ran like mice boldly in under the table, among the trampling feet of the crowd.

But it was not Bluetooth who ruled here, Corban saw, disappointed; it was that same yellow-headed broad-faced man who had come to Palnatoki to insult him, Gold-Harald, who wanted to be King but was not. Many men surrounded him, all trying to speak to him, to get his attention, to hook themselves to his power.

Looking at him, Corban thought he did see something in him of the boy Sweyn. He wondered if he would have noticed, if Palnatoki had not suggested it. He got a cup of ale and a fistful of bread and went out.

All around the edge of the meadow there were games going on. He walked down to a stretch of trampled dirt where men were running races, and suddenly caught sight of Conn, stripped down to his sweat-soaked deerskin breeches, running mightily along in a pack of other men. Hard as he strove, he was behind the leaders and falling back. Corban laughed. Conn would never be good at running. He looked around him and almost immediately found Raef, standing among some other cheering people near the finish line.

Raef was not cheering; he looked hunched up, cold in the warm Danish sun, his arms wrapped around himself. Corban started toward him, to warn him, and stopped, not knowing what to warn him against.

He circled away into the fair, watching men throw big stones, and strive to lift even bigger stones. The ground here gave up a constant crop of rocks, he realized, looking around, seeing pebbles thick in the trampled dirt, boulders sunk in the ground. The dried beaten grass was slippery underfoot. The air smelled of dry earth and dead grass and the winter coming. The barrows' grassy even slopes lay like sweeps of pale brown cloth against the sky. He went off away from everything, down along the broad tableland,

and abruptly where the land sank a little came on a place where stones had been set together into a flat floor in the ground.

His mind flew to the corn dolls; this was a threshing floor, he thought, an old one, not used anymore, seams of tall dry stalks standing up over the flat stones, shivering in the wind off the sea in the distance. But then, coming closer, he saw the great dark stains patching it.

He stopped where he was. Even from here he could see that those leathery crusts were blood, spilled over and over, blood on blood, ages of layers of it.

Here no church, no carved stone stood; they would let this disappear into the lush stands of grass. They would forget this had ever happened. He sank down on his haunches, out of the wind, out of sight of the fair. He thought the place still smelled of blood, ages of layers. He took the corn doll out of his sleeve, trying to straighten out the wild jags of the awn with his fingers.

The quiet settled around him, and as he sat there Benna stole into his mind. In the bustle and crowd of the fair or the ship or the hall, he could sometimes forget about her, but when he was alone like this his mind flooded with her. An unexpected grief pierced him. He went to the edge of the altar, laid the corn doll down on the stones, and went away, up toward the fair again.

He drank more ale. He went around this time looking for Eelmouth, looking for Gunnhild. He watched men shooting arrows into casks filled with straw; some of the men behind him mentioned Gold-Harald, and he pitched his ears that way.

"Gold-Harald's looking for men, still."

"He's going to be too busy making himself King to do anything profitable," one of the men said. They were directly behind Corban, and he could hear them with no trouble.

Somebody else said, "Did you talk to the big man—Skull-Grim?"

"Yes—he says we have no chance—every man in Denmark

who can stand upright wants to wear Bluetooth's bearskin."

There was a general groan. Another voice said, "We have to get on a ship."

"There's always young Sweyn, maybe."

"Not for long," said the first man, and they all laughed.

Corban hung there listening as they chattered on about ships and captains. In front of him one bowman was making shot after shot into a marked circle no bigger than his palm, backing up five paces after each. As he released his arrow, the crowd gasped; as the bolt struck, they all roared.

Corban touched the sling in his belt; he doubted he could do so well. Certainly not from these distances. The archer had backed up, now, a good stone's throw from where he had started, another stone's throw from the target. He raised his bow, down there, and the crowd caught its breath; then the arrow flew, sailed wide, ticked off the side of the cask, and whined away into the grass. The crowd's voice sagged in a collective sigh of disappointment.

Behind him, one of the Vikings said, "Palnatoki would make that shot."

"Old arms are the best arms," said another, and the first laughed.

"Sure, yea, easy to be the greatest archer in the country when you haven't drawn a bow in fifteen years."

Corban drifted away before they noticed him listening. He looked for Conn and Raef at the racecourse again, but now, on the straight stretch of powdery dirt, young women raced, their skirts tucked up between their knees, their braids flying, and the men roaring them on. He stayed to watch them sweep by him, these long-legged women, their faces shining with sweat.

The sun was lowering in the sky. He was hungry, and he made his way back up toward Palnatoki's tent, through a straggling crowd of people. Then ahead of him a sudden shouting rose.

"Fight! Fight!" The shouting billowed up like smoke, full of names. "Sweyn Palnatokisfostri is about to fight Gold-Harald!"

Corban swore under his breath. Around him suddenly people were calling out, eager, and surging forward. He broke into a run, weaving his way through the quickening crowd, up toward the clamor.

—o—

The trick, Raef thought, was to look like everybody else. He went along after Conn, trying to imitate his jaunty stride, the loose, careless angle of his swinging arms. He pretended to be happy. He couldn't bear to make a fool of himself, as Conn did, running in races he couldn't win, and sporting with girls; but there was a lot to eat everywhere around them, and drink also, and plenty to look at. When in the early afternoon they joined Sweyn and the rest of the brotherhood, and they went around in a great roaring wolf-pack, he howled and swung his arms with the rest of them, and began to feel easier.

They reeled from one awning to the next, drinking everything they could find. Boisterous, strutting, Sweyn sauntered along ahead of Raef; the more he drank, the more Raef could see a sort of yellow glow around the head of the King's son. He tried not to see that; that scared him, like the constant little cold thrills along his arms, which he tried not to feel and which meant something bad was going to happen. Conn walked along at Sweyn's shoulder and they talked like brothers. Raef longed to talk so easily to Sweyn, to anybody, but certainly to Sweyn, the golden one; he wanted to laugh, as Conn did, with his head back, and his eyes flashing, and not know, or even care, that something bad was going to happen.

In their wolf-pack they followed some girls around a while, begging for kisses, and then in an increasing haze of ale they joined in contests, lifting rocks, and wrestling, which Raef could not bear to do either.

In the midafternoon they went into the nearest of the great ship-awnings to drink some more. This ale had been watered and there was no bread. Standing there not drinking the bad ale Raef watched a short, square-shouldered, black-haired man moving through the crowd on the far side of the tub, talking to many men but only for a few minutes each. When he spoke he leaned close and whispered into someone's ear. Nobody looked at him directly.

Then this man was strolling by their wolf-pack, and Sweyn went up to meet him, saying, "You are Hakon Sigurdsson, I think? I'm Sweyn Haraldsson."

The black-haired man looked around him; his gaze passed over Raef, who twitched and turned away. "Yes, I'm Hakon. Oh, yes, Sweyn Palnatokisfostri." His mouth drew into a slick smile and he put out his hand. "Enjoy the ale." Without waiting for any answer he turned and went back toward some other men.

Sweyn said, under his breath, "Someday you'll beg to say my name, you dog." Roughly he jerked around and led them straight away out of the awning-tent.

Raef plowed along after him, at Conn's shoulder, through the middle of the fair, with all the colors and sounds swirling around his head. Conn grabbed his arm once and said, "You watch this side and I'll watch the other," and Raef nodded, but he could no more make sense of what his eyes were seeing than he could speak. Conn swaggered along before him, after Sweyn's red-gold charge, and then suddenly somebody in front of them shouted.

They all stopped, jammed together, Sweyn in front of them all. Sweyn said, "Get out of my way, Gold-Harald!"

"I say you back down," a stranger's voice boomed. "Base-born nobody!"

Sweyn strutted forward, his hands on his belt. "Well, you talk a lot of fight, anyway, cousin."

"Don't you call me cousin!" Gold-Harald advanced a little. He and Sweyn moved around each other, circling, in a suddenly broad and empty space in the middle of a vast crowd. Opposite him Raef saw a row of stocky men in leather armor, all bristling with swords, their arms and chests heavy with gold. All along the backs of his hands and arms the nerves prickled up like bee stings. He saw blood in the air like a haze. His knife was in his hand.

People were screaming Sweyn's name. The prince was almost nose to nose with Gold-Harald, one hand on the sword on his belt. Gold-Harald's hair bristled. They shouted at each other, garbage words, fight talk. Raef gulped for air; he felt the whole world coming to pieces around him.

Then abruptly everything split down the middle, half Sweyn's, his, and Conn's, the other half to Gold-Harald, and down the divide walked a huge man.

"What's going on here?" He pushed between Sweyn and Gold-Harald and shoved them apart. His voice sounded as if it came up from the bottom of a well. Raef stepped back, cool all over; he reached out and gripped Conn's shoulder.

"Who is this?" Conn whispered.

Raef shook his head. "I don't know." He had seen him before, several times, during the day—hard to miss, he stood a hand taller even than Palnatoki, and his head was like a misshapen boulder, the bones thick as slabs of stone under his thatch of coarse black hair.

He had thrust the two men far apart, but now Gold-Harald strutted forward, his face red as a turnip, his sword hanging from his fist. "Stay out of this, Skull-Grim!"

The giant put his hands on his hips. He looked down at Gold-Harald as if from the top of a cliff. He said, "No fighting. That's the King's order. Put it up, Harald, or I'll break it off."

In the crowd of onlookers close around them all, now, somebody laughed. Raef looked quickly around, startled, remembering how they had howled for a fight. In the dense thickets of bodies and faces he saw Corban watching.

Sweyn said, "He jumped at me. He came at me first."

The giant Skull-Grim snorted at him. He wore a heavy black

bearskin cloak over one shoulder. Raef thought he was the ugli-
est man he had ever seen. His voice rumbled out again. "Yes,
that's likely, you're obviously too busy drinking to fight. Get out
of here, and stay out of trouble."

Gold-Harald said, "Yes, run, pig-prince."

Sweyn bridled up; Conn said softly, "Help me," and stepped
in to grip him by one arm, holding him back. Raef held him by
the other. Skull-Grim cast one glance their way and turned on
Gold-Harald, and got a handful of his shirt and jerked him up on
his toes.

"Did you hear what I told you? No fighting—on the King's
orders."

Gold-Harald twisted in his grip and wrestled free. "You
can't hide from me, Sweyn, so don't try!" He glared at Skull-
Grim and marched away. The crowd separated to let him
through, and a dozen men followed on his heels.

Skull-Grim chuckled. He glanced at Sweyn; Raef had let
go of him and stepped back a little, but Conn still stood beside
him. "You keep your calm, boy." He nodded. "Both of you." He
slouched away, loose-limbed, his great knob of a head sunk
down on his shoulders.

Conn said, "Who is that?"

Sweyn sighed; he looked around, probably for Gold-Harald,
but Gold-Harald was gone. He said, "That's Skull-Grim. He's
chief of Bluetooth's berserkers."

Conn said, "He's well named."

"Oh, he's got worse names than that." Sweyn nudged him.
They went off again through the fair, looking for more drink.
Raef trailed after them, tired. Sweyn went on, "He's killed
dozens of men. Swords bounce off his head. He has arms like
tree limbs. And he's clever, too, don't let that troll-look fool you.
Just the same, that's odd."

"What?" Conn said.

"My foster-father said if Gold-Harald attacked me, it meant

the King condoned it. Then why would Skull-Grim break it up?"
Conn said, "Who knows? Why make anything of it? It didn't
happen now, but it will happen, someday. Just be ready." He swung
an arm around Sweyn's shoulders. "Now let's find some girls."

Sweyn gave a bellow of laughter. He looped his arm over
Conn's shoulders and led them all along in a rush. "Look! There's
food!" In a clamor of eager voices they went on into the next tent,
Raef just another one among them, his arms still tingling.

⸻

The sun was setting. Corban went back to Palnatoki's tent; it was
all but empty, dark under the pitch of sailcloth, even the table
gone. From the back, Palnatoki called his name, and he went
into the shadows and found the tall man sitting on his bench,
talking to another man beside him on a stool.

Palnatoki said, "This is Corban Loosestrife, Hakon."

The man on the stool was short, with a square chest, thick
black hair, and darting eyes. He said, "Is that supposed to mean
something to me?" He held out his hand to Corban. "I am Hakon
of Lade, anyway, and pleased to meet you, whoever you are."

Corban shook his hand. "I have never heard of you, either, sir,
so we start even." He watched Hakon steadily; he wondered how a
man who seemed so smooth could be edge-on to everything.

Hakon ignored him, turning back to Palnatoki, laughing.
"You see Norway is still Nor, and Denmark still Gor. What's this
about Gunnhild? Everybody said she was finished with Grayfur,
after the squabble they had over that church."

"Is she here yet?" Palnatoki said.

"I don't think she's coming," said the black-haired man
Hakon. "Or Grayfur. Where is Gunnhild, anyway? Why did she
leave Norway?"

Palnatoki said, "Grayfur makes a bad enemy, as you certainly have reason to know. Gunnhild has a house at Hrafnsbeck,

on the big lake at Hedeby." He turned to Corban, his eyebrows raised. "What was that shouting I heard earlier? Somebody getting into a fight?"

"Yes," Corban said. "Sweyn and Gold-Harald."

Hakon laughed. Palnatoki's jaw dropped. He said, "They fought?"

"No—they were getting into it when one of the King's men stopped them."

Hakon said, "Gold-Harald, he's a bag of wind, is all. He won't start anything. You mind that boy of yours." He leaned sideways, his mouth smiling, his eyes moving, always looking somewhere else. "Gunnhild, now, how can she keep herself there? Hrafnsbeck is not a big place, is it."

"She has her ways, and she keeps only a small household. Eelmouth, her servants. Gunnhild Kingsmother is her own army. I thought you were friends with her."

"Oh," Hakon said, "I am friends with everybody," and smiled again. He put out his hand to Palnatoki and went away out of the awning-tent.

Palnatoki swung around to Corban. "What happened?"

"Just some shouting," Corban said. "The King's man came in before they got to blows." He nodded after Hakon. "Who is that, now? There was a Hakon, years ago, a King of Norway."

"No, no." Palnatoki made an amused face. "That was Hakon the Good. The Ericssons killed him. This is another Hakon entirely. Not good. This is Hakon of Lade, as he said. His father had a great holding in Norway, but the Ericssons killed him, too, and Hakon fled down here. He turned Christian, and now he and Bluetooth are like thumb and forefinger on the same hand." His eyes glinted, his face a shadow in the gloom of the gathering night; he levered himself up onto his feet. His gaze poked at Corban in the dimness. "Did you get the impression he already knew about Sweyn and Gold-Harald getting at it?"

"It didn't seem to surprise him," Corban said. It hadn't really seemed to surprise Palnatoki either, but he kept that to himself.

The tall man nodded. "We should go to the feasting, if we are to get any decent meat."

"What did he want with you?" Corban followed him off into the fair.

"Who, Hakon?" Palnatoki looked around him and beckoned, and some of his men came up around them. "I have no idea. That's how it goes with him, you never really can tell what he's up to. Where is Sweyn, damn it?"

They walked through the fair toward a spreading glow of torchlight, in between the howes. In front of the awkward little church, a crowd was gathering; coming closer, Corban saw the table in their midst, all heaped up with roasted meat and baskets of bread, and the tubs of ale were full again.

Behind the table was a carved high seat, twice as tall as a man, and on it sat the King.

Corban had never seen him before. Bluetooth was older than he expected, with crooked shoulders and a long thin beard. He had been a bigger man once. He seemed shrunk down around his bones, a cloak wrapped around him like swaddling. He was looking steadily out over the crowd, his gaze moving over everything. Beside him, standing on the ground so that his shoulder came only to the King's knee, stood a tall lanky man in a white tunic whose hem touched the ground. A white hat poked up from his head like the top of an onion.

Palnatoki said, into his ear, "Poppo, the Bishop, who turned the King Christian." His voice brightened. "There's Sweyn."

He started forward, pushing through the crowd toward the table, and then the King saw Sweyn also.

"Sweyn Palnatokisson!"

The whole place hushed in an instant. Palnatoki went rigid as iron. Over there, by the far corner of the table with its half-picked carcasses, the other men drew back, leaving Sweyn standing alone, facing the King.

Not alone. Conn stepped up close behind him, and then, behind him, Raef.

"My name is Sweyn Haraldsson," Sweyn said, "as you well know, sir. I am here to ask you to give me a fleet of ships, as you did last year, and to hear my right name in your mouth."

His voice was clear and strong in the silence. Nobody else moved or spoke.

Bluetooth rose in his seat. From somewhere behind him the giant Skull-Grim drifted up toward his left hand. "Your real name may never be known, boy. As for ships—I hear today you were brawling, like a common lout, disturbing the peace of my festival! Is that so?"

Sweyn flung his head up; his face glowed with rage. "Gold-Harald—"

"Don't give me any whining excuses," the King said, but he put one hand out. "Hold." Hakon of Lade had come up around the end of the table to the high seat, and the King leaned down over the arm; Hakon cupped his hand over his mouth and spoke into the King's ear.

Sweyn said, "I'm not whining. I only want what's mine."

Bluetooth pulled straight again, Hakon sliding away from him. The King looked angry. He turned and glared at somebody else, across the crowd. Hitching himself around in the high seat, he turned his furious gaze on Sweyn, standing there in front of him.

"What's yours, boy, could be pitched into one of these bread baskets. You arrogant pup! I'll not have you making trouble here. Go back to Hedeby, and wait there at my pleasure." His hand jerked, as if throwing something away. "Get you gone from here this night, now, at once. And Palnatoki, too." His head swiveled, stabbing his gaze at Palnatoki. "But stay by Hedeby—if you want ships!"

"Gladly, then," Sweyn snarled, and turned around. "Let's go!"

The white Bishop, beside the high seat, put one hand up. "Wait. Where is the wizard?"

Corban, who had been turning to follow Palnatoki, jerked his head around, startled. The watching crowd gave off a rustle of whispers. Palnatoki put his hand on Corban's shoulder and, pushing him forward, said, "This is Corban Loosestrife."

The Bishop advanced a few steps from the high seat, leaning on his scroll-headed staff. He had a long lean face, hollow as driftwood, and deep sunken eyes. Lifting his hand, he made the Christian cross at Corban.

"Is it true you are a priest of Satan?"

Corban laughed, in spite of himself. "No," he said. In the crowd also people laughed. The grave face of the Bishop flushed a little, but his eyes were fierce.

"Then are you Christ's man?"

"I am god's man, as are we all, will we or not," Corban said.

"Well spoken," someone said in the crowd, and here and there others called out.

The Bishop braced himself on his staff, his head cocked. "Are you then afraid even to speak Christ's name?"

Corban could feel everybody watching him, their expectations on him from all sides; he fought down a spurt of rage at Palnatoki. He said, "If Christ is God, as you say, then he is just, and will not burn me for a lie."

"If he is God!" the Bishop roared. "Proof enough!" But in the crowd also men were shouting.

"Well said!"

"Leave him alone—he's done nothing!"

"It's him who should be here, not this white priest!"

On the high seat now Bluetooth suddenly rose to his feet. He flung back the heavy folds of his cloak, cast a wide look out across the gathering people, and strode down from the high seat, down to the level of all the others. His gaze bored into Corban, cold with hate. Taking the Bishop by the sleeve he pulled him backward, never taking his eyes from Corban, and with the Bishop out of the way set himself square in front of him.

"Yes!" Bluetooth shouted into Corban's face. "I remember you—but you are nothing. The Lady said you were nothing." He lifted his head now and, looking all around, shouted at the crowd. "He has no power. He is no wizard, it was all in the sister. The Lady herself told me." He straightened around to glare at Corban again. "Get out. Go. All of you."

A great yell went up from all the onlookers. The King turned and went back to his high seat, gathering his cloak around him again, and Corban went quickly back away from the torchlight, into the dark. He realized Palnatoki was walking along beside him, and turned and scowled at him.

"So that was why you brought me here." Conn and Raef came running up behind him, with Sweyn trailing after.

"What are you angry at?" Palnatoki said, smiling. "You did very well."

"For now," Corban said. "You can't think he'll leave it at that. Besides—" He pressed his lips together. Out there, somewhere, someone called his name.

Palnatoki said, "Besides what?"

Corban said flatly, "Besides, now we have the whole long walk back to the ships, don't we."

Palnatoki clapped him on the shoulder. "Oh, it's easier going back, you'll see." He gave Corban a piercing look, and left him to himself.

CHAPTER THIRTEEN

So they went back to Hedeby, to Palnatoki's hall there. On the morning after they got in, Corban slept late; he woke to find the place empty, except for some girls sweeping up. He went out looking for his boys. The day was very fine, but cool and gusty, and the trees around the hall were losing their leaves in drifts whenever the wind blew. He walked down the slope toward the long lean-to where Palnatoki kept his horses. Even before he reached it Raef came up to meet him, slouching, not looking him in the eyes.

"Hello, Uncle." He seemed to search for something to say while Corban greeted him, and Corban turned and scanned the lean-to and the horse pens around it; the Danewirk loomed just behind, a wall of weeds and grass.

"Where is Conn?" he said, turning back to Raef, and Raef flushed and mumbled. Corban grunted. "Let me guess. He's with some girl. I hope you never have to protect any secrets of mine."

Raef jammed his foot against the ground, mumbling. His ears looked hot. Corban looked again toward the stable, saw nothing of Conn, and got Raef by the arm and steered him away, back along the path through the little woods, toward the road to Hedeby.

"Come with me. I want to move the ship."

Raef shrugged. They walked along together down the path, kicking through the masses of fallen leaves.

"That was strange," Raef blurted. "What happened, up there."

"At Jelling, you mean. Yes." Corban swung toward him, eager. "What do you think about it?"

Raef shrugged. "Nothing. I—" He lifted his gaze at last and stared at Corban. "You look strange," he said, and jerked his gaze away.

"What do you think about Palnatoki?"

"Nothing," Raef said, between his teeth. "Leave me alone."

Corban gave up. The boy was Mav's son, he had something of her power in him, but he would not use it. He thought of Benna, who had once feared her own power.

He thought of Benna, remembering what Raef had just said: "You look strange." He felt strange; he had dreamt of her all the night, as he did every night now, dreams as real as waking, that clung to him, more insistent every day; now he almost felt as if she walked beside him, leaning on his arm.

They were coming up to the gate into Hedeby. Corban slowed, not wanting to mix with the crowd waiting there to get by the toll-taker, who was busy with a big wagon. Raef said, suddenly, "These people here call me Raef Corbansson."

"So," Corban said. "I told them to. Does that offend you?"

"No." Raef smiled down at the ground, rubbing his foot against the dirt. Corban suddenly noticed, as if he had not seen him for a while, how tall he was getting, his arms shooting out of his sleeves, his jaw sprinkled with downy beard. He reached out and slapped the young man's arm, as he usually did, but this time he held on.

"You need some decent clothes," he said. "Maybe we can find something, somewhere in Hedeby."

Raef said, "Conn got a red shirt."

"Really. How?"

"He won it from Sweyn at some game."

Corban let out a roar of laughter; the people nearby turned and looked at him. He said, "That's Conn, isn't it. Did you play?"

Raef muttered, "I lost my knife. But he won it back for me."

Corban shook his head. He nudged Raef; the crowd was moving on, and they trudged along at the tail of it, in through the dark hollow of the gate, past the toll-taker and his guards, and into the hot stinking uproar of the city.

—❧—

Raef was glad to be with Corban, familiar as his own hands, who knew who he really was and still loved him. They walked around a while, looking at everything, came on a shop selling cloth, and bought some heavy homespun for a shirt for him. Corban brought out the little sack of silver bits Ulf had given him when they left the island and paid for the cloth, the while haggling with the shopkeeper over sewing it up into a shirt. The shopkeeper agreed on a price, and turned his head and called.

A girl Raef's own age came out of the back of the shop. She had long yellow braids and bright blue eyes, and when she took the cloth and began to measure it against him he went into an agony of heat. Even through layers of cloth her touch was like a nettle over his skin; when she bent to measure his side under his arm, such a rich ripe flavor arose from the folds of her bodice that his legs went watery and he was afraid he would collapse. When she moved away with the cloth, he was sure everybody noticed how his old shirt suddenly stuck out in front of him. He bolted out the door of the shop onto the boardwalk, gulping air.

Corban stayed behind a moment, doing something with the silver, and when he came out he was smiling. He gave Raef a laughing look but he said nothing.

Raef said, "Where is the shirt?"

Corban started off down the boardwalk. Ahead was a place where some of the boards had broken, and they pushed into the narrow stream of people circling the hole. "We'll come back later to get it. She has to sew it up."

"You mean—back there?" His voice cracked. "We're going back there?" Corban laughed, and kept on walking.

They took the little ship down the edge of the lake a few hundred yards, away from the big dragons, and walked back along the shore, sometimes wading in the water. Raef could tell Corban was gnawing on something in his mind; he fought off his own itchy feelings, trying to be stupid.

They wandered into the city. At a big open shop full of people they ate some bread and cheese and drank cups of ale, standing up all the while, as if they had to rush off at once. Everybody in Hedeby seemed to be going somewhere fast.

They drifted along the wooden walkway again, looking at cloth and bells and amber. He wondered if Corban was lost; they had come to the waterfront again. Then, as they walked along the broad street that went along the shore, Corban came suddenly up short, and Raef bumped into him.

As he staggered back, mumbling an apology, he looked down the boardwalk and saw there the roan-haired man with the hole in his face, Corban's enemy, Eelmouth.

He clutched at Corban's sleeve. Eelmouth was sitting on a pier, just above a stretch of sand where some big dragons were drawn up; he had not seen them. "Uncle, come away."

"It has to happen sometime," Corban said, "and call me Pap, damn it." He strode forward. Down there, on the pier, the red-haired man turned and saw them. He jumped down off the pier onto the boardwalk and cocked his fists up, and Corban walked straight up to him.

"I'm tired of looking over my shoulder for you, Eelmouth. If you want to kill me, start trying. But you should give it up anyway. This is between me and Gunnhild, not you."

Eelmouth lowered his fists. He put one hand on Corban's chest and pushed him. "So she told me. I'm not to meddle with you, she says. You'll come to Hrafnsbeck on your own, she says, and when you do, you'll have a hard time getting out of there." He smiled, a long snake-like grin, fallen in a little at the middle.

Corban yielded easily to the push, and gave Eelmouth an

answering shove. "When that happens it happens. In the meanwhile leave me alone."

"I will. I always liked you, Corban, that's what made it so
hard." He nodded at Raef. "Who's that? He has a sort of familiar
look, if you don't mind my saying so."

"He's my son," Corban said. "And I do."

Raef went up on the far side of him from the red-haired man,
who sprayed everything around him when he spoke. Eelmouth
climbed comfortably back onto his post and picked up a battered
wooden cup. "Have a seat. Watch the show, here. These are
Trondheimers, they can use an axe."

Corban leaned on the pier next to Eelmouth's. Raef stood
beside him, watching the men below them, on the sloping mucky
lake shore between the edge of the boardwalk and the prows of
the beached dragons.

The men stood on a clump off to his left; two at a time, they
were throwing axes down the beach at a stack of barrels full of
rocks. Half a dozen half-naked boys were loitering around down
there, picking up the axes and running them back up the beach.

Corban was still talking to Eelmouth. "Where is Hrafnsbeck?"

"Down at the far end of the big lake, on the north shore. It's
an old hall, which is why she likes it, very old. You can know it
by the stone watchtower. They say the Romans built it but I don't
believe that." Eelmouth gave a grunt of laughter. "She's right.
You are going to go down there."

"I have to make amends. I saw you weren't at Jelling."

"No. You were? What happened?"

"Nothing. Bluetooth threw us out before the thing even
started."

"What for?"

"Sweyn was fighting with Gold-Harald."

Eelmouth laughed. "I thought that was the whole idea." He

hailed somebody passing by in the street, who brought a bulging leather sack and filled his cup with ale. Raef's mouth watered; he watched the man with the sack going off, wishing.

"Who else was there? Did Harald Grayfur get there?" Eelmouth said. Down on the beach, somebody called his name, and he waved him off. The sound of the axes striking the barrels was like a slow drum; the topmost barrel was nearly hewn away, its scraps of staves held together only by the hoops, leaking rocks with every blow.

"Grayfur never came," Corban said. "What with him not there, and Gunnhild not, it was very boring."

"Did you see that Bishop? Poppo, his name is."

"Yes."

Eelmouth dropped his voice to a whisper; Raef had to strain his hearing to make out what he said. "If you ask me, that's why Gunnhild didn't go. She can put up with Bluetooth but not Poppo. He says evil things about her, worse even than the truth. These Christians, they can't abide women, I don't know how there will ever be very many of them."

Corban laughed. "I don't think Christ does that much below the gut."

"I don't think Christ does much," Eelmouth said. "The whole issue is a puzzle to me, why people like him. Did you ever hear the story of how Bluetooth was converted?"

"No," Corban said. "Tell me."

"Well, he had decided to do it long before, Gunnhild thinks, for reasons of his own. Anyhow he needed a show, for the people. So he told Poppo he would be a Christian if Poppo would hold hot iron in his hand and his God would protect him." Eelmouth grinned. "So one day we all gather at the forge, and Poppo is out there with the King, and the smith heats up a chunk of iron in his forge and with his tongs lays it down on Poppo's hand, and a moment later takes it off, and Poppo holds up his hand, as lily white and soft as any maiden's. And so Bluetooth was converted, and supposedly everybody else in Denmark."

He drank of his ale and held it out to Corban, who drank a little and passed it on to Raef. Eelmouth was watching Corban with a grin, and finally Corban said, "Well?"

"Nothing. Except when the smith put the iron down, Poppo was standing next to the anvil stump, and that has a burn in it three fingers deep now."

Corban grunted. "So he doesn't even believe it himself."

Eelmouth shrugged. "Who believes in anything anymore? With Bluetooth, you never know. Poppo has a great air of holiness, but it's his holiness, not God's, if you get me." The men on the beach were shouting to him to come down and throw the axe, and he waved them off again. "Have you fallen in with Palnatoki, now? That's a long weak limb, there, Corban."

Reluctantly Raef gave him back the cup. He liked the way the ale felt in his stomach, sour and fat. On the beach, two men came up to the line, each holding two axes in his left hand. Twenty paces down the beach, the barrels were slivered, shards of wood among the rocks. One stave stuck up above the rest, hardly thicker than a finger. The taller of the two men at the line took his first axe in his right hand, squinted down the beach at the barrels, and cast.

His axe sailed away over the barrels and missed entirely; the boys behind the target leapt nimbly out of the way. All the men watching broke into hisses and jibes. The tall man flung his hands up, turning away, his face twisting.

Still at the line, the shorter man stepped back, his eyes fixed on the target. The jibes and laughter of the other men sank into a hush, expectant, intent. The short man strode smoothly forward and flung the axe sidearm, and the flying wedge clipped the stave neatly in half.

The onlookers burst into full-throated cheers. The short man held up his arms and swung around, enjoying the applause. Beside him, the taller man straightened, his face fretful, and with his second axe took a nasty little swipe at the other.

The toe of the axe grazed the shorter man's forearm. He wheeled, his arm coiling, and without a pause sank his second axe into the tall man's neck.

The tall man went down like a hewn tree. Raef gasped. Over the rest of the men a silence fell. The tall man sprawled on the ground, his head all but lopped off, blood pouring out of his neck. The men closest to him shifted backward a little, away from the spreading puddle. Eelmouth said, "Oh, hell. That's not going to sit well with Hakon."

The short man said loudly, "He attacked me first. You saw it." The other men gathered around the corpse, stooping to peer down at it.

"With Hakon," Corban said, looking startled. "Whose men are these?"

"Oh, they're Hakon's warband," Eelmouth said. "They were supposed to have some work to do, but now that's off, and they're going a little mad. That's the second one killed fighting since they got here."

Corban grunted; he said, under his breath, "Well, that's interesting."

Raef realized he had thought these were Eelmouth's men. He jerked his gaze away, not wanting to know any of this. He thought of the yellow-haired girl, and her hands on him, and the yearning began again in his groin. He leaned against the pier, half delirious.

Eelmouth said, "When were you thinking of coming down to Hrafnsbeck? So I can tell Gunnhild. She'll want to make a nice welcome for you."

Corban snorted at him. "I have somebody else to talk to first, and I may not survive that." He looked up at the sun, then turned to Raef. "Let's go get your shirt."

Eelmouth said, "Who else?" Corban ignored him. Raef followed him down the street, running a few steps to catch up with him; behind them, there was a loud yell of anger. Raef wheeled, looking back; they were all fighting, down there.

"Whose men are those?"

Corban's eyebrows jacked up and down. "The question is, why are they here, and not up in Jelling, with Hakon?" He stretched his legs, walking fast around a little knot of arguing people at a crossway. "I wish I could figure this out, Raef."

Raef bit his lips together; everything Corban said made him uncomfortable, and he wanted his uncle to shut up. It was mid-afternoon. They went along the streets, from one little market to the next, and Corban bought a jug of milk at one of them and a pottery oil lamp at another, not saying why. They came to the cloth shop, and Raef said, "I'm not going in." If he saw her again, he would wreck himself.

Corban laughed at him. "Whatever you say. Stay here, then." He went in, and came out again in a few moments, with the new shirt and a linen undershirt also, neatly folded. Raef stiffened himself against the temptation to bury his face in the cloth. They crossed the city to the nearest gate, and there Corban stopped.

"Go back to Palnatoki's," he said. "Be careful."

"What?" Raef said, his hands full of the stacked shirts. "Where are you going?"

"Go up to the hall, show off your shirt to Conn. I'll be back tomorrow."

"Tomorrow," Raef said, astonished. "Wait!" But Corban was already moving away, back into the city.

—⁛—

When dark was coming, Corban went down through the streets of Hedeby to the Lady's house.

Where the Lady's house had been. The dark, overgrown plot of land stretched away from the boardwalk into the fog. Even in

the thick dark he could make out the gallows shape of the remaining piece of wall with its hanging eave. Nobody else passed
by along the street. The dank vapors of the fog drifted around him
in the air, and the night slid in over him like the lid of a trap.

He drove himself down off the boardwalk into the high saw
grass; the ground was slick and stinking under his feet. Something slithered away from him, and he heard splashing, up
ahead. An owl called. He thought he saw the great bird slide
silently off beyond the next fence, its pale breast luminous in the
dark.

Behind the standing wall he found a place sheltered from the
street, and sat down, and lit the lamp, and put down the jug of
milk beside it, and waited.

His heart churned and heaved in his chest. He wore the red
and blue cloak wrapped all around him but he could feel the cold
of the night air. Even in the dark the city was loud, but it all
sounded far away, indistinct and blurry. The fog muffled down
around him. In the hollow behind the wall, the little flame in the
lamp burned clear and straight.

Abruptly the upright fire guttered over flat. The jug tipped
over and the milk spilled. A cold gust blasted over his face and
his hands.

"What is this? Do you think me a house fairy? Why are you
here? Isn't it bad enough what you did to me that you have to
come to trouble my sleep?"

He was trembling all over, his stomach plastered to his
spine. Coming at him so suddenly she had scattered his wits, and
he could not gather himself. His eyes ached with staring, but he
could see nothing; there was only the horrible voice.

He said, into the empty cold, "We didn't mean to hurt you.
You were trying to kill me. I am here to offer you my amends,
anyway, to pay you wergild, if you will, and close the thing between us."

"Amends. What use are you to me now? You are a man, and the other one is already dead."

His teeth began to chatter. He pulled the cloak tighter around him, but the cold seeped in around him, a casing of ice. He said, "I was handy to you once."

"You betrayed me with Bloodaxe. Then you stole your sister from me."

His fingers were numb, his lips, his cheeks. The cold wrapped itself around his throat. His eyes glazed over, as if his tears froze. He could see nothing but the faint blur of the flame in the lamp. He said, reaching for the only thing he knew, "Bluetooth betrayed you worse."

The icy air froze his lungs. His veins were like wires in his arms. He could not move. His lungs had turned to stone. Yet the little flame burned still in the circle of the lamp. He fixed his gaze on it, struggling to breathe.

The frozen silence gripped him. His lips were stiff and numb. Then, abruptly, the pressure eased around his chest. "Yes: Bluetooth." The voice had changed: milder. "You were at Jelling. You saw."

He said, "What is he doing?" He drew in a deep, ragged, grateful breath, his fingers tingling alive. He felt the rush of blood hot under his skin. He pushed on. "At first I thought he was setting Gold-Harald on Sweyn, which seems pretty obvious. But then Bluetooth's own man broke that fight up. Then when the Bishop started in on me, he stopped that, too, although he wanted not to. And where is Hakon in this?" The cold filtered away from him through his cloak, leaving him soft with relief.

"Never mind Hakon. Just get Bluetooth." The lamp grew stronger, its light trapped in the fog, and in that vaporous glow for a moment he almost saw her. "Do you want to even things with me, Corban? Keep going. Bring Bluetooth down."

"Then tell me what's going on!"

His voice fell flat. Before him was only empty space. Nobody was listening. She was gone. The lamp burned steady and clear. The spilled milk gleamed whitely in the high grass.

He put his hands over his face, exhausted. He had no more ideas what to do. She had not killed him, if that was what she had meant to do at first, but she had given him nothing, except more trouble. Getting to his feet, he walked up to the boardwalk, and went down to the waterfront and along the edge of the lake to his ship, to sleep until the next day.

He slept well into the morning, curled in the sheltering belly of the little ship, dreaming of Benna. When he woke he could not rise right away. In quiet like this, alone, he could feel her there beside him, more and more. He hardly dared acknowledge that she was there.

But she was.

He remembered what the Lady had said the night before and knew what price she had paid to come to him. He ached to see her, touch her, not just yearn after the shadow of her, only half in the world, visible to him only when he slept.

At last he got up and waded into the lake and washed his face and hands. He went up into the city, losing her again in the racket and bustle around him. It was nearly midday. In the big market by the waterfront, in among the stalls of fruit and cloth and whiskey, he watched a dowdy woman in a long red dress juggle colored balls and listened to someone play an instrument like a long two-stringed harp. The musician had a deformed face, flat and yellow. Corban gave him one of the last two silver pieces in his purse, and with the other bought himself some bread, and while he was eating it, Eelmouth came up to him.

"Well, now," he said. "You'd better get to Hrafnsbeck

quickly, things are happening. Grayfur is at last come to Denmark, and Gunnhild will surely agree to see him, and there will be a great falling on each other's necks and sobbing for forgiveness, and we'll be going back to Norway in a week, mind."

"So he did finally get here," Corban said. "Will they have this council now?"

"Oh, like as not—Hakon's men have gone, anyway, so something is happening."

"Really," Corban said.

"Somebody came in the middle of the night and they were all over each other getting into their ship. Gunnhild says come soon, Corban." Eelmouth kissed his finger at Corban and sauntered off, slouching, his grizzled hair a nimbus around his head.

Corban watched him go, trying to fit this into what he already knew. He felt the thing turning and turning around him like a wheel of fate. Yet he could make no sense of it. The day was fine, and the waterfront was crowded with people; some new ships had come in from the east, and they were hawking goods right off the beach, glass and honey and wax. He stood among all the people crowding around, each after his own end, wondering what he should do.

Around noon he left the city and just outside the gate came on Raef sitting on the grass, half-asleep. When Corban nudged him with his foot the boy leapt awake, his eyes popping. The new gray wool of his shirt was still clean and uncrumpled, only a little grass-stained on the elbows.

"Uncle." He jumped up. "I mean Pap. Where were you? I've been watching for you all day."

"Well, here I am," Corban said. He walked on up the road toward the woods. The trees with their leaves shed looked like claws in the air. They went down the path to the hall. A couple of saddled horses stood riderless in the yard; a dog lying in the sun by the threshold lifted its head and stared at them. The hall door stood partway open, but there seemed nobody around. Likely

Palnatoki had gone hunting, to get some meat on his table. Corban started toward the hall, and Raef twitched and said, "No!"

"What?" Corban swung around toward him.

The boy was standing rigid behind him, his arms out in front of him, holding something off. His eyes bugged out of his head. He said, "No, oh, no, don't go in there, don't you see it's on fire?"

Corban reached him in a stride, grabbed his shoulder, and shook him. A quick glance around showed him nobody watching them but the dog, still intent. He said, "Raef. What is it?"

Raef reached up and clutched his arms, as if he needed help standing, and turned to stare wildly at him. He said, "It's on fire." But the fit was ebbing; his face settled, and when he turned and looked back at the hall, a frown puckered his forehead. "It was, I swear it." He relaxed; Corban saw the tension flow out of his body as if some spirit left him.

Corban turned and looked back at the hall. His heart began to pound; he had a quick, vivid feeling of seeing everything whole, in one piece, and he realized in a flash why Bluetooth had stopped the fight between Gold-Harald and Sweyn, and why Hakon's men had suddenly disappeared from Hedeby, and what was about to happen all over Denmark, and he got Raef by the front of his new shirt and shook him, hard.

"Pay attention to me. It isn't burning, not yet, but it will, soon. We probably have until sundown, they'll wait until everybody's inside for the night, but we don't have much more than that. You've got to stop ducking and dodging this, Raef. I need your help."

Raef said, "No. Yes." He straightened himself up, drawing his arms together; his eyes glistened. Corban thought he saw the leaping of flames reflected in his eyes. He said, "Tell me what to do, Uncle. Pap."

"Good." Corban let go of him, stepping back. "Quick, find Conn, and find Sweyn and Palnatoki. Try to make them run for it, but certainly don't let them go back to the hall." He looked

Raef quickly over, from head to toe. "Find a weapon, a stick, an axe, I've always liked axes." He gripped the boy again by the arms, looking him in the face. "Be careful. If they don't believe you, keep on telling them. Don't wait for me. I'll find you."

"Where are you going?"

"I'm going to Hrafnsbeck," Corban said. "I think now I have the price of the wergild I owe Gunnhild."

CHAPTER FOURTEEN

Cold under his warm new shirt, Raef watched Corban go off down the road to Hedeby. He looked around him for some way to do what his uncle had told him. He had to find Conn first. Once he found Conn, his cousin would lead him on from there.

He could not go into the hall, his feet would not carry him even a step toward it, although now under the great thatched roof the place looked solid and sound. He wandered around the yard a while, as a few slaves went in and out, trying to see in the door. Nobody came out but the slaves.

Finally he went off looking through the horse barns and the sheds and pens, but still he could not find Conn. When Palnatoki and eight men came back at the middle of the afternoon, with two deer and some waterbirds, Conn was not one of them. Raef kept looking. Moving around eased the rustling of his nerves. His mind stirred up images of flames shooting up out of the hall; once he thought he heard a scream, and turned, and looked around, and saw only the yard, where the men were breaking up the deer, tossing bits of offal to the dogs. Maybe it was a dog he had heard.

Then toward the end of the afternoon he heard a steady thudding, somewhere behind the horse barn, and he followed it around the corner and found Conn, in his red shirt, beating with a long sword at a rotten chunk of wood.

"Where did you get that?" Raef stepped forward; the sword flashed in the air, streaming light. Conn wheeled, lowered his arms, and grinned at him.

"Isn't it wonderful? I found it, up on the Danewirk." He held the sword out, the hilt in one hand, and the tip lying on the other palm. The edge of the blade was nicked. "It was all rusted, it

took me all day to clean it up." He lifted his head suddenly, remembering. "Did you find Pap?"

"Yes. He says—" Raef licked his lips. "Come on. We have to
warn Palnatoki. And where's Sweyn?"

"About what?" Conn strode along beside him. Awkwardly
he stuck the sword in through his belt, and then walked with one
hand holding the blade carefully away from his legs. "What's
going on?"

"I don't know," Raef said. He reached for what he did have:
what Corban had told him. "Pap just said we have to get out of
here. Us and Sweyn and Palnatoki. And not wait for him if we
have to run." His hair was standing on end. He looked up into the
sky; the sun was setting, and the great wings of cloud spreading
across the sky were fiery bright. An awful frizzle went along his
nerves. "Come on," he said, and broke into a trot going around
the corner of the lean-to.

At the last of the horsepens he stopped. They were too late.
Up there in the gloom under the trees the dooryard of Palnatoki's
hall swarmed with men, little blobs of torches blazing here and
there among them, and now, suddenly, while he watched, the
first flames shot up along the thatch.

Beside him, Conn saw it, too. He cried, "What are they doing?"

"Bluetooth," Raef said. "Corban thinks. Some huge plot, to
kill everybody." He knew Corban had not told him this. He looked
around him wildly; he had forgotten Corban's advice, that he
should find a weapon. And already, they had to run.

"They've got Palnatoki trapped in there! Where the hell is
Sweyn?" Conn leapt forward, struggling to get his new sword
free of his belt.

"No—wait—we can't—"

Conn swung up the sword, and a shout came from him that
shook Raef down to his heels. With the sword cocked back over

his shoulder, Conn launched himself across the bloody trampled meadow toward the crowd around Palnatoki's door.

Everything in Raef strained after his cousin, every bone and every muscle. He wheeled toward the horse pen, gripped the top rail in both hands, and broke it free. "Conn," he shouted, "Conn, I'm coming—" With the rail in his hands, he charged up the shallow little slope after Conn.

The whole top of the house was on fire now, and the roar of the flames sounded like a high wind in the trees. The flames were climbing up over the hall from the back; they must have started the fire there to force the people trapped inside toward the front door. There, at the only way out, the great crowd jeered and called challenges to the men trapped inside, and coming at them from behind Conn got in several hard blows before anybody noticed.

Raef caught up with him as the mob turned, howling, a mass of arms and swords and furious eyes, the flames behind them roaring up in a thundering sheet of light, glaring into his face. He swung up the fence rail; keep them away, he thought, let no one near him, strike at whatever came near.

There were too many of them. Charging at him from the crackling light of the fire, they were a single churning swarm of shadows. Two pieces of the swarm detached, came at him in unison, one from either side, howling like wolves. In his terror he almost dropped the rail. Beside him, Conn screamed, "Watch out! Watch out!"

In his mind suddenly everything went cool, went clear, and he saw himself and Conn, side by side, with the men coming at him, and he knew exactly what he had to do. He jabbed the rail at the man on his left, driving him back a step, and then swung his club at knee level, hard, and knocked the onrushing man to his right flat to the ground.

The fire dazzled his eyes. He could see nothing but the hot

fiery blast, but he felt someone leaping at him from behind and dodged and chopped down with his club. Conn screamed. They were surrounded. Raef got shoulder to shoulder with him, and struck hard, and for a long moment the two of them held all the others back, but then Raef in his mind saw them failing, and an instant later Conn stumbled against his side.

Then astonishingly the wall of their enemies burst and scattered. The fire rushed up before them, but there standing between them and it, looking dazed, was Palnatoki, with little flames and smoldering embers all in his hair, and Sweyn, just behind him, bare-chested, his sword in his hand.

Screaming. "Run! Run! They'll gather again—there will be more—keep going!" Sweyn got Palnatoki by the arm and made him run again.

Raef dropped the club; the fighting spirit left him, and he saw again what a good thing it was to get away from here. He followed Sweyn and Palnatoki quickly down across the trampled meadow, strewn with the deer's bones, toward the lean-to of the horse barn. A few other men straggled after them, panting and cursing and whispering prayers. Conn beside him was having trouble carrying his sword as he ran. Behind them the hall blazed up in a sudden whoosh, a great crackle of embers blossoming up into the night sky, and he thought he could hear people screaming.

At the edge of the pens, Palnatoki was waiting, Sweyn beside him; the tall man had gathered himself again, had his hands out, was shouting, "Everybody, listen to me, quickly."

The men all crowded toward him. The horses in the pens were stirring restlessly, and one let out a piercing neigh. Beside Raef, Conn lifted his sword and kissed the blade. He said, under his breath, "I shall be worthy of you."

"You're mad," Raef said. He was suddenly glad of his new shirt; the night air bit, damp and still. The moon was rising, showering its weak treacherous light across the broad meadows. The stink of smoke hurt his nose. Behind them somebody screamed.

Palnatoki was saying, "If we separate we'll have a better chance. I'll go to Funen. You, Sweyn, go to Hollandstadt. There's a ship there, you know the one. Get out of Denmark fast. Go to Jorvik. I'll gather ships and send for you."

Sweyn said, "That's good. All of you, get horses, and—"

A howl went up, behind them. Another horse began to neigh, over and over, like a trumpet blast. Raef wheeled around, seeing men rushing down the meadow, through the coppery dying glow of the fire; he saw the light winking like silver ribbons on the edges of their swords. His skin crept. Behind him Palnatoki shouted, "Here they come! Hold—use the barn—"

Raef yanked out his belt knife, wishing he had not thrown aside the club of wood. Conn grabbed his arm. "This way!" They scrambled toward the nearest of the horse pens; the horses inside flowed in a solid mass against the far wall, their hoofs pattering on the ground. Raef wheeled around, feeling those bright-edged swords getting nearer, and with his back to the outside wall of the pen he braced himself to meet the onrush.

He could not see Palnatoki anymore, or Sweyn, anybody else save Conn, and the half dozen strangers rushing straight at them with their swords drawn. He screeched. The belt knife felt like a piece of grass in his hand. Conn, beside him, whirled his sword up over his head, and the oncoming men crashed into them.

Raef sank his knife into the first body, wrapped his arm around it, and held on, trying frantically to free the blade, desperate not to lose his only weapon. The big man in his arms wrenched around and butted Raef's shoulder, and a moment later a hot pain shot through him.

He yelled, fought the blade free, and stabbed down again, and again, until the great weight of the other man sagged against him. The wall of the pen behind him gave way and he fell backward, the body on top of him. He thrust at it, his breath sawing in his throat. The horses were whinnying and trampling just beyond his head. He rolled the dead man off him. His shoulder still hurt;

the man had bitten him through the thick stuff of the shirt. He lunged up onto his feet, looking for Conn.

All around him, in the pen and outside, men stood swinging at each other. A sword. He had to get one of those swords. He had to find Conn. In front of him a man lurched forward, a sword in his hands, and Raef flung himself on him, one hand locking on the wrist of the man's sword arm, the other wrapped around his head.

The other man screeched in his ear. They fell, fighting for the sword, and rolled on the ground. He came up on top and braced himself with one leg, the other man thrashing beneath him. He caught a sharp blow in the mouth; he jammed his elbow hard into the other man's ribs, felt the stiffness of some kind of armor, and with his other hand still locked on the wrist below the sword reared back and aimed his elbow higher. His elbow went hard into the other man's throat. He reared back, the man going slack under him, but now he could not find the sword.

He bounded to his feet. In the smoky air before him another sword swung into sight, cocked back over somebody's shoulder, and he lunged for it, got both hands on the hilt, and tore it free.

He roared, triumphant, the weapon heavy and strong in his hands. Before him the man whose sword this was now stood with his arms still stretched upward, ready to strike. Then with a low grunt he crumpled to the ground, and beyond him stood Sweyn, with an axe.

He said, "That's twice you've saved me, Raef. Now, come on. They went for the rest of them, they'll be back."

"Conn," Raef said, looking around. The fighting had ebbed. Behind him on the dark ground a man groaned, and another rolled over. Several lay still.

"He's there," Sweyn said. "Come on."

Raef followed him across the horse pens, vaulting over a fence; the horses were huddled in a close pack against the wall of the lean-to. He heard hoofbeats galloping off. Conn was standing in the middle of the pen, holding the bridles of two horses, his fists full of leather, while the animals danced and sidled around him. Then the lean-to barn behind them whooshed up into a hot gusting blaze.

The loose horses bolted, shrilling, their manes and tails fluttering like dark flames. One on either side of Conn, the horses he was holding reared straight up. Sweyn leapt forward and caught one by the bridle.

"Go! You two—" He brought the wild-eyed horse toward Raef. "Go! Follow the Danewirk—"

Raef took the reins uncertainly, a hard lump in his throat; then Sweyn was hoisting him almost bodily onto the horse. He wrapped his legs around the shaggy barrel under him, and the horse bolted.

Conn shouted. "This way! This way!"

Slipping and sliding around on the horse's back, he pulled hopelessly at the reins of the bridle, which were both on the same side of the horse's neck. "I can't ride!" Then another horse ranged up beside them, and Sweyn on its back caught the reins from him, and led him on, and all he had to do was hang on.

He was streaking into the darkness, clutching for the mane, banging up and down on the bare thrusting back under him, sliding sideways, about to fall. He leaned forward, wrapping his arms around the horse's neck, but that made his legs lose their grip. The light of the fires fell away behind him into a cold darkness. The horse's strides jolted him painfully. With his head pressed to the horse's neck, he saw the ground flying away under him. His horse was chasing two other horses down along the foot of the Danewirk, looming high on his left, its crown blurry with trees. The horses ahead of them wheeled and stopped, and his horse ran in between them and stopped, and Raef pushed himself up off its neck, his hands on its withers, gasping with relief.

"Ah, ooh—" He straightened painfully upright, reaching

down into his crotch to ease his abused parts. "How do you keep this from killing you?"

Conn laughed, breathless. Beside him in the darkness, Sweyn said, amused, "Sit up straight, keep your feet in front of you." He turned his horse, and they started on again, slower now. He tried to sit back, but his thighs were raw meat, and every jarring step of the horse tortured him.

Presently Sweyn said, "Where is Corban Loosestrife?"

Raef said, "He went to Hrafnsbeck."

"To Hrafnsbeck!" Sweyn turned wide-eyed toward him. Then nodded gravely, as if Raef had told him something in detail. "Yes—Bluetooth isn't just attacking me, he must be dealing with everybody at once, even Gunnhild." He faced forward a moment. They moved through the shadowy dark, with the Danewirk on one hand and the road, a hundred yards away, on the other. Raef understood why they weren't taking the road. His groin throbbed, exquisitely painful still.

Sweyn said, under his breath, "It's kill or die, now, that's certain."

Raef wondered what had changed. The horses broke into a trot. Jangling along, trying to keep his male parts out from under him, he realized suddenly that he had dropped the sword again. He was useless, a waste as a warrior. He couldn't even keep on his horse. With one hand on the withers he tried to push himself up off the blade of its spine. His legs were already cramping. Grimly he set himself to keeping up with Conn and Sweyn.

Corban had a fair wind most of the afternoon, rowing only enough to keep out of the way of the constant stream of ships traveling up and down the chain of lakes that lay between Hedeby and the river to the sea. The sun slipped down the sky. Just before sundown the wind died, but by then, sailing over the biggest of the lakes, he could see the old stone tower there on the north shore, its foot hidden in a fringe of green reeds. When he rowed in to the dock he saw the hall, on the higher ground behind the tower, its deep thatch yellow among the yellowed leaves of the gnarled old trees around it.

Something about it gripped him, the yellow, the stillness, and he stared until the little ship bumped into the wharf. He came out of himself, caught a pier, and got the ship still against the wharf, and then went quickly up to the bow for the painter and climbed out onto the wooden dock.

The sun was still above the horizon, the sky still blue, patched with long clouds. He thought about Conn and Raef, back there with Bluetooth, and wondered if he should have brought them with him.

He could not keep them safe. They were tangled in this, deeper and deeper. He felt Conn set on his own course, away from Corban, and Raef trailing after, as he always did; in any case, they were lost to him.

Now he had this to do.

A wooden causeway led through the spiky marsh grass toward the hall; during high tides this black muck would flood, probably, all the way up to the bank the hall stood on. Its back wall was flush to the bank, and a wooden ladder set against the dirt ran from the wooden walk to a back door. Corban stood a moment, unsure, thinking of Gunnhild, with her piercing look, and her power.

He looked westward and saw the sun sinking. Grimly he walked down the causeway, climbed up the ladder to the door, and pulled the latch and let himself in.

The moment he stepped inside, into a shadowy darkness, he could hear her voice, clear as ringing silver.

"You are entirely wrong, as usual. The Pope of Rome must always be a man. But the Emperor in Constantinople can be a woman."

"I see woman priests." That was Eelmouth. Corban went forward, into a broad hall, splendidly appointed, with hangings in bright colors, and gold and silver fittings for the torches. Only two of the torches burned, down at the far end of the room, and that was where they sat, leaning over the edge of the table, a chessboard between them. Corban, walking forward, trod on a softness of woven stuff, layers deep. His feet made no sound, but up there she raised her head and looked at him.

She had been beautiful once. She was beautiful still, her hair gray instead of golden, the skin of her face chased with faint wrinkling, her eyes clear and blue and hard, her gaze on him that old familiar punch in the gut.

"So," she said. "You did come, after all." She pushed the chessboard away, so violently the pieces flew off. Eelmouth stood, took a step back and away, and waited, his hand on his sword.

Gunnhild waved him still. One arm draped over the edge of the table, and the other hand playing with her hair, she looked Corban calmly up and down. "Well," she said, "you look no different, really." Her lips turned into a humorless smile, her gaze sharp and not amused. "You know that you are—as we say in Denmark—dreadfully attended."

He made a little gesture with his hand, pushing that off. He said, "Gunnhild, I killed your husband."

She lunged at him; he stepped back, and barely on her feet she caught herself, folded back onto her chair, and began furiously twisting a lock of her hair around her finger. She said, "You did, that. You killed Eric, who was not what I wanted, but was whom I loved. I have lost my children, one way or another, Denmark's gone to the Cross, there's nothing left for me to do, but I have this pleasure left, that I can deal properly with you."

"Eric was trying to kill me," Corban said. "I had no choice—"

"You set up the ambush," Eelmouth said, "and led us into it."

"I led nothing. I set up nothing." Corban kept his gaze on

Gunnhild, utterly still except for the finger twisting and twisting her hair, her eyes unblinking on him. Belatedly it came to him how they could justly see things as they did, with him as the villain; hastily he pushed toward the one chance he had with her.

"But I have wergild to offer you," he said. "Your life, and Eelmouth's. You have to get out of here. Bluetooth has some great plot going; he is attacking all his enemies at once. He meant to do it at Jelling, but when you didn't come—you and Grayfur—you threw his plans off. But now Grayfur is come, and he has set Gold-Harald against Grayfur and given you to Hakon."

Her face went pale. Her eyes shone, and she lowered her hand to her lap. She said, "Hah, what you know, Bluetooth fostered my Harald. Hakon is a friend of mine." But her face trembled; she looked older suddenly, her lips trembling. "What do you mean?"

"Where is Grayfur now?"

"I don't know. He has shut his mind to me. The Cross has taken him from me. What do you mean?"

Corban looked for the first time at Eelmouth, standing there by the table. "I think Bluetooth is playing Gold-Harald against Grayfur, and whoever wins is left to Hakon. The trap is closing. Grayfur is in Denmark now. Hakon will come here before dark. You know they would not strike at Grayfur without her also. And Hakon was asking questions about her—"

"No," Gunnhild cried. She swung toward Eelmouth, pleading, as if convincing him would make all different. "He loved Harald. His namesake. He will not—" She swallowed hard. Her gaze left Eelmouth; she slumped down on the bench, leaning heavily on the table. Her shoulders sagged. "Damn him," she said. "He is not a Dane for nothing, Bluetooth."

Corban licked his lips. Outside, somewhere in the distance, he thought he heard the shrill neigh of a horse. Eelmouth heard it also; he swore, drew his sword, and strode around the table, but not at Corban. He headed toward the main door, in the middle of the hall's long front wall, opposite from the little back door where Corban had come in. Gunnhild lifted her head, her face haggard, old as a skull.

Corban said, "It's them. You see, it's true. Gunnhild, come, I have a ship here. You can escape."

There came a thunderous knock on the door; Corban jumped at the booming sound, his throat closing. Gunnhild jerked, all over, and climbed onto her feet. She pulled at her long gown, as if putting herself back together. Her face smoothed. Eelmouth was already at the door; from the wall beside it he heaved up a great long balk of wood and slammed it down into the brackets on either side, barring the door fast.

"Come on!" He sprang around, heading for the little back door. Gunnhild came spryly around the table, and Corban followed her after him.

"That's the ship?" Holding the door wide, Eelmouth was peering through the dusk toward the wharf. He stepped back, still propping the door, and Gunnhild went out first and down the ladder, nimble, her hair coming loose.

"Yes." Corban went after her. The sun had just set, but the air was still pink beneath the darkening sky. From the top of the ladder Corban saw they still had a chance. Whoever was at the door had naturally sent his men to surround the hall, but the sharp steep bank and the marshy ground had held them up. Gunnhild was already halfway down the causeway toward the wharf, and the men chasing them were only just sliding down the bank at the side of the hall.

Corban bounded down onto the causeway; Eelmouth dropped beside him. From their pursuers there rose a harsh greedy outcry. Then their whoops changed to an astonished yell.

Out there on the wooden causeway, running, Gunnhild trailed the scarves and skirts of her clothes behind her, fluttering in the twilight; for one stride more she was a woman, running across the rackety boards, streaming the fringes of her clothes, and then she was rising, her feathery arms beating, her body stretching into the wind, and on wings stretched wide she sailed up into the darkening air.

Eelmouth gave a roar. He bounded off across the wooden pathway; Corban followed him, glancing over his shoulder to see the men rushing after.

Half a dozen on either side, they slipped and wobbled across the muck, but they had a much shorter way to go, and were certainly going to catch him and Eelmouth.

The hawk circled back over them. Its head turned from side to side, and it swung around toward the ship at the wharf. The tide had the little ship in its grasp, drawing it out away from the wharf, the painter stretched out taut, the stern aimed down toward the narrow way out of the lake to the river. The hawk sloped down toward it, her talons outstretched, to land on the high stern.

A step ahead of Corban, Eelmouth strode out onto the wharf and bent to free the ship's painter. Corban looked back; the men after them were pounding down the causeway, the leaders three strides from the wharf.

"Give me your sword." Corban turned toward Eelmouth. "Quick."

Eelmouth was hauling the boat in, hand over hand; he stopped long enough to yank his sword from its sheath and throw it the ten feet to Corban. Corban snatched the sword out of the air by its hilt.

Its weight startled him. On the first boards of the wharf, he wheeled as the first two men reached him, and slashed the broad blade in a sweep across their path. He had no gift for this; he swung awkwardly, nearly slinging the sword off into the marsh, but the oncoming men shied away anyway, crowded together onto the causeway, scrambling away from the sticky muck of the marsh. He planted himself on the land end of the wharf. Amazed, he heard himself howl in Irish— "Damn you! Damn your bloody hides! Come and get me if you dare!"

They rushed at him. He lashed out, the sword in both hands,

and struck one man down; through the tail of his eye he saw some of them leaping down into the mucky river, circling around him. A man with an axe loomed up before him, and traded blows with him, foot to foot.

"Corban!" Eelmouth shouted. "Come on! Get in here!"

The axe slashed at his head; he flinched, ducking away, and twisted, and the notched blade swished by. He saw the little ship standing away from the dock, its red and white sail filling out with the evening wind, and then the wharf bucked hard under him, and from one side somebody reached up around the side of it and grabbed his ankle.

He fell hard on his knees. He lifted his head; he saw out there the swollen sail, the little ship gliding off onto the breast of the tide, already out of reach, and then they piled onto him, and bore him down onto the boards.

⇒

When they dragged him into the hall, the black-haired man Hakon of Lade was there, standing by the table, looking down at the chessboard with its scattered pieces. He lifted his head, watching Corban come toward him, and his face twisted with a cold fury.

"Who told you?" He tramped three steps up to meet Corban and shouted into his face. For once his eyes looked straight ahead. "Somebody betrayed me! Who was it?"

Corban was still, although the men on either side of him let go of him, and let him stand alone. He said, "No one. I made it out of what I saw." He knew he was about to die. He felt Benna wrapped around and around him; soon he would be with her. He said, enjoying this, "Shouldn't you be going? By now, Gold-Harald or Grayfur has won that fight. You should catch the winner quickly, while he's still recovering, and you can beat him easily."

Hakon jerked his head back. His teeth showed and his hand

went to the sword in his belt. "Damn you. Who else did you tell?" He slid the sword partway out of the scabbard, and then thrust it back into the sheath. The rage was ebbing, sinking back into the hard calculation of his wit. He paced off a few steps and came back. "Who else did you warn? Palnatoki. I should have listened to him when he told me about you."

Corban smiled at him, saying nothing. Hakon paced back and forth in front of him, grinding his teeth together.

"You think I'm going to kill you, don't you."

Corban made no answer. He waited, patient, knowing what would come. Hakon's eyes widened, shining with rage, and his fingers played over the hilt of his sword.

"Well," he said, "I am. But not quickly. We'll see what kind of wizard you really are. Eyvind. Thorleif. Take him over to that watchtower, lock him into the top chamber of it. Throw the key in the lake. Let's see how long you can live on air and sunlight, wizard." His arm jerked, as if casting away the key. "Take him."

CHAPTER FIFTEEN

As soon as they reached Hollandstadt, just before dawn, Raef huddled into the bow of a ship and went to sleep, but Conn was too excited to sleep. In the deep gloom of the moments before daybreak he helped Sweyn check quickly over the ship, counting oars and shields, and looking for leaks. The prince said almost nothing but went swiftly and surely about the work. Conn did whatever he bade him, glad of the business. He marked how Sweyn stopped now and then and looked away intently, up and down the river's shore, and to the east.

The sail locker was full, and the ship, one of a long line of dragons drawn up on the river bar, seemed fit to go. They were short some oars, and Sweyn with no hesitation took them from the neighboring hull. As they worked, the sun's first thin blue light slipped over the horizon, casting long shadows away westward. Inland a cock crowed, and over by the scattered buildings of the little town someone began to chop wood.

Sweyn straightened, rubbing his hands together, and looked keenly toward the east again. "I'd thought more of our bunch got out of the hall with us," he said.

Conn said, although he knew better, "Maybe they went with Palnatoki."

Sweyn shook his head. "Anyhow, we're short a lot of men. I'll have to see if I can find some."

Conn said, "I'll go with you."

"No—stay here, keep an eye on the ship. We can't lose the ship." Sweyn reached out and gripped Conn's shoulder. "Thanks, Conn. That's all I can say, now. Someday, a lot more. Thanks." His hand squeezed tight on Conn's shoulder, and he turned and walked away up the shore.

Conn climbed back inside the ship, where Raef still slept burrowed into the hollow of the prow, and lay down beside him. He was aching with exhaustion, but he still could not sleep at once. Everything was going along very well. For years he had thought all this happened only in his mother's stories, but now he had come into his own story, and he was giddy with the joy of it. He had a sword, and a cause, a true and noble cause, to make the world right again; he had a great prince to follow, who would surely lead him to victories.

The god thing was a little confusing—Corban's ideas about god belonged back on the island, with his mother, in that place outside of story; Sweyn's gods seemed no more than stories. Anyhow, the Thor and Odin of it was incidental, compared to the glory of following Sweyn, of winning the battles to come. He laid his hand on the hilt of his new sword, and thought to himself he would never dishonor it, or his prince.

He slept. Almost at once, it seemed, he was jarred awake by the heavy stamp of footsteps just outside the hull of the ship.

He straightened; Sweyn was standing there, with a dozen strange men, some in rags and tatters, and many still half asleep, yawning. Sweyn nodded at Conn. "Don't say anything. This is our crew. Come on, men, let's get to work here—Conn, help me. You men, get yourselves a bench and stow your gear. Let's go!"

Sluggishly the new men climbed up over the gunwales into the ship and set themselves around. Conn stepped down onto the mud of the shore. Sweyn said, under his breath, "They're all I could find, they'll have to do. Come help me." They loaded some casks and baskets full of food onto the ship. Raef woke up, blinking and yawning, and came to help them with the last of it. Before the sun was a fist above the horizon, Sweyn's dragon was sliding down the slow salty water of the river toward the sea.

Conn rowed a while, with Sweyn at the steerboard. The new men sorted out their strokes and rhythm, and the ship glided along the channel through the boggy lowland between Hollandstadt and the sea. When the rowing was going well, Sweyn called Conn back to him in the stern.

"You steer. I need to sleep. Do you know where to go?"

"I'll figure it out," Conn said. "These men seem all right."

Sweyn shook his head. "I don't know half their names. Some of them could be Bluetooth's men. Who knows what they'll do if we're set on—" His lips twisted with distaste, and he went forward a little, lay down in the hull, and slept.

The mists were still rising from the water, the sun a silver dot in a thickness of sky. Conn steered the ship along in a line of other ships making their way down the boggy river to the sea. The river's sluggish tidal current wound between islands of mud prickly with rushes, their feathery tops blown to wild white fluff. He followed a big-bellied ship like a waddling duck down a channel to the sea.

When he put the ship to the line of breakers at the edge of the sea, Sweyn woke up. He cast a look into the sky and another over their crew, and turned to look along the coast. "So far nothing," he said.

Conn thought that in the clutter of other hulls coming out of the river here no one would notice them. He let the ship work its way through the breakers and into the deeper, rolling water offshore. Sweyn came back and got the steerboard grip and turned to run southerly. The wind was better for this and they put the sail up. Quickly the ship outran the slow traders and shore ships that had come down the river with them, and they sailed along just within sight of a low flat coast.

Conn went down to the bench next to Raef's; they broke out some of the food, and everybody sat around eating. "Is this all?" one of the strangers said, and the others whined along with him; Sweyn ignored them, and they fell to bickering back and forth among themselves. Conn sat getting a feel of these men and decided quickly he didn't much like them. Then he saw Raef lift his head and look hard away over their stern.

"What is it?" Conn said.

Raef mumbled around a mouthful of bread. Conn stood up, looking north; the empty sea rumpled away from him into the misty indefinite distance.

One of the new men, a shaggy, scrawny man named Leif, said, "What's the matter? What are you three running away from, anyway?" Someone else laughed.

Sweyn came up from the stern and stood among them, up above most of them. He said, "That's fair enough. What I'm running away from is the King of Denmark. Does that scare you?"

They gawked up at him, wordless, all but Leif, who said slowly, as if he thought he was being fooled with, "Well, then, who would you be?"

"I am Sweyn Haraldsson, the King's son, and at the end of this, I mean to be King of Denmark myself. If you come along with me, you'll rise with me, I swear it."

None of them moved. One muttered, "Sure, and I'm the Emperor Odd." Leif grunted and put his head to one side.

"Does this mean you don't really have the money to pay us when we get to Jorvik?"

Sweyn said, "I have money in Jorvik. I told you that."

Raef muttered something; Conn glanced backward, over the stern, but he had no far sight and he could make nothing out. The sail was luffing. They were losing the wind, and he said, "We should get to the oars."

Leif stood up suddenly, putting his hands on his hips. He said, "Or maybe we would get more money if we took hold of you now, and gave you to that ship coming there?" He nodded toward the north.

Sweyn wheeled around. Conn stepped up face to face with Leif. "Get to your oar. All of you. Now."

Leif's lip curled. "Or what?"

Conn lunged at him. For an instant Leif stood against him, long arms kinked against Conn's hold, but he buckled, and Conn heaved him up bodily and flung him over the side of the ship.

"Or that!" he roared at the rest of them.

They never hesitated. In a rush they scrambled onto their benches and grabbed their oars; before he had filled his lungs again they were bent to the first long stroke. In the stern, Sweyn shouted, "Come on, men—there's a handful of silver in Jorvik for every one of you, when we get there. Now, pull!"

Conn slid onto his bench and ran his oar out. Raef was already pulling. Conn joined him, driving the ship strongly away over the sea. During the backstroke he looked over his shoulder. Leif's head was bobbing up the next wave, moving toward the distant shore. The sea was turning glassy calm, no wind at all.

There was wind up to the north, because there, against the mist, a sail showed. Hastily he turned back straight to his oar and set himself to the work of getting the ship out of its way.

⸻

Around nightfall, they ran into a little sandy beach, made a fire, and got out more of the food. While everybody was eating, Conn went back to the ship, which Sweyn was settling for the night. Conn helped him lash up the steerboard and drag the awnings down to the gunwales. Sweyn wedged the anchor into a piece of driftwood buried high above the tide line, then came back and went around the ship again, checking it with his hands. Conn could see he loved this work.

"Do you have any money in Jorvik?" he said, thinking of the promise to the crew.

Sweyn straightened to laugh at him. "No." He thumped Conn on the chest. "But I'll do something, when I have to. As you did." He laid both hands on the ship's carved stempost. "She's a good ship. And these will be good men, too, when they've got to know us."

"We'll need a lot more than them. More ships."

"Yes. That's why we're going to Jorvik. Jorvik is full of Vikings."

Conn leaned against the ship; up there, they were laughing, and tossing twigs on the fire to make flares. "My mother was from Jorvik. She always told me it's a great city."

"It is. Not as great as Hedeby, but older. Danes have been living there for a long time, and they like to have a Danish King. Since they threw out Eric Bloodaxe, back years ago, they've had the English King on their necks."

"Jorvik is in England, then." He struggled to get this straight in his mind, where everything was. The only real place seemed the sea around them, that connected it all; everything else floated at the edges, half lost in the mist.

"Yes. And here's something—the English King is ailing now, I've heard, which means nobody will care much what goes on in Jorvik, way off in the corner of his realm." Sweyn took a chunk of stale bread from his shirt, broke it in half, and handed one piece to Conn. "When did you leave there?"

"I have never been there." He felt some halt in his mind, some warning not to speak too much about where he had been. He had to say something, and as usual talking got him in trouble. He said, "Raef was born in Hedeby."

Sweyn's eyes glinted with the firelight. "You have different mothers, maybe? He seems so unlike you."

"Yes," Conn said, glad to be able to tell the truth, and then told too much of it. "His mother is a witch." He clapped his hand over his mouth.

Sweyn laughed at him. "Family secrets? I can see that, there is something eldritch in him. Such men are often luckier for others than for themselves. May he be lucky for me. What of your father, though? Where is he?"

Conn lowered his hand to his lap. He felt a pang of guilt; he had not thought about his father much. "He said he would find us." He glanced toward Raef, already curled up asleep on the far side of the fire, Raef who had seen Corban last—who had said where he was going, a name Conn had forgotten instantly. "My father can do anything," he said, startling himself.

"I believe that," Sweyn said. "Tell me about where you come from."

Conn wrestled with the will to tell him everything, about the island, about the attack, and how Corban had decided to come back and find help; but something curbed his tongue. He was silent so long that Sweyn laughed, and said, "I ask too much. So be it. Now, go to sleep; we have to row a lot tomorrow, I think."

"Is Jorvik far?"

"A few more days' rowing. The wind won't be fair this time of year. Then up a couple of rivers. I can get us there."

"What do we do then?" Conn asked.

"Pick up some more men," Sweyn said. "Raise an army."

Conn said, "And wait for Palnatoki."

Sweyn smiled at him, his eyes glittering. "Palnatoki, where's he?"

Conn gave a snort; he liked how Sweyn was taking this on. "Good. I didn't see he knew what was up."

"Right," Sweyn said. "I'm glad you're with me." He clapped Conn on the arm. "We'll get to Jorvik, then we'll decide what to do next."

With only Conn and Raef on their oars, Sweyn brought the ship down into the mooring at Jorvik, where the hulls lay so thick together there was hardly room between them. The rest of his crew sat gape-mouthed looking up at Jorvik, climbing its low embankment above them, a clutter of high roofs and steeples.

For once they weren't fighting or threatening him or refusing to work. He thrust off the whole issue of now having to pay them, glad just to have reached Jorvik.

He knew he would not have gotten through the last few days but for Conn. That was the way of fate, he thought: Fate would send him what he needed for his destined task. But Conn was more than a trick of fate. Sweyn loved his strength, his endless confidence; most of all he loved that Conn understood him almost by his looks. Somehow under the blood, he and Conn were brothers.

The ship was nosing in against the bank. He called out, and the men slid over the gunwales on either side and lifted the hull up onto the river bar. Sweyn sat a moment, one arm draped over the handle of the steerboard, looking up at Jorvik above him. Since his babyhood he had drunk up the old stories, not from Palnatoki, who never thought of anything but scheming, but from the skalds who favored his hall—stories of Ragnar and Ivar and Hastein. Now here he was, ready to make his own saga, and he thought Jorvik was an excellent place to start.

The men were gathering up their gear, which had scattered around the ship during the days of rowing. Raef and Conn shipped their oars and stood up, stretching, and Sweyn considered again the inconvenience that Conn already had a brother. Sweyn watched them, the fair head and the dark, the shambling misfit and the warrior, and wondered once again how he could get rid of Raef.

The two brothers were looking up at the city, nudging each other and talking; now Raef turned his duck-white head to look around the river bar. Sweyn lowered his eyes, regretting his evil impulses. If he was going to be a king he had to act like one.

Then Raef shouted, "Conn! Look!"

Sweyn swung his head up, startled; the two of them were staring into the ships packed along the river bar and out in the shallow water, and suddenly they were talking an incomprehensible stream.

"That's Euan's ship," Conn said.

"They're here," Raef said. "Why are they here?"

"Come on." Conn wheeled toward Sweyn. "We'll be back." He grabbed Raef by the arm and shoved him on down the ship, toward the shore. "Come on, Raef!" They plunged away, up the river bar.

Sweyn watched them go, amazed. He turned and looked at the ships around him, wondering which had set them off. A moment later, looking at the ships around him, he was thinking he could use a lot of these vessels, and every one came with a crew.

His own crew had vanished, sucked up into the city. They would come back, with them problems, but Conn and Raef would come back, too, proof of his destiny. He got off his ship, onto the river bar swarming with oarsmen and Vikings, and considered how to harvest all these men.

⎯⎯

Too happy to be silent, Arre was singing, as loud as she wanted because Euan who sometimes complained she sang too loud or badly was gone off to London. She cast her voice forth like a lark's, in snatches of songs.

The servants sang with her, when she got into something they knew. They were airing the whole great hall out, carrying linen and blankets to the garden, and sweeping out the old musty rushes from months before. In the garden, she paused, her face lifted to the wintry sun. To be home again contented her past speaking, and she was frankly glad that Euan was gone.

He had driven her wild on the long voyage back across the sea, when she was wild anyway, with the two little girls suffering so. Now they were out of the narrow confines of the ship, they had plenty to eat, the children were thriving, and she had her own boys back, and Euan was away doing what Euan liked best, conniving at something.

That thought left her silent for a moment. What Euan connived at added often to her usual troubles.

"Mama!" Her son Edward stood in the door. "Should we move out the chest?"

"No," she said. "It's too heavy." She went back into the hall, to get them doing what she wanted. On the threshold she stopped to slip her arm around her tall son's waist and hug him. "I'm so glad to be back."

"Mama," he said, and eeled away from her, his eyes downcast.

He had grown much in the months she had been separated from him, turned stringy as a bean. In his face he had her looks, her eyes, everybody said, her mouth. He wanted to be a priest. Euan would not allow it and forbade him to talk of it. In fact he seemed too worldly already for a priest, too curious, too easily seduced. She wondered at his coldness, if it was only because of the long separation, or the influence of his grandmother. Euan's mother and Arre did not get on.

"Come with me," she said to him. "I'll show you what I want done." She led him into the hall, which was now smelling considerably better. The windows were open wide, and the door opening onto the street, and the smoke holes in the slate roof— Euan's pride, that roof, higher and safer than their neighbors' gross vermin-ridden fire-prone thatches. Arre put Edward to cleaning out the hearth, although he wrinkled up his nose and tried to wiggle out of it, and herself led the two women servants to hauling in new rushes for the floor and strewing them around. Gradually they spread rushes back into the end of the room, to the broad bench where the two little girls slept, Aelfu with her thumb in her mouth like a plug and her other arm around Miru.

Arre sat down on the bench and touched them. "Aelfu. Miru. Wake up."

Aelfu's eyes opened. At the far end of the hall, Edward called, "Mama." Arre looked around over her shoulder and saw someone had come into the hall. The two servants went up there; probably it was nothing for her. She turned back to Aelfu and

Miru, wanting to coax them awake, to feed them more, cheese and fresh bread and apples.

Aelfu sat up, her hair in her face, and looked around.

"I was dreaming . . ." She turned to Arre, her arms reaching out, and Arre took her into her lap. "I dreamt of the ship again, Ama, I dream we're on the ship again." She pressed her face against Arre's breast.

"No, no," Arre said. "We're safe now. Go sit on the pot." It touched her the child had made this little name for her. She let Aelfu slide down off her lap to the floor, and bent over Miru, murmuring the little girl awake; she had suffered more than anybody on the long trip. Then Aelfu screamed.

"Conn—"

Arre started, clutching Miru against her, and the baby let out a whine and burrowed down into her arms. She watched Aelfu run straight down the hall and fling herself on one of the men who had just come in.

"Conn!"

Arre swallowed hard. She felt turned to stone, although somehow she had gained her feet, in that first startled rush. Even from here she could see that the newcomer really was Conn, Corban's son. Benna's son.

They had gone on before her, of course, coming back here; she had known they might meet. She dreaded facing him, with the news she had to give him. Miru buried her face against Arre's breast. Arre went down the hall, Conn's sister in her arms.

He had swung Aelfu up in his arms; she was talking in a spate of words. "Conn—they have so much to eat here—look at my dress—" Everybody in the hall had turned to stare at them. Over his shoulder Conn was watching Arre approach, and he called to her, even before she reached him.

"Is my mother here? I—we—" He glanced back, at the other man with him, who she saw was Raef, the other boy from the island, startlingly older and taller, both of them very worn from travel. Aelfu ran out of breath and words and looked from one to the other, wide-eyed. Conn said, "We're here with—with—anyway, we saw your ship—is my mother here?"

Arre reached him and, holding Miru against her shoulder, put her hand on his arm. "Conn, your mother is dead."

Aelfu twitched and put her thumb in her mouth. Conn's eyes widened, white-rimmed. Under Arre's fingers the hard muscle of his arm trembled. "No," he said. "No—how can that be?"

She went on, helplessly, knowing he hardly heard her, unable to stop babbling. "She missed Corban, so much—and she needed him, I think, somehow. She fell sick, I could not—I tried to make her well, I prayed—but she did not waken—it was months ago."

His face was stunned and his jaw slack; Aelfu bent her head to his shoulder, her mouth curled down, and his grip tightened around her. Arre floundered on.

"Without her there, we had to come back, I could not endure it, without her—the devils on the mainland were attacking us, we could hardly hold them off." She looked among the other people around the room, all motionless, rapt, staring at them. "Is Corban with you?"

Raef had come up beside him. "Where is my mother?"

"On the island still—she would not come with us." To her surprise, he lowered his eyes, obviously relieved.

"Is Corban with you?" she said again. It came to her that their appearance here in Jorvik was connected to the word come fresh that morning from Denmark of treachery and murder and uprising, the King of Norway dead, the nephew of the King of Denmark dead. She looked from Conn to Raef, marking the sword at Conn's belt, the knife in Raef's, the silky virgin beard on their jaws, the rasp of their voices, something in the way they stood, their shoulders set, their heads a little forward. Everything about them had altered. They were part of this man's thing now, this war thing. They had grown up.

"We don't know where Corban is," Raef said. He had put his arm around Conn, as if to hold him on his feet, but now Conn broke roughly free of him, and still with Aelfu in his arms went toward the fire, and sat down on the hearth there and wept. Miru stirred in Arre's grasp, lifting her head.

Raef said, "There was big trouble in Denmark, and Corban went off on his own somehow. We came to Jorvik with Sweyn Haraldsson."

"Well, you got here at the right moment," she said. "The Archbishop is gone and so is the Jarl and the Jarl's reeve, too, because the King is sick, down in Wessex. No one will bother you, not for a while, except maybe the Archbishop. Of course you and Conn should stay here, with us."

Raef stood looking over his shoulder at Conn. He turned back toward her, his eyes soft, and his attention went to the small girl in her arms. Uncertainly he said, "Sweyn will want us with him."

He reached out one finger toward Miru's tangled damp curly hair. She shuddered, creeping deeper into Arre's embrace. Raef's voice sank. "She was as much mother to me, too, as I ever had—" He stopped abruptly, his mouth gripped tight, his eyes swollen. His finger brushed the baby's hair. His head bobbed. "We should stay here for a while." He went to sit by Conn on the hearth, and put his head in his hands.

Arre stepped back. Miru's eyes popped open; she had been awake all along, Arre saw, just hiding. Clever baby, Arre thought; she saw much in this to hide from.

Largest of it was that the mess in Denmark had spread to Jorvik. She knew nothing of this Sweyn, but if he was part of what was going on he would draw the city deeper into it, maybe a new war, all the kings attacking one another. Smaller, closer, there were her own nephews in the middle of it. She pressed her lips to Miru's forehead. "Clever baby."

Miru said, under her breath, "Raef. Raef." She turned and

looked toward the hearth. Arre went to get her a sop. Her mind
leapt to Euan, away in Wessex doing man's work among the high
men of England. Much as she wished him away, she needed him
to deal with this. She began to think how she would get word to
him to come back at once to Jorvik.

⸺⸎⸺

Aelfu had thought, at first, when she saw Conn, that surely her
mother was coming back, too. Now she saw that he didn't know
where she was either.

Conn believed Arre when she said that their mother was
dead. Carefully Aelfu drew away from him as he slumped on the
bench, staring into the fire, his eyes brimming. Raef sat with his
hands over his face. She went away up the hall, swerving out of
the way of the servants bringing out a table as big as a ship.

Soon they would sit down to eat, eggs and sweet things to
drink, roasted meats and good turnips and onions and bread.
Things they had never eaten back on the island. She sat down on
the corner of the bench beside the table and looked around. The
whole place smelled deliciously of the herbs and fresh straw on
the floor. Her fingers stroked the ribbon along the front of her
dress, so smooth it made the hair stand up on her arms to touch it.
The feel of the fine clothes on her body made her skin tingle all
over. All around her was the clatter of other people, two maids
putting candlesticks out, the boys whooping outside. Off up the
hill the church bell began to toll, and for a moment everybody
stopped and made some motions with their hands, and then went
smoothly on with whatever the bell had interrupted.

Everybody thought her mother was dead. She had forgotten
why she thought differently. She knew, though, that Benna had
only gone away. Maybe she had gotten lost. Euan might have
driven her off; Aelfu disliked Euan, and so she thought this often. Maybe she was just still there on the island, with Mav. But

she was just gone, she wasn't dead, no matter what Arre said.

In any case, Aelfu hoped a little that her mother wouldn't come back very soon.

That made her feel bad. She was bad to want her mother gone. Maybe that was why Benna had gone, because Aelfu was bad. Her thumb had gotten into her mouth. She wanted to shut her eyes and stick her fingers in her nose and make this all go away.

Not the soft delicious bread, the warm beds here, the many kinds of clothes. That she wanted, more even than there was, every day. When she thought of the island she remembered mostly the bitter cold, and being hungry. It was so much better here.

She hunched up her shoulders. If her mother came back they would go home back to the island.

She blinked against a sudden gush of tears. Maybe her mother had gone away because she was so bad, wanting all these things.

Around her the room bustled with people making ready for their supper. She slid down off the bench and went toward the back door, looking for Miru and Ama Arre. Then, just outside the door, she heard Edward's voice.

The sharp tone warned her, even before she drew nearer and heard what he was saying. The edge in his voice put her hair on end. He said, "This is mad! You can't let them stay here, Mother!"

She froze, one foot on the threshold. But Arre answered him hard, in a stout voice. "They're my sister's children, sirrah, don't you tell me what I am to do!"

Edward cried, "But they're pagans. Mother, you're mad. Wait until Father—"

The crack of a hand striking skin made Aelfu jump. She shrank back against the wall. Edward's voice had broken off abruptly as if his mother had knocked it from him. Maybe she had. A moment later Arre came into the room, and her face was red as fire, her eyes brilliant and her hair tumbling down from her headcloth. She had Miru on her hip. Aelfu went after her, took hold of her skirt, and followed her.

"All this time, you know, I've been supposing they were just back there, on the island," Conn said. "As if nothing could happen to them there."

They were walking down through the Coppergate, the long steep street of shops that led from the upper part of the city to the riverside. Raef was still getting used to being on the land. There was a sharp wind coming up from the river, and he drew his new cloak against it. Arre had fed them a warm lamb pie and given them new cloaks, and it saddened him to leave her. He thought of Benna and his mind slid off the surface of the memory and he thought again of the warm pie.

He said, "Arre is good. And she brought back the little girls." He thought of Aelfu's face when she saw them, her whole face wild. "I don't see why we can't stay up there."

"Clayhead. Clamface. Here we are in the middle of a war, my mother is dead, and all you can think of is your stomach. Because we are Sweyn's men, that's why. We have to help him."

Raef said, "I loved her, too."

Conn was silent, not looking at him. They went on down the slope, here and there threaded with wooden walkways, its hollows foul with scummy water. Raef bunched his hands in the new cloak; he felt Conn pulling away from him, leaving him alone.

At last, his cousin said, "We are Sweyn's men. We have to stay with him."

"I like Sweyn," Raef said, although he didn't, really. They went down a steep mucky bank to the river's edge, where a broad gravel bank made a long bar. Here a dozen ships or more were hauled out, many of them unloading their cargoes. From the little height of the roadway they could see out over all of it. A crowd of men moved along the line of ships, a thick dark moving tangle; above them, on the higher ground of the river bar, several little fires burned, and men milled around there also, oarsmen from the ships, some idle townspeople.

"There he is," Conn said, and turned off toward a little group of men sharing a cup there on the shore under the curling head of a big dragon. Sweyn was arguing with them, but as Conn and Raef came up, he broke away, with a shrug, and walked toward them.

He saw Conn, and his face relaxed into a wide grin. "Good, I'm glad you're back."

Conn said, "We went to my aunt's. My sisters were there." He shut his mouth tight, reddening, avoiding Raef's eyes.

Sweyn gave him a quizzical look, seeing his mood. In silence they walked on down the beach a little, Conn beside him staring at the ground. Raef trailed after them, where he could stay out of it and still hear. Sweyn said, "That ship there just got in from Denmark, they say that Grayfur is dead and Gold-Harald is dead, and Hakon is now lord of Norway."

Conn's head rose. His face was like a stone, hard and angular. He said, "Yes, but we got away. And we're the ones who are going to matter." His voice grated. "Bluetooth is going to wish he had left everything alone."

Sweyn stopped, looking around; Raef saw he wanted to be out of hearing of everybody else on the beach. He said, "There are enough ships here for an army. I've been trying to get these men to come in with us, but nobody is interested. Of course I can't offer them much." He reached into his shirt and took out a thin little pouch. "One of the captains gave me some money. Said to remember him if I win." He laughed. "I'm going to pay the crew who got us here. When I do that, we may lose even them."

Conn said, "If they leave they're worthless anyway. Most of that lot is. We're with you, and we have the ship. My aunt fed us, and she would feed you, too, if you went with us." He gave Raef a bitter look.

Sweyn said, "Yes, we have the ship. And a lot of people don't like Bluetooth. They're all asking what wergild Hakon will have to pay for Gold-Harald, seeing as he was Bluetooth's nephew, but then he had fostered Harald Grayfur at his knee." He said, under his breath, "That's not King's work."

They went on along the river bar, toward where their crew was camped. Raef hoped these men did leave. He liked Jorvik already and did not want to go. This city seemed friendlier than Hedeby. The streets ran up and down hill here, which made it prettier, and great trees grew in among the houses, spreading their branches out over the yards. The markets were smaller, but the food was as good, and Arre's house was as fine as Palnatoki's hall in Hedeby.

He thought of Benna and his heart shrank. He felt them all, the whole family, now scattered around the world, to be broken, one by one.

As they walked into the seamen's camps, some cheers sounded. Here plainly Sweyn was better thought of than among the captains. All around the broad bench of gravel above the beached ships, men called greetings to him, and he waved back, trying to look as if it didn't matter to him much that all these people were glad to see him. Raef thought he had the beginnings of an army already. Conn was sunk in his dull mood, turned away from everybody else, turned inside, shut up around his grief.

Raef was thinking, though, that he had known, somehow, about Benna. He was afraid to say anything of this to Conn. He knew Conn thought he cared too little for his mother's death. But it was only that he didn't really believe it. Looking away from the men around them, down toward the river, he thought about Benna, trying to be sorry, although he couldn't really believe she was dead, and then he saw what was before his eyes and yelled.

"Conn! It's our ship! Look!"

Conn was ahead of him. Conn was already running down the sandy shore, screaming, "Pap!"

For an instant Raef's heart soared. Out there on the river, among the great ships, a little dragon was gliding toward them. A single set of oars rose and fell behind the high graceful curve of its prow, a curve he knew as well as the shape of the moon. It was Corban's ship.

"Pap!" Conn shrieked, again, and bounded forward, toward the shore at the very edge, where the gravel bar of the river met the high-thrusting bank, and the little dragon was touching bottom in the shallows.

He stopped. Raef had never started. Standing there on the shore near Sweyn, he watched the man called Eelmouth climb out of the ship and haul her up onto the shore. On board was only one other, and that was a woman. Corban had not come.

Conn stood in the shallows, his arms at his sides. He shot a furious glance at Eelmouth and turned to the woman. "Where is my father? How do you come to have his ship?"

Eelmouth ignored him. He went back to the gunwale of the beached ship and there with awkward ceremony helped the woman climb onto the shore. It seemed to Raef she could have done as easily without him. He took a step back from her, shy of her, although he was long yards away. Conn came back to his side, silenced. The woman looked calmly around her. She was old, wrapped in a salt-encrusted cloak, and barefoot; the hair that hung down about her shoulders was rough and gray as a wolf's pelt, but in the shine of her eyes, the flare of her cheekbone, and the jut of her chin she gave off a sheen of power. Every man on the river bar was silent, staring at her.

Through this rapt attention she walked up the gravel bar toward Jorvik, toward Sweyn, with Eelmouth trailing behind her. She passed Conn and Raef as they stood there and stopped. Her look was like a shove in the chest, a bolt through the eye. But then her gaze sharpened, intent on Raef.

Her face stiffened with a shock like recognition. He stood fast, mute, feeling her attention like a blast of oven heat against him. For a long moment she stared at him, but she said nothing to him, and finally she went on to meet Sweyn.

"Sweyn Haraldsson," she said, standing there with her hair matted from the sea wind and her bare feet spread on Jorvik's stony shore, "the time has come to take Denmark away from these people, and I am here to help you."

"Gunnhild Kingsmother," Sweyn said, "you are as welcome as thirty ships." He gestured to Eelmouth. "Bring Queen Gunnhild's goods. She will have the place of honor with us."

Eelmouth did not move. Gunnhild said, "I have no goods, Sweyn. I came out with nothing but what I have on, and Eelmouth here. Are those the sons of Corban Loosestrife?" She glanced at Conn and Raef again. Raef twitched in the heat of her look passing over him.

"They are."

"Then I have evil news for them. Their father gave himself up for my sake. He is Hakon's prisoner now."

"Alive?" Conn cried.

"I did not see death in his face," Gunnhild said. Her voice was steady and fierce. She gave him another look, and then faced Sweyn again. "I come empty-handed, but I am not poor, Sweyn Haraldsson. I have some friends of memory in this city; I shall be with them. Call me to your council, soon, that we may plan Bluetooth's fall in detail." She walked on past him, up the road toward Jorvik.

Sweyn wheeled to watch her go. In a stride he reached Conn. "That's worth something," he said, low, "but the word about your father is sore, I know."

Conn said, "You don't know. I have heard today also my mother is dead. But I am your sworn man, always, and Raef, too."

Sweyn said, "Let's talk about this. There may be something we can do together." He draped his arm over Conn's shoulder. "Your father saved my life. I promise you, I will not forget him." He had a gift for promises. Raef followed them up the bank toward the campfire, glum.

CHAPTER SIXTEEN

In the morning at Mass, with the child Aelfu beside her and Miru in her arms, Arre listened to Archbishop Oswald give his long rolling voice over to condemning the pagans and those who harbored them. Saying this he aimed his feverish gaze at her, standing on the women's side of the congregation. She stood calmly. She knew better; God could not want her to abandon her poor orphaned nephews, or these little girls. She thought Oswald was mostly seeking his own advantage, as usual, and she prayed for him, along with her nephews and the girls and all the rest of her family.

As she prayed, she looked up before her, and saw the image of the Mother of Jesus painted on the wall behind the altar. She had always fretted at this picture; Benna would have done much better than these smears of brown and yellow, two lines for eyes. Today it seemed better, somehow. She thought of how the Mother of God had endured so much, and thought she could withstand Oswald, who was not evil, just wrong-headed.

When the time came to receive the Body of Christ she gave Miru to Aelfu to hold, and went to the altar, and knelt down with all the rest. The heavy incense hurt her nose. She heard the swish of the priest's robes as he approached her, and lifted her face to receive the Body of God.

He gave her nothing. He went on by her. He left her perched open-mouthed on her knees, begging for the sacrament, and passed her by.

A hot shame washed over her; she lowered her head, feeling all the others watching her, their scorn and contempt like hot coals poured over her. She teetered. For a moment she thought what Oswald thought, what they must all think, that she was wrong.

She was still kneeling stiffly at the altar. Around her people were drawing away, murmuring. Their looks raked over her, knife-tipped. She got up and went back to the congregation, her face blazing, unable to look into anyone's face. The air seemed harsh as salt against her skin, as if she had been flayed. She went in beside Aelfu and knelt down and put her face in her hands.

Was she wrong? Was this a sin? She knew that all disobedience to God was a sin. She knew also she was often heedless, headstrong, too sure of her own goodness. Certainly she was disobeying Oswald, who was God's man, who spoke for God here.

Around her the others spoke the prayers, knelt and rose again; but she stayed as she was, on her knees. Her mind seemed clogged. It was too confusing. She would do as they wished and be done with it. But then she saw in her mind her poor orphaned nephews, and Aelfu and little Miru; was she to turn them out, too?

She turned and looked down at Aelfu, beside her, her arms wrapped around the sleeping baby, and watching Arre steadily with her wide gray eyes.

Arre bent and took Miru, who would wake soon, and want food. Still on her knees, she put her arm around Aelfu and drew her close into her skirts. She could not abandon these children; God could not want that of her, as he had not really wanted it of Abraham. Maybe Oswald was wrong.

When she thought that, she felt suddenly stronger, as if she had the ground under her again. Against these children, what did Oswald have? A scaffolding of words, mostly empty air, that the Archbishop built and rebuilt, as if that were the real church. It was his own power he built, not the real church. Words, not goodness.

"Mama—"

She straightened; startled, looking around, she saw the church empty around her, even the priests gone from behind the altar, and the whole congregation gone away, except for her sons,

Edward and little Dan, who had been standing on the men's side. Edward fidgeted now in front of her, had just spoken to her.

"Yes," she said. "We shall go home now."

"Mama—" Edward cast a quick look away, and Arre, seeing, knew if she followed it that thread of attention would lead to his grandmother, Euan's mother, somewhere watching. Her skin tightened with alarm. The boy turned his pale face at her. "Maybe we should go back and stay with Grandmother again. Until— later." He flushed, his eyes shining.

She clutched Aelfu's hand, feeling somehow rebuked. She said, raggedly, "Oh—go, then—if you want."

"Mama," he said. "It's better." He moved, drawing away from her, his little brother by the hand.

She looked up at the altar, her heart galloping. God had meant it, after all, the sacrifice of Isaac. She saw no good way out of this. She lost her sons, or she lost these little girls, who needed her. Now she hated Oswald, who had brought this on her.

Aelfu's fingers worked in hers, and she realized she was gripping the child painfully hard. She turned and looked down, and saw the little face, heart-shaped like her mother's, looking up, the wide solemn frightened eyes. "I want to go home now," the child said. "Can we still go home?"

"Yes," Arre said. "Let's go." And walked stiffly out of the church.

⸺⚬⸺

The way seemed very long to her house. She imagined everyone was looking at her; she thought someone might be following her. She heard someone scream, once, from a window, and knew it was at her. Her mind faltered again, and before she reached her own door she was drooping, thinking Oswald right, she was a wicked woman, no one should have to do with her at all, no righteous man or woman.

She sent the children off for some breakfast and went around her hall, rubbing her hands together. The impossibility of it opened out before her. Her own maids and cook would shrink from her. The whole city of Jorvik. How would she get bread, if everyone shunned her—if when she went into the street all turned their backs and shut their doors on her? She should leave, go off and let her family at least get on without her.

Her maidservant Erthia came up to her. "Ma'am, now, there's someone at the garden gate."

The words brought Arre back with a jolt. She looked sharply at Erthia, searching for the disgust in her face, her eyes turned aside, the curl of her lip. The maid's round freckled face was bland as milk. She said, "Ma'am, where's young Edward?"

"Went back to his grandmother," Arre said.

At that, the girl frowned, her lips twisting. "Ach. That one." With a flap of her hand, she went off toward the hearth, and put wood on the fire.

She was taking her side, Arre saw, startled. But of course Erthia needed her—ate her bread, slept by her fire. She wondered who could be at the garden gate, and went out through the back door.

It was the bakerwoman, Gerda, with a basket of fresh loaves. "I thought you might not come to market today," she said, and handed her the basket over the gate.

"Ah," Arre said, pleased. She took hold of the basket, but she was more interested in the other woman's gossip. "What are they saying, out there? About me?"

"Well," Gerda said, "you shouldn't come out, not for a while. There are men who would willingly beat you in the street."

"Ah," Arre said, unnerved; she wasn't safe, after all. Always the men. Gerda, watching her, flipped back one tail of her coif.

"Why don't you just go and apologize, Arre? It would make things so much easier."

"I'll never apologize," Arre said, not thinking, and knew at once that it was true. The idea of men ganging up on her in the street with sticks and shovels faded into the background. She reached out and took hold of the bakerwoman's hand. "Pray for me, Gerda, will you?"

"I will," Gerda said. "I'll send someone over from the brewery." She patted Arre's arm. "But I can't give you the bread, you know, dear; you must pay me for it."

"Of course," Arre said. "Wait here."

She went quickly up to the hall again, feeling better. She would get through this somehow. She found money for Gerda— more than usual, knowing Gerda would spread word of her generosity—and paid her, and when she came back yet again to the hall, she found her husband, Euan, standing there, new returned from London.

She had been glad he was gone, but now she was happy to see him back. She wondered how to greet him—how he would greet her, when he knew. He walked smiling from the hearth to meet her, and she lifted her face and slid her arms around him, and they kissed. The kissing part of their marriage had always gone well. In his arms, her body flooded with desire, the kiss deepened, and she felt herself melting into him.

She stepped back, prying herself from his arms. "You must hear the bad news—before you are a moment longer in the house. The Archbishop refused me the sacrament this morning. I'm in disgrace."

"What?" he said, and his long-jawed face hardened. He looked shabby, dusty from travel, his eyes pouched, his cheeks stubbled. His hands closed on her arms, and his voice took a whining edge. "What have you done now?"

"I took in my sister's orphaned children," she said, and braced herself, ready to fight him. "If that is sin, I am deep in it, Euan."

He turned on his heel and tramped away, and came back

again, frowning. "I don't believe it. Oswald wouldn't kick up trouble over anything so small. I'll talk to him, but this is your fault, for letting it happen. Where are the boys?"

"At your mother's."

He grunted at that. "Meddling old sow," he said, under his breath. "Well, Arre, as usual as soon as I leave you get yourself into the middle of a mess, but I doubt it'll be too difficult to mend. I'll go talk to Oswald tomorrow, and see what I can do. Right now I'm to bed, be it noon or no, I'm that tired. I only waited to see you home."

Perversely now she hoped he had no way with Oswald at all. Rough as a badger, she stood watching him go on down the hall, until he turned and said, "Well?"

She went after him toward the cupboard bed, built into the wall at the end of the room. He put his arm around her, and when she stiffened, he jostled her against him. "What, I misspoke? You're not in a horrible mess as soon as I leave?" He kissed her forehead.

She reined in her temper. This was the price of having him at all. She said, "How is the King? Is he getting better?" She let him pull her against him again, and kiss her mouth again.

"No." He drew back, turning toward the bed, tugging off his coat. "He's going to die. We're on our own up here, for now. The Jarl will not leave London; they're all playing chess down there, using people for their pawns. To them Jorvik is only an annoyance."

"Did you see Gifu?"

"Richard Longsword meddles in it all; yes, Gifu is there. She looks very well. She's very beautiful. They're all very beautiful, the whole court, beautiful and proud, and they know nothing."

The doors of the bed cupboard stood open, to air. He sat down on the mattress, and she helped him take his boots off. His feet stank. His hose seemed to have grown onto his skin. She stepped back, watching him shed his shirt.

She asked, "Who will be King if Edgar dies? Those little boys?" The King had two young sons, younger than hers. She gripped one puffed sleeve and held it while he wormed out of it. "Whoever manages those little boys."

"What about us?" Her mind flew to the sermon that morning. "What about this Danish prince, now, who's escaped from Bluetooth and gotten himself here, you heard of this, with our nephews in tow? He's not been idle, you know. He's trying to gather an army, to go back and fight Bluetooth."

"They've sent someone to deal with this Sweyn," Euan said. In his shirt, his hose still glued to his legs, he lay back on the bed. She hauled the rucked covers out from under his feet.

"Who?" she said, drawing them up over him.

He smiled up at her from the bed like a delighted baby she was tucking in. "Me." Turning his head to one side he was instantly asleep.

Arre straightened. A little warning tingle spread through her nerves. It might not be the best idea, Euan taking her case to the Archbishop. Euan had always to be sniffing after power, or the illusion of it, and that had brought him crosswise of the Archbishop in the past. But the course of things was going out of her hands now—if she had ever had any control over it. She closed the right half of the bed, to give him some quiet while he slept, and went down the hall to send someone out to the shambles, to fetch them a roast for their supper, now that Euan would be home.

⚓

Conn said, "Now we have to leave, for sure, tonight." He wheeled toward Raef; they were walking up through the Coppergate, the crowded market street loud with the yells of vendors and hucksters, the crush of people struggling to buy. "What an evil this churchman is—to cast her out! Of all people—the best among them!"

Raef hunched his shoulders. "Tonight. That's too soon. What about Aelfu and Miru?"

Conn cuffed him. Raef loved comfort all too much. "We can't stay—not if it means trouble for her. You've got to see that. There." He nodded up ahead of them. "That's Gunnhild Kingsmother's house."

"I guess so. There's Eelmouth," Raef said.

They had come to the top of the Coppergate, where it ended at the main road; in the old house on the right Gunnhild Kingsmother was staying. The house had a tall overgrown wooden fence around it, and in the gateway of this fence, her man Eelmouth sat, drinking from a wooden cup and eating nuts.

Conn nudged Raef, and they went up toward the gateway. Eelmouth did not move when they greeted him. Conn braced up at this; he had been Sweyn's second in command for a while, and nobody treated him like a boy anymore. Still slouched against the doorjamb with his legs outstretched, Eelmouth looked from him to Raef, and stared at Raef.

"Your brother here I think she will not see, but you she will."

"What?" Raef said. His voice squawked. He threw Conn a startled look. "No—he and I, we go together."

"Well, then," Eelmouth said, "come with me."

He got up and led them into the hall. It was not a big house, but well set up, with a floor deep in clean rushes, a warm fire, and onions and garlic and great smoked hams and bacon hanging in abundance from the rafters. At the hearth Gunnhild Kingsmother was sitting on a bench.

She had changed her rags for a long gown, all sewn with crystals that glittered when she moved, and her hair was brushed and braided; she looked much younger, smooth and bright. Conn bowed to her, amazed at her beauty, the even bloom of her skin, the symmetry of her cheekbones, and her splendid eyes. She gave him half a look, and stared at Raef.

"Sit," she said. "Eelmouth, call for some ale for these young

men." Her attention turned briefly to Conn. "You are Conn Corbansson?"

"Yes," he said. "And we—"

She cut him off with a glance that somehow stopped the
words in his mind, and turned to Raef. "You are Raef, and also
Corban's son?"

Raef cleared his throat. His voice squeaked. "Yes."

"I think not. I had never seen you before the other day, and
yet I know your face as well as my own. I think you are the son
of Eric Bloodaxe, my husband, who was King of Norway once."

Conn gaped at her, and then turned and stared at Raef as if
he had never seen him before. Raef had flushed to the hairline,
his gaze on the floor, his hands twining around and around each
other, and he muttered something.

"What?" she said. "You are a King's son, boy, speak up."

He jerked his gaze up to meet hers. "I don't know." But suddenly he straightened his shoulders. A servant had come with the
ale, and Gunnhild bade her give each his own cup. The servant
set the pitcher down and left.

She said, "Who is your mother?"

Raef said nothing. Knowing him tongue-tied, Conn spoke for
him. "He is my father's sister's son. Nobody knows who his father
was. She was taken away by Vikings and sold into slavery. My father won her back in a mind-war with the witch of Hedeby, before
they all went into the west. Raef was born in the witch's house."

She still did not look at him, but watched Raef, and her face
softened. She seemed to lean toward him a little, to send forth
some aura that embraced him. Conn shivered; he thought he could
have been in Denmark, or under the ocean, for all she cared.

She said, still, always, talking to Raef, "Where is she now,
your mother?"

"She's—" Raef made a little gesture with his hand, opening
up words. "She's home. On the island. It's all right. She's better
there than here."

"For whom?"

Raef looked startled. "For her," he said, and Conn said, also, "Yes, for her. Even with everybody gone. She never needed us."

The Queen watched Raef steadily a moment in silence. She said, "Eric's last son, born almost as he died. You are the image of him as a young man. But you have nothing of his mind. Which is not perhaps altogether an ill thing."

The ale made Conn's head swim; for an instant he thought he saw golden rooftops somewhere, and heard a horn blow a long low sensuous note. The Queen herself reached for the pitcher and filled his cup again, and Raef's. She said, "Your mother, now, what is her name? What is she like?"

"Mav. She's mad," Raef said. "She lives in the woods, she runs naked there, birds feed her."

"I see." Gunnhild twined the end of her braid around her finger. "But you see her. And you have some of her power."

"No," Raef said, with a twitch.

She smirked at him. Conn cleared his throat. He wanted to end this sparring, this weird unfolding, give himself some room to think it all over; he was seeing layers in this that shocked him. He stepped forward toward her, speaking to her. "We are here to find out where Corban is."

Her gaze never left Raef. She said, "I saw him last going down under a swarm of them at the wharf in Hrafnsbeck. Maybe they killed him there. If not, Hakon's next move is surely to go back to Norway, to lay hands on what he has won, and likely he won't take Corban. Even if Hakon knew what Corban was, since he's turned Christian now, he has no use for him. And Corban outfoxed him. Hakon won't forgive that."

"You said—" Conn and Raef spoke together and Raef stopped at once and Conn went on, "That he wasn't dead. Back at the river bar, where we met you first."

"I don't know what happened to him at Hakon's hands.

Hakon is a vicious man. We were friends once; I know him very well." She curled and curled the braid around her finger, now studying them both. There was a long silence. Conn found himself watching the pattern of lights on her gown; images flashed through his mind, too fast to capture.

Gunnhild spoke suddenly. "All right, then, go, if you're going to stand there like a lump." She waved her hand at them. "Go." They left.

Outside, his head much clearer, Conn said, "Do you believe her?"

"About what?" Raef said. They went out to the street.

"That about Eric Bloodaxe."

Raef licked his lips. "Yes." He met Conn's eyes. "Shouldn't I?"

"Well," Conn said, walking fast. He felt as if this new father had grown up suddenly between them, turning Raef into a stranger. Yet he had always known Raef wasn't his brother.

He saw also that Raef had changed, somehow, bathed in Gunnhild's words like one of his mother's story-heroes dipped in dragon's blood. Conn said, "Corban's always been your true father."

Raef muttered something and looked away. Conn strode along, heading for the river bar, struggling in his mind with this thing he had known one way and not cared about, and now knew differently and it changed everything.

Gunnhild had done this. He still felt the weight of her presence, the cold honey smoothness of her voice.

Now Raef seemed utterly changed. Conn, who had always known exactly what Raef was thinking, wondered now how to speak to him. Cautiously he said, "She sounded us like a ditch, but we didn't get much out of her."

Raef shrugged. "Corban's at Hrafnsbeck, she thinks." His voice sounded steadier.

"Where's that?"

"Down along the fjord somewhere, east of Hedeby."

"You know, this—what she said—" Conn stared at him, intent. "Are you still with me—about going to help Pap?"

"Yes," Raef said. "I've been—" He rubbed his hand quickly over his face. "I've been thinking. All that other stuff—I don't care about that. Raef Corbansson, forever."

"Good." Conn swung his arm around Raef's shoulders, glad. "You're better than a brother, anyway. Now, listen—this is what you have to do."

—⋄—

In the middle of the afternoon Arre went into the pantry and found Raef there, stuffing loaves of bread into a sack.

Startled, she blurted out, "What are you doing?" and he dropped the sack and spun around, his big hands flopping, and his face red. She looked at the shelf; he had taken all the bread, a dozen loaves.

"What are you up to?" she said, stooping for the sack. "Not even you can be this hungry." When he yammered something, edging toward the door, she got in his way. "Now, Raef, you can't lie to me."

His shoulders slumped. He said miserably, "I don't want to."

"Then don't."

"We need food. We're going to Denmark—to find Corban."

"You and Conn," she said.

His jaw jutted out. "You can't stop us. We'll go even if we don't have bread. Corban's in trouble. We have to help him. It's partly Sweyn's idea, too; we're to spy for him a little in Denmark. And we can't stay here and make trouble for you."

She lifted the sack in her hands, thinking of Euan, of Sweyn. This would simplify the whole matter for Euan. The little girls were less of an ember in the Archbishop's eye than the boys. And

Corban might need them. "Yes," she said, and looked up at him. "I think you should go. I'll help you. When are you leaving?"

"Tonight." He reached out and touched her arm. "I didn't want to steal from you, Arre. Or lie. I'm sorry."

She nodded. "No, I understand. You'll need something to drink, too, and some blankets, and maybe we can find you some money. Come with me."

⁓

Aelfu crept in under the big quince thicket at the edge of Arre's garden, where no one could see her. They were calling for her, up in the house, to come and say good-bye to her brothers. She moved carefully in among the thorns of the quince, but still they scratched her arms and cheeks, sharper than rose thorns.

They weren't her brothers. Certainly Raef was not. She curled up in the middle of the great thorny thicket and put her head on her arms.

Their voices faded. They were going away. For a moment a great fat lump hurt in her chest and she blinked and blinked to keep from crying. Everybody went away. It did no good to cry.

Everybody went away. She closed her eyes tight, and her thumb slipped into her mouth. Soon they would come and take her away, too, and everything she loved here would be gone.

Shutting her eyes she curled up around the hollow place in her center. She hurt, there, as if she were hungry. Better to stay here and die, just here, like this. She shut her eyes tight and squeezed herself into a knot and held her breath, waiting to die.

She didn't die, she gasped for breath, and shivered on the cold ground. She began to be tired of being here. Arre was calling her again, and now beneath Arre's call came Miru's voice, lighter and smaller.

"Efu—Efu—"

"I'm coming," she said. Suddenly she had to get to Arre, to her sister, more than anything. She crawled out from under the quince bush. "I'm coming—"

⟶⟵

Conn and Raef took the dragonfly down the river early in the afternoon, gliding away on the swift-flowing brown water past banks shrouded with tangled winter-dead willow boughs; by sundown they were rowing into the broadening stream that led to the sea. The shore was all fen country, and finding no place good to put ashore, they followed the current down into the bay, one sleeping and the other awake all night through. At daybreak, they rowed together out through the shallows and bars at the river's mouth, rounded the southern spit, and rode through the crash of surf onto the great salt breast of the sea.

They rowed well out from the land, and then Raef stood his oar up. "We should raise the sail."

Conn let his oar trail in the water. The sea rolled under them; he loved the feeling of the swell lifting the boat. "We should follow the coast south. The wind's out of the west."

"That's what I mean." Raef pointed to the east. "The wind's dead fair for Hollandstadt if we go that way."

"Sweyn brought us up here following the coast." Conn frowned at him. It was his raid, but he was remembering how Corban had heeded Raef on such things. "You and Pap. Open sea, all the way. We can't find—"

Directly overhead a scream sounded, shrill as the wind whistling through a keyhole. Conn jerked his head up, looking into the sky. "That's a red hawk. I don't think I've ever seen one so far from the land. That's an omen for you, Raef, it's headed east."

Raef was staring up at the great bird soaring toward them. "Red hawks don't fly out to sea." He stood up, his eyes suddenly round. "It's coming at us." The hawk stooped toward them, hurtling from the sky so fast and straight Raef shrank down and Conn looked around wildly for something to hit it with, and then at the foot of its stoop, a foot above the sea, it spread its wings, gathered up all its speed into a rising, wheeling turn, and landed neatly on the sternpost.

Conn's mouth dropped open; he leaned on his oar, astonished. The hawk's breast was speckled like ermine. Black tipped her russet tail feathers. She folded her wings, and glanced at Conn, and cocked her narrow head to stare at Raef. "I'm glad I found you. Where do you think you're going?"

Conn brought in his oar and got to his feet. "We're going to rescue my father. What are you doing here, Gunnhild Kingsmother?"

"You should have talked to me first," said the hawk. "You're going to need help." She spread her wings, teetering a little on the curled prow. "I am better at this than I used to be. Once it took all my strength just to hold the shape." Gliding from the height of the prow, she swooped down to land on the gunwale next to Raef. Her feathers ruffled up along the back of her head, and her eye fixed on him.

"I can see much better than you what's going on in Denmark. If you take me across the sea, I will find Corban for you."

"Done," Conn said, excited; he thought this was a very good sign. He nodded to Raef. "We'll raise the sail."

⸺⸻

They sailed due east. The hawk perched on the stern above the steerboard and directed occasional sharp remarks at them from there. Raef fed her bits of bread, which she was hungry enough to eat. Conn dozed.

Raef watched the hawk covertly. Since she told him who his

father was, his mind had been seething. In spite of his promise to Conn he thought the name over and over: Raef Ericsson, Raef Ericsson. She also gripped his mind, which he thought she intended. He remembered what she had said, that he had some power.

He blurted out, "I wish I could fly."

Gunnhild said, "I had forgotten how it lifts the heart. Then when we were running from Hakon, the thought came into my mind, and the next moment, I was in the air, soaring." She preened the feathers of her breast, pulling each carefully through her great curved beak. The sun was going down. Along the eastern horizon a low line of clouds showed, like a detached mountain range. Raef had tied down the steerboard, and only sat with his hand on the pole; the dragonfly ran true before the wind, working over the steep short seas.

"Could I fly?" he said.

"I don't know," she said, and shook herself smooth. "You are already well on the way to denying whatever gift you have. That's the way of it with most people, they'd rather be ordinary."

That stung him; he had always thought there was no one like him anywhere in the world. "What power does Corban have?"

"Corban!" Her beak gaped. He realized she was laughing. "Corban has no power. Except the very greatest, which is he knows it when he sees it."

"But you said—"

"Tush. You have to stop thinking you understand what I say."

He was silent a while. Everything she said to him seemed like a scolding. Under that, something deeper, as if she had to cover thin skin with a rough hide.

She spoke again, as if she overheard his thoughts. "I had six sons. All that mattered to me. I gave my daughter up for nothing to some Orkney lout; then I swore I would see my sons the Kings of Norway. Four of my sons each wore the crown, but they all turned Christian, and now they all are gone. The last two are nothings and will do nothing. My daughter is far away, Christian, too, and I have only Eelmouth. It's a hard thing, growing old."

"But you're a witch," Raef said. "You can keep from growing old."

"No, I can't," she snapped. "I can do much but not that." She was watching him. She said, in another voice, "Yet looking at you I remember Eric, as he was, and as I was. That's something."

He said nothing, glad of the gathering darkness. She said nothing more; he guessed she was sleeping.

Conn woke, and came to take the helm. "You're certain on this course," he said.

"We're drifting a little north," Raef said. "Not much. Better if we don't go straight at Hollandstadt anyway."

"How do you know this?" Conn burst out. "I've never even seen you use an instrument."

Raef swelled up with breath; he thought Conn had never admired him before. He tried to keep his voice even. "I've been there. I just go back there." His voice sounded foreign to himself, as if he were another person, listening. Raef Ericsson listening to Raef Corbansson.

Above them the sky blazed, strewn with lights. The old moon was sinking toward the horizon; the evening star burnt there already like a lamp at the doorway. Above, across the great sash of the sky, Raef recognized those Corban had called drifters, the big bright one, and the fainter, faster red one. Above them all was the net of stars.

Conn pointed; he said, "There's the star Pap calls the blue sun." He meant the bigger of the two drifters.

Raef said nothing; he knew Conn was straining to find something to say to him. He felt suddenly more lonely than he ever had. He got up and went wearily to find his cloak and lie down in the belly of the boat. Back there in the stern Conn sat by the steerboard, a vague dark shape.

He thought of what Gunnhild had said, that he was denying

himself, making himself ordinary. He understood suddenly why everything seemed so simple to Conn. He lay down in the boat and the weariness dragged him down into sleep. Half in dream, he said, "Well, it isn't worth it anyway, if I can't fly."

"What?" Conn said, startled, but Raef was gone into sleep.

CHAPTER SEVENTEEN

When Hakon's men dragged Corban out of Gunnhild's hall at Hrafnsbeck, they took him out to the little jut of land where the old stone tower stood. One in front and one behind, they pushed him up a narrow ladder tilted against the wall of the tower and threw him into the little round room at the top. On his knees, he heard the bar slam down across the outside of the door; he got quickly to his feet, looking around.

The space shrank down around him. The room was made of fitted stones, with a wide window on the wall opposite the door, which faced the lake and the head of the fjord here. It was a watchtower, he thought, very old. Broken wood and barrels cluttered it, a table, oars, a heap of something like rotten cloth. The floor was sound, but the last sun shone in through slates missing in the tilted roof. He went to the window and leaned on the broad sill and looked out.

Too far to jump. Below him, the brown stalks of the wintery marsh spread out into the margin of the lake. This was the largest of the chain of lakes that led to Hedeby, and here at its top the river ran in from the sea; directly before him he could see easily across to the far shore, another swamp, backed by low woods. A sail slipped by, going to Hedeby.

A black despair fell over him. His head began to pound, his stomach hurt, his arms and legs throbbed where they had kicked and beaten him. He turned back into the room. On the battered tipping table stood an empty jug with a crack in it. There were some broken benches and stools. The pile of moldering cloth was a sail thrown over some old fishnets. He went back to the window. The sun was going down, but he could not see it, no matter how far he leaned out the window, only the spreading cherry glow of its failing light.

The silence pressed in on him. The day faded around him. He could hear bats, fluttering and twittering under the eave of the roof over his head; now they began swooping away into the air before his window like a flock of winged rats. He looked out across the marsh to the uneasy water of the lake, gleaming in flashes and sparkles under the light of the rising moon. Slowly he became aware, close beside him, of a weightless pressure against his shoulder, a steady warmth.

His heart leapt. He was not alone. He had Benna.

He yearned toward her, his mind aching, struggling to bring her closer, to see her, to hear her voice, to touch her, to hold her.

He leaned on the windowsill, his face bathed in the icy air of the night. He would make her appear. He would think her into this world. Carefully he remembered the shape of every finger and every toe, and the curve of her calf against his palm, and the arch of her hip, remembered every inch of her, all over. He remembered how she smelled, how she laughed, how she made faces when she drew, as if she turned into different people.

He began to remember every day they had spent together.

He thought of when they first came to the island. Ulf had brought them across the sea from Hedeby; they were lucky and the weather was mostly fair, and they made a good crossing. Later they would come to realize how rare that had been: Going west was much harder than going east. They had come down the coast from where they first made landfall, looking for some place sheltered, some place safe.

When they first sailed into the great bay with its flock of islands, there had been smokes rising all around, and Ulf had wanted to go on, get away from any other people. But Corban had seen no smoke coming from the big island, and he liked the looks of it, with its southern beaches and thick stands of trees. Mostly he was tired of being on the ship, and the baby and the women were doing poorly, and he had Ulf put them down on the southern end of it.

Ulf stayed only a few days, left them some stores and some tools, and went back east again, promising to come again in the spring. Corban and Benna and his sister made a shelter of stones and driftwood, wadding turf into the chinks. Raef was then a tiny baby, colicky and fretful, with a yellow tinge to his eyes and a thin desperate wail. Mav nursed him, but her milk seemed only to make him cry more. Benna chewed up bread and dried meat for him from their diminishing store; more and more she took over mothering him as Mav wandered off into the forest like a wolf.

The great waterland around them teemed with food. They fished in the bay and found clams and crabs, he hunted deer and learned to catch smaller, stranger animals, and Mav showed them other things to eat, mushrooms and berries, rose hips, ferns, nuts, seaweed.

Raef grew, even if he seemed to throw up everything he was fed. They set about expanding the shelter by digging out the bank behind it and piling sod against the outside.

After they had been there only a little while, the forest began to turn color. He had seen trees change their leaves before but never in such masses, in such vivid color, extreme as everything else in this country. From the height of the island he and Benna sat looking out over the broad mainland just to the east, a great wind-rumpled carpet of a thousand shades of reds and yellows, oranges and rusts, sweeping away toward the horizon, the forest shouting at him in a language of colors. At night now the air bit. He sensed the winter like some great force accumulating just over the northern horizon.

The other people who lived around the bay, whom they saw now and again at a distance, and whose main villages Corban had carefully noted in his mind, were moving away. Fewer smokes rose every day from their villages, and finally they were gone. The blaze of the forest faded, and the leaves fluttered down, like a warning he had no idea how to read.

Then one day Mav came in, saying, over and over, "Snow. Snow." She led them to gather firewood and they filled up the shelter with it, and then the storm struck, a swirling onslaught of snow and wind that seemed to suck them out of the world and into a great dark gray howling nothing. They had almost no food; he sat desperately in the half-dark by the little fire struggling to make willow boughs into webs for his feet so that he could get around in the snow, while the baby cried endlessly and the two women cooked old bones over and over for soup and measured out the last handful of berries one at a time. After five days the storm screamed itself out and he dug a way up to the surface of the snow, and he and Mav went off into the forest. The foot-webs he had strapped to his feet kept falling apart, and he had to stop and bind them up again with freezing blue-tipped hands, his teeth chattering, while Mav glided over the snow on the perfect hoops she had made, and hardly looked cold.

She took him deep into the woods, to a place where the wind had blown snow in a twenty-foot drift against the sheltered side of a hill. From the top of the hill he looked down into the hollow between the drift and the slope of the hill, and imprisoned in this snowy bowl were three does.

He used his sling and his knife and a club of wood to kill one; he hauled all the pine boughs and bark he could gather to feed the others, coming back faithfully day after day, keeping them fat until he needed them. The deer meat sustained them all the rest of the winter, through three more storms, and a bitter cold that cracked the rocks of their shelter. By the beginning of spring, Benna was heavy with their baby.

Conn, born when the sun was warm and bright, when the trees burst with green, and everything smelled of growing: born to be always happy. Soon after, Ulf sailed up, talking of an awful trip, men swept overboard, howling cold winds and rain.

He helped them move their camp up from the southern rim of the island to the northern end, where Corban had found a cove to shelter a boat, and a rock to back his house up to. With Ulf's crew helping, he dug out the foundation of his new house and set the corner posts. When Ulf left, too soon, Corban went doggedly at it by himself, the women always busy with the babies, built strong walls of withy, an inside and an outside, and stuffed the space between with sod. And all the while, furiously, they stowed away food for the winter.

He had been always hungry, those early years. He was hungry now, in the tower at Hrafnsbeck; Hakon had said he would not feed him.

He thought about kneeling behind Benna in the old rock shelter and holding her with his arms around her, and Mav between her knees, taking the baby in her long hands, wet and slick, dark hair plastered against his skull, erupting in a yell of rage. They had burst out laughing, all three of them, held him and each other and laughed and laughed, while Raef watched them glumly from one side, little scrawny yellow-haired boy.

Out there now, in the dark, he saw ships slipping away down the river—dragons, which could be warships. He wondered if Sweyn and Palnatoki had escaped from Bluetooth's plot. He wondered which of the Haralds Hakon would end up fighting, and who would win. He had no view of the hall of Hrafnsbeck; he saw nothing of those who guarded him—if anybody. They could have simply locked him up here and left him.

Benna nudged him, a tingle in his mind. She wanted more of the island.

He was tired, and hurt all over; he leaned on the windowsill. Out in the black night sky in the swarm of the stars he could see two of the drifters very close together, and about to overtake the nimbus of light he thought of as the star net. His throat was aching with thirst. Soon he would be on the same side of death as she was, and then they would be together forever. But now he had to sleep. He dragged the mound of sail and netting around until it made a bed, spread his red and blue cloak on it, and lay down.

He slept fitfully. She seemed there, and not there. Over and over he dreamt of waking and finding her gone, a devastating aloneness. As the night wore on he was burning with thirst, his belly grating with hunger. He wondered how long it would take him to die.

When at last he stirred into daylight, he found three big pieces of bread on the floor by the bed, and a jug half full of water.

He gulped the water down. "Thank you," he said, "thank you," and beside him invisibly she smiled, like a little sun back there, and laid her hand on him; he felt every touch like a quickening in his skin.

Thereafter, he spent every day thinking about the island, and every night as he slept she brought him food, apples and bread and cheese, a whole braid of onions once, and now and then a cup of milk. The winter shut down over him. The bats went away and did not come back. Snow fell, and blew in through the holes in the roof, and he gathered it into the old jug and had more water. He pulled all the broken wood into the bad side of the room, under the holes in the roof. No one from outside the tower ever came to see what was going on with him. He tried making a rope of the old nets, but the first knot came apart in his hands in clots of dust. He walked around and around the room, restless and bored.

"Find a key," he said to her, in the dream, the only time he could see her. She shook her head: There was no key. She pushed at the door and shrugged.

One night in the dream she came to him very excited and tried to tell him something.

He could not hear her; he could never hear her. She frowned at him, and he apologized. She went away and came back with a piece of wood and a charred stick, and she began to draw.

He went close beside her, to see what she made. Under her hand the images spilled out flawlessly, and so fast they seemed to move.

He saw the hall, as he remembered it, with the great front door wide open, and the huge overhang of the roof. Then he saw the inside of the hall, three or four men sitting around a table dicing, drinking, a fire crackling behind them. One of the men had already fallen asleep, his head on the table. He saw how she was able to find food; the table was covered with scraps.

She rapped him sharply. Pay attention, he knew she was thinking.

She drew the men getting up now, going, walking out, and other men coming in. These new men all wore the same coat, red with a big bird sketched on it. After them came a tall man, lanky, with a gaunt righteous face, dressed in a long white robe.

"The Bishop," he said. "Bishop Poppo."

Benna smiled at him, and put away the wood and the bit of charcoal. A moment later he woke up.

He went to the window and looked out; the far shore was white under new snow, the air biting, the lake spangled with whitecaps. He thought about Poppo suddenly appearing here. He had been deep into the memories, and the world outside had fallen away, but now here it was back again. He beat his fists on the windowsill, longing to get out; it was long before he could turn away from the open air, to eat the food she had brought, and feed her with memories.

⸺∘⸺

He gave her memories of the island, of the deep summer nights when fiery bugs twinkled under the trees and the children bundled themselves into their parents' laps and even Mav came down to listen, and she told them all story after story, some she remembered and some she made up, of terrible evil giants and bold great-hearted heroes and magical cities full of marvels, cities called Jorvik and Hedeby.

He had said, "I don't remember it was that good."

She had laughed, and leaned on him, as she did now, pretending to need his strength. "Oh, well, I wish it had been, and now I can make it so."

Then, the next night, just before he fell asleep, he heard footsteps thump on the wooden wharf, outside below the window.

He got up and went to the window. Down below him, on the wharf, stood several men, all staring fixedly out toward the water; one was holding up a lantern. Out on the lake, a ship rowed swiftly toward them.

This startled him. He watched ships go up and down the lake every day, but none had ever stopped here before, certainly not at night. He watched the men tie the ship quickly to the wharf, and then in a crowd they all went up to the hall, the men from the ship, the men with the lantern, and as they went by close under his tower the lantern light showed on their red coats, the black birds spread out on the breast.

He went straight back to his bed and lay down, his heart thumping, trying to force himself into sleep. He lay rigid there what seemed the whole night, desperate to sleep, until, once again, feet boomed on the wharf below the window.

He sprang up again. From the window he watched men in red shirts troop away down the wharf to the ship, bundle themselves in, and quickly row off toward the river to the sea.

He went back to his bed and lay down, and now with morning on him he did sleep, but he did not dream.

All the next day he paced up and down the room, trying to settle himself. He struggled to find the flow of memory, but only bad things came to him, their two little winter boys, Finn and Culm, who died at the breast, one year after the other, in the starvation time of the early spring. He shrank from that, afraid to hurt her, but she nudged him, when he thought that; she wanted that, too. He was gathering himself for that when he heard something at the door.

He turned, surprised. Someone was wrenching at the bar on the door, trying to get it open. A voice reached him through the cracking door. "It's been two solid months, no food, no water, he won't even stink anymore." Then the door burst open, and several men pushed in.

He stood where he was, by the window, watching them. They goggled at him. Three he had never seen before but one he recognized, from the crowd that had dragged him here: the hall porter, who had just spoken.

Leaping into the room, the porter skidded to a stop. His eyes bulged from his head, and he let out a rip of a scream.

"It's him! He's alive!"

The man behind him muttered an oath in some other language. He gave Corban a single hard white-eyed look and tramped into the room, looking all around, one hand on the hilt of his sword, as if something might leap on him from the jumble of broken furniture. He wore a fancy coat with the emblem Benna had drawn, a black eagle on a red ground. The other men huddled by the door, ready to flee. The man in the red coat went to the window and looked out, and wheeled around toward Corban.

"You are Corban? You have been here all this time?"

Corban nodded.

"Who fed you? Who's been helping you?" The man in the red coat had a thick accent. Corban smiled at him, seeing no reason to answer. The German captain glared at him, then turned to the others and rattled off a string of orders. The other men bolted away out the door, leaving it swinging wide; Corban could see the top of the ladder rattling against the little landing there as they scurried down to the ground.

The man in the red coat said, "So. You are some kind of wizard, you want me to believe. You keep yourself alive perhaps on the gleanings of blackbirds."

Corban said, "I don't care what you believe," but his voice had gone unused for so long the words croaked out almost inaudibly. He shook his head. The jug was standing on a piece of wood he used for a table, and he picked it up and took a drink from it.

The German jumped toward him, grabbed the jug, and looked into it. He tipped it and let some of the rainwater pour out into his hand, and sniffed the little puddle on his palm. He gave Corban a wild look. "Witch-wine?" Corban laughed, shaking his head, his voice useless, and the German already too far gone into what he thought he knew. Then someone was scrambling up the ladder again.

"His Eminence says to bring him down. Right away, he says."

The German lowered the jug and faced Corban. "Do I have to force you?" he said. His voice quivered.

"No," Corban croaked. "I'll go." His voice was getting better; he cleared his throat. Picking up his red and blue cloak, he went out of the tower and down the ladder.

⸺※⸺

They went into the hall through the big front door. A great fire burnt on the hearth, spreading heat throughout the room. A small crowd of people stood up at the end where the high seat was, and when Corban went through the door, the German captain behind him, he could hear the voice of the hall porter babbling away. "It's been since he came here, Your Eminence. I—I—there were things missing. Things moved. Doors left open. Someone—one of your people, Eminence, one of yours—thought he saw something, one night when he woke late—something passed between him and the fire, he thought, and yet nothing was there."

Corban went up through the crowd toward him. Beyond the

yammering porter he saw the tall frame of the Bishop, with his smooth bald head and hanging jowls and gorgeous gold-encrusted coat, sitting crookedly in the high seat.

The porter was still speaking. "I thought—we all thought it was him, you know, what was left of him, dead up there—" His voice rose in a wail. "That's why we wanted you to bring him down, to bury him, and get rid of him, but now—now—"

Corban had reached his side, and the porter saw him and recoiled, turning the color of a dead fish. He made a sign with his fingers. Corban was looking all around him, his eyes dazzled by the colors, his mouth watering at the smell of food. They had meat here, great roasts in puddles of fat and blood, crisp-skinned fowl with their legs in the air. Mobs of faces watched him from around the table. The jumble of voices cluttered his ears with an excited murmur. He had been alone so long the mere sound of other people's voices was like music. He went up to the table and put his fingers on the patterned cloth, soft with deep color.

The Bishop was watching him impassively, his eyes unblinking. He said, "I remember you. You are the so-called wizard, Corban Loosestrife."

"Yes," Corban said, and was glad to hear his voice come smoothly out.

"Now, come along, man, you can't have us believe you lived for a month on air and rainwater." The Bishop hitched himself up a little, shifting his weight to the other side; the high scat was piled up with cushions for him, and yet he could not get comfortable. He said, "Someone helped you. Who was it?"

Corban said, "I have seen no one since I went into the tower."

"How did you survive, then?"

"The food was there; I ate it. Water came; I drank it."

Somebody off to his left whispered, "Holy Mary." There was a quick rush of talk quickly hushed. Poppo's face darkened, his eyes narrowing.

"You lie. Someone helped you. You are one like her whose hall this was, that foul witch Gunnhild. By the grace of God we have rid Denmark of her and her kind—by the power of Christian light and truth and order. True God against a crowd of idols—it was this porter, wasn't it, who fed you? One of her men!"

Corban remembered about the test of hot iron; he thought Poppo cared nothing about god, but only held to the faith because it gave him power. He said, "He didn't help me. Gunnhild and I are enemies, anyway."

"I don't believe you," Poppo said.

Corban shrugged. "Believe what you wish." Benna like a warm cloak around him enclosed him.

Poppo studied him up and down. "What I believe may cost you your life. We should have stoned you at Jelling, that time. Yet Bluetooth would not listen, and look what came of it. Who are you? You don't look like much to me. They say you were the apprentice of a witch in Hedeby, before Bluetooth came to God, is that true?"

"Apprentice," Corban said, "is too great a word. I served her. You are right, I am not much."

"You served a witch, a creature of Satan? You admit you serve the devil?"

Corban grunted at him. "Make it whatever you wish. You Christians pick god out of the world and throw it in a little ball into the sky, out of your way, so you can do what you like. This you think makes you superior."

Poppo lurched forward in the high seat, leaning over the table, his eyes blazing. His cheeks were sunken like a starvling's.

"You dare talk of God, you devil-worshiper, you pagan pig. I tell you, we are cleansing Denmark of you, all you ancient necromancers. We'll sweep this witches' kitchen bare and build a clean white church here—let in the bright daylight against your messy dark blood cult, and as for women such as your witch, all such witches, all these women, God abhors them, and we shall drive them into the wilds like the hell-wolves they are!"

Corban felt Benna leave him like a gust of warm wind, the cool dull air rushing in against him in her place, and then on the opposite side of the table, while Poppo was shaking his fist to match the thunder of his rant, his hat flew off his head, and the cup before him leapt up into the air and dumped its contents all over him.

A great gasp went up from the people looking on, who scrambled up off the benches, shrinking away. Then abruptly Corban felt her return, warm around him, clinging to him.

Everybody was gawking at him, including the Bishop, his face shiny with the wine dripping down his cheeks, his eyes black with rage. He bellowed, and someone quickly brought a cloth, and someone else came up and helped clean him. Corban could not keep from smiling. Out of the corner of his eye, he saw the German captain put his hand on the hilt of his sword; if Corban was going to die anyway, he could at least enjoy the Bishop's humiliation.

Poppo flung down a towel. Between his teeth, he said, "How did you do that?"

"I didn't do anything," Corban said mildly. "I stood here. All of these people here saw me do nothing." She was laughing; he could feel her quivering. The onlookers were whispering among themselves, heads turning, but everybody watching him. "Perhaps you slipped."

Poppo said, "Kill him."

The porter groaned, the sound startlingly loud in the sudden silence. Corban met the Bishop's gaze. He heard the snick of a blade coming out of a scabbard; he thought that in a moment he would be with Benna.

The porter said, "If you kill him he'll never leave."

Behind him, somebody else said, "What about the King?"

The Bishop's eyes widened slightly, and shifted from Corban to some space beyond him. His lips pursed. Nobody else moved. Finally Poppo waved one hand.

"We will be merciful. Put him back in the tower. Guard it night and day. I want to know who feeds him." He leaned back, his face slack and his eyes half closed. Wine glistened in the seams of his neck. His grimy white robe wore a broad pink badge all across its front. "I will send word of this to the King."

—⁂—

Corban slept. Benna went to the hall, kicking over the guard's jug as she went. All this time she had been trying to keep from being noticed, but now she saw that was how she could get Corban out of the tower. The trick was to do it without getting him killed.

She gathered up sand and stones, and found where the Bishop slept, in a great cupboard in the hall, and put the stones into his shoes and between his blankets. He slept with his mouth open, and his breath smelled bad. She remembered him ordering Corban's death; she wondered if she could defend Corban against men with swords and thought not.

Going into the hall, where the other men slept bundled onto the benches, she looked for food for Corban, and sprinkled sand into everything else, the jugs of wine, a half-eaten savory. She threw Poppo's cushions from the high seat into the filthy rushes, and then saw a piece of paper spread out on the table and went to look, thinking it was a picture.

It was a picture, lines and marks in some order, but she puzzled over it for a long while before suddenly she made sense of it. It was a view from far overhead of this country, the long wall of the Danewirk with the big gate marked, Hedeby at the end of its chain of lakes, the river itself.

She stood there a while, too tired now to think about this. A pot of dried-up ink and a quill lay beside the picture, and she thought of drawing over it, but that would require mixing up the ink again, and all she wanted now was to go back and rest. Moving things wearied her more and more, and she had done too much this day, flying so furiously at the Bishop. She was beginning to realize she would not last like this, not long. In some time to come she would be gone.

Finally she gathered her strength, took the food for Corban, and made her way out of the hall again. The guard was standing by the bank, fuming over his spilled jug, and beating his arms around himself in the cold. She yanked at his hair as she passed, and he gave a cry, and whirled around, frightened.

She went up into the tower and laid her gifts down beside Corban. For a moment she hovered over him, loving how he looked when he slept, soft and young, his eyelids soft; she loved to kiss his eyelids. Now, she thought, she even had what he was looking for, the reason for the night-ship, the quick and stealthy visit. He stirred, his mouth moving. She bent to kiss him, and sank gratefully down into his sleep, into the world he had made for her in his mind.

—⋙—

Corban prowled around the little room. Now that he had been out of it, if only for a few moments, it seemed intolerably small and bare. He felt Benna leaning against him; she wanted memory, but he could not keep from thinking about Poppo.

What she had said of the map nagged at him. He had to get out of here. He thought, again, Help me get out of here.

She nudged him. To her the memories were real, and Poppo only a shadow. She had drawn him pictures of the tower, of the bar across the door, the ladder on the ground. She could not budge the bar, and when he saw what the effort took from her he was afraid to let her try again. Now there was the guard, night and day. But he had to get out.

In his mind, she said, I'm doing something. Wait.

He felt her warm and snug against him, wrapped around him like a cloud. He forced himself calm, and leaning on the window remembered building the hide boat, all that one summer when Ulf did not come, and Conn and Raef were still little, that whole long golden summer.

She had made a picture of the boat, before they built it; that was when he understood her power, when he saw what she had drawn coming true under his hands.

He remembered one morning when the sun was coming up, and the two little boys had just run out of the house, and he stood on the ledge of the doorway and saw how the sun cast their shadows ahead of them onto the mist, rimmed in rainbow light. He remembered suddenly what he had forgotten for years, how the rainbow streamed around them both in a single halo.

He thought of them with a sore heart, thinking, I brought them into this. Benna poked him, annoyed.

Later the next day, as he stood by the window, he heard his name called in a high piercing faraway voice. He leaned out, looking up into the pitch of the sky. Up there a hawk was circling and circling. Corban stood at the window watching, and on an impulse, he thrust his arm out the window.

The hawk swooped down and landed on his fist. Her talons bit, and he gasped, both at the pain and at the weight of her. Her head turned, the long narrow helmet of skull behind the massive curved beak, the bone curving, flaring back to cup the remorseless eye.

She said, "That's for what you did to Eric. I'm glad I found you, anyway. Maybe now your boys will stop hounding me."

He drew her into the window frame, and she stepped delicately from his bleeding wrist onto the broad stone sill. She picked with her beak a moment at the speckled feathers of her breast, used one dark talon to scratch her cheek, and turned calmly toward him.

"My greeting to my sister," she said. "I'm pleased we meet once more."

Benna leaned against him, soft, alert. Corban said, "Where are my boys? How are they?"

"They are good enough. I left them on your dragonfly, sailing along the coast. I'm to meet them at Hollandstadt. When I am done here we will go back to Jorvik, where Sweyn is raising an army—something he is rather better at than I would have expected." She cocked her head to one side, seeing him in her left eye. "Your daughters, also, are in Jorvik, with the rest of them. They were run out of that place of yours in the west by the local people."

"My daughters," he said, startled, and against his shoulder felt something move, warm, twisting; he glanced at the empty air behind him. Benna, too, had thought them safe away on the island; all this time, they had been imagining them on the island still.

They had imagined the island itself was still there, unchanged, as they remembered it; now they saw that it was all lost.

He wondered, for an instant, if he had ever really been there, if it had not always all been in his mind.

"The word that Sweyn wants men is getting up to the Orkneys and even to Ireland." The cool dry voice of the hawk brought him back. "Some of those men will answer him, with their ships, even if he has no money. He'll have a fit army soon. Bluetooth can see him coming, and is gathering a fleet of his own at the Limfjord. Sweyn will have a task worthy of the King he imagines himself to be."

"What about Palnatoki?" Corban said.

"I have not seen sign of him. I will look."

"Mark this, then," Corban said. "Bluetooth is blind in one

eye. In that eye is the righteous Bishop. He has been meeting German people here, and making a map of Hedeby." Benna was pushing on him. His mind bent away from this, back toward the two little girls, living among strangers in Jorvik. "My children. Who cares for my children? Where is my sister?"

"Your kindred in Jorvik have the two little girls," the hawk said. "I have to go. The light is failing me already." She paced to the outer edge of the windowsill; over her shoulder, she said, "Hold fast, Corban. We shall come for you, soon enough." Leaning out into the wind, she spread her wings, the broad flight feathers fanning apart at the tips, and sailed off onto the breast of the air. She sank into a deep glide, but then tilting her wings slightly curved her path, circling back toward him, and was rising again, her wings utterly still, the flared pinions pressing delicately into the air. She passed by Corban again ten feet away but now above the window, her legs drawn back against her body, her head thrust out, her wings glinting in the last sunlight. She rose away from him, into the still bright sky, and swept off to the west.

He turned from the window, holding his bleeding wrist in the other hand, and thought of his little girls, somewhere in Jorvik, alone. Of Mav, wherever she was. He felt Benna warm and shuddering against his shoulder; walking around and around the tower room, he kept his mind full of memories of the little girls, and almost heard her weep.

CHAPTER EIGHTEEN

In the morning through a dense lifting fog Conn and Raef rowed up the river toward Hollandstadt. Between the city and the sea lay a bleak salt marsh that seemed endless. The fog lifted, and the sun was bright when they finally reached the harbor. Hollandstadt disappointed Raef, hardly a city at all, compared to Hedeby and Jorvik; Tisconum's village had been bigger. When he and Conn rowed into the pond, only five or six ships were moored up there, slow round merchant ships, and a single dragon, its high curled prows carved into snarling heads and covered with shining gold.

They hauled the dragonfly onto the narrow stretch of beach and drifted with elaborate innocence toward the great dragon, drawn up nearer the city. Raef ran his gaze over the ship's long sleek lines, the smooth flare of its waist, the gilded rowlocks down the side; he thought it would be as fast as the dragonfly, maybe, under oars. Several men lounged around it, mending a sail and playing with bones and drinking.

Conn nudged him with an elbow and said, under his breath, "This must be somebody important."

Raef grunted. He wanted to get away from here; the men by the big dragon were beginning to watch them. He was hungry, and he could smell fresh bread baking. His feet longed to travel up the beach to the little town and its offerings. He pulled on Conn's sleeve, and they turned back up the shore; a short bank marked the beginning of the dry land, and they stepped up into crushed broken saw grass and then the trampled dust of Hollandstadt. Raef glanced over his shoulder at the golden dragon.

"I wish we hadn't come in here." The long narrow channel through the estuary felt like a trap to him. He began thinking about the marsh, worrying out another way through.

Conn said, "Pap's likely all the way across Denmark, she said. At the other end of the Danewirk." He waved his hand at the great grassy hill that rose above the marsh and stretched away into the distance. "When she comes back, we have to be ready to do something." The hawk had gone to scout the country.

"What?"

Conn shrugged, his face serene. "When it happens, it happens."

"There," Raef said. "There's bread."

They had walked into the center of the little town. The largest building, a long low hall, faced the shore; behind it was a wide open ground, with a forge at one end and three domed stone huts on the other. In front of the huts was a woman with a basket selling bread, and Conn bought three loaves. They stood there stuffing themselves. Two girls in white headdresses, their aprons crusted with flour, came out of the hall with trays of golden rounds of dough; they opened a door in the front of one of the domed huts and slid the trays inside. From twenty feet away Raef felt the blast of heat from the oven.

He said, "We should buy some meat. For the hawk."

Conn said, around a great mouthful of bread, "She'll find herself something to eat. Let's get some ale." But his eyes turned to the forge, where someone had begun hammering iron.

Raef said, under his breath, "I think we should get out of here." His mind probed and poked at the dense marsh between them and the open sea, threaded through with its narrow, twisting, vulnerable channel.

Conn said, "Come on." He crammed the last of the bread into his coat and strode off toward the forge.

This stood between two three-sided slant-roofed wooden buildings, their open sides facing. The yard between them was full of horses tethered in lines. Conn and Raef went in past a heap of black charred chunks of wood that spilled from a tipped-over cart. In the center of the place, away from all the buildings, a bed of coals shone in a high stone bowl. A boy was working the bellows attached to the edge of the bowl, sending out a rhythmic stream of squeaks and wails. Next to the fire, a half-naked man bent over rump to rump with a slab-sided black horse, one of the horse's feet up in his lap, and trimmed off slices of hoof with a curved knife.

Just behind him stood another man, short, with a neat black beard. His dark coat was splendid with gold, and a great gold chain hung around his neck. Raef started; he had seen this man somewhere before. He slowed, but Conn went straight up toward them, jaunty as a prince.

"Hail, there, fellow, maybe you could help us. We're looking for horses to take us to Hedeby."

The man in the dark coat moved back, out of the way, and the smith straightened. "Who the hell are you?"

Conn put his hands on his belt. "We're fighters. We're looking to get into the service of some great captain and go viking."

The man in the dark coat was staring at them hard. The smith snorted. "Go back to your plows. There's no fighting in Hedeby." Stooping, he picked up the horse's hoof again; the horse groaned, and shifted its weight, and swung its head around and bit bad-temperedly at the air.

The man in the black coat said suddenly, "Who are you? Where exactly did you come from? Some farm around here? Who's your father?"

Raef grabbed Conn's arm and pulled him. Conn was saying, "Just—we're just—from down the way a little—" Waving his hand. The smith shook his head.

"Never seen them before. I know everybody around here." He took a rasp between his hands and scraped at the hoof on his knee.

"Come on," Raef said, and towed Conn off back toward the shore. He looked back over his shoulder and saw the man in the dark coat watching them intently, and now suddenly that man was circling around the forge, coming after them.

Conn at last had caught the urgency in the situation. They

went out of the town and down the beach to the dragonfly, tipped on its side on the beach like a cockleshell. The man in the dark coat was no longer following them but as they were shoving off Raef looked down toward the golden dragon and saw the men down there suddenly bustling around. He bounded into the ship and ran the front oars out.

"Come on. They're after us."

Conn pushed them off the beach. "Who is that?" He climbed over the side and sat down on the second bench.

"I don't know." Raef began to row. "Let's get out of here."

Conn thrust his oars out. "Think we can beat that ship?"

"I don't know." Raef put himself into the swinging rhythm of the work. The tide was coming in, and the ship fought the water a little; he concentrated on keeping them on the straightest course for the channel to the sea. Looking back, he saw the golden dragon sliding down into the pond, and the men climbing into their benches.

"Come on, you sea-pigs," Conn said, "let's race." His back bent; Raef saw the muscles of his arms bunch, and the dragonfly shot forward through the water, across the pond and into the mouth of the narrow channel.

The way twisted and turned through the marsh, sometimes narrow, sometimes opening into wide stretches of water. Over stands of blown reeds the prow of the golden dragon trailed steadily after them. Because of the turns of the channel sometimes they passed close by one another and Raef saw the man in the dark coat, standing in the bow of his ship, staring at him. A wallowing overladen merchant craft coming up from the sea blocked the channel and the dragonfly had to pull over and let it pass, and the great golden head swept closer; it came on the merchant in a wider part of the channel and went by it without pausing.

"What's in front of us?" Conn called.

"More ships." Raef did not have to turn and look; he felt the channel ahead of them as a thick clog of wooden vessels, blocking their way to the sea.

On the dragon, a voice bellowed, "You! In the small ship! Lay to!"

"Is there a way through the marsh?" Conn asked.

"I don't know," Reaf said. "I've never—I don't know it." The marsh felt to him like a watery web, twining deeper and deeper, another trap.

"You in the small ship!"

"Take us in there," Conn said, and leaned forward to thrust his oars down for the drawing stroke.

Reaf pushed one oar into the water and pulled the other; the dragonfly turned neatly and darted across the channel, almost under the bows of another merchant ship. The little craft nosed into an inlet of the marsh. At once the thick clumps of old reeds closed in around them, their butts bulbous above the gnawed banks. He could feel the muddy bottom shelving up, almost to their keel already, and even shallower ahead, but to their right was a slit of an opening, and he felt deeper water that way.

"Oars up," he said, and put one of his oars into the ship, and stood up with the other in both hands. Conn shipped his oars. Raef worked them through the inlet, pushing them along with the oar against the slick mud bank under the stalky dry reeds. The marsh stretched away featureless and brown before them. Great hummocks of mud formed tiny islands above the scummy surface. Like broken gray bones, driftwood lay heaped in the slack water. Here and there the tide ran suddenly fast.

The golden dragon was not giving up. It could not follow into the marsh, but in the channel it kept pace with them, keeping them in sight. Raef saw an opening through the reeds that probably led back to the channel, but if they tried it the dragon would catch them as soon as they emerged. He turned the dragonfly away, going southerly, working through narrow passages and across wide shallow pans of water that would be bald mud when the tide went out. The keel touched something, and then lodged amidships, and he and Conn walked up into the bow and rocked the ship free.

They poled along the side of a long narrow island, dense with dead reeds like broken flutes poking out of the ground. A ridge of driftwood lay all along the far side of it. "All right," Conn said. "He can't catch us here." He leaned out and grabbed a handful of reeds and pulled them snug with the muddy bank.

Raef turned, his oar in his hands. The golden dragon was well away across the featureless flat waterland, only one shape among the constant stream of ships moving down the channel to Hollandstadt. The dragon was not leaving. He said, "I don't know if we can get out of here except by going back." He thought if he were that man in the dragon, by now he would have sent for a small ship. Maybe for people to walk along the shore and come at them that way.

"Wait," Conn said. He climbed out onto the island and walked around it, pushing with his feet; the ground looked solid under him. Raef got cautiously out of the dragonfly, and they hauled it up onto the end of the island. Conn dragged a chunk of driftwood up and sat on it. He squinted at the sun, reached into his coat, and pulled out a chunk of bread. "Do you want some of this?"

Raef sat down on the driftwood, and they ate the bread. "Wait for what?"

"The sun to go down," Conn said. He licked the crumbs off his fingers and got up and started hauling driftwood into a pile.

The sun rolled slowly down the sky; just before it sank into the sea the hawk appeared, circled once over them and the golden dragon, and then stooped down to land on the prow of the dragonfly.

"What are you doing here?" she said. "And what is Hakon of Lade doing loitering out there in the channel?"

Conn turned to Raef. "That's who that is." He bowed to the

hawk. "Welcome back, Queen Gunnhild. We ran into Hakon in Hollandstadt. He's after us. Did you find my father?"

The hawk was settling herself, folding her wings carefully, and fussing with her beak at her feathers. She said, "I did. He is alive and well but heavily guarded. What's more important, there is a huge fleet gathering in the eastern bay of the Limfjord."

"Where's that? Whose fleet?"

"Up at the top of this mainland. The Limfjord runs in across the whole land from the German Sea. It's Bluetooth's fleet, of course. From there he can keep watch on Sweyn in Jorvik and Palnatoki in Funen. We have to get back to Jorvik and tell Sweyn what's going on. Your father can wait."

Conn said, "Where is Corban?"

"He's at Hrafnsbeck. He's safe and well, as far as I can see."

"We should go rescue him," Conn said. But he turned to look out at the dragon, out in the channel. "What's he doing here, then?"

"Hakon has his spies everywhere," the hawk said. "He probably gets news here from Jorvik every day." She walked along the gunwale of the ship into the shelter of the prow's curve. Her harsh red eye turned on Raef a moment and then back to Conn; Raef saw she knew that Conn was the one to convince. She said, "Sweyn's only chance is to attack before Bluetooth is ready. There is no time to go get Corban, who can take care of himself anyway. Do you have some plan for getting us out of here?"

Conn said, "Yes. But I—"

"Then I suggest you do it," she said. She stretched one foot out, the claws gathered up in a loose ball, shook herself in a soft rustle of feathers, and settled down onto the gunwale and closed her eyes. The sun was going down. She was going to sleep.

Conn said, under his breath, "Yes. Look."

Raef looked around, wondering what he was seeing. With the sun down, the night seemed to creep up out of the marsh. The flat reedy islands were already featureless shadows, but the open water caught the last of the light in shining streaks and sheets. In the air above the water, wisps of mist were forming. Just above the band of fog to the west, one of Corban's drifting stars began to gleam. The vault of the sky was deepening to night blue, but the western rim was still red and pink; he could see the dragon's prow against it.

The prow faded a little; the fog was growing up around them, thickening, cold.

"Come on," Conn said. "Help me light this." He knelt beside his heap of driftwood. He had shaved up tinder in a little pile. Raef cupped his hands down around it while Conn struggled to get a spark out of his tinderbox. The sparks flew and died at once, without even making smoke.

"Wait." Conn got up and went over to the nearest patch of dead grass. His hands idle, Raef sat back, lifting his head; a cold warning shiver went down his spine. His eye caught other lights, across the marsh on the opposite side from the channel, fuzzy through the fog: a train of torches, coming along the shore.

"Look over there."

Conn came back with handfuls of grass. "Think they'll come out here by night?" He bent down to his fire again.

"Who knows? Local men would know this place."

"Well," Conn said, "we'll be long gone." He bent, and blew a tuft of fire gently alive under the driftwood. The fire crackled along a dry branch. "There it goes." He sat back on his hams, pleased.

Raef said, "They're coming closer." He squinted, trying to keep track of the lights; hazy in the thickening fog, they blended into a single glob.

Conn's fire leapt high, crackling. Conn said, "Let's go."

"Where?" Raef turned, startled.

"Give me your shirt, so I can muffle my oars." Conn was stripping off his own shirt. "Can you get us back out of here?"

Raef looked away toward the dragon. "We'll come out right by—" He stopped. The blaze of the fire turned the fog into a woolly wall; he could see nothing through it. He realized what Conn had known all along, that the fog could cover their escape. "All right," he said. He went to the ship. "Let's go."

They pulled the ship into the water, careful to keep from getting between the blazing fire and the dragon. Standing in the stern, Raef poled them along, slow and quiet, following the thready pull of the tide going out. He steered well wide of the light. The fog bundled around him, clammy, smelling of rot. Conn sat on the back thwart with the oars cocked up, waiting. Up in the bow, the hawk slept on.

The fog began abruptly a few feet above the water; below that was clear air. Everything else was a thick muffled blank. Raef kept his strokes slow, lifting the blade carefully up and letting the water drip before he swung it forward. He stood with his feet widespread in the hold of the dragonfly, keeping the ship steady with his weight. Behind them the great fire blazed bright even through the fog; in all the marsh it was the only thing to look at. He manuvered them carefully around a great snagged tree trunk and into deeper water beyond. He felt the dragon ahead of them like a vast lump in the night, and now, threading through the damp and dark, a voice reached them.

"How long do you suppose this war will last?"

They were only a few yards from the dragon. A narrow inlet between hummocks of reeds separated them, but the dragon was at the far end of the inlet, like the cat at the mousehole, and the inlet was barely wide enough for the dragonfly. Raef gripped the oar but could not move, frozen with uncertainty. In the middle of the ship, Conn sat utterly still, but Raef could feel his gaze on him.

Another voice came from the heart of the fog, from the dragon. "I don't know. Not long, I hope."

Raef recognized the voice: That was the man in the dark coat. Hakon of Lade, Bluetooth's warrior. His hair stood on end.

He thought of the hawk. Of what she would think of him if he failed. Of Conn, who trusted him. Silently he dipped the oar into the water and nudged the ship forward. He could feel the gentle lapping of a current against the hull of the dragonfly, and he was sure the men on the dragon heard it, too, up there ahead of him. He eased the ship past the reeds, barely moving, the fog soaking his face and his bare chest. His new shirt, he thought, belatedly. His new shirt, wrapped around Conn's oar. The ship nosed down between two eaten hummocks of the mud, and suddenly, above them, the prow of the dragon loomed, a vague tall shape in the fog, closing down over them.

They were near enough almost to touch the stempost, carved with twining serpents. Raef eased the ship along with a little waggle of the oar. Over their heads in the dragon, Hakon of Lade said, "Damn. They're all just sitting out there."

"You don't want to go rushing around in a marsh like this at night. Be patient, sir. I know the island they're on, and there's a good way out through the marsh to it. My boys will get them."

The prow slipped away above them, fell behind them, fading into the gloom. Raef brought the oar carefully up out of the water. He saw Conn moving, now, putting his oars out; Raef sat down on the second thwart and reached down for his other oar.

Conn leapt up, onto the thwart; he had something in his hand. He yelled, "Hakon! Hakon! My name's Conn Corbansson, and don't forget it!" He cranked his arm back and threw the chunk of wood in his hand toward the dragon.

Raef swore; he grabbed his oars. On the dragon a yell went up. The ship was rocking hard under Conn's vigorous leaping. "Why did you do that?" Raef thrust the oars out. "Why did you do that? We were safe!" Conn was laughing, lowering himself down to his oars again. At least they were in open water now, and between the dragon and the sea. A sharp voice back there called orders, and the rumble of oars going out sounded in the fog. Hakon was coming after them. But he was too far behind already;

in his mind, Raef saw the dragon falling back, losing the race. He concentrated on steering them the shortest way up the channel through the dark and the fog.

⌐⚬⌐

In spite of what he had told Arre, Euan knew he would have trouble with the Archbishop. Oswald was shrewd enough, but he was a very devil on sin, and consorting with pagans for him was direst sin. Euan waited a few days, to let the word get around that his nephews had gone, before he went up to the church.

The church in Jorvik had been burned and thrown down and rebuilt any number of times; now Oswald had in mind to raise a minster church, fitting the diocese's high status as the oldest Christian community in England. Behind the church, which stood on the high ground, on the flat near the fountain, the land was already cleared, and a shape laid out with a single course of unpointed stones. Here Euan found Oswald, walking slowly around, and looking up at the back of the old church, black with age and mold.

The Archbishop of Jorvik was tall, with a round belly heaving up his cassock. His short-cropped gray hair grew out in a shock like a straw roof above a face shorter on one side than the other. His small clear eyes were the color of ale. His prominent nose wore a lacing of dark veins. He had been poking with his staff at the ground in front of him, but when he saw Euan he straightened and gripped the staff before him with both hands and leaned on it, solid.

"Well, Wrightson, you again?"

Euan bowed deeply. He was glad he had found the Archbishop here; part of the mending of their quarrel, when he came back, had been a promise to give Oswald money for building his minster. But at first he said only, "God's grace to you, Father, I am happy to see you back in Jorvik. I beg your blessing on me and my household."

Oswald drew a cross in the air in Euan's direction. "God have mercy on you, Euan. And your wife, wrong-headed as she is. Word has it you've been down in London, attending on the King."

"I've been, my lord Father," Euan said, wondering if there were currency in this, if he could parlay some of what he knew into a better position. Oswald was studying the ground around them once more, as if he had lost interest already. Euan edged a little closer, and saw some lines drawn in the dirt there, and realized it was the plan for Oswald's cathedral.

He said, "This is a grand scheme, here, Father."

Oswald poked the stick at the drawing in the dirt. "This is the apse, see. And here, the choir." His voice slowed and dropped to a murmur, as if he talked to himself. "I saw a church in Rome, when I was there, as fine a place as I have ever been. I would make that here."

Euan squatted down; the lines of the drawing were smudged, and he straightened them with his forefinger. "Father, if it please you—" He drew the round outer wall of the choir larger, until his eye told him it married better with the rest of the building.

Oswald grunted, impressed against his will. He stood solid as an oak tree there beside Euan, his legs planted. He said, "That is an improvement, yes."

Still squatting by the drawing, neatening the lines with his finger, Euan said, "Canterbury was much around the court." The Archbishop of Canterbury was Jorvik's archrival.

"Was he," Oswald said, with a sudden twitch; the skirts of his cassock swished around his ankles. "Is the King well?"

"No," Euan said. "He's like to die, but it will take some time, and meanwhile such as Otkar and Byhrtnoth are deciding things."

Oswald made a scornful sound with his lips. "Then I fear for England. Those featherheads."

Euan dusted off his hands. The shape of the cathedral in the dust before him pleased his eye better now, the lines proportioned well, meeting in strong angles. He said, "Have you talked to any masons yet?"

Oswald's skirts rustled again. "I have no money for masons."

Euan straightened, thinking that as he was building traps for Oswald, so Oswald was building them for him; it was a kind of dance. The proportions of that pleased him somehow as much as the drawing in the dust. He said, "I will give you money for it. For the good of my soul, and Arre's." He hoped he had some money somewhere to do this, but he had long since discovered that promising money was often better than actually handing it over.

Oswald's mouth kinked at the corners, his pale eyes steady on Euan's. "In Jesus' name I accept this as your wife's penance. In London, then, you saw all these people? How are they disposed to us here?"

Euan shook his head. "They don't want to think about Jorvik. We have to watch out for ourselves."

"We have always watched out for ourselves," Oswald said. "There were Christian men and women here when those fools in the south were still smearing blood on trees. They made no comment, I suppose, about this current infestation we are suffering?"

Euan smiled, glad to have arrived so nicely at the kernel of the work. "They said I should come back up here and see what could be done."

Oswald's belly shook in a silent laugh. His clear small eyes stayed fixed on Euan. "And what do you think should be done, Euan?"

Euan raised his eyebrows in what he hoped was a gesture of innocence. "I am here, sir, to find out what you think."

Oswald leaned hard on the staff. "These men are pagans. They must leave Jorvik before they pervert my flock. Including and especially those two young men who are taking advantage of your good wife's kitchen and her gullibility."

Euan bowed his head. "Yes, Father. The issue is how to achieve that. There are a number of the Vikings, far more than

any fighting men we can summon, if the King won't help us. So
we can't just pitch them out."

Oswald said, "To begin with, your wife could throw those
imps out of your house."

"Father, the boys have left."

The old man snorted at him. Although his gaze held steady
on Euan, his talk now swerved off on this other path. "Your wife
is herself impudent and dangerously proud. You should restrain
her better."

"Father, I was out of the city. Arre is a good-hearted woman,
as you know, and people take advantage of her."

"She is a woman, with a woman's special frailties. That's
why God gave men dominion over them, because they cannot
manage for themselves. She must learn humility. Which, consid-
ering where she came from, you would think she had already in
abundance, but no."

Euan's ears went hot; he hated having that thrown in his
face, as his mother did often, that Arre had grown up so low before he married her. He said only, "I was not in Jorvik, Father;
she is very humble around me."

Oswald gave a squawk of a laugh. "You lie, boy." His eyes
half closed. He said, "And in spite of what Otkar and Byrhtnoth
said to you, what goes on in Jorvik is my matter, not yours, and I
will not suffer those pagans to remain here. And since those idiots down in London said you should deal with this, then I want
you to go down there to this Sweyn's camp and tell him to get
out." His lips pursed. His eyes glittered, triumphant. "Good day,
Euan. Thank you for your work on my minster." He turned his
head down toward the design, and nodded. "That is well done.
You have some head for this, I think. But first the Vikings. Go
and get rid of them."

Euan said, "Father, that's hard."

Oswald's lips drew back in a humorless smile. "My son, you
have God on your side."

CHAPTER NINETEEN

At Hrafnsbeck the Bishop went around the hall, sprinkling water, intoning prayers, and waving his hands in the sign of the cross. After he was done Benna set fire to his bed. Every night, she went around the house tipping over chamberpots and pails and scattering ashes. The servants sneaked away; Poppo had to send to a nearby village to have his meals cooked. His guards, and the Germans, saw phantoms everywhere, even where she was not, grown men starting up like rabbits at a shadow, and weeping uncontrollably when the wind blew.

Another ship came by night to the wharf. The whole hall boiled with excitement. She watched the Bishop argue furiously, up and down the hall, with the German captain in the bird coat; by his gestures and his haggard pleading face, she knew Poppo was begging the other to take him with him, but before dawn the German and his men hustled into the ship and left Poppo behind. The Bishop paced up and down the hall, pounding his hands together and grinding his teeth.

She reported this to Corban, as she always did, making pictures for him. As if she had only to imagine them, the pictures appeared under her hands, fast and full of life. He frowned, studying what she told him, his fingers knotted in his beard. She wondered what he saw in this, not caring much; she could not fathom why he was so interested in the doings of these men, when their children were scattered all over the world.

She hated Poppo, who was keeping them here. She drew images of him on the walls of his bed, with stakes through his ears and knives in his tongue; all night he moaned with headache, and sores blossomed on his mouth. The next night he slept outside the bed cupboard, in the open, with the covers over his head.

Soon after that, while Corban was telling her stories of the island, and she was wondering how she could drag the table down on top of Poppo, she heard the clatter of the ladder poles up against the outside of the tower. Voices sounded. They were coming for Corban. She gathered herself up, put her arms around his neck, and rode his shoulder down to the hall.

⟶⟵

"Damn you," Poppo said, his voice rough as a burr, his face haggard. He stood behind the table in his gold-trimmed white coat, and stabbed his finger at Corban. "I have stood quite enough of this. Stop it." His voice caught in a desperate rising whine. "Stop it now—all of it!"

Corban looked around him; the hall was a vast dark empty hollow. Only Poppo and three other men sat behind the table, and those men seemed to lean away from the Bishop, their eyes sleek. There were no servants anywhere in sight. A fine meal stood on the table, roasted meat and fresh bread and cheese and cups of wine, but no one was eating.

Corban brought his gaze back to Poppo and said, "I am doing nothing. You it is who keep me locked away in that tower, with nothing to eat or drink, now, for months. Let me go, and see what happens. Maybe then your merciful and loving Jesus will let you live in peace."

Poppo's face went rigid; he was not too afraid to get angry, and he leaned forward, lowering his arm, his fist clenched. He said, "I'll kill you first. Perhaps God is angry with me because I've been letting you live." But suddenly his forehead shone with sweat. His eyes softened with hope. Corban put his hand up to his throat; she was clinging to him tighter and tighter, so strong she choked him. He wondered that no one else noticed.

The Bishop said, "If I let you go, you would leave Denmark forever. And you would never go to Germany."

"I will not," Corban said. "I am not your slave, nor your man, nor your underling. I'll go where I please." At that, he saw the possibility, and turned and started toward the door, walking fast. She pushed on him, eager, laughing. Behind him, someone, not Poppo, said something under his breath. No one else moved. The door was midway in the long wall of the hall; he remembered Eelmouth slamming down the bar across it, when they were fleeing away from Hakon. There was no bar now. He strode down the room toward it, and no one tried to stop him. A surge of triumph carried him the next few strides. He was going to walk free out that door.

Then the door swung inward, opening, and as if he had summoned him with his thoughts, Hakon came in.

Behind him were a dozen armed men, wearing helmets and chainlink shirts. Corban stopped; she pushed him, hard, but he stood fast. He knew he could not make his way through that wall. Hakon stopped also, his jaw slack. He swung a single wild look down the hall at Poppo and fixed Corban with his gaze again.

He said, "I thought if I came here I might find something interesting, but this exceeds my expectations. Why are you loose?" His attention flickered toward Poppo again and back to Corban. "Why are you alive?" His hand moved, and several of his men came around him and stood by Corban. "I'm taking you to the King. Bishop, you should come, too."

Poppo's voice croaked. "Take him—I meant to send him to the King, but there was—there was a matter of transport. I am going to Bremen from here." He came up the hall toward Hakon, his face hollow as an eggshell, his hands moving. "Nothing of interest—I must speak to—to another bishop, a synod of bishops, in fact—doctrinal matters—"

Midway through this Hakon began talking over him, loud. "I see you have supper ready for us, thank you very much. I for one am hungry. I will speak to you later, but you are going to the King,

I assure you, not to Bremen." He started a step toward the table and turned, his eyes on Corban again. "Join me, wizard?"

Corban pulled on his tangled beard, sorting all this out. After so long alone in the tower, he felt the busyness and uproar of the room like a great swarming around him. Getting out of the tower was one thing, getting away from Hakon would be something else, but at least he was moving again. He said, "Thank you. I have not had meat in a long while." He went to the table, and standing beside Hakon he fed on the Bishop's roast venison.

Poppo sank down on the bench opposite, pale in the cheeks. Hakon's men filled the hall, and the food vanished in a breath. Poppo said, "I must go to Bremen."

"First you must go to the King," Hakon said. "Why were you letting this man walk right out of this hall, just now?"

Poppo's eyes were dull. He stared away down the hall, as if he saw more, or less, than anybody else. "Where is the King?"

"At the Limfjord," Hakon said. "With the fleet that will destroy Sweyn Whoever's-son-he-is and Palnatoki and everybody else who opposes Bluetooth once and for all, and make Christ triumphant forever in Denmark. Don't you want to see it?" He waved at the table. "Bring out the rest of the wine. We're all leaving in the morning anyway, it would only go to waste."

—❧—

Corban offered to walk, but Hakon insisted he ride one of their horses. By midday he was already tired of the saddle and they had far to go. Yet all around him was the sprouting green of the fields, wildflowers in rippling sheets of purple and gold; the sky arched enormously above him. He felt as unbounded as the air, and he could not see enough.

Ahead of him the Bishop and Hakon rode along arguing, Poppo in a flat voice insisting Hakon had no power over him, piling words on words, mentioning books and the Roman Pope and Jesus as proofs Hakon had no power over him, the while Hakon was carrying him away into the north. Hakon fended him off with sarcasms and pretended ignorance and deference to the King.

They traveled through woods and wild places, and by broad farms, plowed fields, often a cluster of buildings in the distance; once the people had come out to watch them pass by, had stood there open-mouthed by the side of the road, amazed. In the evening Hakon sent most of his men ahead of them, and shortly they rode up to a hall.

It stood empty, except for Hakon's men by the door; the table inside was set for a dinner, and the meat was on the spit over the fire, and the bread was warm in the baskets, but nobody else was there. Hakon led them all in, and they sat at the table and ate.

"This is the kind of magic I like," Hakon said. He glanced at Corban, sitting on the bench down to his right. "Sword-magic. More reliable than either Thor or Christ."

Poppo made the sign of the cross at him. He was drunk. "God have mercy on you. The wizard at least blasphemes from ignorance, but you, you have seen the truth, and love lies anyway."

Hakon made a wordless snarl at him. Corban wondered where the true owners of the hall were now, probably hiding out in the woods. He said, "Until you face somebody with stronger swords. You handled Grayfur well enough, I guess."

Hakon laughed, a flash of white teeth in the round circle of his trim little beard. "Not Grayfur. Gold-Harald caught him coming ashore in the Limfjord with only two ships of men and took him easily. I had more trouble with Gold-Harald than I expected."

"Why are you still here?" Corban said.

Hakon gave a start. His fingers tapped on the arm of the high seat. "What are you talking about?"

"It was Grayfur drove you out of Norway," Corban said. "But Grayfur's dead now. The Ericssons are finished."

The long fingers drummed hard on the carved wooden lion head at the end of the arm of the high seat. "The King needs me here yet, until he destroys Palnatoki."

Corban was tired, and ahead of him was Bluetooth, whom he was supposed to bring down, but who seemed always stronger than before, whose power was drawing everything into his grasp, not only Corban but Conn and Raef, too, with Sweyn, all of them wheeling helplessly down toward some black center. He said, "Then who will he set on you?"

"What?" Hakon turned and stared at him. Beyond him, Poppo was dozing, his head tipped forward and his mouth ajar.

Corban said, "Why do you think you're any different from the others?"

Hakon met his eyes, for once, direct, intent. "He's the King. I'm only the Jarl. But I'm to have Norway." He paid out the words like money, buying something.

Corban looked away, wanting to sleep; he could feel Benna warm around him, weary also. He said, "Whatever you say. I'm going to find a bed, Hakon. Good night."

⚊⚬⚊

Hakon stared ahead across the hall, his hands fisted in front of him. The wizard had told him nothing that had not occurred to him before.

He had thought about it and pushed it out of the way, into the back of his mind, but now he was thinking about it again.

He had done everything right. When Grayfur moved against his father, Hakon had been in another part of the country; hearing of the old man's wicked murder, he had wasted no time trying to fight back right away. Instead he had taken all his ships, and while Grayfur's fleets waited for him in the inside passages he sailed far out to the open sea and fared south well out of sight of land, and came to Denmark. There, seeing how that sea ran, he had taken Christ for his God, although the rituals bored him and the priests set his teeth on edge. He had made himself so useful to the King, so close in his counsel, that Bluetooth had offered him Norway. In the course of things, he had gotten Grayfur killed, avenging his father's murder, which still gave him a deep satisfaction whenever he thought of it.

Yet he was stuck down here in Denmark, running Bluetooth's errands for him. He had to go back to Norway, which was a wreck and a ruin after years under the Ericssons, but he could not get away. Instead he wasted his time here chasing boys in a cockleshell ship and escorting this bishop, whom he trusted even less than Bluetooth.

All around the hall his men were lying down for the night, moving in on benches already full, curling up on the floor near the fire with their heads on each other's ankles. The Bishop had slumped over sideways on the bench, and one of his servants came up quietly and roused him with some difficulty and took him away. Hakon pretended not to notice. He knew the Bishop was lying about going to Bremen; his itch to be out of Denmark was like a visible rash. Something was going on.

Take him to Bluetooth. Make Bluetooth deal with it.

Then what the wizard had said came back to him, like a knife in the gut, and he set his teeth, and sat there, sleepless in the quiet hall, thinking.

⚯

Eelmouth said, "You know what I'd do. What Bloodaxe would have done. Seize Jorvik and take what we need. The ships, the supplies."

Sweyn said nothing. On the far side of the fire from him, the captain who had joined them only yesterday waggled his knife at

him like a chiding finger. "You should move up to Orkney. You'll
find men there in plenty, all ready to go aviking." His name was
Thorkel. He was cutting his fingernails and flicking them into
the fire. "But Eelmouth is right, burn Jorvik first."

Sweyn grunted at them, irritated at their constant advice. He
wished Conn would come back. He moved his gaze over the
camp around him, once again counting the men there; he had ac-
cumulated nearly a hundred, with more arriving every day, so
many he had moved his camp up from the river bar into the
meadow south of the old Roman embankment. From here he
looked out over a spotty ground of campfires and tangles of gear
and men lying and sitting and walking around, among them people from the city, a bakerwoman with a basket full of bread,
down there, surrounded by Vikings, and idle barefoot town boys,
and here and there some other tradesman, a tinker, a cobbler sitting cross-legged on the ground mending shoes, people with
bundles of firewood on their backs.

But only a few of these. In the beginning many more peddlers
and hucksters had come down here, bringing everything his men
needed. He cast a look up over his shoulder at the city, rising
behind him on its bank, with the spire of the church at the top. Eelmouth, who still knew people in the city, brought him all the ru-
mors and gossip, and he knew that every day this Oswald, the
Archbishop here, was blasting sermons from his pulpit against
Christians who consorted with pagans. People were obeying him:
The bakerwoman in front of him was the first all day selling bread,
and now her basket was empty, and she was walking away, leaving
an angry little crowd behind her.

"Hey! I'm hungry!"

Eelmouth was right, seize the place. He had enough men,
now. This Archbishop was a fool to brace him. He felt the rising
temper in him like a heat, blurring everything.

That was not good. He made himself think cold again. If he

was to be a King he had to stand above pride. He had to avoid making stupid mistakes for pride's sake. Taking Jorvik, he saw, was a stupid mistake, likely to bog him down here, when he needed to get on to Denmark and take up his destiny. Going to Orkney meant going even farther away. He didn't want to be a Viking, he wanted to go challenge Bluetooth, overcome him, and bring justice to Denmark again.

His chest tightened, his belly knotted up. It didn't matter anyway, because he couldn't get out of Jorvik. That was the core of the problem: While he had over a hundred men, his fleet was only two ships, his own, and the battered old dragon Thorkel and his crew had rowed in the previous morning from the north. The rest of his army were men off the ships in Jorvik's river harbor, who could easily disappear as soon as their previous ships left.

Other things were going wrong. Gunnhild had given him some money, but that was used up. She herself had disappeared, and if Eelmouth had recourse to more money he would not admit it. Sweyn had gotten no word yet from Palnatoki, and there was no sign of Conn. Rubbed up against the realities of the world, his great design was unraveling like a worn blanket.

"Who's that?" Eelmouth said, and Sweyn lifted his eyes.

A townsman was coming across the camp toward him, tall and angular, his hat jammed down on his head, and his long coat gripped up in his hands out of the dirt. He was alone. Not important enough to have men to attend him. Or very sure of himself.

Sweyn dusted his hands off and got up. The townsman came up to the fire and said, "Are you the leader of these men?" His gaze rested on Sweyn; he knew already.

"I am Sweyn Haraldsson," Sweyn said. Eelmouth and Thorkel were still lounging by the fire, watching them. Probably everybody was watching. Sweyn's temper edged him again. "Who are you and what do you want?"

The townsman lifted his head an inch, annoyed. Arrogant

purse-fingerer, Sweyn thought. The other man said, in a level voice, "My name is Euan Woodwrightson. I speak for the King, and the Archbishop—"

"Your Archbishop!" Sweyn said. "Tell him if he keeps on preventing your people from selling to my men I'll burn his church around his ears. As for your king, he's not giving orders to anybody anymore, I've heard."

The townsman reared back, his face darkening. "What you've heard. What I've heard, Sweyn Somebody's-son, is you have a great enemy, who will come on you shortly, and we want you well clear of Jorvik when that time comes."

Sweyn could not hold himself back anymore. He bounded on the townsman, got him by the back of his fancy coat, and hauled him off out of the camp. After a brief useless struggle the townsman submitted, snarling. Laughter rose from the men watching. Sweyn dumped him on the ground at the edge of the camp and prodded him with his foot. An easy derisive cheer rose from all sides.

"You want something well clear, try this—I'll get what I need, whatever it takes. Tell that to your Archbishop. Get out." He turned and strolled slowly away, back toward his fire, giving the townsman every chance to jump him.

Nothing happened. Sweyn walked in among the other men; Eelmouth stood with his eyebrows cocked up, and Thorkel was tossing his knife up and down. When Sweyn looked back, the tall townsman was gone.

Eelmouth said, "I know him from somewhere, that one."

Thorkel said, "He's a high-up fahrman, is who he is." He nodded at Sweyn, smiling gap-toothed, his eyes bright. "He's got money, ships—take him for ransom and we'll get somewhere."

Sweyn pulled on his beard with his fingers, his temper cooling, and considered what had happened. He wondered if he had just made another mistake. This one, though, he thought he could work with. "Not ransom," he said. He pulled on his beard, his mind twisting and turning after all the possibilities in this. "But we have to get him in a place where we can lean on him. Eelmouth, come here."

⸻

Euan came home in a black temper, and would not speak to her, but settled over his tallies and his counting board. Arre went into her garden, which she was getting ready for the spring planting. She pulled up beanstalks and chucked away rocks for a while, but she came soon to the end of the garden, where even in the summer nothing grew but flowers, and she sat down there in the dead weeds and prayed.

Oswald the Archbishop had sent to her to come to be cleansed. Now that the boys were gone, he would forgive her. He would hear her repentance, he said, and then take her back into the congregation, and all would be well. She prayed for a while, paters and credos in rows and rows, but she was still angry.

She could not go back there. He had humiliated her for doing good. In front of everybody, withholding the Body of Christ from her. Yet she had done nothing, except obey God.

She sat thinking about Jesus, as she loved to do when she prayed, how he walked with ordinary people, how he worked his miraculous kindness with people as lowborn as she was. That seemed to her the way to follow, Jesus' kindness, his givingness, his everyday goodness. Yet this priest attacked her kindness in Jesus' name. She thought, Oswald has stolen my Christ.

Startled, she crossed herself, warm with guilt: That surely was blasphemous. She prayed again for help, for guidance, and the thought came again into her head, His church is not my church.

She sat rigid, her hands gripped together before her. She wondered if Benna had infected her with some fearful heresy.

But these thoughts made more sense to her than what the Archbishop Oswald said.

She crossed herself again. The whirling uncertainty settled around her, but in a different shape than before. She saw what she had to do. Henceforth she would pray to her own Jesus. And to his blessed mother, who enclosed him in her womb, who nursed him, who stood at the foot of the cross, closer than anybody to him. The Pope's church after all came down from Peter, who was only Jesus' friend, and who three times denied him.

As Oswald himself, she saw with a start, denied Jesus, when he condemned her for doing good.

It all fit now. She felt very calm. She knew what she would do. She saw she could go back to Mass, to the congregation, even accept the Archbishop's silly rite of repentance, because in that false church also lay, somewhere, her true church. And now with a sudden upwelling she felt the grace of God upon her, the comfort she needed, the peace, and she put her head in her hands and wept.

⤙⤚

Aelfu saw Arre in the garden, praying, and went carefully around her. Ama, she thought. Ama. She knew Arre was sad and wished she could make her happy again. Then Arre would love her more than Edward.

She thought of her mother less now. She thought she had been wrong, and her mother was really dead. Or maybe Arre was really her mother and they had to hide this from Edward and Euan. If Arre were really her mother, she wouldn't have to worry about Edward. As she stole out through the garden gate, not opening it, but fitting herself carefully in between two wooden slats, she thought she would find something for Arre, something nice, to make her happy again.

The gate opened in a lane, but just at the top of the lane was the busy street where the fountain was. She ran that way, drawn to the sounds and smells. Sometimes she remembered the island, where everything had been so different, so quiet, so empty of people, but the streets of Jorvik were wonderful and every day she remembered less.

She went up to the big open space where the fountain was, and watched the carts roll here and there, the wheels rumbling on the wooden street, splashing in the muck of the fountain square. She leaned against a wall, her hands behind her. She kept an eye out for boys, who would chase her, but nobody else heeded her ever.

A little herd of swine trotted briskly down from the big bar in the city wall; their skins were pink and spotty and they smelled bad. The woman herding them kept them moving with bangs of her long switch. A moment later the Archbishop himself came by, talking to a monk; they stopped almost in front of her and stood looking up at the spire of the church, and the fierce-eyed old man drew shapes in the air with his hands.

She went on down the hill, toward the Coppergate, looking for something to make Ama Arre feel better. There were no flowers here, but she might find a pretty stone, a feather. She skipped as she went. The air was sharp against her face, but it would not rain; she could feel spring coming, all around her.

Ahead of her voices rose, and she went quickly over to the edge of the street, out of the way. Down there, people were shouting, louder and louder, and—she saw, with a jerk of fear—some of them were Vikings, like her brother and Raef. She went up closer to them, wary, staying in the back of everything. She looked for her brother and for Raef, although she knew they were gone.

That was good, actually. She missed them, and wished she'd told them good-bye, but they didn't belong here. If they came back something bad might happen.

She could see the men arguing now. One was the man who kept the alehouse there, and he was standing in the door of his shop, his hand on the latch, and shouting.

"I can close my shop if I want to!"

"We came here to buy—we have money, damn you—let us in!" The Vikings crowded in toward him.

"My shop is closed!"

"He's closed up, can't you see—" Some other townspeople were pushing into the fight, taking the brewer's side.

"We have money!"

"Damn foreign trash!"

"Why don't you all get out of here?"

"We're not going anywhere until we get some ale!"

"Get out! Get out!" From all over the Coppergate now people swarmed down, shouting, their arms raised. Aelfu crept in along the wall of the alehouse, pressed against the withy wall; the mass of bodies before her hid what was happening, and she squatted down to peer between people's legs.

The crowd around her roared so hard her skin tingled and her hair stood on end. She shrank back hard against the withy wall of the alehouse. The brewer screeched and dashed into his shop and slammed the door. The close-jammed people before her surged ahead, and she heard screams, and a rock thudded into the wall above her shoulder.

In front of her the crowd shattered. Some of it ran down the street and some ran up and some stood and some fell, and the Vikings rushed and charged around them, beating at them with swords and sticks. She hunched down as small as she could get. She put her hands over her face and watched through her fingers. A bloody boy fell to the ground before her. A big man with a horrible round hole in his face where his mouth should have been stormed up toward her, his knotted arms swinging a sword before him to clear his way.

From the top of the Coppergate the crowd rushed back down. Aelfu bit her fingers. She held her breath. The man with the hole in his face stood square, his sword raised, shouting, and the Vikings around him rushed up beside him, and the crowd swept down on them and the sword hacked and blood sprayed up, an arc of blood drops hanging in the air.

The townspeople were scattering away. The bloody boy sprang up off the ground and darted into the lane. The street emptied, except for the Vikings, yelling and stamping around. Two of them ran at the alehouse and began beating on the door. Aelfu cowered down, afraid to move. Then the man with the hole in his face saw her there.

He stalked toward her. His eyes fixed on her, and her breath stuck in her throat. She crouched herself down as small as she could. She felt his gaze like a hot dirty hand taking hold of her. Then a horn sounded, three long blasts.

He straightened, his gaze leaving her, looking up the street. One of the men at the alehouse door said, "Who's that?"

The other said, "Kill him."

"No." The man with the hole in his face held out one hand to keep them where they were. "Everything's on the plan. That's the King's man. Somebody go get Sweyn."

Down from the top of the Coppergate came a lone man, in one hand a brass horn. Aelfu lifted her head, surprised. It was Euan.

She stayed small. She did not like Euan, who had somehow made her mother go away, and it startled her to see him here, walking alone and unarmed down toward the pack of Vikings; she wondered what he would do if he saw her.

His hat was jammed down on his head. He tossed the horn aside as he walked. His eyes were on the man with the hole in his face, who took a long step forward, put his hands on his hips, and shouted, "You! Tell these pigs to give us what we want or we'll take it, and to hell with them!"

Euan stopped; he had on the long coat he wore around the house, its hem and sleeves and collar soft with brown fur, and his soft house shoes; he must have rushed out the door to come here. He said, "Where is Sweyn Haraldsson?"

The hole-faced man said, "That's not what you called him before."

"I'm calling him that now," Euan said calmly. "Where is he?"

"He's not here. We want ale, and bread, and we want it now, or this street will run blood, I'm telling you."

Around the edges of the street, in the lanes, in the windows, the townspeople began to appear, looking out, waiting. Aelfu heard the alehouse door open. Euan stood alone in the middle of the street, his hands at his sides, facing the Vikings.

"Send for him," he said. "I will only talk to him."

The hole-faced man took a step forward. The sword in his hand had blood on it. He was staring hard at Euan now and his forehead creased. "I know you from—" Abruptly his face jerked into a furious scowl. "Now I remember you! You're that trouble-making brat! From when Eric was the King!"

Euan stood his ground. "I remember you, too, Eelmouth, and I wouldn't deal with you if you were God. I'll talk to Sweyn and no other."

Eelmouth let out a roar and strode forward, the sword cocked in his hand, and then another man walked up between him and Euan.

"Wait! Everybody stand fast!"

The whole street fell still. The newcomer stood in the middle of the street, his hands out, as if he pressed Euan and Eelmouth apart. Aelfu held her breath; she had not noticed how many people were out here, the pack of the Vikings, and the swarming townspeople in the windows and yards. She fastened her eyes on the newcomer. He was young, not much older than Conn, his long curly hair red-gold, his wispy growing beard more gold than red. He was beautiful, she thought, and her heart lifted in a sudden gust of feeling.

Euan was still glaring at Eelmouth, but now he turned slightly to face Sweyn. "Your men here were about to get into a lot of trouble."

Eelmouth let out another yell. "I'll give you trouble—
Sweyn, let me kill him. You don't know what he did."

Sweyn's face flushed red; he said, "Put up your sword, damn
you. Everybody get back."

Eelmouth stood where he was. "I'm telling you, Sweyn—"
Sweyn lunged at him, furious. "No, I'm telling you!" He got
Eelmouth by the front of the shirt and pushed him back two
steps, wobbling, staggering, and then stepped away, and wheeled
toward Euan.

"Do you want me to let him loose on you? Start talking to
me, townman, if you want to live!"

A breathless silence fell on the street. Euan stood a little
crooked, one shoulder higher than the other, as if he heaved himself against some great weight. From the corners and windows
and alleys the townspeople peeped out, watching. Eelmouth
waited a moment where Sweyn had left him, the sword dangling
from his hand, and then turned on his heel and strode off through
the pack of the Vikings.

Euan said, "Sweyn, what do you want?"

Sweyn lifted his red-gold head. He had blue eyes, bright and
vivid in his sun-darkened face. Aelfu thought he was the most
wonderful man she had ever seen; she longed for him to look at
her.

He looked only at Euan. He said, "I want what you want of
me, townman—to leave Jorvik."

Euan said slowly, "Then what can I do to make that happen?"

The blue eyes blazed. "Can you speak for that?"

"I have no idea," Euan said, but his voice was smoother and
his shoulders settled, even again. He nodded toward the big oak
tree on the corner. "Come over here, and let's talk about it, and
see."

Sweyn nodded. Turning to the Vikings, he said, "Thorkel,
get them back to camp."

One of the Vikings said, "You need help."

"Get them out of here," Sweyn said, and turned to Euan. "Let's go, then." They started down toward the oak tree. The Vikings burst into low talk; they turned and started away down the street toward the river. Aelfu burst up from the ground by the wall and sprinted away home.

⸙

Sweyn said, "I understand Conn Corbansson is your nephew. He is in my company."

"Not by blood," Euan said. He wondered how Sweyn had found that out and realized the prince had been asking about him. "He's half Irish, anyway."

"Still you might favor his fortunes," Sweyn said.

Euan gave a laugh, startled at the notion his nephews had fortunes. They walked in beneath the widespread canopy of the oak; the buds of the leaves were just opening, and the tangled mass of branches shone with a fresh new green. He said, "I favor the fortunes of Jorvik. Therefore I will help you get out of here."

Sweyn followed on his heels. "I need ships. I have an army. I mean to go against my father Bluetooth, and seize Denmark. If you give me ships, I promise I will remember your help when I am King."

Euan snorted. He moved closer under the oak tree, toward the trunk, away from the curious men in the street. The trunk of the tree was deep-carved with signs and crosses. The city pigs kept the ground under it bare as a street, and the tops of the roots were burnished knobs in the dust. "You have all the chance of snow in August."

"How do you know?" Sweyn turned sharply, following him with his eyes. "What do you know about it?"

Euan leaned against the trunk of the tree, the bark rough

against him even through the layers of his clothes. "Bluetooth has been King forever. This puny little army you have—"

"I'll draw more men, when I blood him."

Euan gave a shake of his head. He had worked on his accounts all morning; three of the captains now in the river owed him money, and he saw all this money vanishing into the air, as money had a way of doing. He eyed Sweyn once more, seeing a green boy here, dewy-cheeked, incapable of seeing what had to be.

Of course, he thought, that meant he might change what had to be.

It was a slim chance. Euan knew better than to think well of it. This money would be lost as soon as he gave it away. But doing this, getting the Vikings out of here, would put him up over Oswald, would make them notice him, down there in Wessex. Even with all else that was going on, they would know of him, down there.

He said, "I will give you ships."

Sweyn surged toward him a step, his hands rising, as if he would snatch these ships out of the air. "How many?"

"Two dragons and a kog. In the harbor now. Your army"— he smiled, to show Sweyn what he thought of this army—"will fit into them easily enough, I think."

"I need bread, and ale. Other supplies."

Euan pulled a face, although he had anticipated that. "I shall have them taken to your camp. But you must keep your men in your camp."

"I will."

"Can you?"

At that the young man's head jerked up, and even in the shadow of the oak tree his eyes blazed. "Yes. Damn you."

"Un-uh," Euan said mildly. "You haven't got anything yet. You need me. And you will leave within the week."

"More men are coming here. I must be here to meet them."

"One week."

"When will you bring the food to my camp?"

"I'll have it there before nightfall. Enough for one week."

"Two weeks."

"The second week when you leave."

"Agreed."

Euan watched him a moment, judging how to broach this, and went straight at it. "And when you are King, you will help me bring a dansker King to Jorvik."

The prince lowered his head a little, the shadows on his face like a mask. "What? You had one. You threw him out."

"Eric was a bad King," Euan said. "Better no King at all than a bad King."

"But now you want another."

"I want a King not English. While the English have a King, we need one." He put the bait out there again, shiny bright. "You could give us one."

"Well," Sweyn said. He put his hand out. "First I shall be King of Denmark."

Euan took his hand, the clasp strong and dry, and for a moment thought, with a heady excitement, that he had won something. But then Sweyn stood back, and started off, and Euan saw again he was just a boy, and he remembered his father talking about Bluetooth, and his grandfather talking about Bluetooth, and he shook his head and told himself he was a fool. He started down to the river, to dicker the ships away from their captains. A hawk screamed somewhere. In the Coppergate, already, people were back to business, as if there had never been Vikings here. Up on the slope the church bell rang nones. He would have to hurry, to get the food to Sweyn's camp. The hawk shrieked again, a piercing cry like a woman's voice. He went down to the river.

Arre stooped and hugged Aelfu tight a moment. "Now, just wait here, until I call you."

"Ama—" Aelfu held tight to her skirt. "Don't go."

"I must. It will be all right." Arre kissed her and Miru again and put the little girl's hand in Aelfu's. "Now, wait. Remember what I told you."

Aelfu felt like crying. She clutched Miru's hand tight. They stood in the doorway of the church, with the warm sun on their backs, and the gloom before them. In there the terrible old man waited. If he called them in, then they would stay here forever and forever.

If he sent them out—if he sent them away—

Her stomach heaved. She wished she had brought something to eat.

"Ow," Miru said, and pulled her hand out of Aelfu's grip.

Aelfu got hold of her sister again. Arre was walking away from them, her hands pressed together, her head bent. When she reached the old man she knelt down before him. He stooped over her slightly. His hand rose. Aelfu through the bleary tears in her eyes saw him gigantic, glowing in the dark. With one word he could send her and her sister into hell. With one word save them. Her knees wobbled.

Then he was straightening. Arre was straightening up off her knees. They were turning toward Aelfu and Miru, and the fearsome old man beckoned to them.

Aelfu took Miru's hand again, as Arre had said she should, and led her forward. "Now, be good, Miru." She could not look at him; she fixed her gaze on the floor at his feet, and walked up before him.

"So these are the small girls." His voice tolled like a bell over them. "Yes, they have a very Irish look about them." He laughed, an odd kind rumble of a sound. "Non anglae sed angelae," he said, and his hand descended onto Aelfu's head.

She flinched an instant, and then steadied, feeling the warmth and weight of the hand, his power, now cast around her and her sister, too. Suddenly her heart buoyed up. She lifted her face up to look at him, and found him smiling down at her. He moved his hand down to cradle her chin.

"We will bring these children to Christ, Arre," he said. "They are too beautiful to be damned."

"Yes, Father," Arre said. She stooped, and picked Miru up. Aelfu stayed where she was, smiling up at him, who had saved her.

"Say 'Thank you, Father,'" Arre murmured.

"Thank you, Father," Aelfu said. She thought she had never been so happy. He was turning away already, making some sign over her as he went, but she was here now, she belonged here. She felt suddenly light as a sunbeam. Turning, she skipped after Arre, walking out of the church.

CHAPTER TWENTY

The sun was hot and bright for so early in the year, and Euan was sweating under his coat. Beside him on the river bar Sweyn Haraldsson was staring at the kog, anchored in the deep water on the far side of the river, and now he turned sharply around.

"I can't use that ship."

"It's a perfectly sound ship." Euan shrugged half out of his coat. He had known the kog would be a problem. Fat as a sow, with the high freeboard and beaky prows of a river trader, the ship had come into Jorvik carrying a load of sheep, and the stink reached him from here.

Sweyn said, "You told me three ships. I need dragons."

Euan laid his hands together, rubbing his fingers, looking for the way through this. He said, "This is a sound ship, fulfilling my promise. You can't change the terms of the agreement now." He saw Sweyn was not listening, was staring away up the river bar, and he turned to look. All over the river bar the crowds of men were quieting, all staring toward the broad sloping way down from the bank.

A woman was walking down toward them. She wore a long white gown glittering with gemstones. The long hair hanging in a thick braid down her back was streaked with gray, but she walked like a young woman. Euan recognized her at once although he had not seen her in twenty years, and remembering what had happened then he stepped back and turned his eyes down and bowed deep to her, getting well out of her way, out of her notice.

She went straight by him. She gave off an elusive dry fragrance he could smell only when he didn't try to. Her gown rustled like feathers and sparkled all over in the sunlight. She went up to Sweyn and said, "Well, Bluetooth's son, are you ready to set forth?"

"My army is larger every day," Sweyn said. Euan knew that only that morning another ship had arrived, with more men to join him. He glanced toward the kog, seeing possibilities here.

Gunnhild Kingsmother faced the young man straight on, with no deference. Behind her stood old Sweyn Eelmouth, carrying her cloak. Everybody was watching her. She spoke in a clear loud voice like an order. "You have to set out at once," she said. "Bluetooth is gathering a fleet; he means to attack you. He gets stronger every day. You must strike first, now."

Sweyn stood solid before her, his hands on the hilt of his sword. "Where is Conn?"

"I left them down at Humbermouth, along with two more dragons of men from Orkney, come to join you. They will hold anyone coming into the river until you get there. But you must go, now, Sweyn, he has fifty ships already."

"Did you see anything of Palnatoki?"

"No. Funen was too far for me."

Sweyn turned to Euan. "I need another dragon."

Euan fixed his gaze on Sweyn and tried to ignore the woman now watching him, too. He kept his mind on what he wanted. He said, "That is the only ship available. It's here, now, when you need it, take it, it will serve." He gave Sweyn a sop, and a chance to accept easily: "I will add three more days' worth of supplies, seventeen days in all, and I'll bring all down at once, this afternoon."

Sweyn didn't bother to argue. He turned to Gunnhild and said, "I'll leave as soon as everything's on board. Where is Bluetooth now?"

"In the Limfjord, in the eastern bay. He has Hakon's fleet with him, and more ships every day join him."

Euan drew back. He knew something of how the land and water lay in Denmark; the Limfjord was a chain of sounds and inlets that reached the sea only at the eastern end, and the bay there was accessible only by narrow passages from the sea. Tucked inside it Bluetooth would be virtually impregnable until he chose to move. Quietly Euan backed up again, eager to get away from Gunnhild. He thought again that this was money gone to hell, all this lavished on Sweyn, although now he saw some chance of recovering the kog, at least.

Aside from that, he had satisfied Oswald's demands, and done it in the name of the King. That was currency he had no way of valuing, yet, especially as word had come from Wessex only that morning that the King was failing.

Sweyn was talking to some other men, giving them orders. He seemed capable enough. Still, it was a lot of money, and likely for nothing. He hoped Bluetooth never found out about it. He wondered if there were a way to get in with Bluetooth, too, so that he won out either way.

As he thought that, on Sweyn's far side, Gunnhild Kingsmother lifted her eyes and looked at him. Euan started. He blinked. For an instant his mind seemed stuck. He wondered what he had just been thinking about. She and Sweyn were moving off. The day was clear and strangely bright and empty. He went up toward his storehouse, to arrange for the supplies.

⸺✦⸺

She had told him to attack Bluetooth. She had not told him how.

Sweyn poked at the fire; the dark was settling down around them, and the day's dank drizzle was turning into a steady cold rain. He had rigged up an awning from his ship for a tent. The rest of his men were spread out in their own quick shelters down the beach. Where the soft waves purred along the high-tide line, the dragons reared up their high curled heads, barely visible in the streaming dark.

So far things had gone smoothly. He had rowed out of Jorvik

with six ships, counting the kog, which Euan Woodwrightson had packed so full of supplies there was hardly room for the crew. They reached Humbermouth and found Conn and Raef waiting there with the dragonfly, and four more ships, men come down from the north, bored farmers, old enemies of Bluetooth's, shiftless Vikings, green boys looking for their first fight, with hardly three swords between them.

Sweyn distributed these men into the nine dragons, divided up the supplies among them, and left the kog behind. He knew the townsman would reclaim it immediately; but Euan had done him some favors, and he might need more from him, later on.

With fair skies and a following wind, they sailed from Humbermouth across the sea to the wild Frisian coast and followed it north, fighting against a headwind the whole way. Now he was hauled out on the lee shore of one of the long sandy spits off the west coast of Denmark, and the rain was tailing off, and when it stopped the wind would likely swing around.

Now he had to do something, and he had no idea what.

Where he was he had been before. He knew that the western edge of the Limfjord began somewhere not too far north of where he was and a little inland, in a chaos of marshes and coves that trickled eastward toward the broad bays and narrow channels that fed into the Danish Sea. Somewhere in that entanglement of land and sea, Bluetooth lay with his great fleet.

If Sweyn sailed on, up through the narrow ways between Denmark and Norway, to attack him from the east, Bluetooth would know he was coming for long days before he got there, would set some trap.

He would have to see the trap first. Lay some countertrap. At least he knew those waters well.

He stared into the fire, trying to pick this apart into some kind of plan. Someone else came in under the awning, dumping down a heavy pack; he glanced around and saw Raef Corbansson settling down nearby.

Raef kept his eyes on the fire. Sweyn knew he would not speak until someone spoke to him. Sweyn remembered wishing he could get rid of Raef, but now he liked him better, not just for Conn's sake. He was strong and sure, and he thought deep: Kveld-Raef, some of the others were already calling him, for his twilight gloom.

Sweyn looked into the fire again. He wondered if he could get his men to carry their ships across the strip of coast between the North Sea into the western end of the Limfjord, wherever that was. He had heard of men doing that in the long river voyaging of Gardarik, to the east.

Off in the rainy dark the other men were still bustling around. Conn had gotten a huge gang of them together to forage, not by giving orders, but by doing it himself. Conn seemed always happy, whatever he was doing. Sweyn endured a pang of resentment and envy. It was evil to think ill of someone for being happy all the time. He felt hollowed out, an unworthy man. He struggled to hold his sense of his destiny, but he felt as if he were dissolving away, all his special graces an illusion, until he disappeared, like a grain of sand into the sandy beach. Maybe he could never be King.

He thought of what a great King would be like, tall and strong, like a father to the whole kingdom, a good father. When he thought that, a deep old knife turned in him. He glanced out of the corner of his eye at Raef, who had taken an awl from his pack and was mending his outlandish bear-fur boots. He thought of what he knew about Raef, but pretended not to.

He said, "Where did you get those boots?"

Raef shot him a shy sideways look. "From—where we lived. My aunt made them for me. Conn has some, too, but he won't wear them."

"Conn's mother," Sweyn said.

Raef cleared his throat and looked away, and mumbled something, and bent over his work with the awl. Sweyn said, "When I was a child I thought Palnatoki was my father."

Raef turned to look full at him. "I thought so, when we met you first. He favors you so much, he always puts you forward. Doesn't he have any sons?"

"Several. They're around. One is famous, Apple-Odd. He's in Gardarik somewhere, a far-voyager."

"Apple-Odd," Raef said. "That's a strange name."

Sweyn rubbed his hands together. "You don't know the story? Well, you wouldn't. Palnatoki used to be a famous bowman. When he and Bluetooth were much younger they were friends, until one night at a feasting they both got very drunk and Bluetooth commanded Palnatoki to shoot an apple off his son's head. He shot the apple clean, drunk as he was, but he's never touched a bow since. That was Odd, the son, so he's Apple-Odd."

"Palnatoki said he would meet us, didn't he?" Raef said. "Where do you suppose he is now?"

"I don't know. There's been no word from him. He's . . ." Sweyn tapped his fingers on his knee, turning his gaze back into the fire. "He's not much of a fighter. I always felt . . . He never repaid Bluetooth for doing that to him. I have always thought that was very small of him." He turned toward Raef. "I don't know if I can count on him for this."

Then suddenly Conn was pushing in under the awning, loud and wet, and carrying a sack. "Thought you were done for the night, hah?" From the sack he dumped out several flat glistening fish. Sweyn yelped, delighted; he grabbed for one of the slippery bodies and pulled out his belt knife. Conn said, "Find some cooking rocks, Raef. It's pouring out there. I'm already soaked." He sat down across the fire from Sweyn, smiling wide, his hair sodden against his head.

They cooked the fish on flat rocks and ate. The rain beat hard on the awning. Sweyn flipped the fishbones into the fire, thinking again of how to attack Bluetooth. Conn laid more wood on the bed of coals; he was steaming, giving off a strong fragrance of sweat and dirt and fish guts. He said, "Raef. Did you tell him?"

Raef hunched up his shoulders, picking the last shreds of white fish meat from the ladder of bones on the rock in front of him. A piece of skin like a silvery tapestry lay under the bones. Sweyn said, "Tell me what?"

Raef glanced at him and back at the fish. "You know Corban is not my father."

Conn snorted. "Not that, clamhead."

Sweyn, pleased, knew something had happened between him and Raef. He said, "I know."

Raef nodded, his jaws moving, chewing up fish. He swallowed, and said, still looking down at the flat rock, "There is a way between the seas here."

Sweyn twitched, sitting up straight, and fixed his gaze on Raef. "What?"

"I can . . ." Raef shut his eyes. "I know this. Don't ask me how. Up a little way the coast opens, there's a way through all this stretch of land here to the sea on the far side."

"Can you pilot us through it?"

Raef's head bobbed. Sweyn stared at him, wondering about this with a tingling excitement; he realized that Raef was talking about the Limfjord. It was true, he had heard in the past that sometimes in stormy winters the western end of the Limfjord breached and the sea rushed in. If it were so now, then they might catch Bluetooth from behind, and unawares. He looked past Raef to Conn, and met his clear gray eyes, and Conn smiled at him.

"All right," Sweyn said. He stood, stooped under the awning, and went to gather his captains.

⸺⸻⸺

They sailed in the murk of a foggy, rainy dawn, Conn and Raef in the dragonfly leading the way. Sweyn had each of the captains put a torch on the prow of his ship, so that they could stay on course in the gloom. Behind the dragonfly the row of fuzzy lights stretched away until the fog swallowed them.

The sea ran northward here. The beach lay just off the steerboard side; Raef tracked it by the sound of the surf. He felt the land ahead of him for a long seamless stretch of sand. The rain lessened, and the air turned colder, icy on his face.

He felt the land sink, ahead, and the sea running over it. The tide was rising and the water was rushing in over the land, threaded through a single deep channel only a hundred feet wide. The fog was thick around him, although at the mastheads the sun shone warm and bright. He said, "Pick up," and when Conn lifted his oars out of the water, Raef pivoted the ship around to face the land. "Rough water," he said.

Conn said, "Let's go."

Ahead of them the shore lay in a broad flat stretch of sand and fen. Where the sea had broken through the water was pouring in, fighting to get in, and it jerked and tossed the ship like a leaf, crashed white up over her shoulder and drenched them, and flung them sideways, the bow rising. Rowing hard they got around and skated down along the slope of a wave and over a boiling pothole into the narrow channel. Abruptly the channel turned in a wild thundering crash of surf, something buried in there forcing the surging water sharply off to the right in a great slick bulge. Shouting back and forth, hauling the oars through the violent water, they kept the ship out of the foam and lined up with the race; then abruptly the dragonfly was skimming out onto a broad, open stretch of water, with the last of the fog seeping up into a cloudless blue sky, low flat shores in the distance to the north, and a headland to the south. The wild water sank down beneath the surface; around them the water turned glassy smooth, and they drifted along on a still lake.

Far off, on the shore, geese were honking in great numbers. Down in the south rose the thin smoke of a village. Raef's neck prickled up; he thought irresistibly of his home, of the island, lost forever. He shook that off. Turning to the east he stared at the distant flat shoreline, feeling for the way through. Behind them the other ships were bolting in through the channel and spilling across the surface of the bay.

Raef settled down to his oars. "Come on." he said. "This is just the start." He bent to the stroke, leading them on.

CHAPTER TWENTY-ONE

The Limfjord lay in a watery chain across the top of the Danish peninsula, opening narrow at its east end from the German Sea, and spreading west, here broadening into bays and coves and there running narrow between headlands until it dissipated into the sands of the country's western edge. King Bluetooth with his army had taken over a village on the southeastern shore, where the lowland swamps gave way to a stretch of beach fit to haul ships out on. The village was only a few huts, some barns and sheds, a church, and a hall, which was now Bluetooth's court. Hakon sent his men on to find him somewhere to sleep, and with the bishop Poppo and the wizard he went into the King's hall.

It was jammed with men, most of them eating something and all of them drunk. A few torches burning here and there kept the place barely lit up enough to move around in and so smoky Hakon's eyes began to sting. He lost the wizard almost at once, but now Poppo also wanted to see the King, and he led the way up to the high seat.

It was empty. On a cushion on it sat the crown of Denmark, a thin round ring of gold.

Hakon growled under his breath, balked. He wanted to rid himself of Poppo at least. He turned and looked around for the wizard. Then Skull-Grim Egilsson loomed up out of the crowd.

The King's berserker stood head and shoulders taller than the men around him. With his misshapen head and thick black thatch of hair he looked like a troll. He saw Hakon and came toward him, pushing men out of the way with his huge hands.

"So you're back," Skull-Grim said. His voice was like gravel jumbled in a bucket. His glance took in Poppo, still frowning at the empty high seat, as if Bluetooth might take shape from his disappointment. "The King will want to see you. Come with me."

"Good," Hakon said. "Come, my lord Bishop. Where's that damned wizard?"

Skull-Grim led them off. "Wizard."

"Corban Loosestrife."

Skull-Grim's gaze sharpened. "He's with you?"

"Was," Hakon said. "He's back there somewhere."

Skull-Grim's face settled, but he said nothing more. They went out the back door of the hall. The rain was still coming down. The sun was just setting, and the sky was a low gray ledge under which the camp lay in a thick murk like a coating of fungus. Skull-Grim took them down across the village, away from the packed and boisterous hall, to the little wooden church. Even here the King's men had made their camps, sleeping in the churchyard among the graves. Hakon tried not to think this was an omen. He followed Skull-Grim across the churchyard to the church.

Skull-Grim pulled the door open. "Go on." He stood back.

Hakon grunted. All this hugger-mugger made him nervous. He himself loved to scheme, but he preferred everybody else to face him square and keep matters simple. He turned to Poppo and said, "Go in there."

Poppo said, "I know the abbot here." He peered around, hopeful. Hakon put one hand on him and thrust him into the church and went after him.

This place was dry, at least. He went slowly up the center of the church, looking toward the altar; another high seat was set before it, just outside the rail. Poppo stood in the center of the little square room, fluffing at his beard with his fingers, his eyes darting around. Suddenly in Hakon's ear Bluetooth spoke.

"You finally got back. What were you doing?"

Hakon spun around. Bluetooth was standing in the shadows just behind him; they must have walked right past him. Skull-Grim came in, and a moment later lit a candle, up near the altar, and then another on the side wall. The King stood fast, tall and gaunt, swathed in a dark cloak. His eyes were sunk deep in the pits of his face.

Hakon said, "I was looking for the bishop Poppo. He turned up in Hedeby, and I brought him back here."

"Poppo," said Bluetooth. "Oh, yes, there you are, Bishop."

Poppo stalked forward, his grave saintly face mellowed in the candlelight. "My lord, as always it is excellent to see you. But you must have other things on your mind than this misunderstanding. Please, if you would, order this"— he shot a look at Hakon—"this man to let me go on my way. I was on my way to Bremen for a very important meeting when he detained me."

The King walked past them, into the flickering web of the candlelight, and sat down in the high seat in front of the altar. He kept his cloak wrapped tight around him. He cut his hair, now, like a Christian. He settled himself in the big carved chair as if those waiting on him could wait forever. Skull-Grim went off and came back with a drinking cup, and the King drank. Finally he lifted his eyes.

"Let him go, then, Hakon," Bluetooth said.

"Thank you, my lord," Poppo said, in an oily voice.

Hakon said, between his teeth, "He's deep into something, not good. That's why I brought him back."

"Let him go. Poppo, go."

"My lord." The Bishop went back out of the church.

When he was gone, Bluetooth said, "He bores me. He's past his usefulness now anyway. I will have a Dane for a bishop, as soon as I can find one I trust who can say the Mass. Now, listen, I have much for you to do."

Hakon said, "You're making a mistake letting him go. He's been spying on you for the Germans."

"He spies on the Germans for me. Besides, Otto is in Italy. I have other interests."

"I see that." Hakon could not keep still; he wanted to go out and seize Poppo and shake him until all his secrets fell out. He paced up and down, making himself concentrate on the King. "You have drawn up a huge army here now. What do you mean to do?"

"You will know everything in due time. Enough now that you do what I set out for you. Today I had word of a fleet in the Kattegat, which I think to be Palnatoki."

"Ah," Hakon said, alert.

"I must have good knowledge of him, at the least, and better he is routed at once. You know what to do, and you have the men and ships to do it. Take your fleet and go out there and find him. Then do whatever is necessary. Do you understand me? Now, go."

Carried along in this, Hakon almost said again, "Yes, Sire." The words stuck in his throat. He turned his head, looking straight into Bluetooth's eyes, and said, "I brought someone else back from Hedeby."

In the heavy bones of his face Bluetooth's eyes gleamed like water. He gave a low growl. "So? Who?"

"Corban Loosestrife."

"The Irishman." The King's voice changed, rougher, urgent, and his gaze abruptly switched away. Hakon blinked, startled, catching a sudden tinge of fear from him. The King licked his lips. Words burst from him in a muttered rush. "I meant to kill him in Jelling. Why did I not? Something crossed it. I should have realized what that meant." Then Bluetooth swung back toward Hakon again, his eyes fierce, intent, desperate, and he said, "Kill him."

Hakon said, "I tried to, once, and it didn't work."

Bluetooth's hands jerked up, his fingers working, claws of hands, clutching the air. His voice snarled. "He is an agent of the Lady. Kill him."

Hakon took a step back. "As you wish."

"And find Palnatoki and deal with him."

"Yes, Sire."

He turned and went out of the church. His chest felt clamped around with bands of steel. He remembered the King's hands, flexed like talons, grasping the empty air. He thought, He is afraid of the wizard. Knowing that seemed of little use.

Skull-Grim was nowhere in sight. Hakon went back around to the front of the church, through the graveyard full of sleeping soldiers, and on across the village to the hall. He hoped he wouldn't be able to find Corban. He thought not being able to kill him the first time was probably a sign of something. The feeling would not leave him of steel wrapped tight around his chest. The rain was lessening somewhat; the crowd still packed the hall, and without trying to get inside the door he decided he had looked enough for Corban and went off down toward the beach.

He has set me on Palnatoki; now who will he set on me?

He shuddered that off. He was still too useful to Bluetooth for that to happen. He calculated how he would know when Bluetooth had decided he was no longer useful. He walked with long strides down the slope toward the water. The beach curved along the bottom edge of the bay; west of the village a low flat-topped headland rose like a wall behind the stretch of sandy gravel. Along the row of dragons, torches glimmered in the rain, and he picked out his own ship, *Sea-Hound,* down at the far end.

It would be good to take his ships and go out. He could make a quick, clean victory over Palnatoki, and then back to Norway, home, and free.

He thought, Too bad Bluetooth let Poppo go.

He thought briefly of going out and finding Poppo and beating the truth out of him. Corban had talked of a map of Hedeby. Whatever was going to happen would happen there, at Hedeby.

From the ocean islands to Gardarik, the wealth of the whole world depended on Hedeby.

The rain had finally stopped and the wind was rising, clean and cold. The face of the headland rose up on his left, giving some shelter. He walked down along the row of his dragons, nodding and speaking to the few men there. With every step the urge grew in him to get these ships and men away from here, away from Bluetooth. Poppo seemed as good an excuse to him as Palnatoki, maybe even better, since it was his own idea. He came at last to his ship, and found his captain there, with a few others, sitting around a little fire on the stony shore, and before they even stood up he was giving them orders.

⸙

Corban saw right away that Bluetooth was not in the hall; he found some bread and a cup of ale and went out again, into the rainy darkness. In the center of the village a crowd had built a fire and was packed in around it. Corban stayed away from the mob, circling around through the village, wondering where Bluetooth was. He dropped the empty ale cup and ate all the bread, since food was so easy to come by here.

He saw Poppo come out of the little church across the way and followed him around to another house in the churchyard, and soon after that men brought horses up to the door and Poppo came out, with a few other men in churchman's robes; they got on the horses and rode away. Corban trailed after them on foot to the edge of the village and watched them hurry away down the road south.

He wondered what would become of the Lady if the Germans took Hedeby. He thought maybe she would make the best of things.

He raised his hand up to his throat, where Benna's arms gripped him. She was heavier and lighter at the same time. She was always weary now, left him seldom, often seemed asleep, even in dreams. She seemed asleep now. He walked back to the village, looking for someplace to rest and set himself to helping her.

First he went to the church, having often spent the night in churches when there was no place else, but the door was barred. There were Vikings sleeping all over the churchyard, between the rows of the humped graves, under wooden markers. He went back out to the common, where the light of the bonfire cast everything into a deep flickering flow. Unconscious men lay thick around the fire; a last remnant of the crowd still stood in clumps in the warmth, passing cups and talking. He went toward the hall, which was also still stirring. He shied from the noise, bending his course to go between it and the big barn next to it. As he reached the corner of the barn, he felt her wake suddenly, and she nudged him, hard.

He turned. The common was a confusion of shadows against the billowing flames of the fire, but his eye fixed at once on the monster shape moving toward him, man-like, but too big, too massive-headed to be a man, and coming fast after him.

His whole body tingled. He turned and ran, looking around for someplace to hide. He heard Skull-Grim pounding after him, every stride closer; he would catch up before Corban reached the corner of the barn, and midway down the wall, Corban stopped and wheeled and flung himself back hard at the big man's knees.

It was like crashing into a tree. His shoulder hit bone and muscle with a jolt that jarred him to his heels. He felt the giant sway, off balance, and bounded up, darting back, but Skull-Grim's hand closed on his left arm and held him.

Corban swung around, facing the berserker, twisting in his grip, but Skull-Grim held him fast. With the fire behind him Corban could not make out his face. Skull-Grim's free hand clenched down on his other arm, and he knew the big man meant to kill him.

She flung herself forward. In a bolt of heat she hurtled into Skull-Grim's face, and with a howl he reeled back, letting Corban go, clutching at his eyes, thrashing his arms, trying to fight her off. Corban whirled around and raced for the edge of the barn.

There, he stopped, gasping for breath, and cold. Cold. She was gone.

He groaned. He felt her absence like something torn out of his body, an unendurable void. He wheeled around, looking back; Skull-Grim had sunk to one knee on the ground back there, shaking his head, rubbing at his eyes. She was not besetting him anymore, but she had to be there somewhere. He had to get Skull-Grim out of the way before he could look for her, and he sprinted down and threw himself headlong into Skull-Grim's side.

This time he knocked the giant over. Skull-Grim roared, sprawling flat, his head jerking around toward Corban. His eyes alternately screwed up and bugged out, still half blinded. His arms flailed out and Corban dodged and ducked and ran behind him, got him by the coarse black hair and dragged him down. Skull-Grim roared at him again, savage, and heaved himself up onto hands and knees again, but Corban kept hold of the great head, both hands fisted in the giant's thick hair, and wrenching with all his weight he brought the big man down again, slamming his head to the ground. Then once again with all his strength he yanked the head-boulder up again, smashed it on the ground again.

Skull-Grim groaned and lay still. Corban wheeled, his hands outstretched, feeling through the air around him, close to the ground, groping around in the cold dark. The firelight fluttered over the ground, catching on shadows. The air was cold and empty. He sobbed. The ache spread up from the pit of his stomach into his chest. His eyes hurt.

"Benna," he said, low. He scrambled around, swinging his hands through the air, just above the ground now, she might have fallen, she might be lying on the cold ground, hurt. "Benna."

A warm feathery touch grazed his cheek. He swayed, loose in the knees with relief, his eyes aching. She gathered herself around him again. He felt her weaker than ever before, thin and fading, but she was back, that was enough, and he carried her off to find somewhere safe, where she could rest.

⸺⸱⸻

The fog was thick as frozen wool around the dragonfly; Raef pulled his cloak up over his head. They had come up against the breast of Sweyn's dragon, and he could hear the men above him in the other ship, but he could not see them.

The dawn was coming. He sensed that like a thin singing in the air, a quickening.

Above his head, Sweyn said, "Now, this is the plan. Their ships are all drawn up on the beach, up there, very spread out. I will go in first, with the small ship, there, and one dragon, and all the men I can fit into it. You keep the other ships back here in the channel. I and my men will hit the very end of the line of their ships. Likely there won't be many men on board, the way the weather's been. We'll capture the ships, as many as we can, and get them under oars. Bluetooth will come off the beach and attack us, coming around like this from the east"—Raef imagined him curving his hand through the air—"and when he comes past the mouth of the channel, the rest of you will take him from the rear."

Nobody spoke for a moment. On the midthwart of the dragonfly, Conn lifted his head and grinned at Raef.

Eelmouth said, "Well, we will attack him from behind. But we have ten ships, here, and he's got fifty, at least."

Sweyn said, "I know this place. The shape of the bay here won't let him hit us all at once. You strike hard and quick from this channel, he'll reel back. He'll have to, to regroup. Then the rest of us will close with you, make a line, and we'll take him on in pieces. If he gets too much, we sail on into the channel and hold him off easily from there."

Thorkel grunted. "You've got a big mind, boy."

"Are you with me?" Sweyn said.

Eelmouth said, "Let's get moving."

Their feet shuffled. Raef drew in a deep ragged breath. He
saw what lay before them as if he stood above it, looking down,
the ships, the blood; he wiped his hand across his forehead, his
skin tingling all over, his insides jumpy.

For a moment, in a sudden clear calm of mind, he thought he
saw the reasons, the purposes, lying in sweet order over the wild
bits and pieces of what was to come, something glorious taking
shape. Then Sweyn jumped down into the dragonfly. Everything
collapsed again into right now. Raef's guts tightened up again,
his ears ringing with alarms. He fended them off from the bigger
ship; Conn was already running out his oars. Sweyn settled down
to use the other set. Raef took hold of the steerboard bar and settled down to get them them on course.

⸻⚬⸻

Corban came awake in the gray fuzz of the dawn light, hearing
horns blasting, and men shouting, and the trampling of feet. He
got up from the straw where he had been sleeping, stiff and
cramped; his upper arms hurt from Skull-Grim's grip. The barn
was full of horses, tethered in long lines, standing dozing in
heaps of dirty straw. He went down to the door and out into the
daylight.

From all over the village men streamed across the common
toward the beach. Horns blasted from the church door, from the
hall door, from the center of the common. As the men ran they
shouted to each other.

"Attack! Attack!"

"Who?"

"Down by the—"

"To the ships! Everybody—"

"Who?"

Corban ran along beside them, staying out of the main

stream of the onrush of men, to where the village ended against the rising side of the headland. There he stopped in his tracks.

Before him stretched the beach, running away under the lee of the headland. More dragons than he had ever seen before were hauled out there, a row of the high coiled heads that went on and on out of the reach of his eyes, looming like monsters in the dawn fog.

Men scrambled and shouted around them, taking down awnings and gathering crews. Right in front of him a bunch of men heaved one great beast-ship back off the beach into the deeper water. Several others already floated in the shallows, oars running out their sides like slatted wooden wings. The others were fighting to get off the beach, jammed together in their haste, their crews shouting and cursing, struggling for rowing room, but swiftly they untangled themselves, and as he watched the whole fleet except one ship stroked away out onto the bay, spreading out as they went, most of them going toward the east.

The wind was freshening, bright and cold, strong out of the west. The fog was burning rapidly off; Corban could see rags of blue sky through it already, and out there on the broad surface of the bay the water began to glint and sparkle. He stayed where he was a moment longer, watching a little knot of men stride down the beach past him.

Looming up among them was Skull-Grim, looking no worse. They were headed for the last of the dragons, where a crew already waited, a big ship with metal trim over its coiled serpent head and high carved gunwales. After them four slaves struggled along, carrying what looked at first like a great open wooden box.

Bluetooth's high seat, Corban thought. He turned his gaze back to the men now climbing onto the last dragon. While they bundled the high seat on board he looked among them for Bluetooth and picked out a tall, gaunt figure wrapped tightly in a dark cloak. The dragon pushed off into the little waves and rowed away.

Corban lifted his eyes. Out there ships spread out across the broad water, striding on banks of oars lifting and falling, bright in the steady new sun. Horns blew, summoning them. Corban stretched his sight, trying to make out what was happening. The fleet had all scattered; under the horns' command they were turning. He could not tell at first which way they were turning, only that they began to line up, but Hakon had said this place could only be attacked from the east.

The last of the fog was vanishing into the windblown sun. The bright water of the bay broke into a galloping fret, waves leaping like horses with manes of foam, leaping into the east. The great mass of ships began to move, began to fight against the wind, against the strong chop of the water.

Heading west. Hakon was wrong. The attack had come from the west. Corban turned and ran back toward the barn where he had slept the night, to get a horse.

Conn leapt across the narrow strip of water between the dragon-fly and the beached ship, landed crouching in the hull, and wheeled to meet the huge bearded man careening down toward him from the stern. As he ran, the bearded man drew a sword out of a loose scabbard. Raef bounded into the ship just behind him. Two other Vikings were running up to meet him, but they seemed the whole crew here. Conn cocked his sword back and met the bearded man's charge straight on.

With a contemptuous swipe the Viking struck his blade aside, and lunged. Conn felt the ship shift under him, rolling, and braced himself against it. The sword whizzed past his thigh and slammed into a bench, and he brought his sword up in the counterstroke and chopped it into the other man's upper arm.

The bearded man screamed, and fell, and Conn threw him

overboard. He ran to help Raef with the other two. This ship was still mostly aground, but he could feel it moving, as somebody shoved it out into the water. With Raef he battered at the two men remaining until abruptly one turned and dove back into the fjord, and the other went down swinging and they pitched his body over the side.

Now Sweyn's men were piling into the ship, grabbing the oars, getting it moving. Conn leapt up onto the gunwale, balancing there crouched on the narrow strip of ashwood, and yelled, "This way! This way!"

The rowers' heads turned. The oars on one side dipped, and the ship pivoted a little, so that its stern swung to cross the stern of the next of the ships hauled out on this beach. Conn could hear the horns blasting now, up there in the distance. The fog was burning off, the sun coming out. On the ship in front of him a few men sleeping on board were scrambling awake, and now somebody on the ship beyond this one was waking, and shouting.

As the two dragons slipped past each other, Copnn sprang across the gap of water. One of the crewmen reared up, hoisting a wooden shield up to block him, and Conn slammed feet first into the shield and knocked the man flat under it. With a bellow he charged up toward the bow.

Raef followed him, and then a steady stream of Sweyn's men; well outnumbered, the few men on this ship leapt off immediately. Conn jumped over the side, into the water, thigh deep, the stony bottom slippery with moss, and helped float the ship, while Sweyn's men swarmed over it, running out oars.

He stayed in the water, wheeling toward the next ship in the line. Behind him the second captured dragon swept rapidly away. The wind was picking up, hard against his back. Raef was beside him; he shouted, "Let's go!" and they rushed at the dragon lying broadside before them, half in and half out of the water.

This was full of men, ready and waiting for them. For a moment Conn was fighting upward, fending off blows and giving none. Some others of Sweyn's men rushed up behind him. Conn edged sideways, got the Viking on the ship above him a little crooked, and chopped him through the waist.

The man careened away. Conn gave a screech and vaulted up over the gunwale into the gap he had cut in the line. Raef bounded up after him. The Vikings on the ship wheeled toward them, howling, but in the narrow ship they could attack only a few at a time. Conn braced his feet apart on the hull; two men rushed him, getting in each other's way, and he hacked them both down with one swing. Then Sweyn's men swarmed in and crushed them from the side.

Conn stood, breathing hard; his arms throbbed from the sword work. Sweyn leapt up beside him, gripping him by the shirt. His nose was broken and bleeding. His eyes blazed. "This is the last one we'll get so easily—look!"

Conn wheeled. The fog was gone. Under the wind the blue water of the Limfjord fluttered with white feathers of waves. Through the blaze of sunlight on water, a great fleet of ships was moving steadily toward them. The prows of the ships at the front blazed golden. The high coiled heads of the dragons seemed alive. Men crowded them so thick they lay down in the water like great swans. They were fighting the wind, struggling against the uneasy currents, and they spread out across the bay, until Conn gave up trying to count them.

Sweyn said, "I told you the wind would come up and slow them. Get ready."

Conn nodded; he lifted his sword, and kissed the blade. He could smell the blood on it. He said, "This will be a good fight, Sweyn." Beside him, Raef, long-faced as usual, was staring away at the oncoming fleet. He turned and his eyes met Conn's and held a moment. A leather sack full of some fiery liquor came by, and they both drank deep of it. Conn slapped Raef on the arm. "We'll take them. Keep your head up." Sweyn hung his arm around Conn's shoulder. They waited, smiling.

———

In the barn where he had spent the night Corban found a horse that would stand still for him to mount and rode up onto the sloping back edge of the headland. A thread of a path ran up through the windblown grass to the top. He followed the path up into the blast of the wind and kicked the horse along the top.

From here he could see everything. On his left the great watery expanse of the Limfjord glittered and thrashed, its surface torn into whitecaps. Bluetooth's fleet was scattered across the center of it like something thrown down from heaven. Below him just off the western edge of the beach, where it fell off into a marshy cove, four dragons waited, drawn up side by side.

There had already been fighting here. This was where the first attack had come. Bodies sprawled in the shallows behind the waiting dragons, and higher on the gravelly shore a few men sat huddled together, watching what was going on.

Beyond, at the point of the beach, lay a ship he knew, his dragonfly.

He could not make out Conn and Raef in the ships waiting down there. He lifted his eyes, wondering how they had gotten here. The cove that spread away from the end of this beach, tending south, shallow and reedy, seemed to have no other way out. He moved his gaze along the shore beyond it, toward the west.

There, below another high-cropping headland, some water gleamed. There was a watercourse over there.

Stretching his gaze, patient, letting his eyes work, he thought he saw some masts of ships waiting, in that far gleam of water. But he wasn't sure: maybe just trees on the shore.

Far off across the water, thin as a gull's cry, a horn blew. He turned his gaze back toward Bluetooth's fleet. For a moment, the dozens of ships were still scattered everywhere. Then they turned, and as if drawn up by a magic string they gathered into a curving line, aimed into the west, at the four dragons waiting for them by the beach below.

He stopped the horse. He had come to the end of the headland anyway, where the outcrop fell off into a stand of trees, and beyond that some plowed fields. He looked back the way he had come, wondering if he should circle back. Far down there, on his track, someone else rode along.

Horns sounded, far down there. His heart began to pound. He swung forward again, looking out at the water. Bluetooth's ships were thrashing their way along, mighty-oared, brimming with men. The strongest were pulling out ahead of the others, but the bay was narrowing here anyway. This tip of Bluetooth's fleet, some dozen ships, swung around to attack the four dragons waiting for them.

Who did not wait. Those four ships suddenly burst forward, striding up on flashing oars, attacking first.

Even on the headland Corban heard the yell from Bluetooth's whole fleet. The main body of ships flailed on, struggling to get into the narrowing neck of the bay. The vanguard swung around to meet the attack, spreading out, and Conn's four dragons drove straight at the center of this line.

Then from behind Bluetooth's vanguard, from the dim gleam of water there, more ships were swarming into the fight. These had the wind behind them. Corban could hear screams from them, and shields banging. Bluetooth's vanguard staggered, struck from the front and the side at once. Corban saw men wheeling around in their ships, and one or two of the dragons began to row eastward, out of the fighting, back into the main body of Bluetooth's fleet.

Down in the cove the oncoming ships closed hard, ships running in beside ships, oars raised up, and men leaping from one dragon to another. He heard the tinny clash of swords. The ships were grappling together, making a rocking wooden field to fight on, and the mass of men surged back and forth along it. Corban could see nothing of what was happening, only a great tangle of wooden ships and men scrambling around on them, and faintly, screams and thuds, and the clank of iron.

He paced up and down on the edge of the headland, trying to see who was winning. Most of Bluetooth's fleet was still struggling in the narrows of the bay, but they would break through finally. The invaders—Conn, Raef, Sweyn, down there, somewhere—could escape back into the inlet, or they could fight this battle; he didn't see how they could do both. They showed no signs of running. On the clamped rocking ships below the men struggled up and down. He sat down on the headland to watch.

—⚬—

Raef gasped for breath. For once nobody was trying to kill him. He swiped at the blood dripping down into his eyes and passed his sword from hand to hand, flexing his stiff bruised fingers.

Then beside him Conn shouted, "Help me! Pull!"

Raef laid his sword down and seized the dripping inch-thick rope just behind Conn's hands. The grappling hook on the rope's other end was caught on the gunwale of the next ship; wrenching and tugging hand over hand, they dragged the ship they were on over toward the one at the end of the rope, their ship's hull rolling up over the other's sagging bank of oars, tipping steeply upward. Conn yelled, "Jump!"

Raef grabbed for his sword and followed him up, over the gunwale of their ship, and as that footing crashed down under him sprang off into the next.

A sword met him. This ship was crammed full of men, fighting, crashing together as they tried to swing, clawing at each other for room. The hot stink of their bodies met him like a wave. Everything dissolved into a wild swirl of colors. He could see nothing but pieces, an arm, heads, shoulders, the leap of blood. Everything had fallen into pieces swirling around him, drawing him in.

He chopped frantically at it, keeping it away, to stay out of it, to stay whole. Pieces roared at him, an arm, a blade rippling with eerie light, two eyes, full of sadness and recognition, looking into his. His arms were numb from the shock of blows. Conn—where was Conn—gripping the sword with both hands, he struck back and forth against an axe for a moment, and then the axe disappeared, swept down from behind.

Conn screamed, "Come on!"

Raef plunged after him, the sword gripped two-handed, cutting his way through the packed ravening mass around him, the sweet beautiful fabric of the world coming apart here into nothing, a whirlwind of chaos sucking everything in. Something struck him hard, and he staggered, and a body slid under his feet. He walked on trembling, shrieking flesh.

He staggered along after Conn's black head, came up with a crash against the hard edge of a rowing bench, and then Conn was beside him. They got back to back again, which always worked. Hacking at the men struggling at them they had a better chance, on more solid ground, and were milling down all comers until the ship suddenly lurched and went over sideways.

Raef screeched; he clung desperately to his sword even in the air, and hit the water on his face. He went down, down. The cold was silent around him, blessed cold silence. He kicked out and swam up, dragging the sword after him, and burst up into the air almost under a ship. In front of him, going up the side of the ship, was Conn. The air was warm on his face. He struggled after his cousin through the lapping water, reaching the next ship just below Conn's feet disappearing over the side, and scrambled up.

He toppled over the gunwale and landed almost on top of a man struggling to get to his feet; Raef struck him down before his knees straightened. He wheeled around, trying to find Conn, and ducked a flying sword and chopped out without looking where and blood sprayed all over him, and something fell on him but it was a body, not a sword. He flailed it off, standing up, dazed.

Conn gripped his arm. "Look—we got behind them somehow."

Raef looked around him, amazed. This ship was empty, except for the two men they had just killed; all the men from this ship had gone on, past them, onto the front row of ships where the fighting was. He gaped across the stretch of open water between him and those ships, where men crowded together so tightly Raef could not make out each from each, could distinguish only their hacking arms, and their surging back and forth, and the bodies pitching off the ship into the water, and the screech and howl of one great mad voice coming from them.

He turned around, to look the other way, and saw the inlet, opening below the headland, the water glistening in the sun, and the sunlight yellow on the grassy top of the headland, the world there all still woven together, all whole.

Conn said, "Come on."

Raef turned toward him, thinking, We could get away. He knew they would have no other chance. He could see already that Bluetooth's ships held the inlet. Sweyn and his ships would not escape. He stared into his cousin's face, but Conn did not even look back at him. Conn was turning back toward the battle; he saw nothing but the fighting over there, that confusion, that coming apart. And now he was running back along the ship, to go back into it, not for Sweyn, Raef knew, not for victory or glory, even, but for the unraveling itself.

Raef drew a deep breath. He had no choice; even while he longed to escape he was following Conn back down the ship. Diving into the water again, and going back there, following.

CHAPTER TWENTY-TWO

Looking inland from the Limfjord, Corban could see, across the woods and fields, people fleeing the distant farms, streams of people headed deeper into the country, driving their animals ahead of them. When he turned back toward the bay he saw wreckage.

Three ships lay on the stony shore below him, their hulls stove in, their oars broken, and men scattered around them dead or dying, in the water and out. Pieces of ships and oars and sails floated in the shallows. Two other ships lay unmanned on the water, one half swamped and listing hard, the other aground on an offshore bar, and more bodies.

He shaded his eyes against the slanted sun. There was no tide here; the water seemed no lower than when the day started, but the fighting had moved away from him. All he could see now was the dark tangles of ships, floating on the water like wooden burrs stuck together. The scream and clang of the fighting reached him in a thin featureless clamor, like a distant music, mostly lost.

He knew his boys were there. When Sweyn's dragons first lined up, he had seen two men run back along them, as the ships rowed together, two men running, leaping from ship to ship, until they reached the shallows and splashed through the water to the dragonfly. He had kept them in sight as they rowed hard up into the line, into Bluetooth's second attack, but he soon lost them in the crowded dragons.

He had watched the fighting all day long. At first Sweyn's fourteen ships had driven back Bluetooth's much larger fleet, whose own numbers hindered it, the ships in front blocking the ships behind, half of its hands useless. Sweyn's fleet had kept

well together, struck hard, overrun some of the vanguard dragons; then they had been much closer to him, he had seen the
surge of fighting men along the narrow length of a dragon, the
ship pitching and rolling, the bodies falling into the bay, living
and dead. Then Bluetooth's men had withdrawn a little, and
Sweyn's fleet had striven toward the inlet they had come in
through, to escape.

Only now the wind was against them, and Bluetooth was
ready. He swung a line of his ships down across the mouth of the
inlet, and pinned Sweyn's fleet in the cove.

There they had joined their lines, lashing their ships together
in rows, and set on each other. Most of Bluetooth's ships were
still stuck behind his vanguard in the narrow bay, but Corban
could see men moving steadily up through those ships, so that
there were always more of Bluetooth's men where the fighting
was. Throughout the main part of the day Sweyn's fleet held its
line, but Bluetooth's weight steadily told on them. By mid-
afternoon the solid line of Sweyn's fleet was breaking up, fighting separate fights against always more of the enemy. Then, at
last, he saw the dragonfly again.

It was floating steadily down toward the cove, while two of
Bluetooth's dragons rowed up and down trying to get some line
to attack it; each time, just as the big ships closed, the little one
slipped neatly between them and away.

Corban let out a cry. He could make out two men on his little
ship—no, as the dragonfly drifted closer he saw there were three;
one had a bow and was shooting steadily into the King's ships.
Still the big dragons rowed up and down, circling, but they could
not pin the dragonfly. Then one of the big dragons ran aground,
just off the beach, in the shallows at this end of the cove.

The other ship pulled abruptly off. The dragonfly veered
away at once, rowing hard back upwind, toward the rest of
Sweyn's scattered fleet. He saw the black hair of one rower, the
white hair of the other. Back on the stranded dragon, the men

jumped off and began hauling their ship back into deeper water.

The day was waning. The wind was fading away, leaving the water calm as a puddle. A haze blurred the air; the far headland was indistinct, the sky milky. Horns blew, out there on the water, brassy bird yells. Suddenly the two fleets were pulling apart. A gap of open water widened between them. One by one Sweyn's dragons swept off into the cove. There they turned; they rowed back up into the opening to the shallow inlet, and turned, and lined up again, gunwale to gunwale, their prows toward Bluetooth.

The last to swoop down was the dragonfly, swifter and nimbler than all the rest.

But they were trapped. The King's great fleet milled around, awkward, struggling to get some rowing room; they could not close on Sweyn's men, but Sweyn's fleet could not escape the cove. Slowly Bluetooth's fleet pulled around in a broad arc facing Sweyn's line, but they did not attack. Instead they drew back a little and set out anchors, and Corban realized they were settling down for the night.

On Sweyn's fleet, they clearly saw this, too. Some of those men began moving down off their ships, onto the far shore of the cove; the dragonfly had run in onto the beach there. Somehow they had made a sort of truce; he wondered how long it would last.

Then, from Bluetooth's fleet, a dragon was striding on its wooden legs toward the shore directly below him, and even from this height, and with the light going, he saw the bulky shape of the high seat in the stern.

He crouched down, not wanting to look obvious against the sky. The dragon ran into the shore, and the crew leapt out and hauled it up on the gravelly beach. The men in the stern got out. They talked a little, and then one led off, and the rest followed him straight up the beach, out of Corban's sight along the sheer flank of the headland. After them, bent double under the weight, went the slaves with the high seat.

Corban went to the edge of the headland, where it fell off

into a stand of young beech trees, hazy golden with their first spring leaf. He strained his ears; he thought he heard voices down there. He rubbed his hands on his thighs, looking over the cliff face here. It was steep. But there was a broken place he could get a foothold, some of the way down at least.

The sun was setting. The night air brushed cold over his face. He felt her snug against him, sleeping, as she did almost all the time now. Slowly he crept down over the edge of the cliff, feeling his way with his feet. After a few yards' groping desperately in the dark he found a little trail angling down, only a few inches wide, and followed it.

Now he was sure he heard noises, somewhere in the beech wood, and through the damp smell of the mast he smelled smoke. He stopped where he could shelter against a tree growing out of the headland, and looked down and saw the glow of a fire through the tops of the trees, out on the low ground.

He saw men passing back and forth through the glow; he heard voices, and somebody laughed.

He crept on down, the cliff now leveling out to a gradual slope, thick with brush. The ground was crumbly. On all fours he wiggled his way through a bramble that ripped at his face with its thorns. Going slowly to make as little noise as possible, he still sounded to himself like a bull charging. The air was flavorful with smoke. He smelled meat roasting. Over there, in the stand of young trees on the lower ground, a great burst of laughter went up. The fire grew brighter, flickering through the trees, sending long streamers of light back and forth through the wood below him. His belly growled. Crouched on the slope above the encampment, he wondered what he could do, after all, against so many men.

He had to kill Bluetooth. Only that would stop this battle and save his boys. He recoiled from that. He hated Bluetooth, but killing Eric Bloodaxe had gotten him into all this. He realized he was fingering the puny little knife in his belt. He had no real weapon to kill with, not with Skull-Grim there, and the other berserkers, not even his sling.

He pulled his cloak around him against the night chill. His belly growled with hunger. Everything he had done, all his life, had brought him down to this, that he had to kill another man, like a wolf on another wolf, and he had no will to do it.

He stiffened; the crunch of leaves came to his ears. Someone from the camp was coming toward him through the trees. He crouched down under some brush, wondering if he had been seen. Huddled on the slope, he looked down through the branches.

A tall gaunt figure slouched in where the brush was thick, and there pulled his clothes aside and squatted down to relieve himself. When he did, he turned a little toward the fire, and the flickering light struck the side of his face. It was Bluetooth.

Corban clenched his teeth. He had his chance now. He drew the knife; he could leap down there now, and kill him with the knife. The old man hunkered long over his bowels, groaning. Kill him in his shit. He gripped the knife but he could not make himself move. He could not do it, not cold like that, like a murderer, not even this murdering king.

Then, from away on his left hand, higher on the slope, something hissed, sped past him, and struck hard. The King squatting below him groaned and pitched forward.

Corban did move, then, scrambled down the slope, breaking through small branches and clumps of brush. Bluetooth lay on his side in a stink of shit, but he was still alive. Corban put his hands on him.

"Help me," Bluetooth said, and then louder, desperate, his breath whistling, "Help me!"

Corban said, "Here. I'm here. Where are you hurt?" and his hand, groping over the clenched body of the King, banged into the shaft of an arrow sunk deep in his lower back. Over by the fire somebody yelled, and then a chorus of bellowing rose, like frogs in the dark.

"Don't leave me alone," the old man said, between his teeth, the pain clenched in his jaws, his eyes wild in the unsteady light. "Don't leave me."

"I'm here," Corban said, and took hold of his arm. Under his hand he felt the life running out of Bluetooth like the stuff in his bowels. The old King shuddered, his teeth chattering.

"God, I can't remember what to say."

He sagged, went limp. Then crashing through the trees came Skull-Grim.

Corban stood up quickly, backing away, glad anyway to be out of the stench. The giant gave him a single glance and bellowed, "Bring a torch." He knelt down by Bluetooth; other men rushed up through the trees, and brought a light, and the thick ruddy torch-light washed over the King dead, Skull-Grim kneeling by him.

Corban stood where he was, knowing better than to run. Skull-Grim's boulder-head swiveled toward him; his teeth showed. "You."

"Not me," Corban said. "See the arrow? I'm no bowman."

Skull-Grim grunted. "Hold him."

Men closed in around Corban, who did not move. None of them touched him. His heart was beating hard; he thought, I will die now for the King I did not kill. He put his hand up under his throat, into her warmth, wondering what would happen to her now, if they would be together.

She hugged him faintly. Not afraid.

Skull-Grim straightened Bluetooth's body out. The other men murmured, some crossing themselves in Christian wise, all craning their necks to see, Bluetooth's name over and over in the ripple of their voices. The arrow had come out the front of the King's body, and Skull-Grim broke the shaft and drew the head out of the wound.

He looked at the arrow, and stood up, massive in the midst of the spindly trees, the smaller men. His face was expressionless. He said, "It wasn't the wizard. Take the King to his ship."

The Vikings who had been standing around Corban left him, going with the rest to lift the body and carry it away. Skull-Grim held out the piece of the arrow; as it moved, the oblique firelight rippled startlingly over the shaft.

Skull-Grim said, "Do you know this arrow?"

"No," Corban said. He stared at the stub of the arrow; now he saw that three gold bands ringed it just above the break.

"Well, I do," Skull-Grim said. He pushed the arrow at him. "Here, you keep this. Come with me." His eyes sharpened, glinting in the torchlight. "No more magic."

Corban said, "I have no magic. I keep telling people that." He put the piece of arrow into his belt, and followed the berserker toward the fire, where the smell of roasting meat was delicious.

—

Sweyn clenched his teeth, his eyes watering, all the pain in the world in his nose, which Conn was carefully molding back into shape with his fingers. He said, to be saying something, anyway, "We gave it to them, we outfought them all day long. All of you, you all fought like Odin's own. Ahh."

Conn sat back on his heels. "You'll never be pretty again, Sweyn."

Sweyn's eyes were bleary with pain; he felt tenderly of the great swollen sore lump on his face. "Ah, you couldn't stand the competition, could you." He blinked, trying to clear his eyes.

Conn laughed. He put another piece of driftwood on the fire. Sweyn looked from Conn to the other men, and said, "I just wish I'd planned it better. We wouldn't be trapped here."

Conn said, "It was a good plan, even if it didn't work." He slapped Sweyn hard on the back. "We beat them today. We'll beat them again tomorrow." His face was clear and open as a child's.

"It would have worked, if I'd held my end." Eelmouth was slumped down alongside the fire, one arm draped over his up-turned knee, the other leg stretched carefully out in front of him. He had taken a hard blow to the shin and could barely walk on it. "We'd have been the other side of the door by now, and him looking in."

Sweyn said, "We made him suffer. We'll get out of here to-morrow." He didn't know how, but he thought something would come to him, somehow.

Conn said, "Is there anything to eat?"

"Lost it all," Eelmouth said shortly. His ship had gone down, in the vain attempt to escape out the channel. He lay down, curved around the fire, his head on his arm.

"We can search the new ships," Sweyn said. "And the wrecks."

"Raef went over there," Conn said. "If there's bread any-where around here Raef will find it."

Eelmouth chuckled; he was going to sleep. "Wake me up if he brings anything."

Sweyn inched closer to the fire. In spite of their problems he felt the swelling in him of a buoyant triumph. He had taken the fight to Bluetooth with a much smaller force, and used him hard, and no matter what happened next he had won a big victory to-day. Going at Bluetooth's vanguard like that had worked, had gotten his men off his own ships and into the enemy's. His men had taken ship after ship, sunk as many as they had captured, and sent their crews down dead or into the water, losing only two ships of their own.

Conn had been much of that, he knew. Everywhere Sweyn had needed someone, Conn had gone and fought, and Raef was everywhere Conn was. But it was Conn the other men loved, for his joy, his quick high spirit, as much as for his eye to the chances in everything—stranding Bluetooth's ship had been his idea, and several other clever moves.

Sweyn stood up, looking around the gravel beach, dotted with low fluttering fires. Night had fallen, clear and cold. The line of his ships, lashed together beam to beam, stretched away into the dark, their crews all come ashore. He went to the nearest of the fires, where the men sat from Thorkel's ship.

They greeted him in a chorus of voices; but Thorkel was not there.

"Got him just at the last," said his prowman. "I'm captain now of this ship, you should know."

Sweyn said, "I hate losing Thorkel. He's feasting now in a greater hall than we'll ever see on earth. But you men fought like Odin's own, and I'm proud you follow me."

They cheered him, and suddenly they were offering him a bit of bread, but he saw they had little, and he said, "No, I have my own. Keep together, and sleep well." He got up, and went on to the next fire.

There also he heard who had died, and praised the ones who had won this for him. These men had something to eat also, but those at the next fire did not, and he put them together.

He went on from fire to fire, making sure his men were as well off as they could be; he thought a King had to do this, but also, it pleased him very much to do it. When he came back to his own place, Raef had shown up with a sack of food, and so he ate, too. He lay down by his fire still contemplating the rightness of this, and when he slept he slept sound.

⚓

Raef jarred awake, hearing Conn's voice, and sat up. It was still dark. He was still tired. He reached for his cloak, wanting to lie down again, but now Conn was coming up to him, and saying, "Let's go. We're going to try to break out, as soon as there's light enough."

"Pagh. Whose idea is that?" Raef looked around. The fire

had died down and the night was still utterly dark, but he could see the other men stirring. He sat down and pulled his boots on; they were still soaked inside and icy cold, and he moaned.

"It's Sweyn's idea," Conn said. "Come on. You know he's right."

Raef growled at him. He ached all over from the hard work of the day before. Two of his fingers felt broken, and his left shoulder hurt whenever he lifted his arm. Now it was so stiff he could barely move his hand. Groaning and muttering, he found his sword and trudged after Conn, down to the dragonfly on the shore.

The black night overhead was still pricked with stars, but off to the east, where the sky sloped down, the clear air thickened into mist and the lower edge of the mist was turning pale. Raef stopped by the dragonfly. Just down the shore from him the other men were creeping out along the chain of their ships lashed together across the cove; they moved along slowly, bent over, trying to keep the ships from rocking, to get to their oars before Bluetooth's men saw what they were at. Raef wrapped his cloak around him and buckled his belt on over it. He liked this sword, which was the third one he had picked up during the fighting the day before.

His shoulder was feeling better. A leather flagon half full of something came by, and he drank deep of the liquor; his head whirled.

He handed the flagon on, his stomach burning, and his head expansive, and looked out toward Bluetooth's dark massed ships; some lights glowed here and there on that line, but it seemed quiet. Then he heard, out there, a sharp yell.

"They've seen us," he said, wheeling, and with Conn he grabbed hold of the dragonfly's gunwale and heaved it down the stony beach into the water. Sweyn stayed behind a moment, bellowing a sudden volley of orders. A moment later he bounded into the ship, and they pulled oars and swung the ship around and headed toward the end of Bluetooth's line.

The sky was turning gray, but it was still too dark to see much. On Bluetooth's line, a dark uneven cluttered wall against the whitening sky, bellows of warning went up, and feet clattered. A horn blasted. Raef leaned into the stroke of his oars and looking back past the dragonfly's stern saw Sweyn's ships, one after another, break out of the line and row after him.

He curled himself into each stroke, hearing Conn behind him groaning with effort, and then Sweyn shouted, "Up oars!" He cocked his oars up out of the way, and the dragonfly, running along over shallows, slid in past the outcurving stempost of a big dragon, the end of Bluetooth's line.

"Go! Go!"

Seizing the sword he barreled up, following Conn, bounding first onto the dragonfly's gunwale and from there up onto the bigger ship. Vaulting into that hull he stood a moment alone, Conn lunging on ahead of them, Sweyn still scrambling up behind, the space of the enemy ship around him, and then from the dragon beyond came a rush of men and filled the space up and he was slashing and stroking at them, his teeth clenched, trying to keep his feet.

He lunged forward; if he could get to the other side of the ship, he could use it for some cover, but the King's men swarmed at him and drove him back, away from Conn. The ship rolled under his feet. He tried to stand fast but three men came at him, two in this ship and now one on the next, leaning over the gunwale to attack him, and he had to leap backward. He had to get to Conn. Conn was out there somewhere. The man in the next ship heaved up his axe, chopping at Raef's head, the blade too high, and Raef saw the gap under and struck. That man pitched backward, stumbling into somebody behind him, and they both went off into the water.

Directly before him two men ran at him together and he flung his sword up between them, trying to hold off their blades, their swords came at him from everywhere, up and down, and both at once. His eyes lost them, they were a glaze of light in the air around him, the sword blades kissing with a sharp shriek of metal, somehow he was holding them off, but soon—a blade hissed by his face and struck fast in the gunwale. That man wobbled, wrenching at the blade, and Raef lifted his foot, still soaking wet in the bear-fur boot, and kicked him over the side of the ship.

Another man came at him with a shriek and a whirl of his sword, but one was simpler than two, and Raef swept him aside. Then he charged forward, into the hole left behind, and going forward like that, and swinging and jabbing with his sword, he cleared half the ship, coming up gasping for breath beside the block for the mast.

Over the shoulder of a falling man he saw Conn's wild dark head. He bellowed to him. A man with an axe reared up before him, toe to toe with him, striking back and forth with his curved blade, and Raef ducked, and the axe swung hissing over his head. Raef bulled forward and shoulder-butted the man off the ship.

A horn blew, somewhere. Raef rushed on, up into the front of the ship, where Conn stood, breathing hard, his sword dangling in his hand with blood dripping off the tip. Sweyn, beyond him, shouted, "Hold!" They were facing the next ship in line, still lashed to this one, where Bluetooth's men packed together. But Bluetooth's men had drawn back.

Raef moved his sword from hand to hand. The sun was breaking through a thin mist, the sky already bright blue overhead, the light steadily strengthening. Raef glanced behind them.

They had opened up the end of Bluetooth's line, and the first few ships of Sweyn's fleet had burst through. Now everybody had stopped, was waiting, which puzzled him. He gripped his sword. "Let's go."

"No, wait—look." Sweyn put one arm out. "Hold on."

Raef looked; now, coming in through the pack of Bluetooth's men, forcing a way up toward him and Sweyn, was Skull-Grim, Bluetooth's berserker.

Conn said, "I want him."

Sweyn said swiftly, "He's not killable. I've heard somebody hit him on the head once with an axe and the axe broke."

"I'll get him," Conn said. He took his sword in both hands, his eyes fierce.

"Sweyn Haraldsson!" Skull-Grim finally elbowed his way out of the massed army, and stood by himself, between Bluetooth's men and Sweyn's. "We need you to stop fighting for a while. Something's happened."

Conn groaned. "It's a trick. Tell him I'll fight him. For everything, him and me."

Sweyn gave him a shove, still facing Skull-Grim, and aimed his voice across space between them. "Yes, I'm beating you, is what's happening. Do you want to give up?"

The pack behind Skull-Grim let out a howl that hurt Raef's ears; they shook their swords in the air, furious. The giant turned slightly, looking over his shoulder, and swung back to face Sweyn again, grinning. "No, we don't give up. Just wait until midmorning. By then we'll have this worked out." The big man shrugged one huge lumpy shoulder. "No need for anybody else to die, if we can settle this in another way."

"What other way?" Sweyn said quickly.

Skull-Grim shrugged again. "We all here have to talk it over."

Sweyn frowned. Raef said, astonished, "Do we let them do that?"

"It's a trick," Conn said, between his teeth.

Sweyn faced Skull-Grim again. Raef watched him keenly, seeing him cloudy with doubt, thinking, but then he gathered himself up straight, and his face cleared. He said, "If this is a trick, and it is Bluetooth we're talking about, so it could be, it's be a vile one. But I am not Bluetooth, and I will give you an honorable truce. Go ahead. We'll wait." He took a step back and sat down on a rowing bench behind him, his sword across his knees.

Raef lowered his sword. He looked around again, and saw the four ships that had already slipped past Bluetooth's line waiting out there on the broader water, the rest gathered inside the cove. Facing forward again he watched as Bluetooth's army walked away off the cordon of their ships onto the far shore, and there circled into a crowd to talk.

A dozen of them stayed behind on the ship opposite this one. Immediately the men on the ships started calling back and forth.

"Hastein! Hastein! Is that you?"

"It's me, Snorri—still bigger than you are!"

That brought laughter from both sides. Somebody behind Raef called, "Hey, do you have anything to eat over there?"

"Think we'd feed you, you shiprats?" But a chunk of bread suddenly traced an arc through the sky from one dragon to the other. At once everybody began to yell.

"How long do we wait?" Conn asked Sweyn, under the uproar.

"Not much longer," Sweyn said.

"I say we run for it," Raef said.

Conn laughed, as if he had made a joke; he stowed his sword along a bench and sauntered up and down the ship, stretching his arms. Raef chewed his thumb. The gash on his forehead hurt, his feet were frozen, and he was hungry and nobody was feeding him; and he could see that they could get away, here, just by starting to row.

Then Sweyn said, "Here they are again."

"That was quick," Conn said.

Raef gritted his teeth. Standing up, he watched Skull-Grim and a dozen men walking back up the ships, leaving most of the others behind. Raef heaved up a big sigh, relieved, and took his sword and thrust it into his belt.

Conn said, "What?"

"Not a one of them has a weapon drawn," Raef said. He folded his arms over his chest. "I think this is over."

Sweyn stood up. "What do you mean?"

Skull-Grim tramped toward them from ship to ship, until he stopped on one beside theirs, facing them. Under the thick black thatch of his hair his eyes glittered with a strange humor. His hands were loose at his sides. He said, "Sweyn Haraldsson, King Harald Bluetooth your father is dead."

"What?" Sweyn said. "When—How?" He glanced at Conn and Raef, his face rumpled with disbelief.

"I'm not sure," Skull-Grim said. "But he's certainly dead. And we all here, after the way you've kept us going, yesterday and today, we all say that as far as we're concerned you're now the King of Denmark."

From the men behind him, then, there went up a yell.

"King Sweyn Haraldsson!"

Sweyn's face cleared, shining bright as the sun. Conn let out a whoop and grabbed him around the legs and hoisted him up into the air. Sweyn flung both arms up in a wild salute, as if he could soar up into the sky; he was shouting, and Raef was shouting, too, but he couldn't hear Sweyn and he couldn't hear himself, for the roaring voices all around him.

"King Sweyn Haraldsson! King Sweyn Haraldsson!"

Let everybody else shout. Raef collected himself, trying to figure this out. But it had all come right, even if he couldn't see how. He was glad he didn't have to fight anymore, and now, of course, there would be plenty to eat. He stood back, letting the other men get in closer to Sweyn, lift him up, and carry him cheering toward the shore. Conn edged his way back beside him.

"Now we can find Pap," he said.

Raef muttered in his throat, watching the celebration around Sweyn get farther away. "Yes." They went down toward the dragonfly.

On the command of the new King, they all put up their arms, and
both the armies sailed back up the bay to the village where Bluetooth had made his headquarters. Sweyn took over the big hall in
the village where Bluetooth had held court, and there sat, and a
steady stream of the men from both armies came to him and took
him for their King. Raef got quickly into looking for food. Conn
hung around near Sweyn, in the big hall, where he had already
seen a girl he liked. Skull-Grim came in and talked to Sweyn,
and when he left, Sweyn called Conn over to him.

"Your father is here."

"What?" Conn said. "That's very good news to me. Where?"

"Maybe not so good." Sweyn gripped his arm. "They found
him standing over my father Bluetooth's body."

Conn jerked back, staring into Sweyn's face. "No. I don't
believe it."

"It's true." Sweyn kept hold of him. "We have to do this the
right way."

"My father didn't kill the King," Conn said. "Or if he did—"

"Don't do anything," Sweyn said. "Whatever happened,
we'll hear it all out, we'll do this right."

Conn stared at him, hot words on his tongue, and Sweyn met
his eyes. They said nothing, but much passed between them.
Abruptly Conn turned and walked out of the hall.

He remembered how Sweyn had likely heard this, and he
went through the village, looking for the berserker, Skull-Grim.
He found him standing on the front step of a little wooden building, his arms crossed.

"What do you want?" Skull-Grim said to him.

"I'm looking for my father," Conn said. "I'm thinking you
may know where he is." He looked up at the other man's lumpy
ugly face, sprinkled with dark beard like spines, into the small
amused eyes, and his blood heated.

"You are Conn Corbansson?"

"I am."

The giant shifted, his back to the door, blocking the whole way in. "In fact I do have your father. I found him standing over the body of the King. The King that was."

Conn's muscles sang; he said, "Let me in."

"I won't. Go talk to the King that is."

Conn reached for his sword. "Let me in, or I'll cut my way in through you."

Skull-Grim's eyes gleamed. He never moved. He said, "I would much like to try you on, boy, but there's a truce on. Your King's truce."

Conn swallowed, remembering unwillingly what Sweyn had told him; it went hard against him to choose between his father and Sweyn. Then Raef jogged up to him.

"What are you doing?" He cast a narrow glance at Skull-Grim. To Conn, he said, "Sweyn wants you. Palnatoki is finally here."

Skull-Grim grunted, his arms unfolding. Conn said, "Palnatoki." He backed up, giving Skull-Grim a raw look. But Raef and Raef's news drew him. "Isn't he a little late? Where is he?"

"His fleet is sailing in now. Sweyn wants to meet him on the shore."

"Very well, I'm coming," Conn said. He turned to the giant, now standing in the doorway staring out toward the Limfjord's flat blue waters. "I'm not finished."

"No, no," said Skull-Grim. "Neither am I." He turned and went back through the door. Conn walked on down to the shore, to greet Sweyn's foster-father's tardy coming on the ground.

⁓

Late in the day Sweyn drank the arvel ale in the hall where Bluetooth had held court; he sat in the high seat, his captains and warriors all around him, and spoke Bluetooth's name and drank deep. The mead and the ale went around, and they ate their fill of meat and bread, and the hall rang with their uproar. Over and again someone heaved up onto his feet and saluted Sweyn with his cup, calling him King, and many other fine things besides, and then they all cheered and beat their hands together and drank.

Sweyn had Palnatoki beside him in the high seat, showing him all honor, but Conn sat on Sweyn's other hand, and Raef beside Conn. Corban, sitting down one bench from them next to Skull-Grim, could not take his eyes from them. They seemed bigger, new men, utterly strange to him, as if the boys they had been when he saw them last had sloughed their skins. Conn had gold around his arms and on his chest and in his ears, and he looked in a perpetual high humor. Raef, beside him, hung his head and drank a lot, his hair milk white, shagging down below his shoulders; he wore no gold.

In the high seat with Sweyn, Palnatoki was enjoying himself. He sat stroking his hands over the carved arms of the chair and smiling. Sweyn turned and held up a cup to him. Now he stood up to lead another round of hard drinking to the glory of Sweyn Haraldsson. Everybody bellowed; the hall fell into a hush while they drank. Skull-Grim turned toward Corban.

"Those are your boys, hah?"

"Yes," Corban said.

"They're great fighters. Sweyn's lucky."

"He's lucky," said somebody on the giant's far side, "that we decided not to fight anymore. He wasn't going to win. We'd have crushed them."

On Corban's other shoulder, another voice sounded. "It came out all right. It was a wolf-war of a fight anyway, although not much gold in it. Skull-Grim, give us a poem about it."

Corban was still watching his boys, paying little heed to all this; he thought it was a joke, about the poem, but then Skull-Grim lifted his head, and his face kinked up, his eyes half closed. All the men around him hushed and waited. Amazed, Corban heard the big man speak skald's words.

"On the Limfjord loom—"

He stopped. His wiry eyebrows jerked up and down and he muttered into his hand, and began again, his voice rumbling out, the phrases in their heavy measure like the thudding of great hammers.

"Weird women wove the ring-gold's worth on the loom of the Limfjord, now the harvest of the one-handed husbandman brings riches for ravens;

"Wine of wounds waters the ash-tree; smith's steel smokes with warm man-mead. The storm-father stalks us, seizing his own.

"When Rig's spawn takes the swan's road home, Egil's stoneheaded son

"Must seek Mimir's meal among the mighty; or maybe make a wolf's way from now on."

Corban understood almost none of it, but the heavy thunder of the words carried him. Around him the other men listened with their heads cocked, their faces rapt. When Skull-Grim was done none of the listeners spoke, although all around them the hall buzzed and roared with other talk. Instead they nodded, solemn as priests, their eyes worshipful on Skull-Grim.

Then the man beside Corban said, "Well, it's not that bad, is it? Sweyn will take us all, for sure."

Skull-Grim nodded his head toward the high seat. "It seems to me Rig's spawn's spawn already has his berserker."

Somebody else, under his breath, said, "Is he Bluetooth's son?"

"He is now," said Skull-Grim. "And the time's come to prove it." He laid his great knobby-boned hands on the table and turned to Corban. "Do you have that thing I gave you, back when the King died?"

Corban started, his mind empty; then he remembered the broken arrow. "Yes."

"Then be ready." Skull-Grim stood up. "King Sweyn Haraldsson!"

The clamor hushed a little. Up there in the high seat, Sweyn lifted his head. The light shone on his red-gold hair. Beside him Palnatoki turned and held out his ale-horn to a servant in the shadows behind him.

Sweyn said, "Speak, Skull-Grim, you've earned it. Although I never thought to hear the name Peacemaker applied to you." At the sound of his voice the whole room fell quiet, listening.

Skull-Grim rumbled, amused. He looked up and down the hall. "Not now, either. There is the matter of the death of the old King."

The hall hushed, all at once, very quiet. Up by the high seat Conn started to his feet, and Corban realized he had heard something of the matter. Sweyn put his hand out and held him down. "Tell us what you know, then."

Skull-Grim said, "I found him dead, and this man standing over him." He tapped Corban on the shoulder.

All around the room a murmur of voices rose. Corban stood up where he was, drawing every gaze to him. He felt naked under their eyes. Some stood up, to see him better, and he heard his name whispered all around him. He had the piece of the arrow in his hand, although he wondered what use it would be. Up there on the high seat, Sweyn was watching him steadily, frowning, and now he got to his feet.

"Corban Loosestrife, you have done me great service, and I know you are honest. Your sons are my right arm, and for their sake also I will believe what you say about this. Tell me what happened."

Corban said, "I didn't kill him. I could have, I was watching him. But this killed him." He held out the arrow.

Skull-Grim took it and passed it to the man next to him, and the arrow went from hand to hand along the table to Sweyn, and no one spoke. But as each man looked at the arrow, he lifted his head, and turned and stared in one direction, and by the time the arrow came to Sweyn, everybody in the hall was looking at Palna-toki.

Sweyn took the arrow, and he went pale. His head swiveled toward his foster-father. Palnatoki got up out of the high seat, backing away from them all, as if their looks drove him off like daggers.

"It's true," he said. From the darkness behind him his own men came, bringing him a cloak, and he shrugged into it. "I am not ashamed of it. I left my ships down at the mouth of the fjord to fool him and came down here alone. I found him by following the wizard. I knew that was why the wizard was here, the first time I saw him back in Hedeby." As he spoke he was moving toward the door, and his men with him. Nobody moved to stop him. The crowded servants near the door parted to let him by. "Why else would she have—would the Lady have called him out of the west, except for Bluetooth? I followed him until he led me to the King. My aim was off, or I'd have got him through the head. I'm out of practice. You all know what right I have to this—how he wronged me, long ago." He stopped, standing with his back to the door.

Sweyn said quietly, "It was all for your revenge, then, not for me. All that you did." He raised his fist and brought it down hard on the table. "Go. If you see me again, have a sword in your hand, or a bow, if that suits you better."

Palnatoki stood tall and thin in the doorway. He said, "I am going. But I won't stay gone." He went out the door, and his men after him.

Corban sat down on the bench again. The whole room buzzed around him with talk, only Skull-Grim sitting there silent, staring at the door, his great head sunk down between his shoulders. Corban got up and went away from the table and out through the small door in the rear of the hall. No one stopped him.

He walked out across the open ground of the village, the noise and bustle of the hall fading behind him, until he could feel her frail warm web around him. His mind churned.

He could not stay clear of it, he was guilty still—he had not killed the King, but he had drawn his death to him. He wondered if Palnatoki was right—if behind all this was the Lady of Hedeby—and remembered the shark, rising from the sea like a messenger, calling him back here. Or was she also just a piece of it? Of what?

He felt bound and hobbled, wrapped around with the bloody ropes of these people's ambitions. Suddenly he longed with his whole soul for the island, for the clear air and the wild wind, and the emptiness.

"Pap!"

He wheeled, and in the depth of the black longing a surge of happiness ran through him like a charge of light. Warm around him she stirred, glad. He shouted their names, and through the dark they rushed on him, whooping, and he flung his arms out and around them, losing himself in his sons' love.

CHAPTER TWENTY-THREE

"Pap," Conn said again. "You can't go back. There's nothing there anymore, I told you. Mam—"

Grown man, hero that he was, he could not speak about his mother. Corban smiled, and slapped his arm, steadily amazed at him, this son he had somehow made, this warrior, with his fine shirt and sprouting beard and blazing gray eyes, and the power he had over all these other men. This stranger.

"For you, everything is here," Corban said. "You belong here, this is your place, now, you and Raef—" He looked around at his sister's son, standing beside him, almost a head taller than he was. "You've got this King now, and all his works to do, and the heads and arms to do it with. And you don't need me for that. And I am going home."

He did not say that every day he felt the need more to get her back there, where she belonged, a panicky itch along all his nerves, every day more urgent.

"He'll be a great King," Conn said, looking down the beach, where Sweyn was coming along after them, hanging back to talk to other men as he passed.

"He'll be a King," Corban said. "I don't get on well with kings, they are unlucky for me. There's Eelmouth coming."

"He wanted to kill you once," Conn said. "Why are you sailing with him?"

"That's all over," Corban said. "And we're both going to Jorvik." He turned to them, and put his hands on their shoulders, thinking he should say something, give them some golden words they could carry on with them forever. There were no words. Instead they curled their arms around him, and all three stood together, close, not even looking at each other, linked.

Corban at last stood back, and raised his eyes to their faces. "I'll see your sisters in Jorvik. Remember them, they're still yours to care for."

"Arre loves them," Raef said. He had taken a long wound across his forehead in the battle, healing into a ridge of scab.

"Yes," Conn said roughly. "So do I. I'll watch over them, Pap." His eyes shone, watery, regarding his father. "We'll never see you again."

Corban thought that was so, but he could not say it; he said, "That happens as it happens, doesn't it." Then Sweyn walked up to them, jovial, hung one arm on Conn's shoulder, and faced Corban.

"So. You are going. You know that I would much like to have you here, for your counsel and your deep thinking."

Corban laughed. Sweyn had also changed since he had seen him last, his red-gold beard growing long, his face grooved with new lines, his eyes more guarded, even when he smiled. Shielding his own deep thinking. Corban did not think Palnatoki would have walked out of the hall, that night, if Sweyn had not allowed it.

He said, "Such counsel as I could give you, I think you would quickly tire of. I'm leaving you my boys, anyway."

"You are," Sweyn said. "I need them both. I must go around the kingdom now, and lay all Denmark under me, and I will have Conn and Raef both by my side, whatever that requires." He took a step forward toward Corban, one hand out. "They have told me of your island, and the trouble there—I will give you ships and men to rebuild what you had there. Only ask."

Corban said, "Thank you. I think you have enough to do here. I'm going alone."

Conn began to weep, and came like a child into his father's arms. Corban's throat filled so that he could not breathe; he felt Benna move around them, and he got back for a moment those old days, when they had been the only people, and the world around them perfect and true. He felt the other men around them like a wall. When he and Conn could let one another go, Raef was next. He gripped Corban hard; he said, under his breath, "I love you. I love you."

Corban wrapped his arms around him. "I'll find your mother."

"Tell her that also," Raef said. He blinked, clear-eyed, his lashes damp. "Benna, also." He blinked again.

Corban let him go, and slung his packs into the dragonfly. He had stocked the ship with new sails and water casks, and had gotten an awning, foreseeing a need for it, Sweyn in the first flush of his kingliness willing to give him anything he asked for. Many of the ships had already pulled away from the Limfjord shore; Skull-Grim had gone that morning, and now Eelmouth came walking along the stony beach, a sea chest on his shoulder, his crew along after him.

He stopped by Sweyn. "Good fighting, King. Call me, if you need any more help."

Sweyn laughed. "Come to me, should your present captain ever let you go."

Eelmouth gave a shrug. "That may happen." His gaze strayed out onto the water. "When did that ship come in?"

"This morning," Sweyn said.

"Looks like one of Hakon's."

"Well, it is," Sweyn said, and smiled.

"Where is he?"

"He's gone back to Norway. He sends that he met some force of Germans, down by Hedeby, who were trying to overrun the Danewirk, and beat them back, very bloodily, he says, thus saving us all. He's no more Christian, he says; he's killed the horse to prove it, and we are even now."

Sweyn's smile widened. His blue eyes glittered; he looked very amused.

Eelmouth said, "Are you?"

"Not really," Sweyn said.

Corban snorted. "The more you eat, King, the hungrier you get. He will be no easy take." He shook Sweyn's hand, and Conn and Raef went to help him float the dragonfly. "Eelmouth! Which way?"

"West!" Eelmouth shouted. "We'll see if I can remember how he did it."

"West," Corban said, and climbed into the ship and reached for his oars. He stroked off into the deeper water. On the bank behind him his sons stood, getting smaller and smaller. He bent his back to another stroke, the little ship lively around him.

— ❧ —

Conn stood to his knees in the water, watching his father row away; his heart hurt. He said, "Will he make it home?"

Raef, behind him, cleared his throat. His voice was unsteady. "I don't know. I can't feel that far."

Out first of all the leaving ships, the dragonfly was a mere dot on the water. Abruptly the red and white sail bloomed over it. Conn tore his eyes away, turned toward the beach, and waded ashore, Raef beside him.

Raef said, "What are we going to do now?"

"You heard Sweyn."

"Sweyn, yes. But us." Raef was watching him steadily. The scab across his forehead made him look tilted. His cheeks were wet.

Conn gathered himself; he felt odd, new, a little tender, as if he had just hatched from some old constricting shell. No Corban here to tell him what to do. No Corban to please or displease. He swelled, suddenly larger, ready for anything. He could do whatever he wanted now. All he had to do was to find out what that was.

"Sweyn's giving us a ship," he said. "Let's start hustling up a crew." He laughed, exultant, and strode off down the beach.

— ❧ —

The spring sun was high and bright in Jorvik. Arre went down the street from shop to shop, buying here and there, and everywhere talking to her friends. Aelfu trailed along after her, leading Miru by the hand.

They had just all come from the church, where after the Mass Arre had spoken to Oswald the Archbishop about the image of the Virgin Mother she had promised as part of her penance. Oswald had taken to this with unusual warmth. They had walked a while around the church, talking of it, the man more and more convinced that he had thought of it himself.

The work now lacked only a workman. He had charged her to find one. She meant to have someone as good at drawing as Benna, and she knew that would be hard, but there was no hurry. She could enjoy the prospect as she enjoyed the sunshine of the late spring day, and the gossip of her friends, and the two little girls trailing after her, whom she was stuffing with honeybuns.

They walked down the side of the Coppergate, toward the big oak tree, and she stopped to smooth Aelfu's hair out of her eyes and put Miru's shoe back on. Kneeling there by the two girls, she looked up the street and saw Corban.

She froze. She had heard that morning some ships had come from Denmark, with news of a great battle, and a new King, but she had not considered that he might come, too. She stood, putting her arms around the girls; her first wicked selfish thought was that he would take them away from her. Her second was a rush of grief for him, who had nothing now.

He saw her, and he called her name. He crossed the street toward her. He looked the same, square and strong, the red and blue cloak wrapped around his waist, his sleeves rolled up, his beard wind-tangled. She wondered how to greet him, but then Aelfu tore roughly out of her grasp.

"No! You can't come back now!" The child rushed forward, not to greet her father, but to scream strange words at him. "I like it here now. You left us and went with him and I hate you! I hate you!" She turned, her face contorted, squirting tears, and bolted up the street.

Corban stood, his mouth open, watching her go; he looked suddenly haggard. He turned his hollow-eyed gaze to Arre, and shook his head. He came the last few steps to her, his feet dragging; he squatted down suddenly, face to face with Miru, and touched his fingertips to the child's cheek. She had hold of Arre's skirt, and when he reached out to her she shrank away from him, pulling the folds of cloth around her, hiding.

Corban stood up. Arre said, "I'm sorry." She put her hand on Miru, buried in her skirts. "Come stay with us a while, they will remember you."

Corban shook his head. "I'm leaving. I'm going back to the island." His face settled. She saw how that purpose carried him; he was halfway gone already. Maybe that was what Aelfu had meant, with her screaming, that he would leave them again.

He looked deep into her face. "Take care of them, Arre."

"I will," she said. "They're like my own already. You won't stay just a little while?"

"I have to go back," he said. He reached out and took hold of her hand. "Thank you." Bending down, he put a kiss on her forehead, and then he turned and went away down the Coppergate.

Arre's forehead burned; for a moment, dizzy, she saw him walking down toward another river, through other trees, in some strange outlandish place. She shook her head, breathless and dizzy.

Down by her side, Miru's sticky hand crept into hers. Drawn back again, Arre looked down, and the child raised her eyes to her, her forehead wrinkled. "Ama? Who that?"

Arre lifted her eyes, and watched him go out down to the river, and she was thinking of Benna, that he had taken Benna away, that she had died in the wilderness because of him and his otherness. Tears blurred her vision, and when she had wiped her

eyes he was gone. She stooped and picked Miru up. "Just someone who knew you once," she said. "Now let's go find Aelfu."

⸻

Corban sailed first to Iceland, with some trading ships, and there
took on more supplies. In a market on a windy coastal bluff he
heard talk of newfound lands to the west, and a man trying to
start a settlement there. He listened fearfully to the talk until he
realized their new land was well north of his island.

He set sail again, and went on, heading southwest. The days
went one after the other. He sat thinking of the island, how it
looked in the heat of the summer, with all the grasses and the
blooming flowers, how it would be when they got there.

He knew he had to reach the island quickly. Benna slept almost all the time now. Even in dreams she slept in his arms. He
gave her memories, but they did not make her stronger.

They made her happy. Whenever she roused herself, snug-
gling against him, she was happy.

For a while he thought over and over of Aelfu, what she had
screamed at him, how she had run away. It was Benna she had
screamed at, and yet Benna seemed untouched, while the child's
rage burned him to the heart. He remembered sitting with her on
his lap while the fireflies glinted under the trees and Benna told a
story of wizards and warriors in a fantastical city called Hedeby.
His arms ached for the warmth of the child, her close-nestling
trust.

He longed for that moment when everything had seemed
whole and good, and bound to last forever.

A storm blew up, and he rigged the awning and set a dragging anchor. The rain passed. The dragonfly sailed on over the
broad swells of the ocean. One morning he woke up to find the
little ship floating in the middle of a great herd of whales, black
bulges lying on the water. One barnacled head rose up right beside

the ship to stare at him. When the beast dove, the flukes of its tail blotted out the sun for a moment and the splash carried the ship up over the next wave.

Aelfu faded away behind him, back with her brothers, back in that other world. Better that way anyway, he thought, and somewhere deep in his mind Benna nudged him. She had thought so all along.

He thought forward now. He thought of home again, the island, their house there. Everything she had made there. He fell to trying to remember every image she had made. He thought of the house, how as he built the house what she had drawn became true. The power in her seemed to run through his arms into the walls of the house. Into the dragonfly itself, later, which she also drew, countless times, bringing it steadily into the world.

Nobody knew but him what she was. Nobody would ever know. Yet she had made their world. What would happen to her when he got her back to the island, he did not know. He dreamt she came back to him. He dreamt also she disappeared and he lost her forever.

He lay awake one night, staring the stars into shapes, and a burst of falling stars rained down on him, one after the other for a long while, some bright and some small. It amazed him to see them squiggle suddenly out of nothing and then blaze away to nothing again. He wondered if there were some meaning to it, some intent, some message.

He thought the meaning was the thing itself, but then he caught himself wondering what that meant.

One gray morning a low barren shore appeared on the western horizon. He sailed on to the south, following the coast, the days bright and the nights very cold. Gradually the nights grew warmer. The shore along the western horizon turned green and soft. He went steadily on, until at last he raised a shore he recognized, a headland with trees along the edge, and a long row of sand dunes.

He rounded the treacherous bars at the tip of the great cape, his heart singing now, and Benna more awake, eager, seeming stronger. Below the cape, the land fell away, and he followed the broken coastline around into the west. On a fine noonday with the tide slack, the vast waterland opened up before him, island after island floating like clouds on the blue water of the bay. He waited for the tide to make and went up the narrows, to the tip of the big island, and brought his ship ashore there.

His legs trembled, feeble. He climbed out of the ship and went up the slope, through grass to his waist. Everything was overgrown in brambles and weeds. He nearly fell over the ruins of a stone wall, buried in the green riot. He stood looking around him, astonished. His house was fallen apart. The thatch had sunken in and the walls were sagging. The storehouse was buried under a mound of berry vines; her garden had vanished into the wild overgrowing weeds. The whole place was going back as fast as it could to what it had been before he came.

His legs would scarcely carry him. A sharp pain was beginning in his chest. He stumbled around looking for familiar things. He found her grave, coming on it very suddenly, almost tripping on the mound of earth. He stood looking down at it, his whole face aching with grief.

He felt her slipping from him; he gasped at the shock of it, after so long together with her, as if she pulled roots up from his body. He felt her leave him, and then, for a moment, as she turned toward him for the last time, he saw her.

She was real as the air, her small heart-shaped face, her wide eyes, her lips parted. She seemed about to speak to him, and he called her name, joyous, reaching for her, and then she sank down into her grave and was gone.

He dropped onto his knees, exhausted. On the weatherbeaten mound of earth a rock lay, and he reached for it, because he thought he saw an image on it. But it was just a flat rock.

He slumped down, his spirit sinking into his belly. He saw

what a fool he was. He had made here only what he had brought
with him, laid on like a scab over the land, without roots or vigor,
and now vanishing. He had lost Benna, for his follies, and his
children. He was alone, with nothing, in an enormous wilderness.

"Corban."

His name struck him like a bolt of lightning. He lifted his
head, turning his gaze up toward the line of the trees. He saw
nothing, until she moved.

Mav came down out of the trees toward him. Her hair was
like blackened silver around her, threaded through with flowers.
Her skin was like silver. She walked light as a deer on the grass.

In the shadows behind her, he saw the dark man, waiting.

He rose to his feet. His sister had stopped, there, halfway to
him. Calling him. He felt his body creak and settle into life
again. He stooped a moment, and put his hand down flat on the
grave at his feet, and whispered Benna's name. Then he stood
and walked up after his sister, toward the forest.